Twisted Tracks

Lesley Horton

First published in Great Britain in 2008 by
Orion Books, an imprint of The Orion Publishing Group Ltd
Orion House, 5 Upper Saint Martin's Lane
London WC2H 9EA

An Hachette UK Company

1 3 5 7 9 10 8 6 4 2

A CIP catalogue record for this book is
available from the British Library.

ISBN (Hardback) 978 0 7528 9058 6
ISBN (Trade Paperback) 978 0 7528 9060 9

Typeset by Deltatype Ltd, Birkenhead, Merseyside

Printed and bound in the UK by
CPI Mackays, Chatham ME5 8TD

The Orion Publishing Group's policy is to use papers that
are natural, renewable and recyclable products and made
from wood grown in sustainable forests. The logging and
manufacturing processes are expected to conform to the
environmental regulations of the country of origin.

www.orionbooks.co.uk

FRANKLEY LIBRARY
FRANKLEY COMMUNITY HIGH SCHOOL
NEW STREET, FRANKLEY
BIRMINGHAM, B45 0EU
Telephone: 0121 464 7676

Loans are up to 28 days. Fines are charged if items are
not returned by the due date. Items can be renewed
at the Library, via the internet or by telephone up to
3 times. Items in demand will not be renewed.

Please use a bookmark

Date for return		
1 9 JUN 2017		
2 9 MAY 2019		

Check out our online catalogue to see what's in stock, or
to renew or reserve books.

www.birmingham.gov.uk/libcat

www.birmingham.gov.uk/libraries

Birmingham City Council

Birmingham
Libraries

Twisted Tracks

This book is dedicated to my husband who has given me his full support through the bad times.

Acknowledgements

My thanks go to the Keighley News Editor, Malcolm Hoddy, and News Editor, Alistair Shand for allowing me to use articles referring to the remains of miners buried in the hillsides of the villages around Keighley. Also to Ian and Helen Pepper for their information on forensics and to Mike and Bob at Doughty Brookes garage for spending time explaining how staged car accidents are planned and carried out. I would like to make mention of my late father-in-law, Amos Horton, a miner who used to tell stories of the strikes, of manning the picket lines and of the rifts caused between families on different sides of the divide. Special thanks go to Linda Regan who picked me up when I felt very low and persuaded me to carry on with the novel and to members of the Airedale Writers' Circle who supported me throughout. Finally I would like to thank my agent, Teresa Chris, and my editors Kate Mills and Genevieve Pegg, all of whom have put up valiantly with the problems I faced while writing this novel.

prologue

1975

If anyone had asked her, she could have explained why she wasn't afraid. Why should she be? She'd been more afraid after the rape than she could ever be now. Afraid of going outdoors in case he was waiting; afraid of her father who'd thrashed her for lying and called her a mucky tart and of her mother who'd let him. Afraid of the police she knew didn't believe her and afraid of the looks people gave her, of the comments they made in stage whispers and the blame they apportioned to her. She was lucky she wasn't pregnant, they said, or had some nasty grubby disease – she probably had, the filthy whore. They felt for her parents, decent hard-working religious people; what they must have gone through – still be going through. It said something about their level of forgiveness that she was still living in their house. She hadn't even been able to name him because she knew that in everyone's eyes she was the tart and he was educated, respected, not the type to rape anyone, least of all her.

If anything it had been worse in school. Her ears still rang with the remarks in the corridors, the name-calling, the boys salaciously asking if she'd give them some of what she'd given him. She'd carried on until she could stand it no more and then she'd dropped out. They'd sent education welfare officers round to persuade her back in – they said they weren't there to judge, but to help. But she knew from the way they looked at her that it wasn't true and finally she locked herself in her room and refused to come out and they washed their hands of her.

But more than anything else, she was afraid of the dreams. Nightly dreams in which his face contorted as he loomed over her and then backed off, grinning; in which as he pushed inside her, her body shuddered and the harder he thrust, the more violently she convulsed so that eventually she thought she would go mad. And still no one cared.

So why should she be afraid now? She was looking at freedom.

Halfway up the concrete stairs, she stopped out of breath, and for a moment leaned against the wall. It was rough and cold and it reminded her of his roughness and the coldness of the grass onto which he had thrown her. She looked up. Her eyes saw the wooden ceiling, but her brain transformed it into the canopy of trees she'd tried to concentrate on as he'd raped her, but they were quivering in the breeze and she closed her eyes. She continued to climb until suddenly the door onto the roof was in front of her. She opened it and stepped out. The wind was fiercer up here; it had been no more than a puff of air at street level. It blew through her long hair making it dance around her face. She pushed it back as she climbed onto the turreted edge of the church's tower, then leaned forward and allowed herself to fall.

chapter one

2007

Detective Chief Inspector John Handford stared out of the dining-room window of the neat semi at the garden where figures dressed in protective clothing were digging. A white tent covered the area, partly to shield it from inclement weather, but mostly to block the scene from onlookers and the gathering media. The house was the last in a row and behind it and to the side the field was cordoned off with the blue and white police tape and monitored twenty-four hours by officers.

Handford watched as the scene-of-crime personnel worked slowly and methodically, as if they were carrying out an archaeological dig. They couldn't afford to make mistakes or to put back together anything they might undo in a momentary lack of concentration. They had only one chance to find the body (if there was one) and preserve the evidence.

It was unusually mild for mid-November and the bulbs that hung from the ceiling of the crime-scene tent and the more intense lighting of the movable electric arc lamps added to the heat. The men and women drew in their own air as they breathed into the masks covering their mouths and noses. This, Handford knew, added to their discomfort, but the sooner they found – or failed to find – the body of twenty-six-year-old Bronwyn Price, the sooner their discomfort would end.

Bronwyn had been missing for almost eight weeks now, but it hadn't been her parents who had finally reported her as a MISPER. In fact, when questioned, her mother said she didn't know where her daughter was living or where she was working now, except that she had moved from the travel agency in Bradford to their office in Leeds. Bronwyn had refused her calls when she had rung there and she had only seen her once or twice in the past eighteen months and that was more by coincidence than arrangement when they had visited a neighbour at the same time. As far as the Youngers were concerned, Bronwyn had been considered a missing person a long time ago. 'She packed her bags and left when I told her I was marrying David,' she said, her Welsh accent becoming more pronounced as she went into detail. 'She never liked David, always arguing with him she was, so I said, "I deserve a life too, you know. I'm marrying him whether you like it or not. If you don't like it you're the one who'll be going."'

Bronwyn's boss at the travel agency in Leeds eventually called the police. Bronwyn hadn't returned to work after a week's leave, which wasn't like her. If she was ill or had had an accident she would have let them know. The manager had attempted to get in touch more than once, but each time her answer machine had clicked in and although he'd left several messages there was no response. At first he was angry; her absence left them short-staffed, but after three weeks and no news concern took over from anger and he drove to her flat in a village a few miles north of Bradford. Her car was parked against the kerb. He asked the young woman pushing a pram if she knew where Bronwyn was, but she said she hadn't seen her for some time nor, when she thought about it, had she heard any noises coming from the flat. So he knocked on the door several times and peered through the windows. The woman had been right: there were no sounds he could hear, in fact no movement at all, not even the flicker of a curtain.

At first she was treated as a missing person. The constable assigned checked the mortuary for Jane Does and the hospitals for amnesiacs. When this failed to find her, he contacted the airlines to establish whether she'd taken her flight to Cyprus. She hadn't. The inspector said it didn't mean much – she may have decided not to go, but it would be worth checking with her bank. If she was still drawing on her account then there was nothing to worry about. The bank manager was helpful and although he was not prepared to go into detail, he confirmed there had been no movement from her credit and debit cards or her bank account for several weeks. Finally, the police sought permission to enter the flat. A partially packed suitcase was on the bed and on the dressing table were her flight tickets, hotel reservation, her passport, a bundle of Cypriot pounds and some traveller's cheques. There was no sign of Bronwyn Price. Wherever she was, she hadn't taken her holiday.

The case was passed to CID who appealed for anyone who knew of her whereabouts to contact them and Lynne and David Younger sat in front of the television cameras and pleaded for their daughter to let them know she was safe. All possible sightings were followed up; the hills and wooded areas in the district were searched and divers plunged into the waters of the river Aire and the Leeds–Liverpool canal; all attempts to locate her came to nothing. Finally, a serious-faced senior officer told the media they were very concerned for Bronwyn's safety and the case went to the Homicide and Major Enquiry Team and on to Handford's desk. HMET, as it was known, had been set up to investigate serious crimes throughout West Yorkshire and although he was still based in Bradford, he enjoyed the freedom of going where he was needed rather than working within the confines of one sub-division. To say the Bradford inner city patch had become claustrophobic was an understatement. It frustrated him when he had not been able to move beyond his own boundaries unless he had permission from his boss as well as that of the DCI in the area into which the investigation had slipped.

Handford opened the window and smelled the air. There was the aroma of autumn, but no stench of death or of a decomposing body. It was near here that the rivers Aire and Worth met and during heavy rain the neighbourhood was prone to flooding. If there was a body then the decomposed flesh and body fat would inevitably have come into contact with water and given off the particularly repugnant smell well known to all detectives involved with buried bodies, exhumations or victims of drowning. There was none of that, only the pungency of the soil.

Four feet down, they had come across clay and concluded it was unlikely anyone burying a body in a hurry would dig through that. The garden was also criss-crossed with land drains taking the water from the hills to the rivers. It had turned the soil immediately above the clay into mud. The conditions were not ideal and progress had been slow but now they were nearing the end of excavating the third quarter.

A scene-of-crime officer looked up and shook his head. He was telling Handford what deep down he already knew: there was no body and they would move on to the final quarter. Handford thanked him with a wave and motioned that he was leaving the site. There was nothing more he could do here; he would be better employed back at the station. Murders without bodies were the very devil to work on. They started with what his new boss, Detective Chief Superintendent Mike Paynter, called victimology, in the hope that the possible victim would set them in the right direction, but so far they had little background on her, except what her employers and her mother and stepfather had told them. She had come to Yorkshire from Wales after her parents separated. She had few close friends, but there had been a boyfriend from whom she had split – quite acrimoniously apparently – and now as far as her colleagues knew she was involved with an older man, foreign they thought, but they weren't sure because she had kept him very much to herself.

Handford shrugged on his overcoat but as he was about to leave, the sound of raised voices broke the silence and a tall, muscular, shaven-headed man burst through the door, pursued by a uniformed officer. 'I'm sorry, sir, he pushed his way in. I couldn't stop him.'

Handford waved the constable away and turned to Bronwyn's stepfather. 'Didn't I make it clear that you were not to come here, Mr Younger?' he said.

David Younger glared at him. 'It's my house.' His tone was belligerent.

'Nevertheless, you have to stay away while we get on with our job.'

'You mean the job of digging up my garden to find a non-existent body?'

Handford ignored the question.

Breathing heavily, Younger took a step closer and faced the detective. His breath stank of alcohol and noticeable was the small gap between his front teeth, which rubbed out the brute and replaced it with the boy. More the petulant teenager than the outraged stepfather. 'She's not buried here. She's not even missing. She's doing this on purpose, but you're too stupid to understand. We went through that farce of a television appeal and now you're wasting tax-payers' money digging up my garden.' His face was puce and he pulled a handkerchief from his pocket to wipe away rivulets of sweat. 'I've said it before and I'll say it again – in words of one syllable if you like – you're not going to find her because she doesn't want to be found; and she doesn't want to be found because she wants to make our lives – mine and her mother's – as miserable as she can.'

Handford made no reply, but kept his eyes firmly on the man's face.

Uneasily and less decisively, Younger said, 'It's her way of getting back at me. She's hated me from the moment we met. The bitch would do anything. She's probably sunning herself on some beach as we speak.'

'Not without her passport, Mr Younger; we found that at her flat.'

'Oh for God's sake, man, she works in a travel agency and she has a boyfriend no one knows anything about except that he is a foreigner, which probably means he's an illegal. Work it out, it's not rocket science.' He was surer of himself now and when Handford still didn't answer his exasperation showed. 'He's got her a new passport.'

Handford had had enough of Younger's illogical observations. He opened the door and called the constable. 'Go back to your wife, Mr Younger. You are not to come here again until we've finished.' He glared at him. 'Do you understand me?'

At first it seemed as though Younger would stand his ground, but when the uniformed officer grasped him by the arm, he pulled himself away angrily, and marched out of the room, stopping only to fling 'She's not here, I tell you,' at Handford.

Handford turned back to the window. As he surveyed the

scene below, instinct told him Younger was probably right: there was no body hidden in the garden. But instinct also told him that Younger's ranting had an element of *my lord thou doth protest too much* in it. He'd been like this since the start of the investigation: angry, argumentative, confrontational even. Whatever the reason, he wanted the police off his back, for if Bronwyn wasn't tucked up under the last quarter of the lawn then there was something he didn't want the police to find that may well have nothing to do with his stepdaughter. He'd been right in as much as the television appeal had been a farce. Mrs Younger was naturally upset – Bronwyn was her daughter and however much hurt she had caused her mother the bond was still there. But not David Younger; he had had to be persuaded to display a modicum of concern. In the end, apart from re-iterating his wife's plea, he had remained silent. It had not been missed by the police officers in the room. That was part of the reason for a television appeal – to scrutinise the family closely. Handford buttoned his coat. If he had to gamble, he would lay his career on a hundred-to-one bet that Bronwyn wasn't under the lawn or in any of the flower beds and then an accumulator on Younger knowing where she was and wherever that was, it wasn't on some beach enhancing her suntan.

Douglas Handford closed the door of his office and walked to the window. The new building of which the County's Social Services department was a part perched on the hillside like a sleeping dog and gave a clear view of the metropolis sprawled along the valley. It never failed to surprise him that cities could be this beautiful, particularly as dusk fell when the house and building lights mapped out its geography and the street lamps covered it in an orange glow. Although the temperature outside was beginning to fall, it was stuffy in the room and he pushed open the window. The sounds of the boys playing football on the nearby all-weather pitch floated towards him. He smiled. Young people never felt the cold. Suddenly the smile left him and abruptly he shut the window and dropped into the chair behind his desk. Why? Why now after all this time? Surrounding him was the fulfilment of everything he had worked for, the years he'd spent protecting and supporting dysfunctional families, many of whom didn't want to be either protected or supported except with money. But like it or not he had tried to give them a chance at a future that was better than their present and with some he had succeeded. At the same time he had climbed the career ladder, moving from district to district, county to county, until eventually he had been rewarded with the post of Chief Executive. And now one letter had resurrected the past and threatened a bitter end to his career.

He leaned back and took the envelope from the inside pocket of his jacket and stared at the address. It had been delivered to his home; they must have taken a lot of trouble tracking him down. Social work had taken him the length and breadth of the country over the years, so much so, that when he was offered his current position his wife had told him quite categorically that this was the last time she was boxing up the contents of their house. This time it was for keeps. He supposed the police could have spoken to John, after all he was one of them, but he wasn't even sure his brother had his new address. They hadn't been in real contact for years – ever since ...

He pulled out the letter and read it slowly for the fourth time. It was headed with the West Yorkshire Police logo and signed by a Detective Chief Inspector on behalf of the Chief Constable. New advances in forensic technology, it said, were allowing them to open up past cases. They intended to re-investigate the alleged rape of Josie Renshaw, and as he had been at the venue when it had occurred an officer would like to go over his state-ment with him and allow them to take a sample of his DNA. It was his right to refuse, of course, but he must understand what that refusal would convey to the investigators. His anger rose. Typical of the police – the smile followed by the knife.

He stared into the distance. He hadn't thought of Josie Renshaw for a long time, but he remembered her – how could he forget? Time was not always the great healer people thought it was. Even now when he closed his eyes images of her played against his eyelids. Images of her falling from the roof of the church tower. Had she plunged to the pathway below like a rock or had she twisted and turned, her arms and legs flailing?

He didn't know, he hadn't seen her throw herself off and at the time he had pretended not to care. It was his seeming lack of compassion for a girl who had never been able to get over the fact that she had been raped that had been part of the reason for he and John going their separate ways. And the fact that he had asked John to give him an alibi for the time of the rape, and the fact that she had committed suicide, and the fact that he had refused to attend her funeral. So many facts. It was only after her death that John had questioned why it had been necessary to give his brother an alibi. At first he'd laughed it off, tapping the side of his nose and saying he had been otherwise engaged. Then he'd feigned anger and demanded to know if John seriously thought he could rape anyone. The answer was 'no, of course not', but his brother's eyes told a different story. He wasn't sure. At that moment any bond that had existed between them was severed. They hadn't spent more than a few months in each other's company for over a quarter of a century. Of course, the reason they gave was that for most of the time they lived distances apart and that both were busy men, but Douglas knew that was only part of the story.

He turned back to the letter. It mentioned new technology – that meant they would be able to link the DNA found on her clothing with the man who she alleged had raped her. She hadn't given a name because she said she didn't know who it was, she hadn't seen his face; he had jumped her from behind, clapped his hand over her mouth, pulled her into the bushes, and raped her. But his DNA would be there.

As would his own. He had gone to the disco that night, a newly graduated student, full of his own importance, and he'd had sex with her. He hadn't cared that she was only fifteen nor he doubted had she. She was the village tart – he knew it, she knew it, and more often than not she was the instigator; she flirted, she gave the lads the come-on, they followed. But that didn't make it right – not then, not now. He swallowed hard as he felt the fear building. He'd quit smoking several years ago, but the desire for a cigarette to calm him had never been greater than it was now. The worst of it was he hadn't used any protection so yes, they would have his DNA. Could they really match it after all these years? They must think they could or he wouldn't have received the letter.

He felt sick and opened the window again. The boys playing football were remonstrating with the small goalkeeper who had let the ball through. Douglas took several deep breaths and as he watched them, he began to think more rationally. Whatever the DNA said and whatever John believed, the fact was it was proof they needed, a confession that the sex he'd had with Josie Renshaw was against her will. They couldn't get the answer from her because she was dead and he would never admit to any such act. So what did they have? Nothing except a double helix of DNA.

If only it were as simple as that. In the present climate one whiff of anything sexual, particularly with a girl who hadn't reached her sixteenth birthday, and his career would be finished. The fact that this case was thirty years old or that he had been fresh out of university at the time would mean nothing to those to whom he was accountable.

He had given the police his alibi then; he would stand by it now and insist a DNA test was unnecessary. Whatever John believed, he would have to back him up again. He was a senior police officer now; he couldn't risk his brother being arrested or himself being accused of lying all those years ago any more than Douglas could.

John Handford entered the incident room. A year ago Central Police Station had relocated to Trafalgar House, a new building away from the city centre. It had been a controversial move and many had protested the lack of a police station where it was needed most – in the centre of the city. As far as he was concerned, the move was coming not a moment too soon: it hadn't taken much of a downpour for buckets to be dotted strategically along corridors and in the offices. It was embarrassing steering visitors around the failures of a building only thirty-four years old. He pulled up a chair next to Detective Constable Andy Clarke and sat down. 'Anything more on Bronwyn Price?'

The silver-haired detective looked up, took off his glasses and rubbed his eyes. Handford thought he seemed tired. At fifty-five he was probably ready for retirement, but he had entered the service as a mature recruit and was adamant he wanted to serve his thirty years. Perhaps the pressure of working in the Homicide and Major Enquiry Team was beginning to get to him or perhaps it was no more than too long spent in front of a computer screen. As soon as possible he'd get him out on the road – it was what he preferred and what he was good at.

'Not really,' Clarke said. 'No one knows much about her and what they do know shows her to be an unremarkable young woman, liked, but not loved and certainly not hated, except perhaps by her stepfather who has nothing good to say about her.' Which was why they were currently digging up his garden – that and the fact that most murders were committed by a close family member. Even if her body wasn't there, David Younger wasn't off the hook, not by a long way.

'What about the new boyfriend? Have you found him?'

'Not yet. She hardly spoke about him.' Unremarkable she might be, but neither it seemed was she one to let people into her life – especially her love life. 'The consensus is he's foreign, not Asian, possibly Polish or Ukrainian. We're currently trawl-ing the various churches, organisations and aid centres but it's going to take some time.' Clarke paused. 'I assume there's no sign of her in the garden.'

'None. The nearest we've got to anything like remains are the skeletons of two small dogs.' He pushed himself up from the chair. 'Get me something more on her, Andy, something that might tell us where she is, and while you're about it the name of her killer.'

Clarke's round face burst into a smile and his eyes twinkled. They both knew their long-term friendship still counted for a lot. 'I'll do my best, John, but as I said she's an ordinary young woman. The boyfriend might be the key. If we could find him, it might help. Is it worth using the press?'

Handford wasn't a great friend of the press; he'd been mauled by them more than once, but they had their uses. 'Why not? It would give them something more to do than hanging round that garden like vultures.'

He had reached the door when Clarke asked, 'How's Gill?'

Handford turned and pulled a face. He didn't like being reminded his wife was thousands of miles away. 'She's fine; in fact, she's more than fine. She loves it in the States. I think if it was possible she'd stay.'

Gill had secured an exchange appointment teaching English literature in a high school in America for a term. When she'd told him she wanted to apply for it every nerve in his body had shouted, 'No way.' What he actually said was, 'Why not?' It was only an application after all and there would probably be thousands; the chances were she wouldn't even be offered an interview. When she was offered an interview and then a posting, his heart sank into his boots, but it was too late for objections and instead he took her out to celebrate. That night she'd asked him more than once if he was sure. He'd said he was, when what he was really sure of was that he didn't want her to go, but that he wouldn't stand in her way. She'd supported him throughout his career, now, for better or for worse, it was his turn to support her. Watching the plane take off for Florida and disappear into the clouds at the beginning of September he knew how much he would miss her for the next four months and had difficulty holding back the tears. His daughters, Nicola and Clare, though only seventeen and fourteen, were coping better than him. But he'd comforted them nevertheless in the hope that some of that comfort would rub off on him, but it hadn't. It was like there was a deep hole in his life, a hole he was permanently trying to fill – usually with work. They'd been over to Tallahassee to see her during the girls' half-term holiday and they'd talked on the phone every day but as time passsed Gill's enthusiasm for the job and the lifestyle became more spirited. And each time he replaced the receiver, the pain in his chest became more intense.

What worried him now was how she would cope when she returned. 'I'm not sure what she'll do when she comes home; she'll have to go back to Cliffe Top Comprehensive for a while, but I can't see her wanting to stay, not after this.'

The screen saver on Clarke's computer jumped into action and a series of pipes began to form a geometric pattern. Handford watched them for a moment and then said, 'It's not been the same there since the investigation into Shayla Richards' death. I turned that school upside down for her.'

Clarke was phlegmatic. 'It would have been turned upside down whoever had been SIO.'

'Yes, but I was, and that made it worse. I could have asked to be relieved of it if I'd wanted to, but I didn't. I think some of the staff still haven't forgiven Gill for Graham Collins' resignation.'

'Then I pity the kids they teach if they're so short-sighted they couldn't see that she had nothing to do with it.' As Handford made to argue, Clarke waved his hand. 'All right, so they don't know the whole story. So what? Let it go, John.' He shifted the mouse and turned to bring back the report he was writing. 'Try looking on the bright side for once. She'll be back soon and in the meantime you and the girls have the pleasure of your mother living with you, now what could be better than that?'

Christine Blakely slammed down the receiver. She'd had enough of this. Bloody, bloody Patrick. Tom was her husband, Patrick his brother. Why couldn't he believe her when she said she had no idea where Tom was, that he'd been missing for ten days, that she was desperately worried for him and that she couldn't care less that his father had willed him his half of the business? She wasn't interested. She'd had more than enough coping with Patrick's constant jibes about Tom being the enemy and having no family loyalty. The miners' strike had happened over twenty years ago; Patrick and his father had been miners, Tom a police officer. They had been on opposite sides. But not any more. Tom had retired and was working as an investigator for an insurance company, so why couldn't Patrick forget the past and move on? His father obviously had.

Normally she wouldn't have been too worried about Tom. It wasn't exactly the first time he'd stayed away, usually with some woman half his age. But then she'd always known what he was doing – he was hardly discreet. Not that she'd ever understood. She was no beauty, but she was petite, slim and reasonably attractive, and no matter what, she'd always been there for him. Perhaps that had been her mistake. Perhaps she should have thrown him out the first time he cheated on her – but she hadn't and that mistake seemed to have given him carte blanche to carry on. It was a pity she allowed her love for him to over-ride everything else.

But not this time, this time her worry stemmed not from blinkered love, but from fear. Fear that she would never get him back. She knew Tom well and she knew when he was having an affair and when he wasn't. That was her trouble. And at this moment in time she was absolutely sure his absence didn't involve a woman. She thought back to the day she'd last seen him and shuddered. They were at breakfast and a police officer he'd once worked with had telephoned.

'It's Ian Gott,' he said when he came back into the kitchen and sat down. 'He walked out of an open prison a few days ago.'

Ian Gott? Ian Gott? She tried to bring his name to mind. 'Am I supposed to know him?'

'I arrested him for a series of aggravated burglaries, mainly of old people. He threatened them with a knife, used it occasionally then beat them up for good measure. He was given fourteen years and he blamed me, said I'd set him up.'

'Did you?'

'No.' He winked at her. 'Not this time. Not that I wouldn't have liked to just to make sure. Low-life like him is better off locked away. But I wouldn't because that's not the way I work and I wasn't going to start with him and anyway I didn't need to. I got a tip-off from one of his cronies who didn't like it that he was beating up old folks. Knowing how Gott worked, he was worried he might try to rob his elderly aunt.'

'So why blame you?'

'Gott didn't know; he assumed he was caught because I'd set him up. If he had known he'd have made sure Billy suffered, probably by beating the old lady up himself if he got off or setting someone on the outside onto her if he didn't.'

'So instead Gott blamed you? So what? It's happened before.' Being threatened by a criminal they'd helped to get off the streets was an occupational hazard. Normally it didn't mean much and he'd shrug it off, so why was he so upset about this one?

'Not from Gott it hasn't. If he's in the area, and George thinks he is, then he's here to carry out his threat, otherwise why come all the way here from Ford? It's in West Sussex, for God's sake.' For a moment he'd been quiet. Then suddenly he banged his fist on the table, startling her. 'What in hell's name is this government doing sending someone like him to an open prison? What did they think he was going to do, stretch out and enjoy it? No, he was going to leg it. Talk about no room in the inn.'

As he'd gone off to work, he'd kissed her more fervently than usual and told her he doubted Gott would come to the house, but not to open the door to anyone she didn't know and if she was worried to ring John Handford. She'd known then he wasn't going to be around otherwise he wouldn't have suggested contacting John rather than him or George.

She watched him until he was out of sight, fear lurking at the back of her own mind. She'd tried to shrug it off, but when he hadn't come home that night or for the next four nights, she'd spoken to John Handford at his home. He'd rung the station there and then to check on the status of Ian Gott. As yet he hadn't been apprehended. Other than that there was little he could do personally, except insist it was passed over to CID, and tell her not to worry. 'Are you sure he's not with another woman?' he'd asked. She'd shaken her head. 'Not this time.'

CID had been even less helpful. Adults are allowed to disappear, many do every year. The sergeant didn't seem to think Gott was an issue. There was no evidence to say he was in the district. Finally he agreed to check up on Gott again and ask uniform to keep a look out for Tom. He told her not to worry, but she was left with the distinct impression that the man, like John Handford, thought her husband was up to his old tricks. If only it was as easy as that. His infidelity she could cope with; his disappearance was harder, particularly when no one was taking it seriously.

She pulled aside the curtain and stared through the window in the front room. A man was leaning against the wall to the school playing fields on the opposite side of the road and looking towards the house. She thought she'd seen him this morning and possibly yesterday evening, but she couldn't be sure. Tall, slim, probably in his mid-thirties, with dark hair. That was about as much as she could make out in the gloom, except that he seemed nervous and constantly smoked cigarettes. A burglar? Possibly. The houses in this part of town were detached with four or five bedrooms and a double garage and were a worthwhile target for burglars.

She didn't think so. He had made no attempt to hide himself and seemed to be waiting rather than watching. Could it be Ian Gott? She didn't know because she'd never seen him in the flesh and probably wouldn't have recognised him if she had. There'd been no photograph of him in the paper, indeed his escape hadn't been mentioned – but then there had been so many escapes from open prisons over recent months it was hardly surprising. And anyway, the more she thought about it, the surer she was that if Gott was in the district, Tom was out looking for him, probably luring him away from the house. The CID sergeant would have laughed at her had she put that forward as a hypothesis.

She let the curtain go. It didn't make sense to her, but while she was desperately afraid for her husband, she had no fear for herself and the obvious thing to do was to talk to the man. It would be more sensible to call the police but he might be gone before they arrived. If Tom, one of theirs for thirty years, wasn't a priority then what chance did she stand of a quick response? As stupid and as dangerous as it might be, and as much as Tom had warned her to be careful, there was only one way to find out who this man was and why he was there and that was to ask him.

chapter two

Back in his office, Handford set about building a mental picture of Bronwyn Price. They had three photographs, none of them recent. One had been taken at school when she was sixteen and another on her eighteenth birthday and judging by her demeanour she was anything but comfortable. Her mother said it didn't mean anything; she'd always hated having her photograph taken and more often than not would look away or pull a face. 'She'll be mortified to see these in the newspaper and on television,' she said, keeping her daughter well and truly in the present tense. The most recent photo had been given to them by a woman with whom she worked and showed Bronwyn sitting in a bar with colleagues, and even in this she seemed uneasy. He wondered what it was that caused the embarrassment. Her looks? Possibly. No one would ever have said she was pretty, her eyes were too close together and her nose crooked. It hadn't always been like that, Lynne Younger had been at pains to tell him, it had been broken at school during a hockey match. Handford smiled to himself, his daughters had had a few bruises caused by over-enthusiastic hockey players. Had he not been a police officer and known what people were capable of, he would never have believed girls could be so rough in what, after all, was meant to be a game. The most striking aspect of Bronwyn's appearance was her red hair, a mass of uncontrollable curls. She must have inherited it from her father, since her mother's was straight and, judging from the roots, uninterestingly mousy. One thing was for sure, unless Bronwyn had taken to wearing a wig or had had it coloured and straightened, she would have been easily recognisable, even in a crowd. Another reason to presume she was dead.

Handford glanced at his notes. She was born in Aberystwyth in west Wales, but brought to England at the age of five when her mother left her husband. More accident prone than unhealthy, Bronwyn had sustained a broken leg at ten and an arm at twelve but had rarely been ill. Academically she was of average ability and at sixteen had managed a mixture of C and D grades at GCSE. From school she had moved on to the local college to study for an NVQ in Leisure and Tourism. As a child she had dreamed of becoming an air hostess or a rep in some hot climate, but it had never been more than a dream, and at twenty-six her reality was a nine-to-five job in a travel agency.

Her mother described her as a happy girl, bubbly and full of fun, or at least she had been until David came on the scene, when she had changed and become morose and quarrelsome. He said she was a bitch, never happier than when she was arguing or complaining. Her colleagues painted a picture of someone who was quiet but not so reserved that she was distant, while her boss said she was a reliable and efficient worker who was good with clients. Her ex-boyfriend, Peter Bolton, shrugged and said she was OK, but nothing to write home about. Although he insisted it was he who had ditched her, it could have been the other way round and his portrayal of her no more than sour grapes. There was talk that she was going out with another man – older and possibly foreign, but no one seemed to be sure whether it was one, both or either description that fit.

Clarke was right: Bronwyn Price was an unremarkable young woman. Yet not so unremarkable that, even without a body, it was looking more and more likely someone may have murdered her. So if she hadn't had an accident or committed suicide – and currently there was no evidence to suggest either – what was there in her life that had roused someone to do just that?

So far nothing. He supposed it was possible they were reading too much into her disappearance. Perhaps she was just another missing person, someone who didn't want to be found – like Tom Blakely. Handford hadn't thought much about him since he'd passed the information over to CID. He knew Tom, but not too well. Blakely had been an inspector when Handford was a sergeant. A clever detective, but something of a loose cannon. They'd called him a good thief-taker – police speak for someone with a high arrest rate but slightly dubious methods. It was questionable as to whether he had ever actually set anyone up, but if he had, he had done it so that it got the result he was looking for without it back-firing on him. When Handford had a minute he'd contact CID and let Christine know what progress they'd made. In the meantime Bronwyn Price was his priority.

As he turned to the task of setting out actions for the next day, there came a tap on his door and Detective Chief Superintendent Mike Paynter popped his head round. 'Busy?' he asked.

Handford smiled. 'As always.'

From their first meeting, Handford felt at ease with his new boss. Everything about him was the direct opposite of his former DCI, Stephen Russell, including his appearance. He hardly ever wore a suit, except when he was summoned to the Chief Constable's office or to court or a press conference, preferring a more casual approach. In summer he discarded the pullover. His voice too was less cultured than Russell's, still with traces of his native Cornwall. He carried his rank well and while he was not aloof nor was he one of the lads.

He had joined the West Yorkshire force some twenty years ago when he married a girl from Leeds. Married life obviously agreed with him for they had produced five children, two of whom were still at home. 'They just won't go,' he said. 'I blame Millie's Yorkshire puddings.' Millie's Yorkshire puddings were obviously an integral part of his diet, for now in his mid-fifties he was solidly built. He sported a good head of thick dark hair which was beginning to recede at the temples and his moustache, of which he was inordinately proud, was bushy but neat. If the rules about facial hair became stricter, Handford was sure Paynter would leave the service rather than shave it off.

Although Mike Paynter referred to his rank as 'having been knighted', he was a hands-on detective. Paperwork had to be completed, but not at the detriment of the investigation. No journalist could ever accuse him of never visiting the scene or the relatives. He was a hard taskmaster but his manner was frank and honest and everyone from the most senior to the most junior detective knew exactly where they stood with him. And that was what Handford liked about him; he'd had enough of Russell's flowering plants and freshly ground coffee beans; now at last he was on the same wave length as his boss.

Paynter pulled up a chair. 'I assume, since all hell hasn't broken loose, they haven't found her body.'

'Not yet, sir. The ground-penetrating equipment found some hot spots, but so far they haven't been her body, just the dogs'. They're on to the last quarter, but I'm not holding out much hope.'

'No, me neither. But we had to give it a go. If they don't turn her up, at least we'll know where she isn't and the bigger question will remain as to where the hell she is.'

'We'll find her, eventually.'

'With our luck it'll be some man walking his dog who'll come across her first.' Paynter picked up the photographs and flicked through them. 'Do you think it's worth searching the front garden as well?'

The row of houses faced the main road that ran between the city of Bradford and the smaller town of Keighley. It had once been the main link and often gridlocked, but these days the new relief road took the bulk of the traffic. Nevertheless, it was still used by enough vehicles to make anyone contemplating burying a body think twice. The semi-detached properties, each pair bordered by a wall, stood some eight metres from the road, with a medium-sized garden between the frontage and the footpath. On the opposite side the houses eased themselves up the hillside. Anyone looking out of their window from there would have a good view of the Youngers' front garden

Handford shook his head. 'I can't see him burying a body there, can you? Assuming she was killed eight weeks ago, that takes us back to September and the nights would be drawing in and the street lamps on. He wouldn't do it in the day-time, and even at dusk he could be seen. Neighbours would be bound to wonder what he was doing digging up the garden in the darkness and someone would have mentioned it during house-to-house inquiries. Even if he waited until the middle of the night, there would always be the possibility of police traffic or insomniacs to see him. It would have been too much of a risk.'

'The field then?'

'Sir, we've tramped that field so many times we're on nodding terms with every blade of grass. There is absolutely no sign of any soil disturbance. She's not there.'

Paynter smiled. 'I believe you. So while we're waiting for her to turn up, let's get as much as we can on Younger and Peter Bolton. That young man might not be admitting it, but she could have dropped him for the new one – whoever he is. It's interesting he hasn't come forward. Could he be an illegal, do you think?'

'Younger seems to think he might be, but that doesn't mean much. He's frightened and clutching at anything that will take the attention off him.' Handford described the encounter at the house. 'If she's dead, he'd be our prime suspect. Certainly he hates her enough to have the motive and if she's in the garden we will find out whether he had the opportunity and the means. I can't help feeling that if she's dead she's somewhere we haven't even considered looking and unless we get a flash of inspiration the chances are we'll never find her.'

Paynter stood up. 'Inspector Ali is back from leave tomorrow, isn't he?'

Handford nodded.

'Then put him onto it. His brain is younger than ours, more prone to flashes of brilliance. He might come up with something we haven't thought of. And don't worry, John, it is possible to charge someone with murder without a body. I've done it; it's not satisfactory, but it is possible with the right kind of evidence, so while we're waiting let's work on that.' He walked to the door and was about to leave when he turned abruptly. 'Nearly forgot, John, I had a phone call from a DCI Noble ...' He raised his bushy eyebrows interrogatively.

'Brian Noble?'

'That's him. Do you know him?'

'I worked with him on an investigation about eighteen months ago. I didn't know he'd been promoted.'

'About the same time as you, I think. He's on the unsolved cases team. Apparently he wants to talk to you about a Josie Renshaw.'

David Younger sat at a table in the corner of his local. He'd already downed several pints in the hope they would lift his mood, but all they had done was add to his despair. He looked round. For the first time in years the pub had been refurbished. When it was reopened the manager of the brewery had described the decor as relaxing – but not today, not as far as David Younger was concerned. Today, its forty-watt bulbs, heavy burned-umber flock wallpaper and chairs and benches cushioned in material of the same pattern only added to his anguish. Its saving grace was that it was empty. There was no one to disturb him, come up and ask how the investigation was going, or worse still ignore him. After all, what did you say to a possible murderer?

The copper had been right: he was frightened. Frightened that Bronwyn was dead. Not that he would cry over her coffin, he wouldn't; she'd been a cow ever since he'd met Lynne. Friends said it was because she didn't want to share her mother and he could have understood that had she been fifteen, but she was in her mid-twenties and should get over it. They didn't interfere in her life; she had no right to interfere in theirs.

The landlord came over with another beer and a whisky chaser. 'It's a bit early for you, isn't it?' he said, placing the glasses on the table. 'Do you want to talk about it?'

Did he want to talk about it? Was there anything to say? They were digging up his garden hoping to find a body.

'They think I killed Bronwyn.' He was surprised at the strength of his voice, because he felt like shit. He picked up the pint glass and took a long drink.

'You driving?'

Younger began to laugh, at first softly, then more loudly. He'd just revealed that the police thought he'd killed his stepdaughter and the only comment the landlord could make was to ask him if he was driving. What was the use? Without a word he pushed his keys towards him.

23

The landlord picked them up. 'It's better you leave your car here and take a taxi home. You don't want to be done for drink-driving – not in your job.'

Younger glared at him. 'You're right. Better I'm banged up for murder, than for drink-driving,' he said, his tone overflowing with sarcasm. Suddenly he felt as though someone had pulled the plug on him and his strength evaporated. 'I'll tell you what, mate, just do me a favour and leave me alone.'

The landlord stood up. 'I'll ring a taxi when you're ready.'

Younger watched him until he was safely ensconced at the other side of the bar. Fucking idiot. Why should he worry? It was all money in the till to him.

Money, that's what it had been about. When the police started to delve into his background, as they surely would, a simple check into his personal bank accounts would expose his other life. Once they'd started, it wouldn't take them long to follow the thread between him, his estate agency and the charity offices and blow the whole enterprise wide open. He should have kept it under the mattress or in the loft, at least then it would be safe from prying eyes. He could feel hysteria taking over. If it wasn't so awful it would be funny. Even in his drunken state he could see the irony of it. Bronwyn could turn up suntanned and alive and with what the police would find out, he could be sent down for something else altogether. What did a charge of drink-driving matter?

Over and over again he'd asked himself why he'd become involved with them. The answer wasn't rocket science, he'd needed the money and if he hadn't come up with it he would have lost the business and the house and given Bronwyn, saintly Bronwyn, the chance she'd been waiting for. He was nothing more than she'd always said he was – a waster. Lynne should leave him. It had sounded so easy and at the time it was the answer to all his problems – just let them use a long-term empty property as a mail box.

He felt sick. The flavour of the beer mingled with the smell of the hollowed-out soil clung to his nostrils and soured his taste buds. He dragged himself from the chair and stumbled towards the toilets. Inside he pushed open the door of a cubicle and fell to his knees just in time to heave a stream of foul-smelling liquid into the bowl. For a few minutes he remained where he was, dizzy, unable to focus. Finally, he raised his head, pushed himself to his feet, flushed the toilet and staggered to the wash basin. His hands were shaking as he turned on the tap to sluice his face with cold water. As he dried it with a paper towel he stared at his image in the mirror. He hardly recognised the man who returned his gaze. Memories of the past few hours, days, weeks scrolled across the pock-marked mirror and now, in this moment of truth, he knew he wasn't fooling anyone, least of all himself.

Bronwyn wasn't hiding herself away, Bronwyn was dead.

Brian Noble came towards Handford and shook his hand vigorously. Physically, he hadn't changed since they had worked together on the child prostitute case. Five foot seven and well rounded, his trousers sat uneasily beneath his plump belly, the bright red braces straining against his large frame. He had cast his jacket to reveal the sweat that had gathered under his armpits and in the small of his back.

Handford patted his colleague's stomach. 'Still on the junk food and not getting any exercise, I see,' he said.

Noble laughed. 'And I expect you're running on the treadmill every day, or is that the beginnings of a paunch?' He moved away and indicated the chair in front of the desk. 'Thanks for coming,' he said, suddenly serious. He picked a sheet of paper from the folder in front of him and studied it for a moment. 'The chief superintendent has told you what this is about?'

'You're re-opening the case on Josie Renshaw.'

Noble nodded. 'You remember her?'

'Yes, she lived in the village where I grew up. She committed suicide.' He frowned. 'But that's North Yorkshire, Brian. Why are you investigating? '

'Because she also alleged rape and the village in which that happened is in West Yorkshire, therefore it's ours.' Noble's voice was smooth. Explanations over, he pulled another sheet from the folder and handed it over. 'You gave this statement at the time.'

Handford glanced at it. 'That's right, the local bobby took it. We all gave one – everyone who was at the disco. It was only a village hall event, nothing big.' He was prattling and he knew it.

'Can you remember if she was there?'

'Not specifically, but she would be. She usually was.'

'With anyone in particular?'

'I doubt it. My recollection is that she tended to flirt, usually with anyone who took her fancy and would reciprocate. Boys or men, she wasn't fussy.'

'Did that include you?'

'Not as far as I was concerned. I'm not saying she didn't try it on once or twice, she did with all of us, but I wasn't interested.'

'So what you're saying is that a young lad wouldn't have to rape her to get what he wanted.'

Handford leaned back in the chair, attempting to appear calm, pretending this was no more than a discussion of an ongoing case between two officers. But it wasn't and his unease was growing. He tried to muster an element of disgust into his voice. 'No, I'm not saying that, Brian. Don't put words in my mouth. All I'm saying is that she liked the company of the opposite sex. More than that I don't know.'

'So when she said she'd been raped, did you believe her?'

'At the time probably not. To the villagers she was a tart, a prostitute even, and to some of the village lads an easy lay, although I doubt she was any of those things. She was just a young girl who liked enjoying herself.'

'You said "at the time". Do you believe her now?'

A venomous pain began to stab Handford behind the eyes. He rubbed at his forehead, trying to dislodge the physical and mental hurt he felt. Josie Renshaw's suicide had badly affected his relationship with his brother and he didn't want to relive unhappy memories. He tried to make light of the question. 'God, Brian, I was only seventeen and busy with A-levels and university applications at the time.'

Brian Noble raised his eyebrows to show he needed an answer.

Handford sighed. 'As far as I remember there was no real proof one way or another and no charges were brought and even if she'd been telling the truth the consensus was that it was her own fault.'

'And do you think it was her own fault?' Noble interrupted.

Handford flinched at Noble's use of the present tense – not 'did you', but 'do you.' His current opinion was important – the type of question a barrister would throw at a witness in court. Noble was good, he had to admit that. 'No of course not, Brian. I'm not sure I even thought it then, but rape wasn't taken that seriously and it was difficult to prove. Even if she had had sex—'

'She'd had sex; there's no doubt about that. He was a secretor; his blood group was O.'

'Which covers a good proportion of the male population. You know as well as I do that eighty per cent of people leak blood cells into their bodily fluids and since O is the most common group, him being a secretor with blood group O was hardly evidence – not even then.'

Handford saw Noble's lips tighten. 'You're prevaricating, John. I asked you if you believe her now and you haven't yet given me an answer.'

He shifted his position. 'After the allegation she changed, became withdrawn, isolated. I think she dropped out of school, wouldn't leave the house – that sort of thing. Anyway, at eighteen she threw herself off the church tower.'

'John, do you believe her allegation?' Noble emphasised each word.

Handford scrutinised his hands momentarily. He wasn't going to be allowed to evade the question. Then he let his eyes meet those of the man opposite. 'Yes, I think I do.'

'Can you tell me why?'

'Because she was a sexually active young lady and as far as I know had never alleged rape before. Why should she? As you suggested earlier, a young man wouldn't have needed to rape her to get what he wanted. She'd have given it to him.'

'An older man might.'

'I suppose.'

'So it could have been an older man? Someone she wouldn't have considered going with.'

'Possibly.'

'Or a younger one she'd already been with and didn't want to again?'

There was silence for a while until Handford said, 'Even with DNA, which is presumably why you're opening the case, you're going to find it difficult to get a conviction. It was over thirty years ago; most of the older men in both villages will be dead by now and the younger ones could be anywhere. Rape tends not to be witnessed, so unless you know something you're not telling me and there was a witness who has come forward, then the only one is Josie Renshaw and she's dead.'

Noble replaced the statement in the folder. 'When it comes to something like this, John, people's memories are long and we have managed to locate many of those who lived in the villages or who were at the hall that night. How do you think we found your brother? Douglas is your brother, isn't he?'

Handford tried to suppress the cold sweat that threatened to swamp him. 'Yes,' he said, then, 'I don't see much of him – we lost touch years ago.' He wasn't sure why he'd given out the information, probably because 'yes' seemed too inadequate a response. Noble made no comment, but Handford knew he would be salting it away for future use. He would do the same if he were in Brian's position.

As Noble stood up, indicating the conversation was over, Handford's eyes followed him. Physically he may well not have changed, but he had grown in confidence. It isn't easy questioning one of your own and he had managed to get out of him that little bit more than he would normally have been prepared to give. He had always been good, but rank had made him even better. This was not going to go away.

'I really only asked you to pop in to get your permission to check your DNA against what we have,' Noble said. 'It is on file for elimination purposes, I presume?'

Handford eased himself from the chair. 'Yes it is.'

'So, can we check it against the DNA from Josie Renshaw's clothing?'

'If you think it will help.'

'Every little helps, you know that.' As they reached the door, Noble said, 'I shouldn't be telling you this, John, but it's not only Josie Renshaw we're interested in. There were several rapes in the area at the time, all carried out between June and October of that year, all during discos on victims roughly the same age as Josie and all by a man who was a secretor with blood group O. For the moment we're assuming there may be a link. The DNA from each victim's underclothing has already been checked and so far we've matched two from the same man. Once we've collected samples from everyone we've traced we can start to eliminate them. A conviction might not be as difficult as you suggest.'

'You've still to prove rape.'

'And we'll only get that from victims who are prepared to be cross-examined, which means they have to stand up in court and re-live something they'd probably rather forget. As you say, we've lost Josie, but if the DNA samples match on the girls' clothing we're halfway there. The rest are alive and at least one of them wants closure; the others ... ' He shrugged. 'Well, for the moment they say they don't want it back in their lives, but you know as well as I do that it often only takes one to agree to give evidence to break the reluctance of the others. That as well as the DNA results may do it.' He took hold of the handle. 'Whoever he is, John, he didn't push Josie off that tower, but as sure as hell he contributed to her death and I'd like to get him just for that.'

As the door closed behind him, Handford found himself trembling. However informal it had been, that had been an interview in a rape case. He'd hardly seen Josie himself on the evening in question, but instinct told him that Douglas might have done. Why else would he have pleaded with him to back up his alibi – the only explanation given a playful tap on the side of his nose? Handford had agreed because even as a child Douglas had been adept at getting what he wanted. Nevertheless, the questions remained: what had his brother been doing and where had he been during the time Josie alleged she was being raped? Why had he needed a false alibi to protect him? And why had he refused to attend her funeral when almost everyone in the village had been there, many of them filled with remorse at the way they'd treated her? At the time it had been his brother's lack of concern that a young girl had been so traumatised that she'd climbed the winding staircase of a church tower and thrown herself to her death that had angered Handford so and it was then he realised he didn't like his brother very much and wanted as little to do with him as possible. But now that he was being honest, he knew it was more than that, his absence from the funeral had been no more than a useful tool to push the more serious questions to the back of his mind, hiding them among the other detritus. It was easier than believing his brother was a rapist.

Christine Blakely wrapped her coat round her thin body and ran across the road. When the man saw her, he began to back away. If he jumped over the wall or darted down the street then he could disappear into the park and she would lose him. The drizzle had become a light shower, and with it the temperature was falling. She quickened her pace.

'Please,' she said, 'I've only come to ask if I can help.'

He stopped, obviously unsure as to what to do or to say, but at the same time it was equally evident he didn't want to leave. Christine approached him. From the house she had been unable to distinguish his facial features, but now she could see his tousled hair glistening wet in the light of the lamp which was beginning to glow orange. The colour of his skin and the shape of his face suggested he was probably Eastern European. He couldn't be much more than thirty-five, she thought, but his features were haggard and he appeared old beyond his years. At first glance he seemed unkempt, as though he'd been sleeping rough, but as she drew nearer she could see his coat was of good quality and his shoes, though smeared with mud, were solid enough to give his feet protection. There was also a smell surrounding him that she couldn't quite pin down. It wasn't repellent, in fact quite the opposite. A natural, countryside smell. Soil – no not quite, more than that. He turned towards her, his head down, as though he wanted to remain invisible. If he couldn't see her, she couldn't see him. But as she got closer he remained where he was, holding his ground. 'Are you looking for someone?' she asked, stripping her voice of challenge.

'Tom,' he said warily. He spoke in a thick foreign accent – Polish perhaps or Slovakian.

Her heart missed a beat. Tom, her Tom? 'Tom Blakely?' she said.

He nodded.

'I'm afraid he's not here.' Tom would have been furious with her for letting a complete stranger know she was on her own.

He seemed deflated. Whatever the reason, the man wasn't aware her husband was missing and had been for almost eight days. 'I'm his wife, can I help?'

'No. It is Tom I must speak to. I come back tomorrow. I have to go now. Sorry, sorry.' He turned and darted towards the main road.

Christine attempted to call him back. She wanted to ask who he was, how he knew Tom and where he lived. Why had he come here at all? Why not meet him at his office? As he disappeared round the corner, she knew she had missed her chance and the first signs of hysteria built up inside her. First Ian Gott, then Patrick and now this foreigner. What was happening? Tom hardly ever spoke about his work or about his shattered relationship with his family. If he'd been more forthcoming she might have been able to understand. She had no one to turn to – the police didn't care, not even John Handford. Tom had been one of their own, and all they had done was make assumptions – the wrong assumptions.

The rain, which had become heavier, mingled with the tears streaming down her face and she ran back across the road. She flung open the door, banging it behind her. How dare they? Her husband was not screwing some other woman. She knew it so why wouldn't anyone else accept it? She wanted him found. She wanted him back with her. Exhausted, she leaned against the wall, and allowed her fears to take over. She felt dizzy and weak; her legs no longer supported her and she slid down to sit on the floor where she covered her face with her hands and wept.

Ian Gott shivered as he lay across the seats in the bus shelter – now there was a fucking contradiction in terms. He hadn't seen a bus in a long time and there was certainly no means of shelter. He pulled the foul-smelling blanket up to his chin. The stink was enough to make him throw up. His lips curled at the thought of the homeless bugger he'd pinched it from. That would teach him not to leave his pitch. Survival of the fittest, mate, survival of the fittest – and he knew all about that. If life had taught him something, it had taught him that.

God, he was hungry. Since he walked out of the prison he'd got by mainly by snatching handbags, sometimes at knife-point if they'd fought for it. The money had kept him going until he arrived here, but the purse in the last one had been all but empty. Five pounds and some change; it wasn't enough for a decent meal, let alone for anywhere to stay. He needed to find somewhere he could doss down, somewhere he wouldn't be found and somewhere a bloody sight better than this fucking bus shelter. A hostel would be the cheapest, but he couldn't be sure they hadn't been warned to keep a look out for him – not that it was likely, not up here. In Sussex possibly, but not up here; it was miles away from Ford Prison. Even so, it wasn't worth the risk. He'd probably be safer in a B&B.

It was raining more heavily now and swathes of water were gathering at the edge of the road. Cars and buses sped past, some drivers enjoying the thrill of drenching pedestrians as their wheels closed in on the puddles. A woman walked by. For a moment it looked as though she was going to take refuge in the bus shelter, but when she saw him, she changed her mind and scurried away. Up yours, he thought.

He'd picked up a discarded newspaper from one of the seats and as far as he could see, there was still no report of him being on the run, nor any pictures of him. In fact, no one seemed bothered. There was a time when an escaped prisoner would have had his name and picture over the papers – but not now. Now they didn't seem to care – not about anything; if they had they wouldn't have let Blakely and his side-kick Clarke stitch him up. He owed the two cops for that. His fury mounted and he banged his fist against the wall of the metal and Perspex shelter. The sound echoed round him and he was back inside again with a pillow over his head to shut out the racket of the inmates punching the cell doors at lights out. There was a lot of anger in prison; he had fed on it – his own and theirs – and it had kept him going through the past six and a half years. It had caused him some grief, too, but it didn't matter, the grief was worth it because the emotion and the hatred it fed was shoring him up now and it would keep him on track until he had done everything he came to do. Phase one had been accomplished. He fingered the knife; now all he needed to do was to get hold of enough money to give him time to complete the rest.

chapter three

He'd been watching the nursery for days now, so long in fact that he was surprised someone hadn't noticed and asked him what he was doing. But it was six o'clock and almost dark and those that hadn't already were all too busy collecting their kids. Anyway, it wasn't the kids he was interested in – he hated them, noisy little brats. It was the mothers who were important to him. This time it had been easy to pick her out. Young, with two little ones here and another no more than three months old. He didn't know whether it was a boy or a girl; he didn't much care, although he had wondered what she did with it during the day, probably left it with its grandmother. What interested him more was that it was always crying. The time for picking up the older kids must coincide with its feed time or something because the mother's aim was to get them in the car and drive home as quickly as possible. He'd followed her for most of the week and knew her habits better than she knew them herself. She was always so engrossed in her irritable brood that she never paid much attention to the road or the rest of the traffic. It was a miracle she hadn't been involved in an accident before he could set this one up.

Her route took her in the right direction for a hit – along the relief road towards the roundabout. A roundabout was always the best place for it to happen, so much traffic to watch, so much to think about. The car was right too. New, expensive and insured. She didn't look the type to flout the law. Even the weather was on his side. It had been raining heavily, but had now settled into a light shower, enough for the water to run down the windscreen, but not enough to force the wipers to speed up. The roads were wet, with stretches of water in the notorious flooding spots. Such a lot for the woman to think about.

He raised his mobile to his ear. 'I'm going with this one today. She's just gone in, so they'll be out in about five minutes. It's a silver Ford Mondeo, registration BN06HOR. Give it to Kowalski; it's about time he learned why he's with us.' He closed the phone and watched as the woman unhitched the car seat, trying all the while, but without success, to pacify the baby. She was harassed, he could see that, and he almost felt sorry for her. Almost.

She disappeared into the nursery and a few moments later reappeared, gripping the boy's hand. He could hear the baby more clearly now. The girl ran after her, clutching a picture, obviously keen to show it to her mother. The boy pulled away from her and ran towards another child. His mother called him back, her impatience growing, and when he refused to comply she strode back to him and dragged him roughly from his friend and his conversation. The girl was more compliant and climbed into the car, but again the boy tried to free himself from his mother's grasp. He was in exactly the frame of mind the man watching wanted him to be – bad tempered and unmanageable. The worse he became, the less attention the woman would give to her driving.

Finally, all of them safely and noisily installed in the car, she drove off and he switched on the engine and followed her. Eventually he overtook her and pulled in front. He could see her through his front mirror, driving with one hand and stroking the still crying baby in his chair in the passenger seat, from time to time turning to speak to the children in the back. At the roundabout he spied Kowalski in the Mercedes. He had his hand out of the window and was fiddling with his wing mirror – the sign he was ready, the brake lights disabled. On the footpath next to the kitchen warehouse was a group of men apparently deep in conversation. They were ready too.

What happened next was stealthy, quick and in the man's mind quite beautiful. As she pulled onto the roundabout, Kowalski swooped in front of her and slammed on his brakes. There was nothing she could do and she hit his rear end. The damage to the cars was substantial; it was of no consequence to the driver of the Mercedes, but it would matter to her. It was her fault; she had hit him. Other cars on the road swerved round them and continued on their way; it was none of their business. The group in conversation ran over and surrounded the vehicles as a grey Fiat Punto stopped and the driver jumped out. Almost unnoticed his passengers climbed into the Mercedes.

The woman was hysterical. The baby and the two young children shrieked. Their mother screamed that he had no brake lights. Not true. The Mercedes engine was still running and Kowalski stepped on the pedal. The lights gleamed bright on the wet road.

The man in charge smiled. A job well done. It would be worth fifty or sixty thousand in insurance. He let out his handbrake and drove off unnoticed.

chapter four

As he drove home that night Handford was a worried man. It was raining heavily now and the road in front of him glistened as black as the excavated soil in David Younger's garden. The scenes-of-crime officers had completed their task and packed up and left without finding Bronwyn Price's body. She was not there and they had no idea where she was. He turned on the CD player and pushed the Play button. Soon the car was filled with the sounds of the Brighouse and Rastrick brass band. The first thing he'd done when his promotion came through was to discard the old cassette recorder from the car and replace it with a CD player. He needed the rousing music that only a brass band could produce. He wished he still had time to play himself; he'd always enjoyed the practice sessions and the concerts, but once he'd transferred to CID he was never sure of making either of them. Now, he was so out of practice that he doubted he would have the breath or the energy to sustain a note.

Every problem that had arisen today had added to his concerns and, under normal circumstances, he would be glad to get home. Not tonight. He wasn't being very fair on his mother, she had given up her own life to look after them and he ought to be more grateful, but he missed Gill. Nothing felt the same without her.

They still lived in the detached house in the secluded cul-de-sac they had bought early in their marriage. There were twelve properties lining the road, all built to the specifications of the original owners, each of whom had stamped their own personality on the design. Not for them a series of identical boxes. Situated on the hillside, they overlooked the valley and the gentle lower slopes of the Pennines beyond. In summer it was beautiful and in winter, whether swirled in mist or topped by dark thunderous clouds, the view conjured up a drama all of its own. It had taken only one visit for John and his new wife to fall in love with it all those years ago and they had offered the full asking price to make it theirs. And from the day they moved in they had been happy there, or at least as happy as anyone deserved to be.

Handford turned into the drive, brought the car to a halt and turned off the engine, but made no attempt to climb out. Instead, he gazed at the outline of the house, silhouetted against the darkness of the sky by the light from the security lamp and he wished he was coming home to his wife and not his mother. What he missed most about Gill being away were the evenings when the girls were doing their homework or in bed and they sat and talked. He could tell her anything and he knew she would listen, would understand and would be honest with him. She was his conscience and he trusted her like he trusted no one else. He often joked to her that not many people could say they had a conscience they could make love to. And today, right now, he needed both her conscience and her love. Today everything had crowded in on him – Gill, Bronwyn Price and Josie Renshaw, but uppermost in his mind at this moment was the re-investigation of Josie Renshaw's alleged rape and those of the three other women. He hadn't been aware there had been others and if his parents knew they had never discussed them in his hearing. Nor could he discuss them with his mother now, although he would have to tell her the case was being reinvestigated, if only because his father would probably be asked to give a sample of his DNA. What he couldn't do was mention the false alibi he'd given Douglas – for the moment it was better she didn't know.

Not so Brain Noble, he had to be told. This afternoon he had handed his thirty-year-old statement back to Handford. *You gave this statement at the time.* There had been no question mark in his tone, but the comment had demanded an answer.

Handford knew that. He knew also that he had dissembled and given him the obvious one – not a lie, but not the truth either. In a job where you mixed with criminals you quickly learned their methods of avoidance. He'd seen it in suspects, but he'd also seen it in officers worming their way out of trouble. Was that what he had been doing this afternoon – worming his way out of trouble? And if so, had he been protecting himself or Douglas? Probably both, because to protect one meant protecting the other.

The security light switched off, the only illumination now was that from the street lamp. He leaned over to the passenger seat, picked up his briefcase and overcoat. Even if Douglas's absence from the hall meant nothing, it should at least be investigated. He'd assumed his brother had been smoking dope or perhaps having sex and wanted it kept from their father. It might have been the seventies when free love and drugs were part of the culture, but it would have horrified his parents to think their sons were involved. The one thing he hadn't even considered was that his brother was the alleged rapist – that he had taken what he wanted by force. After all, this was Josie Renshaw they were talking about. Indeed, since it was Josie, streetwise Josie who was old beyond her years, he hadn't thought much at all. Not until she had committed suicide, then he had questioned Douglas about his need for an alibi. Douglas had been furious, demanding to know if John believed he had raped her. He had said 'no, of course not', but he'd seen a glimmer of relief in his brother's eyes and it was at that moment the bond between them had been broken and they had gone their separate ways, a decision made more by mutual unspoken consent than angry words. But he had kept Douglas's trust, such as it was, and had told no one. There had been no reason to until now.

Now he was a police officer who had, when the question had been posed at his interview for entry into the service, said he would investigate anyone who he thought had broken the law, even if that person was a family member. To change his original statement now for the truth was not far removed from that pledge. So like it or not, he had to go back to Noble and rescind his statement. It would be better if he admitted it straight away, though he supposed in theory he could wait until the results of the DNA tests were known.

Handford pulled himself from the car, pressed the key fob to lock it and let himself into the house. As always the hall was bright and welcoming and the aroma that met his senses told him his mother had cooked his favourite meal of sausages and mash. He hung his coat on the hall stand, catching sight of himself in the mirror as he did so. Was Noble right? Did he have the beginnings of a paunch? He couldn't deny there was a suggestion. Checking no one was looking he tightened his stomach muscles but couldn't hold them for any length of time and accepted reluctantly that his fellow officer was indeed right. He'd have to do something about it before Gill returned. She might be honest with him, but sometimes there was only so much truth a person could take. Low-fat meals and a few long walks in the Dales would sort him out. In the meantime, sausage and mash was a comfort food and at this moment in time he was sorely in need of comfort.

Christine Blakely had no idea how long she'd been sitting on the floor, first crying then staring into space. The telephone broke into her misery. Tom. She made a grab for the receiver, but it was someone selling kitchens and she shouted at them to go to hell and slammed it back on the rest. The effort had taken all her strength and for a moment she sat breathing heavily. Finally, she forced herself upright, holding on to the banister until the dizziness passed. She began to shiver; it was cold in the hall. She turned her head to look up at the clock. Five forty-five. She'd gone out to talk to the man as dusk was falling, which meant she'd been here for over an hour.

She walked unsteadily to the kitchen where she turned on the cold water tap and swilled her face, dried it with the tea towel and sat at the table. For the past week she'd tried to maintain some level of normality in her life by putting her faith in the fact that eventually Tom would be found, but tonight she knew differently. No one believed he was anywhere else but with some woman and because of that they hadn't made any serious attempt to search for him. There was no doubt in her mind that if he was to be found it would be down to her to do it.

She shrugged off her coat and hung it in the utility room, then opened the fridge. It was almost empty; she needed to do some shopping and she would – tomorrow. Tonight a boiled egg and some toast would suffice. She put a pan on the hotplate and a slice of bread in the toaster. When they were ready, she placed them on a tray and walked into the lounge. In spite of the central heating, the room felt cool and she turned on the gas fire, setting it several notches higher than normal and then switched on the television to the local news. She watched it as she ate. The headline story was the disappearance of Bronwyn Price. The search of her stepfather's garden had revealed nothing and had been discontinued. The police obviously didn't think *she* was screwing. It was so unfair. Tears sprung into her eyes, but she brushed them away. Tears, she decided, were a waste of time.

When she had finished her meal she returned to the kitchen where she washed the few pieces of crockery she had used and then sat at the table to think. Still chilled, she should have gone back to the warmth of the lounge but was afraid that would lull her to sleep and there were decisions to be made as to what she should do next, so for the moment it was better she didn't get too comfortable. She cupped her chin in her hands. How did you go about finding someone who was missing? As she trawled through the recesses of her mind, she realised that in spite of having been married to a police officer for more than twenty-five years, she didn't know. She supposed she could have pictures of Tom printed and posted in shops and on noticeboards but in her experience they gave back little information for the time spent on them. Perhaps later. Apart from that, nothing came to her – at least nothing more than she'd already done, like speaking to his employers. They hadn't seen him for over a week, but that wasn't unusual, they said, investigators work very much on their own and could be away from the office for days. If the comments were meant to encourage her, they had been mistaken. He might not go the office, but he would have contacted her. She'd also been in touch with his friends, even with the mistresses whose names she was aware of. None had seen him but most agreed to let her know if they did. One of his lovers said that if she never saw him again it would be too soon and yelled at her to leave her alone. In spite of herself, Christine felt sorry for the woman – she must still be hurting. Tom had a lot to answer for.

In desperation she tried his mobile as she had done so many times since that day and the answer was still the same: either the phone was switched off or the battery was dead. Anxiety clutched at her. To prevent being swamped by it, she pushed herself out of the chair and went into the lounge where she turned the gas fire to full and poured a glass of red wine then settled herself on the settee, pulling her knees under her. She had always tried to make this room central to their lives, the place where they spent their evenings, watching television, talking or reading. Tom was a great reader – anything and everything, but most of all science fiction. He joked that it took him out of himself, but what he really meant was it took him as far away as anything could from the horrors he witnessed and had to deal with. She smiled for a moment, remembering; no one knew Tom like she did. They knew the working Tom or the police officer Tom, but not the real Tom, not the man she loved and who, in spite of everything, loved her. She wasn't denying life with him had been hard, but this time, for the first time, she knew in her heart he was not with someone else. It was much more likely his disappearance was connected to something else. The last time she'd seen her husband was the day he'd been told Gott had escaped from prison and it had unnerved him. A check on the man's crimes and on the trial that put him in prison would give her more. There must be something in the archives of the local papers or even on the internet. Also she could ask the insurance company what case he was investigating – that might give her a clue as to where to start.

Finally there was the man who had come looking for Tom – the foreign gentleman. He'd seemed desperate to talk to him; why else would he have spent so much time outside the house? Perhaps he was linked with the case Tom was working on. She had to find him; she had to know what he knew – discover why it was important he spoke to Tom. He'd said he would

42

come back, but she wasn't so sure. Talking to her had unnerved him. There were organisations, charities that looked after immigrants, perhaps she could find him through one of those. She went into the hall and pulled the copy of the Yellow Pages from the telephone table. There were several and it would take a long time to contact all of them. However, he seemed to know the district, therefore it was possible he lived locally, so she'd start with those close to home. Maybe he worked locally too. She remembered the smell that reminded her of a farm, perhaps, or stables. Again she flicked through the Yellow Pages. There were not so many of the first, but quite a lot of the second. Nevertheless, she would visit all of them, see if he was one of their employees.

She sat back, suddenly weary. The warmth of the room enveloped her, comforting her, and she allowed herself to drift into sleep. The last thing she remembered was thinking that perhaps by tomorrow or the next day or the end of the week she could tell the police where Tom was.

The call came in the middle of the night. Automatically John Handford stretched out an arm and picked up the receiver. He listened to the usual obsequious opening comment: *Sorry to wake you, sir, but ...* The 'but' this time was the body of ninety-six-year-old Mrs Annie Laycock found in her home by officers in a passing police car. There were a number of pensioners living in the area and the night patrol often drove round. It didn't take long and it made the old folk feel a bit safer. Tonight they had seen a light in Mrs Laycock's window and investigated. Her door was open and they had entered and found her. It looked like a robbery, but she had been stabbed as well as badly beaten. The detective sergeant sent to the scene doubted it was a robbery that had gone wrong, but rather that the perpetrator had taken pleasure in killing her. Apparently he had said that to his mind whoever had killed her had done it with relish.

Handford closed his eyes for a moment. Why had these people to be so violent? How much of a fight could an old woman put up? She would more than likely have been terrified

43

and let him take whatever he wanted. 'All right, tell them I'm on my way. Ring Inspector Ali; I'll join him there.'

'Inspector Ali's on leave, sir.'

'He's back today.' Handford glanced at the illuminated figures on the clock. They flipped over to 2.59. 'And by my reckoning we're three hours into today.'

Annie Laycock's bungalow was part of a small estate of privately built dwellings near to the Youngers'. It was cordoned off with police tape as was the street leading up to it, and the scenes-of-crime officers were already there. The police tried to make it as easy as possible for the residents, but this was the second time in as many days rings of blue and white ribbon had prevented them from going about their normal business. Some, Handford knew, would be understanding, others would be angry and blame the police, and the more ghoulish amongst them would find it exciting and talk about it for weeks with anyone prepared to listen.

Ali was waiting outside for him, already in protective clothing.

Handford surveyed his inspector's lithe figure. That was the trouble with tall, slim, good-looking men; they could wear anything with style – even paper suits.

'Good leave?' he asked as he struggled into his.

'It would have been if I could have completed it with a decent night's sleep,' he said.

Handford grinned. 'Why? Your leave ended at midnight.' He tapped his watch. 'Now is today. And since it'll be your case you ought to be here.'

Ali returned his smile. 'You're a hard task master, you know.'

Handford pulled the protective suit over his shoulders and zipped it up. 'I always was, it's just that you never noticed. Now, do you want the case or not? I can always give it to someone else.'

'Don't you dare, John.' For as long as Handford had known Khalid Ali, he had been ambitious, so ambitious that often he had overlooked the fact that he was part of a team and had cut his own path – sometimes to the detriment of the investigation.

44

Now he was about to run his own case he would have to learn the importance of that team otherwise he would have detectives sitting around twiddling their thumbs.

'Right then, that's settled. Now, let's see what we've got.' Handford approached the SOCO. 'Can we go in?'

'If you keep to the tread plates, but I warn you, she's not pretty.'

As soon as they entered, the stench of blood and faeces hit their nostrils and they pulled their masks over their mouths and noses. They didn't keep the smell out completely but they made it bearable. The SOCO had been right. She wasn't a pretty sight. She was lying on the floor in the sitting room, dressed in a flannelette nightgown that was scrunched above her knees and drenched in blood. Handford would have liked to rearrange it to preserve her dignity – albeit in death, but protocol and scene preservation demanded the body should not be disturbed. He hoped with all his heart she hadn't been raped as well as robbed and murdered. There were several visible stab wounds to her chest and abdomen and the distortion of her body the way her limbs were splayed suggested she'd been thrown around as though she'd been used in a pillow fight. She wore one light-blue slipper; the other was a metre away, its sole upturned. Her long grey hair fanned out like a halo around a face whose features had been almost completely obliterated and there was a deep trench from forehead to the leathery wrinkled skin of her neck where the bones had caved in as a result of a blow by something very heavy. Handford couldn't even begin to imagine what she looked like in life and for a brief moment Ali turned his head away.

'You all right?' Handford asked.

'Yes.' Ali swallowed hard. 'Yes. Yes, I'm sorry. After a fortnight away this kind of thing comes as something of a shock.' He let his eyes wander the room, still avoiding the body. Furniture was upturned, drawers out of their housing, ornaments smashed, some of them almost powdered, as though the perpetrator had stamped on them. Papers and what looked like birthday cards were strewn over the floor. Under the SOCO's watchful eye Ali carefully picked up one between forefinger and thumb and opened it. 'Ninety-six today, have a wonderful birthday. Not so wonderful,' he said.

'No.' Handford surveyed the scene, thoughtful for a moment. Finally he asked, 'Do you know anything about an Ian Gott?'

'Never heard of him. Should I have?'

'Probably not. He's something of a career criminal – has spent more of his adult life in prison than out of it. In 1999 he was sent down for fourteen years for aggravated burglary. He'd served half and was transferred to an open prison before being released, but about ten days ago he decided not to complete his sentence and walked out of the open prison he had been transferred to. He hasn't been seen since.'

'And this is his MO?'

'Yes, just about.'

Ali frowned. 'I'm confused, John. Escaped prisoners tend not to come into our actions for tomorrow, so what's your interest in him?'

'Nothing, except ... Did you ever know Tom Blakely?'

Ali shook his head.

'He was a detective inspector – retired some time back. It was Blakely who arrested Gott; Gott decided he'd set him up and when he was sentenced he threatened his revenge. Yelled it all the way down to the cells, apparently. I wouldn't have known he was out except Mrs Blakely came to see me at home a few days ago. She hadn't seen her husband for over a week and she was worried for him. I handed her over to CID.'

'But now you think Gott may have carried out his threat?'

'No, not really, I think Tom is doing what Tom does best and is with another woman, but if Mrs Laycock's murder is Gott's work it means he's in the area and if he is we've got to ask ourselves why has he come here. It would have made more sense for him to have gone off to some city where he would be anonymous. Anyway, after Mrs Blakely left I checked on him. He picked on the vulnerable – old people, the disabled – anyone he could rob easily.'

'There was nothing easy about this,' Ali pointed out.

'Not for Mrs Laycock certainly. Usually he did no more than frighten his victim with his knife – he didn't need to – but if anyone fought back he wasn't against using violence. Looking at this scene, I'd say Mrs Laycock fought back, wouldn't you? I might be wrong, Khalid, it might have nothing to do with Gott, but he's been on the run well over a week now and he's bound to need money. At least keep him in mind is all I'm saying. You never know, you might actually find him in the process and ...' Handford winked at the SOCO, 'that's bound to earn you a gold star.'

Ali was about to retort when a scenes-of-crime officer came into the room, a grin lighting up his face. 'You'll never guess what the cheeky bugger's done,' he said.

They turned towards him. 'He's only gone and had a bath. Is he thick or what? Doesn't he know his DNA will be all over that room?'

There weren't many places to hide in November where he could be warm and at the same time not be seen by the cops, but to Ian Gott the far side of the lake in the grounds of the seventeenth-century manor house just off the main road was about the best. He had known it well as a kid, used it as his hide-away when he was bunking off school or when his father came home drunk and in the mood to use him as a football. The lake was home to ducks and swans and sometimes herons and at the far side there was a small bank of trees and reeds among which he could hide. No one would venture near the hall at night because of the tales that it was haunted. He didn't believe in ghosts, except those that had haunted him for the past six years, but if he did see the phantom coachman who was supposed to have lost his life in this duck pond, he'd tell him to fuck off. He wasn't sharing his hiding place or his blanket with anyone, least of all a spirit. Although, as he looked across at the hall, he had to admit it was a bit eerie. It went back a good few centuries with its tall chimneys and dark windows, not to mention the ruined building next to it. As a child he'd pretended there'd been highwaymen in the district. If he'd lived then he would have been a highwayman and ended up with the kind of treasure he now had in his possession.

The box he'd found hidden under her clothes in a drawer in

the old woman's house lay at his side. He wasn't sure because he hadn't counted it, but there must be a good few thousand in it. She'd fought hard to keep it, he'd give her that, although goodness only knew why. She must have been ninety if she was a day. What would she want with that kind of money? Her strength had come as a bit of surprise to him. He'd picked her because she was small and frail-looking, almost bent double, but she'd had the strength of a dozen – and the spirit. That had shocked him; he hadn't expected it.

He settled down under the blanket. No point worrying about it; what was done was done. Collateral damage that's what it was. His war was with Blakely and Clarke; she was just a means to an end. A means that meant he could go to a charity shop tomorrow to kit himself out and then find a B&B. where he could get a decent night's kip and a good breakfast, maybe enough for a car as well. He cuddled the box containing the money – he wouldn't want the phantom coachman getting hold of it. He grinned – fat chance. Then he closed his eyes, still smiling.

That night Ian Gott slept better than he had for many a night.

chapter five

Christine Blakely was not a religious woman, rather a lapsed Catholic who from time to time needed the help of a being she didn't really know or understand, which was why the next morning she went to light a candle in her local church and to sit quietly offering up her hopes and fears to whoever might be listening. She wasn't in a position to know whether it would help, but when she finally walked through the large wooden door into the dreary November day the doubts that had amassed during a fitful night had dispersed and she had boosted her courage enough to take the first step in finding her husband. Leaving her car in a side road close to the church, she set off to walk into the town centre where the nearest of the charity and welfare organisations were located.

Sandwiched between a hairdresser's and a dog-grooming salon, the offices of Help International stood in a double-fronted Victorian terraced house in a street off the main thoroughfare. For many years it had been a desirable residence, but as the town grew and industry boomed the middle-class inhabitants moved out into the more select villages and in common with others the building was turned into offices. It was first bought by a group of solicitors then latterly by the charity, on the grounds that although the location was poor it was cheap. To concur with the many acts of parliament, they had added a disabled ramp and widened the entry with double doors, but otherwise it was pretty much the same as it had always been. Generally few people ventured down this street, partly because it was away from the banks and the shopping centre, but mainly because it was narrow, edged by tall buildings and always in shadow – the perfect blanket for anyone needing to conceal themselves for their actual or imagined protection or for the fulfilment of more dubious activities.

Christine required neither and if she felt at all nervous, it wasn't because she was afraid of the surroundings or a possible mugging, but because she was afraid that if she found the man who had been standing outside her house he might tell her something she didn't want to hear. She stood for a moment, reading the notice in one of the windows. It was written in several languages and scripts; one or two she recognised but could not understand, others she had no knowledge of. The English told her that Martin Neville and Leon Jackson welcomed anyone who needed welfare advice and it listed health care, benefits, family credits, housing and finance as examples. She wondered if missing husbands came into welfare advice – probably not.

She pushed open the door. In front and to the right was a flight of stairs and to her immediate left a glass door which led into the offices. The interior was welcoming, probably much as it had been when the solicitors were there. The reception area was empty but for a curved desk and three chairs, all of which were unoccupied. On the wall were racks of leaflets, again in different languages and scripts. Behind the desk was a partition of dense opaque glass, part of which appeared to be a sliding door and through which she could see the hazy outline of a man – at least she assumed it was a man since the names on the posters were those of men. Whether he had heard her or not she didn't know, but he made no effort to check or to come out to her. To the left was an open door. She peered through. It seemed to lead into a darker corridor lit by low-energy light bulbs. At the far end was what appeared to be a kitchen and on either side several rooms where presumably clients could unload their problems or be given advice in comparative privacy. From one of them a well-dressed man and a not-so-well-dressed young woman emerged dragging two toddlers behind her. One was crying and the woman yelled at him to shut up or she'd give him what for. Either the child didn't hear her or he was too far gone to take any notice and the wailing continued. With a weary smile the man stood aside while the woman entered the reception area and then opened the front door for her, suggesting as he did so that she should come back if she needed them again. Then he turned to Christine and, with fingers crossed, said, 'Please God she doesn't need me, at least until that child is old enough to be at school.' His smile widened, adding to his already boyish image. He seemed too young to be helping people of her age – indeed of any age – with their problems. 'Sorry,' he said, 'but he was beginning to get on my nerves.'

She knew how he felt.

He walked towards her. 'I'm Martin Neville, can I help?'

'To be honest, I'm not sure,' she said.

'Try me.'

Now she was here, it was difficult to know where to start. Finally she said, 'My husband is missing.'

'I'm sorry, Mrs ...?' He raised his eyebrows interrogatively.

'Blakely.'

He made no reply until he was at the other side of the desk. When he spoke the smile had gone, but his tone was kindly. 'We don't deal in missing persons, Mrs Blakely. Surely you would be better going to the police.'

'No, no. You don't understand.' Of course he didn't. She hadn't begun to tell him what she wanted. 'I haven't come here for you to find him. I've already been to the police.' She wanted to add that they were little or no help, but he might have asked questions she didn't want to answer. For a moment she struggled against the tears that were threatening to fall.

He must have noticed for he came back round the desk and manoeuvred her gently towards one of the chairs. 'Can I get you a drink of water perhaps?'

'Please.'

Mr Neville hurried through the side door. She thought she saw him in the glass-fronted office, but she couldn't be sure and when she looked again he had disappeared, returning eventually with a glass. He handed it to her. Her hands shook as she lifted it to her lips and took a sip. 'I'm sorry,' she said. 'It's been a difficult week.'

Neville took the seat next to her. 'I understand. Take as long as you need. When you're ready you can explain exactly how you think I can help.'

'A man has been watching my house morning and evening for a few days now ...' Neville opened his mouth to speak, presumably to tell her they didn't deal with stalkers or burglars either, but she didn't let him get that far. 'Last night I asked him what he wanted and he said he had to speak to Tom – my husband. I told him he wasn't home, and he said he would come back today, but he hasn't. I need to find him, to find out what he wanted of Tom, see if it has anything to do with his disappearance.'

When Neville seemed not to understand, she said more firmly, 'The man was a foreigner, Mr Neville, probably Polish or Slovakian. He might have come to you for advice. He was in his mid-thirties, tall, slim, dark-haired. I think he might work on a farm or at some stables. He was nervous, smoked a lot and was obviously worried about something he thought Tom could help him with. I wondered if you knew him or of him, if he'd been to you to ask advice.'

She watched Neville as she spoke and more than once thought she saw a flicker of concern in his eyes. But if there was, his words belied it. 'You have given me a description that could fit many men, foreign or otherwise, Mrs Blakely. I couldn't put a name to him, and to be honest even if I could I wouldn't. We are an advice centre, people expect us to preserve their privacy and that means their names.'

A few moments ago she had been attempting to stave off her fears with a glass of water, now she wanted to drench him with it. He was no more help than the police; it was just that his reason for refusing to help her was different. There was a man out there who may have information about Tom, who may have been to this advice centre and who Martin Neville may well know. What harm would it do to give her his name? Seething inside she wasn't sure how she managed to maintain her composure. She handed him the glass and stood up. 'I do understand your dilemma, Mr Neville,' she said quietly. 'I just wish you understood mine.'

Whether the comment stirred his conscience or whether he was attempting to placate her, she didn't know, but he said, 'I can't say I recognise the man you have described – or at least he might be one of a few. I'll tell you what I will do: if anyone fitting that description comes in, and there's no guarantee of that, I'll ask if they have tried to make contact with your husband and if someone has, I'll ask if he is prepared to get back in touch with you. Let me have your name, address and telephone number and he can do the rest. It's the best I can do, I'm afraid.' He pulled a piece of paper from under the desk and handed it to her. She scribbled down the information.

Martin Neville walked her to the door and as he pulled it open he said, 'I do hope your husband turns up, Mrs Blakely. I'm sure he will, missing persons often do.'

Martin Neville peered through the window and watched as Christine Blakely walked towards the town. From the back she looked as world-weary as she had when she'd been sitting on the chair sipping the water he'd brought her. He ought to have felt sorry for her, but it wasn't an emotion he was prepared to waste on anyone, least of all Tom Blakely's wife. The man had been a thorn in their flesh for too long now and as far as Neville was concerned missing was the best place he could be. The last thing he or Help International was ever likely to do was to make it easy for her to find him. From behind him came the sound of the door sliding back. He turned to see Leon Jackson approach and lean forward over the desk. His long face was as gaunt as ever, made even more so by the shoulder-length fair hair that framed it.

'Did you hear any of that?' Neville asked.

'Enough.' Jackson frowned, his thick blond eyebrows almost meeting in the middle of his forehead.

Neville sat down on one of the chairs and crossed his legs, attempting to appear unconcerned but he could feel his facial muscles tightening round his clenched teeth. 'You know she described Marek Kowalski. It couldn't have been anyone else. We should have warned him off properly when he wanted out.'

He could feel the rage building up in his partner and worried, not for the first time, that Leon was so volatile. One day his temper would get them into serious trouble.

'The bastard's talked, hasn't he?' Jackson said.

Neville attempted to placate him. 'I doubt it, not yet, otherwise he wouldn't have gone looking for Blakely. And if he'd said anything to her, she wouldn't have needed to ask who he was. At least we're warned.'

If he'd heard it, Jackson ignored the comment. He turned on Neville, his eyes blazing. 'I told you he was trouble. But no, you had to take him on. "He looks the part", you said. What good's that if he goes running to the law at the first sign of trouble?'

'It wasn't the law he ran to.'

'As good as. It's a bloody good job Blakely's out of the frame or God only knows what Kowalski would have said.'

'So we teach him a lesson.'

Jackson glared at his partner. 'If I had my way I'd cut his bloody tongue out.'

He would too. That was the problem with Jackson; he was irrational, bordering sometimes, Neville thought, on the psychopathic. He was quite capable of carrying out what appeared on the surface to be no more than an angry threat. 'Don't be ridiculous, Leon, we're not the Mafia, we can't go around cutting people's tongues out.' The telephone rang in the back office. 'Go and answer that – and calm down.'

When Jackson had gone, Neville stood up and returned to the window. It had begun to rain heavily now and the clouds had stained the sky a deep blue-black so that although it was only morning the street was almost in darkness. The image of Christine Blakely loomed in front of him, cowed and despondent as she walked from the offices. Had he done enough? Would she wait for him to ask around or would she continue to look for Kowalski? Her husband was missing, the police had been informed, but reading between the lines, they were doing little or nothing to find him, so she had taken it upon herself to do so. He hadn't been with her long, but she seemed to him to have considerable strength of character. Most people would have left it to the police, but not her. More worrying was that she was observant. Kowalski carried the scent of horses like an aura and she had noticed. Sooner or later she would visit farms and stables and eventually she would find him. The owners wouldn't be as interested in Kowalski's privacy or think twice about telling her when he would be working. He was legal so they had no reason not to talk to her. Jackson was right: the man would have to be persuaded not to give her any answers.

Leon Jackson came back into reception. 'That was the hostel,' he said. 'They have a couple of places if we need them.' His hard blue eyes ran over Neville's face like a sensor. 'What do we do about Kowalski?'

Neville turned from the window. 'If Mrs Blakely's got it right, and I think she has, then she's left us with no choice. We warn him off. Point out that he was happy enough to take our money when he was on his uppers and that he doesn't repay us by discussing our business with an insurance investigator. And if that's not enough, we teach him the meaning of gratitude.'

Jackson smiled broadly, a smile Neville knew meant he was enjoying what he was thinking. 'A few days in hospital – yeah?'

Neville nodded. 'Yes, that should do it – but no more than that,' he warned. Suddenly he smiled as though he had been infected by Jackson's obvious satisfaction. 'He can always say he was kicked by a horse.'

Douglas Handford had phoned the office that morning, pleading a migraine. 'I'll be in later,' he told his secretary, then he left the house and drove to the cemetery where Josie Renshaw was buried. Now in the cold mist and rain, he stood over her grave. He wasn't sure why he'd come, except for some inexplicable need to see her final resting place. The inscription was simple.

JOSIE RENSHAW BORN 5 AUGUST 1957
DIED 19 SEPTEMBER 1975. REST IN PEACE.

He hoped she was. From what he'd heard she hadn't

experienced much peace in the two years between the rape and throwing herself off the tower.

'Are you a relative?' The voice came from behind him. Unexpected, but friendly enough.

Startled, Douglas turned. A man, huddled in a dark grey coat, a scarf wrapped round his neck and his hands in his pockets, was standing above him on the path leading to the gates. 'Er, no, just someone who knew her a long time ago.'

The stranger freed one of his hands and held on to a headstone to steady himself as he stepped onto the grass. 'I'm the vicar here,' he said, waving in the general direction of the church. 'Sorry if I startled you, it's just that I was surprised to see you; she doesn't get many visitors.' Douglas made no reply.

The vicar watched him for a brief moment and then said, 'Not a bad girl really. She just lost her way a bit, don't you think?'

'Probably.' He didn't know. He wished the vicar could refrain from making her seem more of person now she was dead than he and the other young men had done all those years ago when she was nothing more to them than someone who could give a few minutes' pleasure.

'The grave has become so neglected,' the vicar continued, his words hovering over Douglas's thoughts like piped music. 'It's sad but the Renshaws don't seem to have the spirit to keep it tidy and Bill, our volunteer groundsman, is getting on a bit and can't bend down as he used to. To be honest, even after all these years, I think it's still too distressing for her parents to come here; I think it reminds them not so much of the fact that she's dead but of how she died and why. One sin compounding another, you know.' He glanced up at the church tower, silent for a moment. Eventually he said, 'Do you know them?'

Douglas had let the vicar's words wash over him; he didn't want to hear about the Renshaws but the question penetrated. His immediate reaction was to say 'no' but he could hardly deny them when he hadn't denied the daughter so he said, 'I used to.' The next question found the same spot.

'In that case, do you think it would be possible for you to drop in on them? I'm sure they'd like to see a friendly face.'

Douglas felt the colour rising in his cheeks. A friendly face. If only the vicar knew. How could he explain he didn't want to be part of their grief? 'I'm sorry—' he began.

The vicar interrupted. 'No you're right; it's not fair to ask you after all these years. I thought since you were here ...' His voice trailed off. 'I'll leave you with Josie.'

Douglas watched him climb onto the path and walk away. Perhaps it was something to do with being a vicar, but there was a man who could say the wrong thing that was so obviously the right thing – the thing that hit where it hurt. Leave him with Josie. Josie whose parents he didn't want to know, whose features he could barely remember. Desperately he tried to bring her to mind but she was a blur, nothing more than a shape rolling around on the grass with him. He could still feel the warmth of her body, his own on top of hers, the trees above them, the sunlight flickering through the leaves. It had been good, he remembered that. Although not quite sixteen she had taught him a thing or two.

Not quite sixteen. The words jarred and his fear returned. They sounded better than fifteen, but they meant the same – she was under the age of consent. At the time it was a law regarded more seriously by the Establishment if not by the youth. Now it was regarded seriously as a law only by those who wanted to make capital out of it – like the media. He could see the headlines: *Social Services boss admits to sex with a minor*. No one would care that it was thirty years ago; that information would be hidden in the small print. It was the headline that would stick in readers' minds.

He lifted his head and let his eyes take in the view. At one time this had been his home. Two villages linked by a road and an indefinable boundary line. One of them, the one where he was now, housed the church, the pub and the school where he and John had been pupils and his father one-time head teacher, the other the chapel and the institute where discos were held. Through both ran the canal where he had fished for sticklebacks – tiddlers they called them – with a piece of string and a home-made hook. On the opposite side of the valley was the river Aire and high up the hillside behind the villages the moors where they had played and picnicked as children. Life was less complicated then.

Not now. Now things had moved on. Now he had to think rationally, take his relationship with the girl in this grave out of the equation and there was only one way to do that. If the police were able to match his DNA with that on Josie's clothing – and old as it was, they obviously could, otherwise why take samples – he would become a suspect. It couldn't happen. He would not, could not agree to the police request. With his DNA they might have something; without it they had nothing except an allegation from a dead girl. He had to pull himself together, return to the office and contact the police. He would go through his statement, but that was all and whatever interpretation they put on his refusal, there was little they could do. Any attempt to take a sample against his will would constitute assault, and providing John upheld his alibi, they would have no evidence on which to question or arrest him.

He stooped down and laid the flowers he had brought on her grave then he walked away. It was the best he could do for her and her family.

After the morning briefing into Annie Laycock's death, John Handford set up a meeting with Khalid Ali and Andy Clarke. Now they were settled in his office, he was aware it wouldn't be the easiest he had ever called. Although Ali had discussed the possibility of Ian Gott's involvement in the murder with his team, he had, on Handford's instructions, not given out any information as to why the man might be in the district. Some things were meant for a need–to-know basis and this was one of them. The last thing he wanted was the press getting hold of a story of a possible miscarriage of justice caused by corrupt police officers. Nor did he want either Tom Blakely's or Andy Clarke's name pulled through any mud the media might manufacture.

Briefly Handford outlined what he knew, keeping nothing back and allowing no interruptions. 'What we need to be sure of first,' he said finally, 'is whether or not Gott is in the district. Annie Laycock's murder suggests he might be and the DNA in the bathroom will tell us more, but until we get the results of that – and even when we do – I don't want you or your team assuming he killed her. You investigate all leads.'

Ruffled, Ali said, 'Of course.'

Handford ignored his tone. This was nothing to what was coming up. 'Next, if he is here, we must ask ourselves whether Tom Blakely's disappearance and Gott's reappearance are no more than a coincidence or whether they are linked, and if they are, has he come back to carry out the threat he made when he was sentenced?' He turned to Clarke. 'I'm sorry, Andy, but before we go any further I need to know if there is any truth in Gott's claim.'

Clarke stiffened and his eyes locked onto Handford's. 'That Tom and I set him up? Of course not. I know what people said about Tom but as far as I was concerned he was a good copper; he didn't need to mess with evidence.' He leaned towards Handford and, restraining his obvious anger added, 'And for the record, nor did I.' For a brief moment, he remained quite still, then he sat back and said, 'I'm surprised you even asked.'

Handford understood how he felt. Although he hadn't accused Clarke, it would feel like it to him. He said, 'Take me through the investigation as you remember it.'

For several seconds, Clarke made no reply. Eventually, his voice tight with controlled resentment, he said, 'Gott was a career burglar; he broke into old folks' houses, usually at night when they were asleep, ransacked the place and took their savings, even their pensions if that was all he could find. Some of the old folk he had robbed said he had a knife, so this was something of a departure for him. We found one on him when we arrested him. He insisted it was for his own protection, but a couple of the ladies had nasty wounds on their arms and legs that could only have been made by a knife. We wanted him caught. It was only a matter of time before he killed someone.'

'So what happened?' Ali asked.

'For some reason he'd changed his routine and broken in during the evening. Allan Widdop, the victim, was watching television and took exception to someone stealing his things so he fought back. Gott knifed him and beat him up, put him in hospital for a week or more. It was a vicious attack, he could have killed him. But Widdop was a strong old boy and although he wasn't found until the next morning he survived. God only knows how. If he hadn't Gott would have been on a murder charge. We sent Gott's knife for forensic examination and small amounts of blood were found between the blade and the hilt but seven years ago DNA investigation wasn't as refined as it is today and it was too small a sample to get a definitive match. All they could say was it was Mr Widdop's blood group.'

Handford digested this in silence and then said, 'You said stealing his *things*. This time it wasn't just money?'

'He took some war medals as well, probably to teach Mr Widdop a lesson for standing up to him, show him he wasn't a war hero any more, just an old man. They weren't worth much – a few pounds at the most.'

'Did they turn up?'

'Yes, in a skip in the town. It didn't appear as though he'd tried to sell them on, at least none of the usual suspects would admit to being offered war medals. Presumably they were no use to him, so he'd thrown them.'

'Any fingerprint evidence?'

'Yes, mostly smudged, but there was a clearer partial thumb print on the box containing the medals.'

'Enough to say it was Gott's?'

In spite of his confident tones, anxiety veiled Clarke's features. 'The expert said so and the defence and the jury believed him.'

'But you're not too sure?'

'Mr Blakely had no doubts.'

'That wasn't what I asked, Andy.'

'There was no reason to assume a mistake had been made.'

Handford wondered if the detective really believed what he was saying or had he been uncertain about the evidence at the time and was now shielding his one-time boss? 'Anything else?'

Clarke relaxed. 'Small amounts of glass were found in the soles of Gott's trainers; they were matched to a tumbler belonging to

Mr Widdop, which had been broken in the scuffle. We also carried out an identity parade and the old man picked him out. The defence made a big thing of the fact that his eyesight was fading and that he couldn't possibly have been able to identify Gott, but the jury didn't agree.'

'Was anyone else ever in the frame?'

'Yes, a gang of lads, but we ruled them out pretty quickly.'

'Why?'

'Because they were in the process of vandalising a park at the relevant time and there were witnesses to that.'

'No one else?'

'No.'

'Did you ever wonder why Gott changed his method, breaking in during the evening rather than during the night, stealing goods rather than money?'

'Of course we did, and it wasn't rather than money, but as well as, nor was it goods, it was one set of war medals. And as far as breaking in during the evening instead of at night was concerned, Gott was good at playing games.'

'What about his alibi; did he have one?'

'Oh yes, he had an alibi, three in fact, all different and not one of them stood up to investigation. When it was put to him that we hadn't been able to validate any one of them and that they were a figment of his imagination, he agreed – finally – that he'd been in the house, although he insisted it was later. He said he'd found the old man unconscious, on the floor, blood everywhere, so he'd left. He didn't even stop to ring for an ambulance. He had no real explanation for his thumb print on the war medals except that he might have touched the box while he was in the room and that it must have been someone else who took it and threw it away.'

'Did he suggest who?'

'The police, of course. Who else?' Clarke took a deep breath. 'Whatever Gott says, there was nothing wrong with our investigation; it was done by the book, sir.' There was no hint of pleading to be believed in his voice, but rather an indication in the word 'sir' of the disgust he felt at having to defend himself at all. Before Handford could comment Clarke continued,

'The Police and Criminal Evidence Act had come in when we arrested Gott, and you know well enough that at the beginning we always read the book before we did anything. So for the record, in spite of what he says happened, Gott wasn't set up; he wasn't leaned on and he was as guilty as hell.'

'And Mr Widdop, where is he now?'

'I don't know.'

'Then if he's not dead we need to find him, and I want a full report on the investigation in to the attack on him, Andy. As soon as possible please.'

Handford saw Clarke's hackles rise even further. 'Why?'

'Because if Gott is back on our patch and if he has killed Annie Laycock, then we want to be ready for any allegations he might make and not scrabbling around at the last minute for information.'

Clarke pushed back his chair and stood up. Suddenly he looked much older than his years. That's what a suggestion of dishonesty did to you in this job. You didn't need to be found to be corrupt – the intimation was enough. 'Then I'll get on with it, sir. I'll let you have it by the end of the day.'

Handford watched in silence as Clarke disappeared through the door. They had known each other since they were coppers on the beat; Andy was Nicola's godfather. It was unthinkable that he had set up Gott, but it had to be checked out. They were accountable to the public and the villains alike; that was how it was in the police service and there were times when Handford's rank got in the way of friendship. They were detective chief inspector and detective constable – the distance between them vast, and at times like this almost impossible to bridge.

'Do you think Gott is right, that they did set him up?' Ali asked, breaking into his thoughts. 'I know Clarke's a friend of yours, but you have to admit their evidence was a bit thin. The best is the glass in the soles of Gott's trainers and he could have picked that up during the night as he said. But if you assume he didn't, what else did they have? Not much. A knife on which they found a small amount of blood that told nothing more than the victim's blood group, a partial thumb print

62

on a box of medals found in a skip, an identity parade out of which a partially sighted old man picked him and the fact that he changed his MO in order to play tricks on the police. Any half-decent brief should have been able to demolish the prosecution's case.'

Handford couldn't argue with Ali's reasoning. Yet Andy Clarke was the most honest man he knew. He would never knowingly set someone up. If the evidence against Gott had been questionable in any way, then it was down to Tom Blakely not Andy. Perhaps they had it wrong and his wife was right. Tom Blakely was not having an affair with some woman; he had gone AWOL. Frightened that Gott was back he had made himself scarce. But that didn't necessarily mean he had set the man up. The chances were that wherever he was, he was safer there than at home, but Clarke wasn't, neither from Gott nor from the service if he was thought to be involved in a miscarriage of justice. Blakely was crucial to the investigation into Annie Laycock's murder and to Clarke's future; they had to find him.

'I don't know whether Gott was set up or not,' he said finally. 'And I agree the evidence was thin, but my question would be why didn't the defence demolish the prosecution's case? Look, Khalid, I know you've got a lot on with Annie Laycock's murder, but if Gott is responsible then there may well be a link with the original investigation and the chances are all this will come out. I want you to go through it; I want every statement checked and re-checked. Find out whether those boys were vandalising the park at the time Clarke said they were. If there is anything to suggest it wasn't sound, then I'll pass it over to Complaints and Discipline. Get Warrender to help you.'

'Warrender? You don't really mean that?'

'Yes, I do.' Handford had worked with Detective Constable Chris Warrender for the past four years and he had a lot of time for him. Ali, on the other hand, had come up against the worst in the man, mainly his prejudice against the Asian population in general and Ali in particular. Their relationship had improved during a case involving the death of a pupil from a local school, but Ali would never trust him entirely. Nevertheless, in Handford's eyes he was a good detective and because his methods were sometimes unorthodox, he would understand the workings of a mind like Tom Blakely's better than most. 'Bring him up to speed and warn him this is between you, me and him and if necessary Clarke and no one else; I don't want any leaks.'

When Ali had gone, Handford ran his hands over his face. He was tired and his head ached. He opened his desk drawer and took out a box of painkillers. Pushing two from their bubbles, he walked into the incident room. It was deserted except for Clarke who looked up and then away. Handford drew a cup of water from the dispenser, threw the tablets to the back of his throat and swallowed. He said nothing to his friend – perhaps later when they were both feeling less stressed. He was about to leave when the telephone rang. Clarke stretched over to pick it up. He listened for a moment and then handed the receiver to Handford. 'It's for you,' he said. 'Mr Noble.'

Handford took it from him. He'd almost, but not quite, forgotten about Noble, Douglas and Josie Renshaw. He had intended to speak to Noble when he arrived at the station, but Annie Laycock's murder had delayed him. He knew the longer he left it, the more difficult it would be to say what he had to say, but he was not prepared to discuss it over the phone in the incident room in front of Clarke. 'I'll take it in my office,' he said.

A few moments later he picked up the receiver. 'Brian—'

Noble interrupted. 'John, I've just had a message from your brother. He's refusing to give us a sample of his DNA. Talk to him, will you? Show him the error of his ways.'

chapter six

KEIGHLEY NEWS   25 OCTOBER 2007

MINING DISASTER RIDDLE DEEPENS

By Alistair Shand

Since the *Keighley News* reported in last week's edition that dozens of bodies could be hidden beneath our hillsides, amazing new evidence has revealed that several more collapsed coal pits may also conceal victims.

Research into an alleged mining accident at Thwaites Brow has unearthed previous undisclosed information about other possible incidents. Now, a former police officer has claimed that his great-great-grandfather was one of the miners whose remains were never recovered.

Retired Detective Inspector Tom Blakely maintains William Ratcliffe died in a mine in the Riddlesden area in 1861 but his body was never retrieved. Mr Blakely, the son of a miner himself, is convinced that underneath the moors and hills around Keighley are the remains of other men who failed to return to their families.

'As far as I understand it, there was considerable danger and expense involved in recovering the bodies so it was the usual practice for victims of accidents to be left underground,' he said. 'There's no official documentation of the pit fall or of his death, but my father often told us how his own grandfather had waited as a young boy and watched night after night with his mother for his father to come home. He never did.'

As Mr Blakely presented a petition signed by more than a

hundred people to the council urging them to fund a memorial to men like William Ratcliffe, he said, 'We must not forget them. They are part of our history and our heritage.'

A council spokesperson said that since there is no firm evidence of bodies of miners in the area, they have no plans to build a memorial at this time.

Readers who wish to support Mr Blakely in his campaign can contact him through this newspaper.

The weather during the first two weeks of November had fluctuated from bright sunshine and unseasonably warm temperatures to cold, clinging mists and threatening skies. Today, the day chosen by the local historical society to visit the site of one of the disued mines, the deep blue-black clouds fractured occasionally by ribbons of winter sunlight plodded across the sky. For the majority of the members, whose ages averaged fifty plus, this was not the best kind of morning for a ramble across country, but to Rosemary Harker, the society's secretary, it was worth the extra effort of pulling out warm clothing and heavy walking shoes and trudging up the wet and slippery hillside.

The group had met the previous evening to discuss the expedition. Tom Blakely, the retired police inspector, was the authority on the mines and the miners and Rosemary had hoped to persuade him to join them, give them a commentary of what he knew and describe the life of William Ratcliffe. However, when she rang his home his wife had said he was away and she wasn't exactly sure when he would be back but had suggested Rosemary contact James Amery, a solicitor and friend of Mr Blakely who might be able to help. This she had done and while Mr Amery was too busy to accompany them to the site, he had met with them to relate as much as he knew about the workings in the Keighley district. As he talked, she doubted his knowledge was as extensive as Tom's and his interest certainly didn't lie with the miners. There was little passion in his words, instead an impenetrable reserve, which made Rosemary wonder why he had become involved with Mr Blakely's cause in the first place. Still he had enough information on which they could hang their own imaginations and he did warn

66

them amid laughter that ghosts were said to walk the nearby fields.

Now, away from the cheerful warmth of Rosemary's fireside, the dark, claustrophobic clouds hung heavily, generating an atmosphere that, if not ghostly, was distinctly funereal. On a day like this it was easy to imagine the men digging at the poor quality coal, listening all the while for the warning rumble of the wooden props about to collapse under the weight of the mud and water above them, hoping they could reach safety in time. The party stood quietly for a moment before venturing closer.

The entrance to the mine was at the end of a pathway approximately a hundred and sixty metres long, while the mine itself was blocked off with a stout brick wall and heavy wooden door. As the path descended, slatted structures had been erected to shore up the side of the hill and even though it was almost a quarter of a century since it had last been worked, there was still evidence of the ruts formed by the wagons as they trundled the coal to the carts waiting to transport it to the canal barges for distribution.

Rosemary suggested the others should wait while she tested the ground, then pulled a torch from her bag, switched it on and made her way cautiously down the path. The terrain was rough and she slipped, slithered and tripped over tufts of grass or mounds of soil, stretching out her arm to prevent herself from falling. She was about halfway along when the beam of her torch caught what appeared to her to be a pile of rubbish tucked against the retaining props. Fury bubbled inside her. Why did people do this? Why did they have to dump their waste? Didn't they have bins? But as she moved forward and let the light play on it, the bundle took on a different shape. She couldn't make it out clearly and prodded it with the toe of her boot. It shifted, skewed to one side releasing the sickening stench of rotting flesh. Nauseated, she turned her head away.

'Come on, Rosemary, hurry up.' The voice came from behind her.

She tried to speak, but no sound came. The smell was obnoxious and she covered her nose and mouth with the stray end of her scarf. It could be a dead animal; she hoped it was, but even she knew animals didn't wear mackintoshes, not even on the Pennines in winter and this body was wearing a mackintosh.

It was curled in a foetal position and obviously dead; Rosemary had been a nursing sister in A&E before she retired and she knew the signs of death when she saw them. She was aware she ought to leave it exactly as she had found it and call the police, but a morbid sense of excitement took over and cautiously she pushed at it again with her foot. It shifted, unfurled and then lolled to one side and this time fear superseded excitement and she couldn't prevent the bile rising from her stomach. It was an older man – a tramp, maybe, who had come here to shelter. His hair, though wet and streaked with mud, was greying and as well as the raincoat he was wearing dark trousers and shoes. There was some decomposition, maggots crawled around the mouth and nose and what was left no longer resembled a face. Some of it was gone, and scarring the rest were rivulets of blood that had dried hard on his skin. A sudden shaft of sunlight caught an eye which stared up at her, demanding nothing, telling her nothing. Rosemary reckoned she'd seen most injuries, many of them sickening, but the sight of this body out here, infested with insects and its features broken and wasted, nibbled at by the foxes that roamed the hillsides, repelled her. Suddenly the fear became too much and she backed away banging into one of the party who had crept up behind her.

'Found something interesting?' he asked.

Deep in thought, Christine Blakely idly stirred the spoon round the coffee cup as she sat in the shopping centre café. Even though she understood Martin Neville's reluctance to help her, she was still disappointed by his response. It was her fault; client confidentiality wasn't something she had considered when she had decided to trawl the advice agencies. Nor had it occurred to her that the description of the man outside her house could apply to a few. She had seen him, talked to him, even absorbed the smell of horses surrounding him – to her he was an individual, not one of several.

Nor was he to Martin Neville – whatever he said. He'd recognised the description, of that she was sure. There was that scrap of concern in his eyes when she had mentioned the farm and the stables; it was no more than that but she was positive she hadn't imagined it. She placed the spoon in the saucer, lifted the cup with both hands and took a sip. Was she right about Neville, or was it that she wanted to find the man so much that she had seen something that wasn't there? Or perhaps she'd been married to a police officer for so long that his cynicism had rubbed off on her. Believe no one; trust no one was his maxim, in that way you get to the truth. She had never been sure she agreed with him – until now.

The trouble was she didn't know what she could do about it. There was so little to go on – a flicker of concern in a man's eyes and the smell of horses. She could hardly go back to the charity and demand Neville tell her the truth and if she went to the police they would laugh at her, not to her face, of course, but she could imagine the discussion after she'd gone. Tears threatened to overflow and run down her cheeks and savagely she brushed them away. Damn Tom. Why had he had to have so many affairs? No one, particularly those who knew him, was able to look beyond him rolling around a bed with some woman. Suddenly she felt very tired. All she wanted was to go home and sleep. And she could do just that, go home and wait and hope – no one would blame her – except herself. She'd had a week of doing nothing but waiting and hoping and where had it got her? Nowhere. The police hadn't come back to her, nor would they. She could feel her anger against his former colleagues rising and as it did it renewed her determination. If they wouldn't do anything, she would; finding her husband was down to her.

She pushed the coffee to one side and lifted her handbag onto the table. Out of it she pulled a notebook and flicked through the pages. There had been several farms and eleven riding schools and stables listed locally in Yellow Pages. She would leave her tiredness behind her and start with the stables. If she worked out a sensible route she could probably get through some today, the rest tomorrow. Then once she had found the man he would tell her why he wanted to speak to Tom and she would have more to give the police.

She replaced her notebook and glanced at her watch. Eleven o'clock. Time to visit a couple of the nearest before lunch.

Handford sat erect in his chair and stared at the telephone. Brian Noble's news had stopped him in his tracks, so much so that he had lost the opportunity to confess his own misdemeanour. Instead, he had done nothing more than give his agreement to talk to Douglas.

That his brother would refuse to give a sample of his DNA was something he hadn't reckoned with. Didn't he realise what it would mean? That they would consider he had something to hide. Handford slumped backwards and ran his hands through his hair. He would talk to him all right, although he was sure Douglas would have an answer to all the arguments. Handford could hear him: it was his right to refuse; once they had his DNA it would be stored on the National Data Base and since he wasn't a criminal it was against his human rights. All irrefutable arguments. But then Douglas's arguments had always been irrefutable, even as a child. Not that it mattered, for whatever the polemics, the investigating team would assume the worst. Innocent until proven guilty in law, but as far as suspects – or even would-be suspects – were concerned in the eyes of the police it was more a case of guilty until proven innocent. And that's what Douglas would be. There would be questions and more questions, probably at the police station, and they would delve into his background and that of his family: his parents and siblings, and his way of life all those years ago. Did he know Josie Renshaw? Had he ever had sex with her? Had he had sex with her that evening? Had he raped her? Then they would question him about the other girls – the same questions and they would go over and over it again and again until either they were sure he was telling the truth or they were sure he wasn't. They might even arrest him on suspicion, in which case they would be able to take his DNA whether he wanted them to or not. Whatever his reasoning, Douglas hadn't thought it through.

Or perhaps he had. Perhaps he knew what it would mean and was relying on the alibi Handford had given him. His assumption would be now John was a senior police officer he wouldn't be able to retract it. After all, giving a false alibi could be considered perverting the course of justice – a serious charge both then and now. He would be unlikely to put himself in that position. The lie would have to continue and if he had any doubts that his brother would retract his statement then he would play on Handford's sense of morality – he had often mocked it when they were growing up. What about Mum and Dad? Decent, ordinary people who didn't deserve to have their lives shattered by something that had happened years ago. John, the police officer son of whom they were so proud, arrested for perverting the course of justice; John, who had always considered others, would not want to be the one doing the shattering. He could almost hear the sarcasm in Douglas's voice.

How could he have gone along with him all those years ago? How stupid was it? At the time he had idolised his older brother. He had been so different from Handford, more exciting, more charismatic, more persuasive, and as such had always got what he wanted. 'No' had never been a word he had understood. If he had been refused sex, would he have taken it anyway? If he did, as streetwise as she was, Josie Renshaw would never have stood a chance.

Or the three other women? Handford's heart lurched into his stomach. His mother had said nothing and he hadn't been aware of them, but was Douglas? In theory, he shouldn't know they were part of the case, but in practice ...? The stupid, stupid, STUPID man. Handford's fist banged down onto the desk at the same moment as the telephone rang. He grabbed at the receiver and growled 'Yes?' into the mouthpiece.

It was Philip Thackery, an inspector in CID. He sounded taken aback by the anger in Handford's voice. 'I'm sorry to bother you, sir, but we have a suspicious death. The body's on the path leading into one of the old mine workings above Riddlesden.'

Christine Blakely drew into the stable yard of the Moor Top

Equestrian Centre, the third riding school on her list, and parked between two four-by-fours close to the fence. The first stables she had visited had been a non-starter since it was a family business and they did not employ outside staff. 'No need to with my brood,' the woman had explained. At the second the owner had told her all her workforce came from the village and none of them were foreign. 'Try Moor Top,' she had advised. 'One or two of their stable lads come from away.'

Christine climbed out of the car and glanced round. The centre was not quite as Moor Top as its name suggested, for beyond the boundary wall were a couple of sizeable fields and then the moors. To one side of the yard was a Portakabin which she assumed doubled as an office, and opposite a huge grey shed the size of an aircraft hangar, from which she could hear the sound of children's voices. The fine drizzle that was falling clung to her skin and hair, and avoiding the potholes she hurried towards the noise. She found herself in a rectangular arena about eighty metres by forty lined with bales of straw and a wooden fence against which several adults were leaning and chattering.

It must have been the start of a lesson, for the children were clambering lithely on to ponies twice their height. Christine stood in the doorway and watched them for a moment. She had tried horse riding once and once had been enough. 'Show him who's boss,' the instructress had shouted from the ground. She didn't need to; the horse knew full well who was boss. The children here had no such problem. With their sense of their own security, they moved off confidently round the arena.

One of the instructors caught sight of her and came over. 'Can I help?' she asked.

Her name tag read Winnie. Christine wondered if it was short for Winifred – a name that hardly suited the bright, smiling young girl standing in front of her.

'Yes it is Winnie,' the woman said, reading her thoughts. 'I was born, named and christened Winnie. I can't say I like it, but it was my father's choice, and let's face it I was too young to argue.' She smiled. 'Now what can I do for you?'

'I'm looking for a man,' Christine said.

Winnie smiled. 'Aren't we all?'

Christine wasn't sure she was ready for flippant comments. 'No, I mean ...' Uninvited her eyes flooded with tears and she turned away.

Winnie's smile faded. 'Oh God, I'm sorry. I didn't mean to upset you. That's me all over; speak first, brain in gear second.' She rested a hand on Christine's arm. 'Let's go into the office where we can be warm.'

The office was a single room of DIY proportions. Along one wall were sets of cupboards, drawers and a sink unit and on its work surface stood a portable television whose picture flicked from one view of the yard to another, a microwave, a kettle and an array of mugs. A shorter length ran adjacent to it with a telephone, a diary and several pens and pencils. In the back corner was a battered grey filing cabinet and on hooks along the walls hung riding hats in varying sizes. In the space in the middle were two office chairs and one that was more comfortable.

Winnie patted the latter. 'I'm sorry about the mess. One day we'll have a proper office. For the moment the Portakabin will have to do – another of my father's gifts.' She switched on the electric fire. 'Tea, coffee?'

Christine shook her head. 'I'm sorry about earlier,' she said, looking at her hands. 'It's just that my husband's missing and ...' Suddenly the words flooded out. Everything from Tom's concern about Ian Gott through the disinterest of the police and the stranger who had come to the house looking for her husband, to her fear as to where he was and whether anything had happened to him. She had never articulated her worries fully before, not even to herself, but this young girl was the first person to really listen to her. Christine wasn't even sure whether she had actually understood, but it didn't matter because she listened and didn't judge Tom.

Instead she said, 'Would you like that cup of tea now?'

Christine's head was spinning and her breath coming in gasps. She was frightened she might make a fool of herself again by hyperventilating. She took a deep breath to steady herself and nodded.

Winnie busied herself preparing the drinks. While she was waiting she took a photograph album from one of the drawers. 'We have three foreign stable lads,' she said. 'I have photographs of all my workers which I also display in the arena so that the children will recognise them when they come for their lessons. We're quite isolated, but very open up here and it's important all our pupils, particularly those riding out on the moors, know who are the workers and who are the strangers. It's a statement of the times I'm afraid.' She passed the album to Christine. 'Look through and see if you recognise him.'

His photograph was on the fifth page. He was exactly as she had seen him, his features serious, his smile nervous. 'That's him,' she said.

'That's Marek,' Winnie said. 'Marek Kowalski. He's been with us a couple of years. He's a good worker, loves the horses and gets on well with the children.' Winnie took the album from Christine and scrutinised the picture. 'I'm not surprised, actually. I've been worried about him for a while; I'm sure he's had something on his mind, but he won't talk about it. I thought at first it was girlfriend trouble, it still might be because she hasn't been around for a while, but I have this feeling it's more than that and since he's reluctant to talk, I don't want to press him too much. Now, after what you've told me ...' She sighed. 'I just don't know.'

Christine leaned forward. 'Can I see him, talk to him?'

The kettle switched off and silently Winnie poured water into the cups. She handed a mug to Christine. 'Help yourself to milk and sugar,' she said and sat on one of the office chairs. 'He's not here, I'm afraid; it's his day off.'

'Then I'll go and see him.'

Winnie spooned sugar into her mug and stirred. 'I'm sorry, Christine, but I don't think I ought to give you his address. Showing you the photographs is one thing – they're pinned up on the wall in the arena, and everyone is happy with that because they understand the need for it. But handing out addresses is quite another.' She paused furrowing her brow. 'I'll give him a ring if you like, tell him you're here.'

That wasn't a good idea. Much as Christine wanted to speak

to him today, she didn't want to frighten him off. He'd been scared last time she'd spoken to him and he hadn't returned to the house. Better he was among friends when they met again. 'No,' she said. 'I'll come back tomorrow.'

John Handford stood at the bottom of the hillside looking up. The fields stretched as far as the eye could see – large open spaces, dotted at intervals by individual houses and copses of trees. It was difficult to imagine that at one time shallow coal mines had existed here. Groups of police officers had been given the task of looking for a weapon and were carefully trawling the rougher edges of the fields, and halfway down the slope the tent protecting the body stood out against the green of the grass. He checked the sky. The clouds had dispersed and it seemed as though it would turn into a fine autumn day – bright, but crisp.

The woman who had made the gruesome discovery was sitting in a police car and he had spoken to her briefly. She was calm, and described clearly and concisely why she and her party were here and what she had seen. She said she had kept everyone else away, as much because the sight was too shocking for some of them to witness. Handford thanked her and she agreed to come into the station to make a statement the next morning. The shock, Handford was sure, would set in later.

The hill was steep and the ground wet and climbing to the crime scene was hard on his thighs. He steadied himself by catching hold of clumps of grass until the slope flattened out and he was able to walk more safely. The heater in the car had kept him comfortably warm but now the cooler air up here was beginning to penetrate his clothing. He pulled his coat round him and ducked under the police tape.

He was met by Philip Thackery, the inspector from CID who had contacted him. 'Not a pretty sight, sir,' he said.

'Are any of them? Do we know who he is?'

'Yes, I'm afraid we do. It's Tom Blakely, not that you'd be able to identify him from his features – they're almost gone, but his wallet was in his pocket and I recognised the ring he's wearing.'

Handford groaned. 'Are you sure it's him?'

The inspector shrugged. 'As sure as I can be without a post mortem and a DNA test.'

'His wife reported him missing; she came to me ... I thought ...'

'We all thought the same thing and there's going to be hell to pay over what we thought. I hope you don't mind, but since his disappearance had been passed over to us and we were supposed to be investigating I've let Superintendent Russell know. I tell you, he's already jumping up and down. When I hinted that no one would have thought to come up here, he said that given Blakely's interest in the miners' remains, it was one of the places we should have looked – and he's right, of course. He wants a report on why we did nothing to find him and he wants it yesterday.'

Handford chuckled. 'So you won't be expecting a coffee when you see him?' Russell's coffees were legendary at the station. He ground his own beans each morning and you were only offered a cup if you were in his good books.

'You might laugh,' Thackery said. 'He told me to inform you he will go with you to tell his widow.'

'I don't think so.' Handford had left Stephen Russell firmly behind when he was promoted into HMET. 'Any sign of the press yet, Constable?' he said as he struggled into the protective suit handed to him.

'Not yet, sir.'

'Then let's have the outer cordon extended as far down as the road and all the way to the top of the hill. That'll stop 'em coming too close when they get wind of what's happened.'

The inspector had been right – Tom Blakely was almost unrecognisable. The description Rosemary Harker had given him had been accurate in every detail. He turned to the doctor. 'Eaten or beaten?'

The man looked up from the body. 'Both, I should think. There's no doubt he's been hit with something and it looks as though he's been a good feast for some animal, foxes, probably, given the area. He's been stabbed as well, six or seven times.'

'Stabbed?' Handford groaned inwardly; it was beginning to show the hallmarks of Ian Gott's MO.

'How long would you estimate he's been here?'

The doctor shook his head. 'Difficult to say, but a while. There's some insect activity, although I'm not sure what, you'll have to ask the expert about that.' He picked up his bag. 'That's me done. I'm pronouncing life extinct at twelve thirty hours on Wednesday, fourteenth November. Although why I need to do it I don't know. It's obvious to anyone who looks at him that he's dead. Give me a ring if – when – you need me again.'

Handford smiled his goodbye then turned back to the body. He would need a post mortem to verify what came first, the stab wounds or the head wounds, but either way, it seemed to him that Tom Blakely had gone through a trauma very like that inflicted on Annie Laycock. 'I assume you've notified the coroner, Philip?'

Thackery nodded.

'Then contact him again, would you, and say I would like a pathologist up here, preferable the one who will carry out Annie Laycock's post mortem.'

'You think the two murders are linked?'

'I don't know, but we'll find out more quickly if the same person covers both post mortems. And while you're about it, ring through to HMET and ask Inspector Ali to join me.'

'Yes, sir.'

Thackery moved out of the tent, leaving Handford to stare at what was left of Tom Blakely. Had Gott killed him? Had he carried out his threat? It angered him that they had let one of their own down. And he bore his share of the blame, because Christine Blakely had come to him expecting help. Every one of them had broken the first rule and made assumptions – there was little point in looking for Tom because he would be with some woman. Christine had said he wasn't; they hadn't believed her. Why did they think they knew Tom better than his wife? It was arrogant in the extreme. Now he was going to have to break the news to her, take with him the ring and other bits and pieces to see if she recognised them. He couldn't allow her to see him, which meant she couldn't say her goodbyes.

Sitting with the body often helped the relatives; it gave them the opportunity to pour out their grief. Christine Blakely would not get that opportunity.

A photographer slid past him. 'Excuse me, sir,' he said.

Handford was in the way; it was time for him to leave. Outside the tent, scene-of-crime officer Joe Norton was carefully treading the ground as he manoeuvred himself towards the entrance to the disused mine. He flicked on his torch, allowing the beam to arc deeper into the darkness. Suddenly he pulled his mask over his mouth and nose then turned. 'Sir,' he called, then again more urgently this time. 'Sir.'

It didn't take an expert to guess there was a problem. Inexplicably Handford's stomach curled and he sprinted down the pathway.

Norton looked up at him. 'There's another body, sir,' he said. 'What's left of it.'

chapter seven

Joe Norton hadn't been far wrong when he said there wasn't too much left of the body – more a carcass than a corpse. Notwithstanding the considerable decomposition, body parts and clothing either had been eaten or were missing altogether, probably carried off for dessert by rats, foxes and crows. What there was left was bloated and any skin that was visible had taken on a marbling effect of purple and green. Orifices were infested with maggots.

'There's a lot to be said for cremation,' the SOCO said as he took a pace backwards.

Handford nodded. Life's finale was not always pretty. They had two bodies here to prove it. The one discovered this morning was likely that of Tom Blakely, but the second? Could it be Bronwyn Price? Again it would need DNA tests to confirm it, but unless they were suddenly in the centre of an epidemic of killings, it had to be her. He stretched out his hand. 'Let's have your torch,' he said. Norton handed it over and Handford shone it over the corpse. The features were unrecognisable, but not so the hair. It was dirty and plastered to what was left of the face, but it was unmistakeable – a mass of red curls. There was in no doubt in his mind they had found the young woman who had been missing for eight weeks, presumed dead for most of them. He turned and looked up at the SOCO who was bending over him. 'How long would you say?'

'Not sure, but weeks rather than days.'

'Eight?'

'Could be.'

Handford handed back the torch and pulled out his mobile. 'Get the doctor back and ask Inspector Thackery to notify the coroner and the pathologist,' he said. Then into the phone: 'I think we've found Bronwyn Price's body, sir, a few metres from Tom Blakely's.'

As he waited for Ali, Handford leaned on the bonnet of his car. Away from the crime scene the air smelled fresher, but eventually the aroma of death and decay would seep towards the village. Even out of the protective covering, it was already clinging to his suit, face and hands. Once back to the station, he'd need a shower and a change of clothes to rid him of the surface smell, but he knew nothing but time would take away the lingering biting taste that had burrowed into his throat or the images of the dead fused on his consciousness. They would haunt him until something worse came along to displace them – and it would, it always did.

His eyes wandered the contours of the village. Not that it could be considered a village any more, creeping and linking as it did with other small communities to become an appendage of the nearest town. In its early days – and it was mentioned in the Domesday Book – Riddlesden had been farmland and orchards, but with the Industrial Revolution and the obvious advantage of the roads and canal, it had fallen victim to urbanisation and now with easy access between town and city it had once again become a place rich for developers. But even though the tentacles of the large conurbations had crept ever nearer it had managed to hang on to its identity and while it could no longer be considered rural, neither was it crime-ridden – some drug dealing, shop lifting, the odd burglary or two, but little else. The last real excitement was years ago when a man held his girlfriend and her children hostage at gun point and a negotiator had to be brought in to end it. Now, inexplicably, it boasted three murders, none of them pleasant.

A dog barked in the distance and he could hear the cries of the children in the school playground. Life went on; everything normal. But not for Christine Blakely or the Youngers. At some point today and before the press got hold of it, he had to break the news to each of them that a body had been found. It was never a pleasant task, but this time he was dreading it. He could pass it over to someone else, but given the past few weeks of little or no information and in the case of Tom Blakely, little or no help from the police, it was something he needed to do personally. Better him than a couple of police constables and better him and a family liaison officer than Mrs Blakely opening the door to the hypocrisy of a chief inspector and a superintendent. He swallowed hard. If he was honest, he didn't know which he was dreading most: telling Christine Blakely, who must already feel let down by the service, or telling the Youngers. Mrs Younger would want to see her daughter and he would have to refuse her. It was a cliché, but in this case it was better to remember Bronwyn as she had been, rather than as she was now. David Younger, on the other hand, would be smug in an 'I told you so' frame of mind but at least Handford would have the satisfaction of letting him know that now they had a body, he was still a suspect, probably even more so. There was no doubt he had a motive, even he must see that. But it was a motive that accounted only for the murder of his stepdaughter, not for that of Tom Blakely – at least not for the moment.

Were the deaths linked? The two victims had been found at the entrance to a disused mine about which there had been a feature in the local paper. Because of that he could link the place with Tom Blakely – although not necessarily with his death. You didn't kill a man because he wanted a memorial erecting on an out-of-the-way hillside, but you might leave his body there. His killer was more likely to be Ian Gott. He could easily have followed him up here, done the deed and fled. But not Bronwyn Price. She'd been dead for several weeks, long before the news broke about the remains of buried miners and long before Ian Gott walked out of the open prison. So if the locality was the link, then somehow both Tom and Bronwyn figured in it.

She'd had a new boyfriend. Her colleagues had hinted at a man older than her and possibly foreign. Tom Blakely was undoubtedly older. Had he been having an affair with her?

Certainly not over the past eight weeks. But before that? Perhaps she'd wanted to end it – or he had. He'd brought her up here, they'd had an argument and he had killed her, possibly accidentally – difficult to know, since there were no obvious signs as to how she had died; the how would be down to the post mortem, which given the amount of decomposition could well come up with an inconclusive result. If Tom had killed her, he would have left her body here, knowing there was little possibility of it being discovered, but when the news broke about the dead miners and the place had become a sight-seers' paradise he would have needed to come back to hide it. If Gott had followed him, here would have been a perfect place to carry out his threat.

All plausible theories, but they couldn't work on the assumption that Gott had murdered Blakely any more than they could assume he had murdered Annie Laycock. Tom would have more enemies than him and they already knew that Bronwyn had at least one: her stepfather.

Christine Blakely lay on the settee, exhausted but unable to sleep. She had thought doing something would help, and it had while she was doing it. Now, alone in the house, she knew it didn't make a bit of difference. No one knew where Tom was and it seemed to her no one cared. She wanted him found; she needed him back with her. She had put her faith in locating the stranger and although now she had a name – Marek Kowalski – it was quite possible he wouldn't talk to her; it had been Tom he'd wanted to see; he'd been adamant about that.

The television played softly in the background. She had switched it on to watch the local news in the vain hope they would mention her husband; they hadn't, of course, but she had left it on anyway to give some background noise. Normally silence was her friend, now it rolled round her head her like an attack of tinnitus. She flicked through the channels. Nothing much – a quiz show, racing, a 1950s film which she doubted she had the concentration for. Perhaps the racing. Tom always enjoyed it; maybe it would bring her closer to him.

She must have dozed, for the knock on the door startled

her. It was loud, urgent, rapid. Marek Kowalski? The police? Tom? She pulled herself off the settee. For a moment dizziness overcame her and she waited while it abated. The knocking continued, louder than ever now. She staggered into the hall. The light from the road cast the person on the other side of the patterned glass into shadow. A dark shape, big. Tom. Her heart thumping, Christine pulled at the door.

'At last.'

Patrick. She slumped, clinging to the framework. Why couldn't he leave her alone?

He pushed his way past her, neither noting nor seemingly concerned about her distress. 'Where is he?'

'He's not here,' she said wearily. 'I told you that when you rang. He's not here, Patrick, and he hasn't been here for over a week. I don't know where he is.'

'Liar.' He marched into the lounge, through into the dining room and then into the kitchen, and finally up the stairs. Enraged she slammed the door, not caring if the glass shattered. How dare he? Not content with abusive phone calls he was now harassing her in her home.

Adrenalin pumping through her body, she shouted after him, 'He's not here, I tell you.' But the man was past reason.

Finally he loomed over her from the landing, breathing heavily. 'Where is he?'

'For God's sake, Patrick, I can't make it any plainer, I don't know where Tom is; I only wish I did. Please come downstairs; you're not going to find him up there.'

For a moment it appeared as though he was not prepared to move, then slowly he made his way down and followed her into the kitchen.

Her anger spent, she turned to him. 'Tea?' It was an inane question, but at least it gave her something to do and time for Patrick to calm down.

He hesitated, then nodded begrudgingly. It was as if taking something from his brother's wife would negate his reason for being here. And Christine knew exactly why he was here.

She busied herself while he paced between the window where he stood looking out into the gloom for a few seconds and the door. She couldn't take much more of this. 'For goodness sake, sit down. Tom's not going to jump out at you.'

Noisily he pulled out a chair and sat next to the table. 'How long has he been gone?' He almost spat the question at her.

'I've already said, over a week.' She wondered whether to tell him about Ian Gott and his threat to Tom, but decided against it. Patrick would have sided with Gott, insisted it was typical of Tom to set someone up. She handed him a mug and pushed the sugar basin towards him. Patrick spooned some into his tea and stirred it. For a moment they were silent. Christine watched him. He was so like Tom. Patrick was two years older, but they could easily have been mistaken for twins – the same height, same build, stocky but not fat, the same black hair, now greying at the temples, the same deep brown eyes and the same slightly hunched shoulders. He even held his mug in the same way as Tom – the first two fingers through the handle and his thumb round the front, so that when he drank his chin and nose were completely obscured from view.

Patrick placed his mug carefully onto the table and stared into the contents. His jaw worked as he controlled his anger. Finally he said quietly, 'I just want what's mine, Christine,' then in a raised voice, 'and make no mistake, I'm going to get it.' He leaned towards her. 'You tell him that when he comes back from whichever whore he's sleeping with.'

A door slammed shut in her head. No matter how often she denied it, it seemed everyone on the other side wasn't listening. And Patrick would never listen. If he could think the worst of Tom he would. There was no point arguing with him, no point insisting Tom was not with another woman. Instead she let the tears fall.

'Don't start that,' he said. 'You married into the police you live with it.'

'And you had a brother who didn't want to follow you both into the pit. You live with that.'

Patrick guffawed. 'Yeah, and what did he do instead? He slept with the enemy.'

'Don't be ridiculous; Tom's not your enemy.'

'Get real, woman. *The police* are the miners' enemy. They

were in 1926, in the seventies and in 1984, and they still are; they're as corrupt as they can be – and so is he.'

'No he isn't; he wasn't then and he isn't now.'

'Then why did he fight us during the strike and why has he stolen what is rightfully mine?'

She studied him. How had it come to this? Two brothers so far apart there was nothing between them but a valley of hatred. 'He didn't steal half of your business,' she said as calmly as she could, 'his father willed it to him.'

That wasn't what Patrick wanted to hear. He pushed back his chair and stood up. 'I've had enough of this,' he said. 'You tell him from me it isn't finished. I worked my balls off building up the business after Thatcher closed the pits and left us with nothing, while the likes of Tom lived off all the overtime money he made pushing us around.' He strode towards the kitchen door then spun round. 'I'll tell you another thing, Christine: I don't care what that scab of a husband of yours says or what my father put in his will. That business is mine – all of it. I told him when the will was read I'd do whatever it takes to get what I'm entitled to, and by God that's exactly what I meant.'

Marek Kowalski shrugged on his coat as he left the warmth of Cinema One. It hadn't been a bad film, better than some he'd seen over the past couple of years. In the early days when he'd had few friends he'd looked upon his visit as an attempt to perfect his English, then it had become something of a habit, but for the past few weeks he had had other reasons. The cinema was the only place he felt safe. If he was there, his mobile turned off, Martin Neville and Leon Jackson couldn't contact him. Ever since he'd told them he wanted out and they'd refused, they'd rung him at the stables, in the evening, even during the night to warn him when he was next 'on duty', as they put it. Try as he might he couldn't break their hold over him. If only he had Bronwyn, but she'd gone when he'd told her how he was earning the extra money and now the police were suggesting she was dead – not in so many words, just that they were concerned for her safety, but it meant the same. Even Tom Blakely had disappeared. It was irrational to suppose he had gone because of Neville and Jackson, but the thought had niggled away at him and he couldn't rid himself of it.

He pulled his cigarettes from his pocket and shook one out of the packet. As he turned to the wall to shelter the lighter from the breeze that had sprung up he felt a hand grab at his arm.

'Enjoy the film did you, Kowalski?' Leon Jackson's voice rattled deep in his throat.

Marek's heart pounded. As he turned the pressure on his arm strengthened and he was pushed back into the glass of the publicity window. It was cold and hard against his cheek.

'Let's go for a drink, shall we?' It was not an offer, more of an order.

Marek tried to answer but could manage no more than a whisper. The blow to his right kidney was cushioned by the thickness of his coat.

Jackson's breath feathered Mark's ear. 'You turning my offer down, Kowalski?'

'No, no, I come with you for a drink.'

'That's better.' Jackson spun him round. He brushed his hand down Marek's coat. 'A nice piece of cloth this,' he said. 'Must have cost a pretty penny; pity to spoil it.'

They set off towards the town hall square. The trees edging it were festooned with Christmas lights, not yet turned on and lights played on the war memorial in the centre, illuminating the wreaths of poppies laid on the steps to commemorate Armistice Day. As they walked, Jackson fenced him against the wall of the building so that there was little chance of him making a dash for it. Even if he could, the traffic was heavy; to attempt to weave his way through it would be suicide. And anyway what was the point? Jackson knew where he lived and where he worked; he could get him any time he wanted.

They turned into the main thoroughfare, Jackson urging him on more fiercely now. Marek's feet scuffed the ground as he tried to stay upright and his body banged against the stonework of the pub. People rushing by avoided him, assuming no doubt that he was drunk. A man appeared in the doorway, lighting up as he did so and tottered towards the crossing. Jackson pressed his fingers deep into the sleeve of Marek's coat then shoved him into the next opening and from there into an alley that ran along the back of the shops. The windowless gable of the single-storey nursery on the opposite side connected to a high wall which hid the pathway from the supermarket and its car park. It was in this secluded passage, amongst the dirt and discarded rubbish, the dealers sold their drugs and winos drunk themselves into oblivion away from the eyes of the police and the public, and it was here Jackson had brought him to do whatever he intended. Fear bubbled in Marek's gut. As he stumbled along he could smell the stale urine. Any minute he would be sick. He wanted to beg Jackson not to hurt him, not to kill him even, to let him go, but malevolence shone in the man's eyes and he knew his pleas would be worthless.

The first blow knocked him to the ground. He sprawled onto his stomach. Jackson stood back while he attempted to stand and then kicked at him. This time Marek fell onto his back, cracking his head on the ground. Jackson leaned over him, his hands resting either side of the prone figure. 'You've talked.' It was a statement not a question.

'No.'

'Yes.' Jackson kicked him again, this time in his side. Marek felt a rib crack. The next blow caught his arm. 'You went to see Blakely.' The man's boot found the side of his head.

Marek curled into a ball. 'He wasn't there. I didn't speak to him.'

Jackson began to kick out again, each blow pounding a different part of his body. 'You went to him to grass on us.' He lifted his foot. 'Didn't you?'

Marek spread his arms to protect himself. 'Yes.' The tears came more quickly now. 'I wanted it to stop.'

Jackson straightened himself. He was breathing heavily. 'If I had my way, I'd kill you, but Neville's too much of a pansy for that.' He pulled his mobile from his pocket. 'Instead I'm going to spare you.' He thumbed in a number. 'It's done,' he said. 'He's learned his lesson.' He bent towards Marek his strong fingers squeezing his cheeks and thrust the phone close. 'Tell him you've learned your lesson.'

Hardly able to speak, the answer came in a whisper. 'Yes.'

87

'All of it.'

Marek was crying now. 'I learned my lesson. I'm sorry.'

Jackson's hold relaxed and he straightened up to stand over him like a great shadow. When he spoke his voice was silky. 'Good and just to show you there's no ill-feeling ...' He thumbed in another number, placed the mobile to his ear and waited for a reply. He grinned. 'Ambulance please. A man's been mugged here; looks like he ought to be in hospital.' Then one final vicious kick and he was gone.

As soon as Christine Blakely opened the door and saw John Handford and Family Liaison Officer Connie Burns he was aware she understood why they were there. She was – had been – a police officer's wife; bringing bad news was part of the job. As police officers they cultivated the appropriate expression for the task. He hoped she appreciated that this time he meant it.

'You've found him?'

Handford nodded.

There was no need to ask her if they could come in; she stood back and extended her arm in the direction of the lounge door. The central heating was on as was the gas fire and the room was over-warm. He would like to have discarded his coat, but couldn't until she invited them to stay. He opened his mouth to speak.

'Don't tell me to sit down,' she said. 'Just say what you came to say.'

The comment was unexpected, harsh even. It would be easier for her and for him if they sat down. Nevertheless, he remained where he was in the middle of the room, feeling like a naughty schoolboy who had come to confess. 'I'm sorry, Christine, we've found a body. We believe it to be Tom's.'

Slowly she lowered herself on to the settee. Handford watched her. Judging from her expression, there was obviously no doubt in her mind they had got it right. 'We believe it to be' was no more than a euphemism. The body was that of her husband. There was no necessity to ask if they were sure. They wouldn't be here if they weren't. Finally she looked up at him and said, 'Where?'

'On a pathway leading to one of the old mine workings.'

She gave a short laugh. 'Patrick will love that.'

'Patrick?'

She ignored the question. 'How was he killed?'

'He appears to have been hit with something heavy.'

'Was it Ian Gott?'

'We don't know, not yet. It could have been.'

'So he wasn't with another woman?'

'No ... at least ...' He had discussed with Paynter whether or not to disclose the discovery of the other body to either party, but since they couldn't keep it from the press, they had no choice. He had remained standing all this time, but now moved to sit next to Christine and told her about the corpse they believed was that of Bronwyn Price, then before she could ask the obvious, he said, 'We don't know if their deaths are linked, Christine. It could be coincidence they were found at the entrance to the mine.' It was a weak argument, said as much to excuse the police's ineptitude as to give her comfort. It wouldn't and it didn't, for after a moment's silence she turned to Handford and slapped him hard across the face, then just as suddenly grabbed his coat, leaned against him and sobbed. Connie Burns made to go towards her, to pull her off but, his cheek burning, Handford shook his head. When the sobs subsided, he motioned to Connie to take over. Gently they changed places. There were questions he needed to ask, some of which would not wait until tomorrow. Tom Blakely had probably been dead ten days, Bronwyn Davies eight weeks. A lot of time had been lost, not to mention forensic evidence. Christine would know that.

He pulled off his coat and signed that he would make some tea until the two women were ready. As he passed the mirror in the hall, he glanced at his cheek. It was reddening and there would probably be a bruise by tomorrow. Christine Blakely could certainly pack a punch; anyone else and he would have arrested them for assaulting a police officer, but in all conscience he couldn't blame her; at this moment he represented everyone who had let her down.

When Handford returned from the kitchen with three mugs

of tea balanced on a tray, she was calmer. She looked up as he came in. 'Would he be dead now if you'd listened to me?' Her voice trembled and her eyes accused. He wished he could give her an answer that would not sound as though it was a justification for his non-action.

'I don't know, Christine. We don't know how long he's been dead, but at least a week I would say, possibly longer.' He handed her a mug.

She took it and held it as if warming her hands. 'Can I see him?'

'Not yet.' For once was better to prevaricate. 'He's still up at the scene; perhaps when he is taken to the mortuary.' He pulled a couple of brown evidence bags from his briefcase. The first contained the ring, the second the wallet. 'I would like you to look at these, though, and tell me if they are Tom's.'

For a long moment she remained silent. She picked up the packet containing the ring. It was distinctive – a decorated buckle ring fashioned in nine-carat gold. She nodded. 'I had it inscribed round the inside. *Yours forever.* Silly really, but I was young. He put it on and has never had it off his finger – until now. The wallet, I'm not sure of; it could be his.'

Again there was a silence which finally he broke. 'I do need to ask you a few questions,' he said.

Christine nodded.

'When did you last see, Tom?'

'Ten days ago when he went off to work.'

'So that's a week last Tuesday?'

'Yes.'

'I'll check it out myself, but did he arrive at work do you know?'

'He didn't go into the office, if that's what you mean. But that wasn't unusual; he might not go in for a week or more if he was following up a lead.'

'And you don't know what he was working on?'

'No. He didn't talk much about his work; he never has, not even when he was in the police force.'

'Did he say anything about going up to the old mine workings?'

'No.'

'Did he often go up there?'

'Sometimes. He was hoping to persuade the council to erect a memorial to the dead miners. It was important to him they were remembered.'

'Tell me what happened the day you saw him last.'

Christine Blakely related the phone call that had upset her husband. 'He told me not to open the door to anyone I didn't know and if I was worried to ring you. And I did – you remember?'

Handford nodded. 'Yes, I know. I'm sorry, Christine, I should have listened to you.'

Her eyes found his. 'I always think sorry is such a useless word in situations like this, John. Sorry we didn't get here in time; sorry your baby died; sorry we didn't listen.' Her voice rose as grief caught at it. 'Tom is lying on a cold hillside and I've lost my husband. What use is it to be sorry?'

For a moment he thought she was going to hit out at him again, but instead she seemed to collapse into herself and began to sob.

There were more questions he would have liked to put to her, the identity of Patrick for one, but now was not the time. Tomorrow would be soon enough; it would have to be.

'Do you have anyone who can be with you, Christine? A relative, a friend, a neighbour?'

She shook her head. 'My sister,' she said, 'but she'll not be able to get here tonight.'

'In that case Connie will stay with you; it's better you're not alone.' He glanced over to the FLO, who nodded. He was about to say he was only a phone call away if she needed anything but it hardly seemed suitable in the circumstances. Christine Blakely would remain angry with him for a long time.

He pulled on his coat and walked to the door with Connie. 'Ask her about Patrick, will you?'

Connie nodded. 'Leave it with me, guv.'

As he left, Handford's mobile rang. It was his mother, no doubt checking on his movements for the rest of the day.

He sighed. That was the problem with living with his mother

– she treated him as though he were still a child. 'Yes, Mum?' Thank goodness there was no one here to listen in.

'John, Douglas has been in touch. He needs to see you so I asked him to have dinner with us. You will be home in time, won't you?'

.

chapter eight

Khalid Ali lifted his head and rubbed his eyes. He'd been reading statements and listening to taped interviews made during
the investigation into the case that had led to the incarceration
of Ian Gott and his threat to Tom Blakely all afternoon and
he was tired. The small incident room was deserted. Various
members of the team were out questioning known criminals
who would think nothing of stabbing an old lady then beating
her to a pulp, others were checking on the gang of youths who
had been causing mayhem on the estate. All were in line for an
ASBO, but although he doubted they were far enough down the
line to do what had been done to Annie Laycock, their movements had to be checked. They had located her only daughter
who hadn't been interested. 'Serves the old witch right,' she'd
said through a haze of alcohol. There was a man in his twenties
or early thirties, who visited her from time to time, but so far
they hadn't been able to find him and if he existed at all, he
wasn't a relative. Ali had also instructed everyone to meet up
with their informants – if anyone knew the whereabouts of Ian
Gott they would. So far no one had checked in and since the
results of the DNA harvested from the scene were not yet back,
he had been able to get on with the task Handford had set him
without interruption.

For the first time in his career he had his own office; it was
small, built in to one corner of the incident room, but it gave
him the privacy to get on with the job in relative peace and
quiet. As a sergeant he had used Handford's room occasionally
when the DI was away, but mostly he had been at a desk at the

end of CID – not part of the team, but never far away from their noise and the telephones. He had often wondered how he would furnish an office when he was given one – casual like Handford's or efficient like that of his former DCI. This was too small to be casual; it was much more likely to descend into chaos, so efficient it had to be and if he was honest he preferred it that way: formal, but not too immaculate, and nothing that would imply an arrogance he didn't think he possessed, but certain others thought he did. So he'd decided against anything that could be considered flattering to his ego, but equally he refused to leave coffee-table books and magazines around as Handford did. As far as he was concerned, an office was a place in which to work, not to relax. He did however allow himself a photograph of Amina and the children on his desk.

He turned back to the papers, making notes as he went along. He worked logically, always had, unlike his boss who often let instinct and gut feeling take over. Handford never called it that; to him it was experience, which was followed by detailed investigation, usually delegated and usually to Ali. Perhaps he was right, for they were a good team. Instinct and inspiration working in tandem with systematic evidence-gathering and rational thought. It worked and he was happy with it, though he couldn't say he was happy with what he was doing now, but he was prepared to accept the necessity in checking the investigation into the burglary had been carried out with absolute integrity. He hadn't known Tom Blakely and didn't know what he was capable of, but he did know Clarke. He was a skilled detective and a transparently honest man and if he'd had even an inkling that Blakely was doing something wrong he would have tried to talk him out if it. What concerned Ali was that if indeed Gott had been framed by Blakely, it would be Clarke who would take the blame, whether he had been part of it or not. Should it become common knowledge, as it surely would, that there had been a miscarriage of justice, the senior officers would need a scapegoat and Clarke would be it.

When he had left Handford, he had called Warrender into his office and updated him on what the DCI wanted.

'Don't be ridiculous,' the red-haired detective had snapped.

Ali was aware he had little time for the newly promoted inspector. Nevertheless, he had listened and as he left the office to check out the original statements – a task he considered a waste of time, since the witnesses would insist they couldn't remember – he had turned and said, 'I'll tell you this, Ali, Clarke would no more set someone up than you would and you're a fool if you believe a toe-rag like Ian Gott,' leaving Ali with no opportunity to reciprocate with a suitable comment. He knew the level of mistrust between them would always be there and in Warrender would continue to manifest itself as, if not rudeness, then disrespect. Indeed, since his promotion, Warrender had refused to address him as 'gov' or 'boss', let alone 'sir'.

Ali doubted it would ever disappear since it stemmed from a time when Warrender, his parents and his sister had been involved in a terrible road traffic accident caused by an under age, uninsured, unlicensed Asian driver who had disappeared immediately afterwards. He had been caught and, to Warrender's horror, had only been given a six-month custodial sentence while his parents had been killed outright and Katie left paraplegic. To argue with him that it was not Ali's fault was a waste of time so instead he had attempted to bridge the gap by visiting Katie in the hope he could show that he abhorred what had happened every bit as much as any right-thinking person. She had believed him. When Warrender returned home and found him at the house, he had floored him with a well-placed left hook. Now they tolerated each other, but no more than that.

Deep down he knew Warrender was right about Clarke: he would not be involved in any shady investigation and as he read through the statements and listened to the tapes of the interviews with Gott, there seemed little in them to suggest the man had been set up. The problem was neither was there anything to say he hadn't been. Blakely and Clarke's voices in interview were quiet and calm and there was no apparent attempt to hassle the suspect or persuade him into a confession. Gott, for his part, blurted his way through several alibis and finally agreed he had been in Allan Widdop's house, but insisted it was after the burglary. He didn't deny it had been his intention to steal

95

from the man but – and here he enunciated his words slowly, as though to make himself clearly understood – someone had got there before him. If that were so, Clarke asked, why, when he had come across a badly injured Mr Widdop, hadn't he called an ambulance? Gott had mumbled something about not wanting to be framed for a burglary he hadn't committed. Blakely had also put to him that Mr Widdop had picked him out at an identity parade. Interestingly, Gott hadn't replied as Ali would have expected that the old man was blind and senile but had said instead that it was because Gott was the last person he had seen and therefore he was the person he had remembered. At interview Mr Widdop had strenuously denied he had made a mistake. 'I might be old, but I'm not stupid,' he said. 'I know how many people came into my house that night – one – the man wielding a knife that stole from me and attacked me.' Questioned further, he remained insistent that the man was Ian Gott. So far they hadn't been able to ascertain the whereabouts of Mr Widdop, but Clarke had learned that he wasn't dead, nor was he living in the house in which the burglary took place, so that meant he was either with relatives or in a nursing home. Once he was located, Warrender would re-interview him.

Ali checked the forensic report. There were no fingerprints on the box that contained the medals except those of Mr Widdop and the partial thumb print which appeared to match Gott's. At the trial the forensic expert was adamant it did belong to the defendant and Gott either couldn't or wouldn't give a reasonable explanation as to how it got there. Ali remembered the concern that passed over Clarke's face when he was asked if he agreed with the expert and how he had, when pushed, given an answer that gave away little of his own feelings. Ali also noted how Clarke had relaxed when Handford had moved the questioning on. Was it possible the scientist owed Blakely a favour? He made a note to track down the man or, better still, to contact a friend and have the print re-checked. Whatever the truth of it, they hadn't been able to persuade any of the local dealers to admit to being offered war medals, but that didn't mean they hadn't been. It would be impossible to rely on anything most of them said.

What was certain was that when Gott was arrested he had a little short of two hundred pounds on him. Ali glanced back at the evidence. No one seemed absolutely sure how much Mr Widdop had stashed away in the biscuit tin in the cupboard, but it was thought to be a considerable amount. What could be considered a 'considerable amount' to a pensioner? Two hundred pounds? Gott was picked up a couple of days after the burglary and his explanation as to why he had so much money on him was that he had won it on the horses. Here the evidence against him was sound. He had lost the ticket, he said, but when checked out not one of the bookies in the area had a copy of it or could remember seeing him in their establishment – and anyway, no ticket, no payment. Worse, the horse he said he had backed had fallen at the first fence, so wherever the money had come from it had not been from the unfortunate filly. Once that had been established Gott had exercised his rights and given a no-comment interview. Ali sighed. That was the best evidence against Gott, but it was not good enough and most of the rest was questionable and should certainly have given the courts reasonable doubt. So what had made Blakely go after Gott in the first place? Was it simply that he was a known villain who burgled old people and beat up any of them who crossed him or was there something else – something that he hadn't mentioned and didn't come out at trial? And if that were so, did Clarke know of it or was it known only to Gott and Blakely? Could that information be the reason for Blakely's disappearance and ultimate murder?

After his visit to Christine Blakely Handford met up with Mike Paynter and they went together to alert the Youngers that a body they believed to be Bronwyn's had been found. While he was in no doubt two senior officers visiting Christine Blakely would have been wrong, he was equally convinced that was exactly what was needed for the Youngers – particularly David.

It was David Younger who opened the door to them, a glass in his hand. He staggered forwards as he demanded to know what they wanted.

Paynter asked if they could come in.

Younger brushed his fingers over his shorn head. 'If you must.' As he stood in the doorway, Handford saw for the first time how much weight the man had lost – the opening seemed to swallow him whole. His clothes hung on what had once been a stocky frame and although he was flushed with drink and deep purple veins criss-crossed his cheeks, his appearance was gaunt. His eyes were rimmed with black and seemed to have sunk deep into their sockets. If he hadn't come to know Younger so well over the past weeks, Handford could have been forgiven for thinking his appearance was a result of anxiety for his missing stepdaughter, but given the man's growing resentment towards Bronwyn and his unremitting antagonism for the police he was sure there was more to it than that – in fact, he would stake his pension that there was.

Younger stood back to allow the men through into the hallway, thrust the door shut and pushed past them to lead them into the lounge. Mrs Younger was hunched in one of the chairs, small and frightened, her eyes wide and questioning. Younger ignored her and went to refill his glass. He offered them neither a drink nor a seat.

'Well?'

As soon as Paynter had told them of the discovery, Younger asked if they were sure it was Bronwyn's body. From anyone else a reasonable question – hope is always the last emotion to be given up.

'As sure as we can be without a DNA test,' Paynter said.

As Handford watched him, it seemed there was a flicker of relief in Younger's eyes, but it was gone almost as soon as it appeared. Was it relief that Bronwyn was dead and out of his hair or was it that the DNA results could still prove the police wrong and the body wasn't hers? Younger would love that. He did.

'Like you were sure she was in the garden?' he sneered. 'Like you were so sure you dug it up and found nothing?' He took an unsteady step forward. 'In other words, you're not sure.'

Handford exchanged a glance with Paynter but said nothing. With Younger in this mood, there was little point in mentioning it was unlikely there was another young women in the district with tightly curled red hair who had been missing for some time or insisting that DNA was no more than confirmation. Handford had been on a murder investigation when they had got the identity of a dead girl wrong and he wasn't prepared to go through that again. Images of the cold anger of the father and the absolute relief of the mother as they stared at the body returned each time a relative was taken to identify a victim. As far as he was concerned, it was better to allow David Younger his continued attack on the police by inferring they were incompetent. That Handford could cope with.

He walked over to crouch beside Bronwyn's mother. She didn't need the result of a DNA test. She knew they were sure and she was bereft, but so far she had sobbed alone. Gently, he laid his hand on her arm. 'I'm so sorry, Mrs Younger,' he said. It was not much, but it was better than nothing and she nodded her head and attempted a smile. Such as it was, it was the only comfort she was going to get. Her husband was giving a good impression of an angry and maligned man and there was no doubt his concern was for himself and not for her or for his stepdaughter. Handford couldn't give a reason, except the experience of instinct, but now more than ever he was sure Younger was hiding something beneath his bluster. He had lots of questions to answer, but not today. Tomorrow when he was less drunk would be soon enough.

Tomorrow was not a day Handford relished, nor if he was honest was this evening. Like it or not, he had to confront Douglas before he talked to Brian Noble and although his mother believed his brother's visit was a social one – hence the invitation to eat with them – it was much more likely an attempt to find out how far Josie Renshaw's case had progressed and to insist John stick with the thirty-year alibi.

Douglas's car was in the drive and as soon as Handford opened the door his mother was in the hall, disappointment clouding her face.

'Really, John, I did ask you to be on time tonight. The meal will be ruined. The girls needed to get on with their homework, but they must be starving by now, you've missed Gill's call, and Douglas has been waiting for some time.'

He took off his coat and hung it up. 'Sorry, I've been busy,' he said tersely. 'Where is he?' He wanted to get this over as quickly as possible. When Noble told him his brother was refusing a DNA sample it had shaken him, but there had to be a reason and the only one he could think of was that Douglas expected his DNA to be found on Josie's clothing. At best he'd had sex with the girl and at worst he'd raped her and Handford needed to know which. He couldn't force his brother to comply with the request, but if he pushed hard enough he might get at the truth. If not, he could warn him of the repercussions if he continued to refuse and let him know that this time he was not prepared to back his alibi as he had when he was younger. Things were different now and Douglas had made his choice. It was up to him to deal with the consequences, just as Handford was going to have to.

He found Douglas in the lounge watching television. As Handford walked in his brother pulled himself from the chair. The greeting was formal, no hugs, no pats on the back, no smiles, just a brief handshake. Douglas spoke first. 'You must be busy,' he said, pointing to the television. 'Two bodies in one day and in the same location.' He regained his seat.

Handford grimaced as he settled himself in the corner of the settee. Once the families had been told, the press office had alerted the media. This was not something they could keep quiet for long.

'No names yet?' Douglas asked.

'No.'

'They think one is the missing girl.'

Handford remained silent.

'You're not saying.'

'I can't until the DNA test has been completed.'

Douglas contemplated his fingers for a short while, probably working on his next words. Finally he took a deep breath but before he could say anything, Handford leaned forward. 'Why have you refused to give a sample of *your* DNA to the police?'

Colour flooded Douglas's cheeks and when he spoke his voice was spiked with sarcasm. 'What did they do, John, ask you to persuade me to change my mind – or did it come as an order?'

Handford looked at him in disgust. 'Don't be ridiculous, Douglas, of course it wasn't an order, it was a request from a colleague. But does it matter? Because even if it was an order, DCI Noble is doing you a favour by giving you the opportunity to change your mind. Continue to refuse and he'll pull you in, interview you and if he's not satisfied with your answers, arrest you and take your DNA legally; he won't need your permission. Do it quietly and no one need know, fight it and you'll be all over the media.' He pulled himself from the settee and walked to the patio windows. The heavy curtains were closed and for once, instead of feeling comforted by their warmth, he felt stifled. He dragged one of them open and looked out into the night. The moon was full, but as he watched, the clouds scudding across the sky hid it from view. The wind was gusting and the trees under which the cats slept in summer bent and swayed. Suddenly, almost without warning, the rain cascaded down, bouncing off the patio and off the window and he shivered and closed the curtain. He didn't know whether the SOCOs had finished at the scene yet but weather like this would destroy what was left of any evidence. At least the bodies had been moved to the mortuary in Halifax. The post mortems were scheduled for the next day, Tom's in the morning with Mike Paynter present, Bronwyn's in the afternoon. Handford was to go to that one and he wasn't looking forward to it. Of all the parts of his job, he hated post mortems; he hated the sounds and the smells, and he hated that he couldn't rid himself of the thought that the body on the table had been a living, breathing person until someone had taken away their most basic human right – that of life. He avoided post mortems whenever he could. This one he couldn't. The image of what was left of the young woman flashed into his memory, followed by that of Josie Renshaw as she must have lay on the ground, blood oozing from her shattered head, her body broken beyond repair because no one was prepared to believe her, and with a sudden rush of anger he swung round to face his brother.

'Don't you care, Douglas? If not for Josie, then for Mary and the kids. Can't you see how it looks? To refuse suggests you have something to hide.'

'And you think I have?' Douglas's anger matched that of his brother.

'Have you?'

'No.' Douglas's voice was dangerously loud, but this time it was also laced with fear.

'Then why have you refused to give a sample?'

Douglas remained mute, breathing heavily.

Handford marched over to stand in front of him and with his hands resting on the arms of the chair he leaned over him until he could feel his brother's breath on his face and bellowed, 'Why, Douglas, why?'

The force of Handford's question must have panicked Douglas because he pushed at his brother and shouted, 'Because I had sex with her that night. My DNA will be on her clothing.' The words came out in a strangled cry. 'Are you satisfied now?'

Handford straightened. He wasn't satisfied, far from it. There was another question to be asked, but before he could speak, Douglas said, 'She was under age, John. Can you imagine what would happen to me if this got out? I'd be finished. It doesn't matter that it was all those years ago and that I was young. Once it gets into the press – and it will because this kind of thing always does – I will be pilloried and you know it. I can't risk it.'

Handford walked over to the drinks tray and poured them both a whisky. He handed one to his brother. Douglas took the glass, his hand shaking. For a moment he stared at it and then drained it. He handed the glass back to Handford who poured him another and then sat down. 'Even though she was under age,' he said, 'was the sex you had with Josie consensual?'

Douglas's head jerked up, his eyes blazing. 'You think I raped her? For God's sake, John, you're my brother.'

'Was it consensual?' His words were measured.

'Of course it was. You knew Josie; she was up for it at any time?'

'Was she up for it this time?'

'Yes.' Douglas was shouting again.

Handford let his eyes rest on his brother. Much as he hated it, he didn't know whether to believe him or not. He'd been a detective for a long time, had seen this kind of anger displayed before and in his experience it was never as straightforward as it seemed. What was important was what lay beneath Douglas's fury? His brother's questions and mistrust of him or something else? There were always secrets buried deep in a person that were impossible for them to reveal even to themselves, let alone to anyone else. Was Douglas keeping such a secret? He hoped not. There was only one easy way to find out.

His voice was soft when he next spoke. 'Give them a sample of your DNA, Douglas. Refusing is not a way to cover yourself with the police or with your bosses. At the moment you are one of a group of men who were at the disco that night. If you continue to refuse then you become something else.'

'And once they have the results of the test I will become that something else, as you put it.' He gave Handford a dark hopeless look tinged with something like contempt.

'For a while, possibly.'

'I can't afford a while, John. In my position a while is too long.' Whether he was aware of the other rapes, Handford didn't know and he wasn't about to ask him or tell him. Even though Douglas was his brother, Noble wouldn't thank him for passing on privileged information.

Handford placed his glass on the floor and with his elbows on his knees he contemplated his hands while he weighed up his warning to Douglas. 'You do understand I can't help you this time, don't you?' he said quietly.

'I don't think you have much choice, John.' Douglas's voice was equally soft, but there was a suggestion of malice beneath the words. A hint of if I go down, then so do you. 'You lied in your statement; you tell them that and they'll throw the book at you. Then it won't be just me without a job, it'll be you as well. I can't see Gill being too happy if you're unemployed when she comes home from America.' He settled back in his chair and relaxed, as though he believed he had won the battle if not the war. Then, when it was obvious Handford was not persuaded by this argument, he said, 'If you care at all about

Mum and Dad, John,' Douglas said, 'you'll have to. They'll be devastated and they don't deserve it at their time of life.'

At this moment Handford had never disliked his brother more. His anger flared. 'Don't even go there, Douglas; don't bring Mum and Dad into this. They are not important. Josie Renshaw was raped by someone ...'

'So she said.' In spite of his scornful tone, anxiety clouded his eyes. Douglas was frightened. This was not going to go away.

Handford leaned back, weariness overtaking him. Perhaps Douglas hadn't raped Josie, perhaps he had. Whatever the truth of it, he hadn't come here to be persuaded to do anything that might implicate him; he had come to make sure his brother would continue to back his alibi, for in his warped imagination that was the only way he would be safe. And whatever the events of that night, it was important to Douglas that the lie was preserved. And that worried Handford.

Douglas left before the meal was served and Handford followed him shortly afterwards after an argument with his mother about wasted food – could he tell her what was she meant to do with it?

'Do whatever you want; freeze it or throw it away, just don't bother me with it,' he flung at her and he banged the front door as he left. He spent the rest of the evening at the local pub where he ate nothing and drank more than he ought. He stayed until he was so tired he could hardly keep his eyes open and when he finally arrived home the house was in darkness and the phone ringing. Late-night calls were his preserve and he hoped to God it wasn't the night duty inspector. He was in no fit state to go anywhere.

It wasn't. 'John, it's me.'

He giggled. 'Hello me.' It was silly but since Gill had gone to America they had opened their conversations with each other in the same way.

'You're drunk.'

Was it that obvious? Of course it was – he hardly ever giggled – laughed, but never giggled. 'I know,' he said. 'I've been at the pub.'

'With Andy, I expect.'

His heart plunged into his stomach. 'No, not with Andy. I was on my own.' He doubted he'd ever be able to drink with Andy again. And before she could delve deeper, he said, 'I've had a bad day, that's all: three bodies and Douglas. How's Tallahassee? What time is it and what's the weather like today?'

'It's half past six and it's hot and don't change the subject. Bodies don't usually turn you to drink, John. Tell me about them.'

Briefly he explained about Annie Laycock, Bronwyn Price and Tom Blakely.

'And Douglas?' Gill asked when he had finished. 'My guess is that it was because of him you went to the pub.'

He made no reply and in the silence the sound of her breathing filtered through the earpiece.

Eventually she said, 'You're worrying me, John. Tell me what happened.'

Handford wasn't sure he wanted to. She knew nothing of Josie Renshaw nor that he had lied for his brother.

'John.' Her tone was insistent. 'I'm staying on this telephone until you tell me, even if I have to take out a bank loan to pay the bill. So tell me.'

There was no getting round it so he gave her the whole story: Josie Renshaw's alleged complaint, her suicide, the false alibi he had given Douglas and the re-opening of the earlier unsolved rape cases. It was a relief to talk about it. 'Those of us who were there that night have been asked to give a DNA sample and Douglas has refused. Why should he do that, Gill?'

'Did you ask him why?'

'He said he'd had sex with her earlier that evening and they're bound to find his DNA.'

'But that doesn't prove he raped her.'

'No, but he's worried that if it comes out, then given the current climate he'll be obliged to resign.'

'Why? It happened years ago.'

'She was a minor, Gill, not quite sixteen, and he's right, it won't go down well; there's certain to be publicity; these things have a way of getting out.'

'Could it back-fire on you?'

'What, *Brother of police chief in sex scandal* kind of thing? Probably.' He leaned against the wall, the drink stirring in his stomach. 'But that's not what's worrying me. He's insisting I stick with my original statement and I told him I couldn't. If – and heaven forbid that I'm wrong – but if it's found he did rape her and the other girls and I stick with my statement, I could be charged with perverting the course of justice. I might just get away with it as a seventeen-year-old, but not now. I can't do it and that was what the major row was about. He's frightened, Gill, and I can't help feeling there's more to it than that she was under age.'

'Did you ask him about the other girls?'

'No, it's privileged information.'

Again there was a short silence while Gill assimilated everything she had been told. Then, 'Do you want me to come home?'

Yes, oh yes please. 'No, Gill. I wouldn't ask you to do that. I'll be fine.'

'Would it do any good if I rang Douglas? Had a word with him?'

'I doubt it. In fact, it might make things worse.'

'Then you ring me every night. Promise me you will, or I'll be on the next plane home. And, John ...'

'Yes?'

'I love you.'

As he replaced the receiver, John Handford was very close to tears.

He was in his office early the next morning. When he had driven into work he doubted he was within the alcohol limits. His mother had still been in bed, as were the girls, and he didn't know how much if anything they had gleaned from last night's raised voices, but they must be aware that it was something to do with Douglas and that it was serious. Tonight he would apologise, but whether he could give a reason for his behaviour he wasn't sure. So much depended on what happened today.

As soon as he arrived and before he took off his coat he

left a message on Noble's voice mail to say he had spoken to Douglas and he needed to see him; could he contact him on his mobile to arrange a time convenient to both of them. His hands were shaking when he replaced the receiver, but if he hadn't done it as soon as he got in he might never have done it and Douglas would have been let off the hook and Handford caught securely on it.

He spent the next hour drinking coffee and attempting to force his mind onto the actions for the day. The last thing he needed was his brother's idiocy muddying his mind. It was nothing unusual to be working on several cases at once, but he needed to make sure that should he find himself an integral part of the cold case investigation and, heaven help him, suspended, he would to be able to hand over smoothly. For as long as he was allowed – and he hadn't yet told Paynter what had happened – he would lead the inquiry into Tom Blakely's death himself, and although he would need to square it with the chief superintendent, Ali would take over the investigation into Bronwyn Price's murder as well as Annie Laycock's case. It was more than likely that Ian Gott had killed the old lady, so most of the leg work could be done by a team overseen by a sergeant, and it would do Ali good to work on the two simultaneously. If he was going to fast-track up the ranks then he needed as much experience as he could get.

He was sure the three murders were somehow linked, however tenuously, and eventually the pieces would come together, so the investigations had to be systematic and detailed. Although at the moment there seemed to be no connection between Tom Blakely and Bronwyn Price, it surely couldn't be coincidence their bodies had been found at the same site, nor could it be coincidence that Ian Gott had walked out of his open prison and was in the district. There was no doubt in Handford's mind that Annie Laycock's murder was down to Gott; he may not have meant to have killed her, but his MO was written all over it. Blakely's was different but Gott had, or thought he had, a motive, otherwise why would he have come back here?

Perhaps Christine Blakely could give them the answer.

chapter nine

It was ten o'clock when John Handford and Khalid Ali knocked on the door of Christine Blakely's house. Connie Burns let them in.

'How is she?' Handford asked.

'Bearing up, but she wants to see him. I did warn her it wouldn't be easy for her, but she's insisting so I said I'd ask you.'

'It's the post mortem this morning. Give the pathologist a ring; if he's happy, then I can't see how we can refuse.' Handford changed the subject. 'Anything on Patrick?'

'Yes, he's her brother-in-law and it appears there's no love lost between them. Patrick and his father, Amos, were miners and Tom was involved in policing the picket lines in the 1984 strike. Patrick's never forgiven him for that, or for the fact that a few months later he and his father were both made redundant when their pit closed.' There was a hint of bitterness in her voice that Handford had never encountered before. He gave her a searching look. 'I'm sorry, guv, but my father policed the picket lines and I know what it was like for him and for us. He was away days at a time and when he came home you could see he had aged that little bit more. There are only so many missiles you can dodge in a day and stay sane – but try telling people like Patrick Blakely that.'

Handford knew exactly what she meant. He hadn't long been in the police at the time of the miners' strike and hadn't been involved himself, but he couldn't help but be aware of how it had affected those who had, and he knew the extra money they earned didn't make up for what they went through. He waited until Connie's anger dissipated.

Finally, after a deep breath, she said, 'Anyway, Patrick and Amos pooled their redundancy money and set up in business selling and hiring out equipment for outdoor pursuits. It did well and by the time the old man died, they had three shops as well as a sideline in family adventure package holidays. After his father's death Patrick assumed the business would be wholly his but when the will was read he learned Amos had left his interest in it to Tom, with the proviso that Patrick remained in overall management.'

No wonder Patrick was angry. 'Does Mrs Blakely have any idea why Amos by-passed Patrick?'

'She says not. Perhaps he didn't trust Patrick with the whole business or perhaps it was his way of forgiving Tom. Whatever the reason, Patrick is furious, considers his brother stole what was rightfully his and wants it back.

'The terms of the will seem very specific. Was there any mention of what happens to the business should either Tom or Patrick die?'

'Yes, Amos wanted it to revert to the other, and then to the grandchildren. Although from what Christine understands it's doubtful that would happen. Providing Tom's and Amos's deaths were twenty-eight days apart, then Amos's will is out of the equation and Tom's share would pass under the terms of his own will.'

'To Christine?'

'Yes, which is why Patrick has been harassing them; he wanted Tom to will it back to him or better still to give it back. He felt Tom owed him.'

'And Tom refused?'

'Yes.'

'Do you think Patrick killed his brother?'

Connie Burns shrugged. 'Who knows, sir. According to Christine he tried to have the will overturned, but when that didn't happen he resorted to threats towards her. Presumably because he thought it would be easier to get at Tom through his wife.' She pulled a face. 'He obviously doesn't know her; she's a strong woman and stands up to him.'

Christine Blakely was dressed and in the kitchen filling the kettle with water when they walked in. At first sight she hardly appeared the grieving widow, but when she turned, pain and misery were etched in her face.

Handford introduced Khalid Ali.

'Do you want a drink?' Christine's voice was toneless, the question a mere courtesy.

'A coffee would be welcome,' Handford said.

She switched on the kettle and stretched to the wall cupboard to take out the mugs, but as she did so her fingers caught the sugar basin and it crashed to the floor. In silence she stooped to pick it up, but then slumped wearily on to a chair as though to clean the mess was too much to contemplate.

Handford would have liked to leave the questions, but he knew, and he was sure she knew, this was not possible. 'Let's go into the lounge where we can talk,' he said, 'and leave Connie to clear up and prepare the drinks.'

Wearily, Christine stood up and followed them into the hall. At the door she stopped. 'I'm sorry about yesterday,' she said. 'I shouldn't have hit you.'

Handford shook his head. 'You have nothing to apologise for; you were angry; we let you down.'

She turned to face him, a tinge of contempt in her eyes. 'Yes, you did, and not just me, but Tom as well.' Her voice drifted off and she shrugged. 'Not that it would have made any difference to him if you *had* made the effort, but it might to me. You might have found him earlier and I wouldn't have to beg to see him to say goodbye.'

Handford wasn't sure that was true; the location of the body was probably the last place they would have looked, in spite of Russell's hindsight comment that it should have been the first. As so often happens, it took a member of the public to be in the right place at the right time to stumble across it. But since Christine Blakely didn't want excuses, he made no comment.

'You shouldn't have assumed he was with another woman, John,' Christine went on. 'I knew my husband better than any of you; you should have listened to me. I *knew* he wasn't with another woman.' Her eyes were a bright blue and for a moment, as the anger took over, they flashed a deep azure. Then coldly and with calculated precision she said, 'He was one of yours; whatever your private thoughts you should have shown him some loyalty.'

Ali, who had been listening intently, appeared to be about to refute the criticism, but Handford pre-empted him by suggesting they move into the lounge.

The barrenness in the room was palpable; it was as though it too was suffering from Tom's absence; missing was the scent of his aftershave, the smell of his cigarettes, and his habit of ending the day with a couple of glasses of whisky. It wasn't as though he hadn't been away before when he'd had affairs, but then his presence had seemed tangible. Now it was eddying away and the room was in mourning.

Christine perched on the edge of an easy chair and motioned that the officers should take one of the others. Ali made himself comfortable in the corner of the settee; Handford sat opposite. He studied her for a moment. She had vigorously defended her husband, but what did she really think of his lifestyle? He couldn't believe she would sit back and accept it. How many arguments, he wondered, had there been over the years? How many times had she threatened to throw him out and how many times had he promised to remain faithful only to break that promise? To his colleagues he'd been a joke – the officer who couldn't keep his trousers on. But to Christine he would be the husband who found other women more attractive than her. Perhaps he *was* the older man linked with Bronwyn Price. Perhaps she had been the affair too many. Perhaps Christine had killed him. He hoped not, but he couldn't discount the possibility. However painful, the questions had to be asked, but before he could begin there came a knock on the door and Connie Burns entered with a tray of coffees. She placed them on the low table. 'I'll make that telephone call now, sir, and then, if you don't mind, I'll pop home and change.' When Handford nodded his agreement, she turned to Mrs Blakely. 'I'll be back before your sister arrives,' she said.

Ali offered the coffees round. Without taking a sip, Christine placed hers on the table and waited for Handford to speak.

'We think Tom has been dead between a week and ten days. You last saw him on the seventh of this month when he went to work, so it's likely he was killed on or close to that date. I know it must seem like adding insult to injury, but I do need to ask if you can account for your movements between the seventh and, let's say, the tenth.'

Without a word Christine stood up and walked over to a small mahogany desk in the alcove. She opened a drawer and pulled out a personal organiser, which she opened. 'Here's my diary,' she said, handing it to him.

He flicked through to the dates he had suggested. It was full; she was a busy lady.

'I work part time in the library and the rest of the time I'm either at the Heart Foundation shop in the centre or at home or with friends,' she said by way of explanation. 'As you can see, at first I carried on as normal; but for the last few days ...' She shrugged. 'You can take it; use it to check my movements.'

Calm, efficient and prepared as well as strong – definitely her own person; perhaps she'd had to be with a man like Tom Blakely for a husband. Yet niggling away at the back of Handford's mind was the thought that she was too calm, too efficient and too prepared. He passed the diary to Ali.

She sat down and picked up her mug, but still didn't drink. 'I had to fill my life,' she said, as though reading his thoughts. 'My husband had affairs; what else could I do? Sit back and wait for him to come home?' A sad smile ran along her lips. 'I'm not the first woman to have an adulterous policeman for a husband and I won't be the last. Don't look like that, John, you've been in the service long enough to know that, for some officers, unfaithfulness goes with the territory – the power of the uniform perhaps, I don't know. My husband was one of those officers and whatever the reason, I accepted it because none of the affairs was serious and he always came back.'

An explanation of sorts, but Handford wasn't sure it was enough. 'Do you know Bronwyn Price?' he asked. If the question was unexpected, Christine Blakely wasn't thrown by it.

'The young woman whose body was found with Tom's? No I don't. I hadn't heard of her until her name came up on television and in the newspapers.'

'Is it possible Tom could have had an affair with her? We know she was dating an older man. Could it have been Tom?'

Christine hesitated. 'I don't know, John. If he was, then he was being much more careful than usual. As I say, the first I heard of her was from the media.'

'Did you discuss her disappearance with Tom?'

'No more than to wonder where she was.'

'How did he react when you talked about her?'

'He didn't, except to say what the police were saying – that she'd been gone so long she was more than likely dead.'

Handford had to admit that even in these circumstances Christine Blakely was good. She gave all the right answers and for the moment there was little to be gained by pursuing any relationship Tom might have had with Bronwyn Price. If he had been having an affair they would uncover it once they began to delve into the back streets of their lives and discover if at any point their paths merged.

'Tell me about Patrick, Christine. When we told you where we had found Tom, you said, "Patrick will love that". What did you mean?'

'Tom was trying to persuade the council to place a memorial to the miners who died working the shallow mines in the late eighteen hundreds. Patrick always thought Tom's interest in them was hypocritical since he seemed to care so little about living miners. Patrick would think he couldn't have died in a more suitable place.' Christine went on to explain the relationship between Tom and his brother in much the same words as Connie Burns. 'He'll never forgive Tom for joining the police,' she said. 'He rang on Tuesday and was here yesterday demanding what he thinks is rightfully is.'

'Does he know about Tom's death?'

'Yes, Connie told him last night. He said he wasn't interested and hasn't been near. I imagine he's been too busy consulting with his solicitor to see if his father's will can be reinstated. It can't and he's further away than ever now from taking over the entire business. Tom willed it to me.' She sighed. 'To be honest, it's the last thing I want; he can have it, but not if all he does is threaten me.'

Handford looked over at Ali; he was the one with a degree in law. 'Is that true?'

'Yes, although I suppose he could make an appeal in court,' Ali said, 'But that will take a long time and will be very expensive.'

Christine smiled her thanks. It was a tired smile.

'Are you all right? Can we go on?' Handford asked.

She nodded.

'Describe again the last time you saw Tom?'

'It was at breakfast. He took a phone call from a former colleague, telling him Ian Gott had walked out of an open prison. It worried him. Gott thought Tom had framed him and when he was sent down he had threatened to "do him over". I think those were his words. I'm sure it was nothing more than he'd heard before.'

'But even so, it worried him?'

'Yes.'

'Do you know why?'

'Because for some reason this time Tom believed him.'

'But you don't know what that reason was?'

'No. I asked him if he *had* framed Gott and he winked and said it would have served him right if he had because low-life like him are better off locked away, but he hadn't because that wasn't the way he worked. He said he didn't need to because there was plenty of evidence against Gott and also he'd had a tip-off from someone who knew him.'

Ali looked up from the diary. 'He said he'd been tipped off? From an informant?'

'That's what he told me. But not an informant, just someone who drew the line at beating up old people – apparently he was worried for his elderly aunt. She'd practically brought him up and he was very close to her.'

Ali pushed further. 'If that were so, why did Gott believe your husband had framed him?'

'Apparently Gott didn't know about the other man.'

'Tom told you that?'

'Yes. He said if Gott had known he would have taken his revenge on Billy, probably by beating him up or by robbing the old lady or both. So Tom kept him out of it.'

Ali turned to Handford. 'That makes sense. There was no mention of an informant, named or unnamed, at the trial or in the prosecution or defence papers.' Then to Christine Blakely, 'He mentioned Billy, but did Tom give you any idea what other evidence he had against Gott?'

'No, why should he?' Suddenly Christine Blakely's eyes blazed with anger. 'You think Billy gave him the information and Tom built a case round it. You're investigating him, aren't you? He's dead and you're investigating him.' Tears flooded her eyes. She brushed them away angrily, jumped up, slamming her coffee cup onto the tray and made towards the door. 'Go; I want you to go.'

Ali stood and took a step forward, ready to protest, but Connie Burns had been right when she said Christine Blakely was a strong woman; inspector or not, she had the measure of him even if he didn't have the measure of her. 'Don't even begin to defend your actions or your questions. You couldn't be bothered to investigate his disappearance; but you're prepared to blacken his name just because he tried to keep a young man and his grandmother away from a thug. Well, not with my help, Inspector.'

Handford was furious with Ali; he had no right even to hint at the allegation, never mind question the wife on it. Even though he had never met her, he ought to have realised from her demeanour in the kitchen that you never underestimated a woman like Christine Blakely. Ali might be a fast-track officer, but there were times when his grasp of human psychology was that of a first-year student instead of a senior detective. He went over to Christine and laid his hand on her arm. She snatched it away. 'I'm sorry, Christine,' he said, 'but we have to. When we find Gott, he may make the allegation again. If he's charged with Tom's murder he could well use it as his defence or at least in mitigation. If that happens, it will become public knowledge. If we can look into it now as part of the investigation into his death there's a possibility we can prevent that. Better us than an official inquiry. Now please ...'

He eased her gently back to her seat and although she acquiesced, he knew from her expression that his explanation had done nothing to calm her anger, nor had a forced apology from Ali. It was all too late; they'd lost her and while she continued to answer Handford's questions it was with minimum information or, if it seemed the truth might tarnish her husband's reputation still further, with 'I don't know' or 'He never spoke to me about it'.

As they prepared to leave, Handford turned back. 'Just one last question, Christine. Do you know the whereabouts of Tom's car?'

Marek Kowalski was in considerable discomfort. His body ached mercilessly and no matter into which position he moved – standing, sitting or lying – he was uncomfortable. At first he hadn't been allowed painkillers because of the injuries to his head. To take them might mask any change in his condition, the nurse had said, so he had spent the night shifting his position and attempting to calm his fears. The beating was a warning and Leon Jackson had made it perfectly clear that once working for them there was no way out. When the doctor had insisted he was badly concussed and it would be better if they could keep an eye on him for a day or two, he hadn't argued. At least for the moment he was safe; after that, when he was discharged from hospital, he would gather his things and return to Poland.

It was ironical he had come to England to secure a better life for himself and ultimately for his parents. A year and a half on his bank balance showed he had done that, but he had sacrificed his integrity in the process. His family would be ashamed of him; he was ashamed of himself.

At home he'd been an engineer with good qualifications but he'd known that because his English was so poor, he would not be able to step into the same level of employment in the UK. Nevertheless, he was determined to become proficient in the language so that eventually he could return to doing what he knew best. What he hadn't bargained on was that the engineering industry in England was in decline, and no matter how good his mastery of the language, the work simply wasn't there. So he had remained at the stables. The wage was low and just about covered his rent, his food and his bus fare, but he enjoyed being with the horses and the children, and Winnie gave him overtime when it was available. He should have been satisfied and would have been had he not met Bronwyn. Not that he blamed her – she had been prepared to love him for what he was; it was his fault entirely.

It was the Saturday before Christmas when they met for the first time. They were in a pub. He was on his own, leaning at the bar, trying to make his drink last; she was in a booth with a group of women, but not really part of them. She wasn't particularly attractive, but he had been mesmerised by her red hair. And although she was with others, she had an air of loneliness about her that made him sad. It wasn't in his nature to pick up women, but when she came to the bar to replenish the drinks, he had spoken to her. Something inane like: 'It's busy in here'. And she had smiled at him, a smile that seemed to light up her face. Although he could barely afford it, he offered to buy her a drink and she accepted. She took her order back to the table and to a chorus of 'Oooh' came to stand next to him. They had talked – small talk at first – and finally by mutual agreement had left the smoky atmosphere to sit on one of the benches in the Town Hall Square. It was well past midnight when he had walked her home. He remembered that because of the lateness of the hour and his lack of money for a taxi, he had had to trudge a mile and a half back to his own flat.

After that evening they met regularly and at first they were just friends, then more than friends. He would like to have taken her to Poland to meet his family, but he could barely afford to take her out in town, let alone find the money for the fare to his country. She said it didn't matter, but to him it did. Then one day when he was feeling particularly depressed, he had let his frustration loose on Martin Neville and Leon Jackson. They understood, they said, and, almost as an afterthought, offered him a way of earning more money – a place on their team. That was what they called it: their team. It was dodgy, he'd known that, but it didn't hurt anyone, no one was badly injured, no one died. All he had to do was give a witness statement to a road accident for insurance purposes and for that and keeping his mouth shut he would be well paid.

They were as good as their word and for the first time in their relationship he was able to buy Bronwyn presents and take her places. But eventually – inevitably – she became suspicious about where his extra money was coming from. Then one evening when they were lying in bed, she had confronted him. At first he said Winnie had given him a rise, but she hadn't believed him; then that he had a part-time job – which in a way was true – but because he couldn't think of one that would pay the kind of money he was spending on her, begging her not to be angry with him he had told her the truth.

Enraged, she had pulled herself from his arms, jumped out of bed and begun to open drawers and throw the presents he had bought her into the bin. They were tainted, she said, paid for with dirty money and she wanted nothing more to do with them or with him. She threw words at him like immoral and illegal. He wished he could make her understand that it wasn't that he didn't know it; he'd known it all along, but he'd never had money, not real money, and for the first time he had been given the chance to have it. That was something she would never empathise with – the meaning of what it was like to be poor. She had more than him and that made him ashamed. He had tried to explain. He rented a small one-bedroomed flat in a four-storey building in a less than respectable part of the town. He had second-hand furniture and a small colour television. He travelled to work on a bus that stopped a distance from the stables and he had to walk the rest of the way whatever the weather. She drove the few miles to her office in her own car; she had a flat of her own which was bright and cheery, a television with a big screen and an expensive music centre. She had a good life and he wanted the same. What was immoral about that?

Nothing, she had said. It was the way he was going about getting it that was immoral. And it was then he had told her about David Younger. If he was immoral, Marek had shouted at her, then so was Younger, and her mother who wanted more than her husband could give her. The scene was still vivid in his memory: Bronwyn throwing his clothes into his arms and pushing him towards the door; him pleading her forgiveness and begging her not to leave him.

He hadn't seen her again. He'd tried to contact her, tell her he was sorry, but her mobile had been turned off and she hadn't returned his calls. The man at the travel agency had told him she'd gone on holiday. Then the police said she was missing and eventually began to suggest she was dead – not in so many words, just that they were concerned for her safety, but it meant the same. They had asked for anyone who knew her to contact them, but he hadn't, because deep down he was sure that if she was dead it was because of the staged car accidents that he, David Younger and Help International were involved in.

A hand feathered his shoulder. 'Marek.'

Slowly he looked up. A nurse stood beside his bed. 'You have a visitor,' she said. 'I told him it was not visiting time, but he seems concerned about you so I said he could have five minutes.'

She stepped to one side and Leon Jackson came into view, a newspaper under his arm. His water-colour eyes leered down at him. He drew a chair to the bedside and made himself comfortable. There were no questions about how Marek was feeling, although it must have been obvious that his every movement was agony. Instead he opened up the paper and threw it on the bed. 'Something for you to read,' he said. 'You might be interested. Seems the police have found a body. Bronwyn Price, apparently. Wasn't she your girlfriend? They want her boyfriend to get in touch with them.' He balled his fist and gave Marek what would appear to anyone watching a friendly punch.

Marek barely felt it. His head was spinning as he looked at the picture open on the bed. Bronwyn gazed out at him with that embarrassed half smile she always gave photographers. Tears sprung to his eyes and ran down his cheeks. He picked up the paper, but the words misted in front of him. He lifted his head to focus on Jackson. 'No. Please no.'

Jackson grinned. 'Looks like it,' he said. 'It's murder they say.'

'You killed her?'

The man at his bedside gave a full-throated laugh. 'Not me, Marek. I'm just here to give you the news.' He stood up and replaced the chair. 'I think my five minutes is about up so I'll leave you to read the newspaper in peace.' His expression darkened. 'Don't even think about getting in touch with the police, not if you know what's good for you. Oh, and don't worry about getting home when you're discharged – I'll pick you up.'

Christine Blakely wasn't only tired; she was furious. She scrubbed at the kitchen floor where the sugar had spilled out. Connie Burns hadn't done a very good job of cleaning it up, the tiles were still sticky. Her anger mounted with each movement of the brush. She wouldn't have believed anything could have overridden the grief she was feeling, but this had. How dare they investigate Tom? How dare they even think he would set someone up? At times he'd been a loose cannon, she didn't deny it, or that his methods could be described as unorthodox, but for him to deliberately frame a person for something he hadn't done was unthinkable. Tom might have been less than honest in his love life, but whatever Detective Inspector Ali thought, he was honest in his work. Someone ought to tell him that by now he should have learned to look deeper than the surface and Tom's affairs had been his surface, not his depth.

It had occurred to her when John and his inspector had gone that she'd been so angry she hadn't mentioned Marek Kowalski. And nor would she now – not until she knew why he had come to see Tom that night and why he was so desperate to talk to him. If what he told her was detrimental to Tom, then the police would have to do their own dirty work. There were times during their marriage that she had hated the police service, but never more so than now and because of that she was not about to help them. Nevertheless, she had to know what Kowalski had to say and she had to know before the police.

She pulled herself off her knees, poured the dirty water into the sink and put the bucket and scrubbing brush away. Tom's name hadn't yet been released to the press and wouldn't be until the result of the DNA test. It would take all the strength she could muster, but if she went up to the stables she could talk to him and make him talk to her before he was aware of what had happened. She walked through into the hall, took the notebook out of her handbag and flicked through to find the telephone number of the stables, hoping there was someone there to answer. At the third ring a voice said, 'Moor Top Equestrian Centre, Winnie speaking.'

'It's Christine Blakely, Winnie. Will Mr Kowalski be in this afternoon? Will he talk to me?' The words tumbled out.

Winnie sounded less cheerful than she had yesterday. 'Marek's in the Royal, Mrs Blakely. He was mugged yesterday and I haven't had a chance to speak to him yet. I don't think he's too bad, but I'm popping up tonight to see how he is; I could ask him then, if you like.'

Christine offered her commiserations, thanked her and rang off. She slumped onto the step. Marek Kowalski mugged. She tried to feel sorry for him, but had little emotion left. All she knew was that if she waited for Winnie to get back to her it would be at least tomorrow before she could talk to him and she couldn't wait that long. By then Tom would have been named and once that was out Winnie, being Winnie, would have done her maths, linked her to Tom and to Marek and probably contacted the police. As weary and as desolate as she felt, it had to be today and it had to be before her sister arrived and Connie Burns returned. She would visit him this afternoon. Her mind made up, she pulled off her apron, picked her coat and her car keys off the hall stand and ran out of the house.

chapter ten

When Handford arrived back in his office there was a voice-mail message waiting for him from DCI Noble saying he would be free after five thirty and suggesting they meet up then. He sent back his agreement and then rang Tom's solicitor, James Amery.

Amery's secretary answered. 'I'm terribly sorry, Chief Inspector, but Mr Amery is in court all day. Would you like me to pencil you in for tomorrow morning?'

There was nothing to do but agree, although he would have preferred to talk to Amery today. He might have been able to throw some light on the legacy left Tom by his father. He wanted also to visit the insurance company where Tom worked, and this time Handford would drop in – with three murders on his hands he wasn't prepared to let appointments slow the investigations down. Clarke could go with him to the Bronwyn Price post mortem, after which he would drop him off at the travel agency where Bronwyn had worked. Yesterday he'd steered clear of Andy, leaving his friend to get over what he thought was Handford's betrayal. Now he would have to be over it. He didn't need a prima donna on his squad, whatever the reason. He rang through to the incident room. 'You're with me at Bronwyn Price's post mortem,' he said. At least Clarke would be a captive audience during the journey to the Halifax mortuary: like it or not he would have to listen to him.

They travelled the first few miles in silence. Eventually Handford said, 'Have you found Allan Widdop?'

'Yes, he's in a nursing home the other side of Harrogate.

He's eighty-six and apart from a touch of arthritis he is, to quote the owner, as bright as a button.'

'Is he happy to be questioned again?'

'Apparently, although he's not happy the case is being re-examined. Any more than I am.'

'For God's sake, Andy, stop it. If Gott—'

'I know, if Gott killed Blakely ... And what if he didn't? I'm going through this for nothing.' He turned to face Handford. 'Do you know what really gets to me, John? That it was you who set it in motion. I could just about have accepted it if it had come from Paynter, but not from you. You should know me better.'

'I do, but it's not me you have to convince. It's Gott's solicitor; he'll be the one asking the questions, and more than likely in open court.'

'That's if he killed Tom ...'

'No, that's if he killed Annie Laycock. The question is bound to arise as to why he came back here in the first place, and his answer will be to take revenge on the officers who set him up seven years ago. To accuse and name you in open court is one way of getting his revenge and that's all it will take to set up an inquiry and you know it. All I'm trying to do is to pre-empt it.'

'And if Ali has reason to believe that Gott was set up?'

'Then it's out of our hands.'

For the rest of journey nothing was said. Finally Handford pulled up in the mortuary car park. Clarke climbed out of the car and leaned against it, his arms resting on the roof. 'Can I ask you something?'

'Go on.'

'Am I off the investigation into Tom Blakely's death?'

Handford sighed. He ought to say yes, but Clarke was a good detective and he couldn't afford to lose him. 'No, not for the moment. Why?'

'Well, it occurred to me that we're assuming Tom disappeared because he feared Gott was in the district and after him.'

'Are you suggesting that wasn't Gott's reason for coming back here?'

'No. I'm suggesting that Tom wasn't afraid of Ian Gott. I knew him and he didn't care about threats from the likes of Gott – water off a duck's back, as far as he was concerned. I'm suggesting he didn't disappear at all; that he intended to go home after work, but he was killed sometime that day by someone else. I'm not sure whether his death had anything to do with a woman and an irate partner taking his revenge; they've never done before, so why now? But I don't necessarily believe Gott killed him either. I'm not saying that wasn't why he came here in the first place, but if he did carry out his threat, why is he still here and why stay around to murder Annie Laycock? If it was just for money, he could have got that anywhere; there's no shortage of old folk for him to rob. Surely once he'd got rid of Blakely he would have high-tailed it out of the district.'

'Perhaps he wants his revenge on you as well. You were working closely with Blakely.'

Clarke shook his head. 'No, he threatened Tom, not me.'

'He's been in prison almost seven years. He'll have done a lot of thinking in that time.'

'Then we need to find out. Let me check into Tom's background; let me see if I can come up with another reason for someone to kill him.'

The post mortem was as awful as Handford had expected it to be. Bronwyn Price's body was badly decomposed and at first there was doubt as to whether the pathologist would be able to determine the cause of death, but finally he looked up and said, 'She's been hit with something heavy – you can see the damage to the skull, but I would say whoever killed her attempted to strangle her. Difficult to be absolutely sure because there are no outward signs left and none to speak of in her mouth, but the hyoid bone has been fractured.'

'That couldn't have been done by an animal?'

'Unlikely, I would say. Manual strangulation would be my best bet, although whether it was the blow to the head or the ligature round the neck that actually killed her, I'm not sure yet. I suspect the strangulation came first and when it was obvious she was not dead, then the blow. I don't suppose you've found anything that could have been used?'

Handford shook his head.

'Pity.'

'Is there anything to tell us that it is Bronwyn Price?'

'Apart from her red hair and no DNA results?'

'Yes.'

'Well, as you can see there's not much left of her, but if it helps she has suffered a broken leg and a broken arm at some-time, probably when she was quite young.'

'Ten and twelve, according to her mother.'

'Yep, that would do it.' He walked across to the light board where two X-rays were attached. He switched it on. 'Look, you can just about make them out. The fracture to the leg was a spiral, probably quite a nasty one. We can check that against her medical records.'

The two detectives peered at the faint lines crossing the limbs. 'She had a broken nose as well,' Handford said.

'No, sorry, most of the nose has gone. Probably back in some bird's nest.'

Handford wished the pathologist didn't enjoy his job quite so much. He was still feeling the after affects of last night's binge and he swallowed hard. 'What about Annie Laycock and Tom Blakely? Would you say we're looking for one killer or two?' he asked.

The pathologist walked towards his desk and opened a couple of files. 'Mrs Laycock died of internal injuries. Most of her major organs were damaged but the main problem was that the femoral artery burst, probably when he threw her around, and basically she bled to death – it would probably have taken three, four minutes. A pity because despite her age she was reasonably healthy, could have lived a good few years if she hadn't put up a fight. And I suspect it was quite a fight. There are several defence wounds on her arms and hands, some bruises, but some cuts, which could probably have been made by a knife being waved around. I say this because there was also a twenty-centimetre scratch across the surface of her abdomen; no real depth to it, and certainly not life threatening. Oh, and she sustained a broken toe, which could have occurred when she kicked out at him. She was an old lady and her bones were quite brittle.'

'Was she raped?'

'No, there's no sign of any sexual activity. What makes you think she had been?'

'The position of her nightgown – it was pulled well above her knees.'

The pathologist's voice softened. 'He did a lot of things, but not that.'

'Such as?'

'The wounds to her face and her head are post mortem.'

Clarke exploded. 'You what?'

The pathologist gave him a long look. 'I imagine he didn't like the way she was staring at him, Constable, so he obliterated her features.' He turned to Handford. 'The eyes of the dead frighten some people, those who don't care walk away, the rest ... well, Mrs Laycock is the result.'

'And that leads you to suppose ...?'

'Oh, Chief Inspector, I work on facts, I don't suppose. But if I was in the pub and you were to ask the same question, I would hazard a guess it hadn't been his intention to kill her, but she'd fought back and that made him angry. There's no doubt in my mind the original wounds were made by an angry man – the facial injuries by a frightened one.'

'And Tom Blakely? If you were still in the pub, would you say he had been killed by an angry man?'

'I would say determined rather than angry, at least at first.'

'At first?'

'He was stabbed seven times: once in the back and six in the abdomen and chest. There's little sign of a struggle at all, no defence wounds and nothing except dirt under his fingernails. I've sent it for analysis, but the chances are it came from the pathway to the mine. I suspect he tried to crawl away from his killer – there is a considerable amount of mud on the knees and lower half of his trousers. That said, it was the trauma to the head that killed him. You can see here at the right temple there's a depressed fracture of the temporal bone. As a result the artery ruptured and bled around the brain. He had to be alive for that to happen. The stab wounds would render him almost immobile and he may well have died from them eventually, but as I said, it was the blow to the head that killed him. Whatever it was, it caused an eight-centimetre gash to the right temple and the force behind it shattered the temporal bone.'

'Have you any idea what he could have been hit with?'

'Something heavy like a wine or spirits bottle or perhaps a metal post or even a golf club; a five iron would do it nicely. As with the fingernails, there's little in the way of debris in the wound so the weapon needs to be something smooth; had it been stone from one of the walls or wood from the trees, we would have expected to find fragments we could link to the area.' He surveyed the body. 'One thing's for sure, whoever did this wanted him dead, or at least didn't want him to live.'

Handford grimaced. Unlike Clarke he wasn't prepared to rule Gott out, but although he couldn't see him as the golfing type, he was likely to wield a gin bottle. He would check if the SOCOs had found fragments of glass at the scene; as for the golf club, there were public links in the area. He sighed, that would mean checking on everyone who had used them over the past week or ten days and who knew or knew of Tom Blakely. And that meant slog and shoe leather. He made a mental note to ask Superintendent Paynter for more uniformed officers to help out – at least in the short term.

'What kind of knife was used on Tom Blakely?'

'Kitchen knife, smooth not serrated, fourteen, fifteen centimetres long and three to four at its widest end. Probably not enough to do the damage the killer was after, hence the blow to the head.'

'Could the same knife have been used on Annie Laycock?'

'Oh, yes, I would think so, but I'd need to examine the knife to be sure.'

Finally Handford asked, 'Would you say Annie Laycock and Tom Blakely were murdered by the same person?' When he saw the pathologist's expression he added, 'In your opinion, in the pub.'

'I'm sorry, I can't answer that – not even in the pub. The

injuries sustained are different. Tom Blakely was stabbed, but died as a result of being hit with, to quote Agatha Christie, a blunt instrument; Mrs Laycock was kicked to death and as I said the mutilation of her features came afterwards. The only real link is that the killer had a knife, but it was used much more ferociously on Mr Blakely, probably only to frighten in Mrs Laycock's case. What I can tell you, though, is that Mr Blakely's killer would be roughly his size.'

'So are we looking for a man or a woman?'

The pathologist smiled. 'We're back in the pub again, Chief Inspector.' He thought for a moment. 'For what it's worth, I would say Mrs Laycock was killed by a man; I've never known a woman mutilate the features like that – at least not post mortem. As for Mr Blakely or indeed Miss Price – it could be either.'

Handford ran his hands through his hair. He still considered Gott as prime suspect for Annie Laycock's murder, but as for Tom Blakely, except that it might have been a golfer, male or female, who killed him they were no nearer to an answer. Perhaps Clarke was right. Perhaps the motive for Tom Blakely's murder was nothing to do with revenge, but more to do with his work or his lifestyle.

Christine Blakely found Marek Kowalski without difficulty. When she'd enquired, the receptionist had typed his name into the computer and then told her which ward he was in and given her the directions of how to get there. For a few moments she lingered in the corridor. Would he want to talk to her? Would he be as nervous as he had been when he had come to the house? And more to the point, was it a coincidence he had been mugged? Her husband dead and the man who had obviously wanted to speak with him badly beaten? A coincidence – possibly, they did happen. If it was it had been one that had concerned her on the journey to the hospital and twice she had almost decided to turn back and ring John Handford. But she knew how these things worked and once it was out of her hands, there it would stay. It was *her* husband who had been murdered, but if the police decided any information given to her might prejudice their investigation she would be left out of the loop. And she wanted so badly to know what Kowalski had that could link him or anyone else with Tom's death. He had to tell her; she needed to know.

He was in a four-bedded bay, and for the moment alone, the other patients probably having treatment or in the day room. He was sitting up in bed staring at a newspaper and as she approached he seemed unaware of her. She walked quietly over to him, not wishing to startle him, but eventually he must have become conscious of another person in the room and lifted his head. His expression was one of great sadness, but as he realised who she was, it changed to one of fear.

'No,' he whimpered. 'No, go away, go away.'

She sat on the chair next to the bed. 'Please, Mr Kowalski, I'm not here to hurt you and I do need to talk to you.'

His eyes followed her. 'I can't, I can't. I'm sorry, you must go.' His voice was hoarse, and she wondered if it was a result of the beating. Her husband had been beaten too, 'hit with something heavy', Handford had said.

For a moment grief overcame her and she fought to stem the tears. 'I'm sorry too, Mr Kowalski, but I can't go until I know why you wanted to speak to my husband.'

He avoided her question and instead he asked, 'Who sent you?'

'No one sent me. I came because I need you to talk to me.'

'Then how did you find me?'

She smiled. 'When you came to the house, I detected the smell of horses – it's quite distinctive, you know – so I thought perhaps you worked with them, rather than just ride them and took a gamble and visited the stables in the area.' Although she wasn't sure why, she didn't mention her visit to Help International. Perhaps it was that fleeting look of concern in Martin Neville's eyes when she had described Marek. 'I recognised your photograph from those displayed at Moor Top Equestrian Centre. Winnie was helpful, but I promise you she didn't pass on any personal information, like your address or telephone number. She said you would be working again today, but when I rang her again this morning she told me you had been attacked and were in the hospital. Please, Mr Kowalski, I know you've had a bad experience, but you've nothing to be afraid of from me. All I want is for you to tell me why you needed to talk to my husband.'

He lowered his eyes. 'I can't,' he whispered.

'Why? You were desperate to talk to him two days ago.' Was that all it was – two days? It seemed like years.

He shook his head. 'I was wrong; I didn't need to talk to him. I thought I did, but I didn't.' He looked up at her, his eyes pleading and filled with tears, then he picked up the newspaper and handed it to her.

Bronwyn Price's picture gazed out at her. The woman whose body had been found near to Tom's. Her head spun. 'You knew this girl?'

He nodded, unable to speak.

'She was your friend, your girlfriend, someone you loved?' She wanted to put her arms round him to comfort him, but couldn't be sure that if she did she wouldn't break down as well. 'Was Bronwyn having an affair with my husband? Is that why you came to see him?' It was harsh and when she saw the look on Marek's face and the tears spill down his bruised cheeks the answer was plain enough. If she was, he didn't want to believe it. 'Bronwyn wasn't like that,' he sobbed.

'Then why did you want to speak to my husband? You have to tell me. I need to know.'

In spite of the urgency of her tone, Marek insisted, 'I can't tell you, please don't ask me. Go away.'

She leaned over to him. 'Why can't you tell me? What is it you don't want me to know?'

Marek pushed his legs beneath the sheets, lay down and pulled the top cover over his head. Christine grabbed at it and wrenched it away from him.

'Mr Kowalski, the police know you were Bronwyn's boyfriend and are looking for you. So far I haven't mentioned your visit to them, but if you won't talk to me I shall be obliged to tell them where you are and they will certainly want to question you.'

He looked up at her, his eyes pleading and shook his head

vigorously. 'No, Mrs Blakely please, I can't.' His voice subsided to a whisper. 'I can't,' and he pulled the cover back over his head.

She looked around and saw a nurse watching her. She had pushed him too far and if she tried again they would send her away. Perhaps tomorrow. Suddenly weariness overcame her. She had changed since Tom died. Become less understanding. Perhaps it was part of the grieving process or perhaps she was just tired of fighting for everything: her marriage, her husband, and now it seemed something someone else knew about him and she didn't.

Wearily she picked up her bag; all she knew now was that she wanted to go home and sleep. She looked down at the hidden form of the man under the covers. He was grieving for Bronwyn; she could understand, but couldn't feel sorry for him; she hadn't enough emotional energy left for him. She pulled out her notebook and wrote down her telephone number, then tore out the page which she placed on the bedside cupboard. She bent over Marek. 'I have left you my telephone number,' she said. 'Think about what I have asked and ring me. It is important to me that you tell me what you had to say to my husband that made you come all the way out to the house. If it wasn't I wouldn't have come here. If I haven't heard from you by tomorrow night, I will have go to the police and ask them to find out for me.'

The offices of the Dart Insurance Company were situated on the Keighley to Skipton road where the town ended and the leafy suburbs began. It was a modern building set back from the highway, newly built and landscaped by experts, proving beyond doubt in Handford's mind there was money in insurance. Its only acknowledgement to its past history was the date 1890 above the door and a portrait of the founder, Josiah Dart, in the reception area.

Handford was shown into the office of the senior partner, a room as plush and as dignified as he expected. At one side were two comfortable chairs, a settee and a low coffee table for informal meetings. At the other end and facing the door stood a rectangular mahogany desk and a high-backed swivel chair for the more formal business of insurance.

Graham Dart met him with an outstretched hand. A portly man, Handford gauged him as being in his mid-fifties. His dark grey suit was created rather than manufactured and his shirt was a pristine white broken only by a tie in blue silk, patterned discreetly in a mixture of the same darker and lighter colour. His brown hair was immaculately groomed and when they shook hands Handford noted the well-manicured nails. Such was his image one could be forgiven for thinking the man had never done a real day's work in his life, yet behind the faultless exterior his shoulders were hunched and his eyes were drained of emotion. The dark smudges beneath them spoke of what? Money worries, personal problems or something more? Whatever it was he was in the presence of a care-worn, even worried man.

Yet his voice showed none of that and when Graham Dart spoke it was strong and the accent was that of a solid Yorkshire man, one who took every problem in his stride and dealt with it – or not.

'Please do sit down,' he said as he indicated the chair in front of the desk. This was not to be an informal meeting – at least not as far as the senior partner was concerned. 'Can I offer you a drink – tea, coffee?'

Handford had not been away from the mortuary and the post mortem for long enough to rid himself of the taste or the smell and would have liked something stronger, but agreed that tea would be good. It wouldn't go all the way to quelling the acrid tang, but it would help.

Dart picked up the telephone and spoke to the receptionist. 'Two teas, Jamilla, please,' and then he settled himself in the swivel chair and asked, 'How can I help, Chief Inspector?'

As Handford explained the reason for his visit, Dart shook his head. 'I can't believe it. We weren't aware he was missing from home until his wife rang to ask to speak to him, and even then we assumed he was busy investigating or – well, you knew Tom – that he was playing away. But dead? Murdered, you say?'

'Yes, sir, he died of stab wounds.'

'Is he the other body found with that of the young woman?' The man was quick-witted and there was little point in prevaricating – it would be in the press by tomorrow anyway.

Handford nodded. 'Yes, although his name will not be made public until we receive confirmation of the DNA sample from the lab. We should have that by the end of the day and then it will be released to the press.'

'But you feel confident it's him?'

'Yes.'

Dart lay back against the headrest of his chair and closed his eyes. Handford waited. Finally the senior partner regained his composure and sat forward. 'I'm flabbergasted, Chief Inspector; you read about this kind of thing, but you don't expect it to happen to someone you know. It didn't pass through our minds to worry when we hadn't seen him for a few days or even when his wife rang. Investigators are a law unto themselves, particularly someone like Tom, and we don't interfere.'

They were interrupted by a knock on the door and the receptionist came in with a tray of tea. She placed it on the desk, smiled and left. Dart handed Handford a cup. 'Help yourself to milk and sugar,' he said.

Handford poured milk into his cup and stirred. 'What do you mean, sir, particularly someone like Tom?'

'He's the best investigator we have. Your loss was our gain. But unless he was on a straight insurance job we left him alone to get on and investigate.'

'A straight insurance job?'

'You know the kind of thing, a minor burglary when we're sure the client is adding goods to the list that we suspect he didn't have. It happens all the time. We can spot 'em a mile off.'

Handford smiled. 'So what would he be working on the rest of the time?'

'Fires, large life-insurance claims from policies that had been taken out a short while before the person died – that sort of thing.'

'Anything else?'

'Yes, there was something else, although ...'

'Sir?'

Dart spoke carefully as though he didn't want to give too much away. 'I'm not sure how far he'd got, but he was building up a file on staged car accidents to hand over to the police.'

'Staged car accidents?' Handford knew of them, of course, but wasn't aware the police were interested; he'd always thought of it as an insurance company problem.

'It's always been big business among smaller gangs, but now the organised gangs are getting in on the act it's a question of fraud on a large scale.'

'In Bradford?'

'Most definitely in Bradford and in a good deal of the rest of the district. The favourite place for an accident of this kind is on a roundabout. A driver disconnects the brake lights then pulls onto the roundabout in front of the chosen car. Once in position he brakes sharply and we have a rear-end accident for which the victim is considered responsible. When they claim, they use fake passengers who also make a claim and fake witnesses. It's big business, Chief Inspector; we're looking at over two thousand staged accidents in the past seven years and the number of claims is increasing. There are suggestions that the money we pay out is going to fund terrorists. I don't know, but whatever the truth of it, it's costing us a lot and you drivers even more. Tom Blakely believed there's a group operating in Keighley and was investigating them. According to him it includes the gang organisers, although I have no names, but also dodgy professionals – doctors, solicitors, garage owners – anyone who is prepared to or needs to earn money out of a scam like this, plus other vulnerable men and women who they coerce into working for them as phantom passengers or witnesses.'

'Insurance company employees?'

A wave of uneasiness passed over Dart's face. 'Possibly, but I hope not and I particularly hope it doesn't involve any of my staff.'

'And the victims? Are they just unlucky, in the wrong place at the wrong time, or are they carefully chosen?'

'Usually they're carefully chosen; in fact, the gang may have been watching them for some time. The car will be comparatively new, licensed, and most certainly insured. More often than not, it's a family car and the gangs don't care that there are children in it.'

'And the scam car?'

'If it isn't extensively damaged in the accident, then they may well crash it again, perhaps into a wall to make sure it is. The more they can claim the better.'

'And Tom was investigating this?'

'Yes.'

'Where would he keep his information?'

'In his office, with back-up in his safe at home.'

'Can I see his office?'

'Of course, but I have to warn you we had a burglary just over a week ago and Tom's room was turned over.'

Handford's eyes widened. 'You had a burglary?' It never failed to astonish him that information of that kind was dropped into the conversation as an 'oh, by the way'. When he was being questioned about the murder of one of his employees, didn't it occur to an obviously intelligent man that a burglary of that man's office might just be important? Or were they so run of the mill that he couldn't see it?

Dart smiled. 'Yes, but don't worry, we're insured. Just don't tell anyone; it would be most embarrassing.'

'Did you bring in the police?' Handford had heard nothing of this, but then why should he? It would have been passed on to CID.

'Of course, if nothing else we needed a crime number. They sent their scenes-of-crime officer down and since then we've heard nothing. Perhaps you could find out how far they've got with it for us?'

Handford nodded. He certainly would. He attempted to keep his anger under control. Tom Blakely had been notified as a missing person and it didn't occur to them that the burglary of his office might have had something to do with that. He wouldn't have stood for that type of sloppy work – he was surprised Russell did. But then, he'd be happy in his paperwork. Now he would have to do their job for them.

'Was it just Tom's room?'

'Yes. We assumed they were disturbed.'

'Can you tell me what was stolen?'

'His computer and they had broken the lock on his filing cabinet. Papers were thrown around. It's not unusual; burglars often like to make a mess. It confuses the issue, makes it difficult to know what's gone. Some may be missing, but we were waiting for Tom to come into the office to let us know.'

'When exactly was your burglary?'

'Three days ago.' Suddenly Dart understood. 'You think it might have something to do with Tom's investigations – or, God forbid, his murder?'

'I don't know, sir, but I can't rule it out. Who would know what he was working on?'

'I did, and anyone he told – although as I said, investigators can be a law unto themselves and like to keep what they are doing quiet. It's a question of Brownie points.'

'Someone he might have interviewed?'

'I suppose so, although they tend not to come to the office. I'm not being very helpful, am I?'

No you're not, but you are about to become so, like it or not. 'I want to bring in two teams,' Handford said. 'One to check through all Tom Blakely's paperwork and another to interview your staff. With your permission we'll make a start tomorrow morning. I would also like a list of visitors who came to see Tom over the last month.'

If Graham Dart felt the need to challenge the request, he thought better of it. 'I'll make sure a room is made available and that you have your list in the morning.'

Handford replaced his cup on the tray. He couldn't say the tea had rid him of the taste of the post mortem, but it had been welcome. As he was leaving he turned to Dart. 'Just one more question, sir: we're trying to locate Tom's car. Have you any idea where it is?'

*

The civilian behind the desk wrinkled her nose as the man walked into Central Police Station. She'd met his type before – unwashed, unkempt and probably never done an honest day's work. She ignored him as she reorganised the papers in front of her, hoping that someone else would take him on. He fidgeted, shifting from one foot to the other, occasionally wiping his hands down his coat or scratching his head, and more than once he glanced over his shoulder as though he was expecting someone he didn't want to meet. Finally, when it was obvious everyone else was busy and she was going to have to deal with him, she pushed the papers to one side and asked, 'How can I help you?'

He leaned over the desk, his body odour sluicing round her. 'I want to talk to someone about that old lady as was killed.'

'As was killed.' Education as well as soap and water had obviously passed him by – or had he passed it by?

'Which lady?'

'The one as was robbed and killed. The one as was in the paper. I want to talk to Tom Blakely.'

She stared at him. Rumour had it that it was Tom Blakely's body that had been found with the missing girl's but even if she was sure, she couldn't tell him. 'Mr Blakely doesn't work here; he retired,' she said.

'Then that other one, the one what worked with 'im; Clarke 'is name was. He needs to know he's out.'

Puzzlement showed on her face. 'Who's out?'

'The one as killed the old lady; the one I told on last time.'

She shook her head. He'd lost her completely, but he was obviously distressed, frightened even, so she pulled the book towards her and ran her finger down the signatures. 'He's on inquiries at the moment. You can wait if you like, but I don't know how long he's going to be.'

The man glanced over his shoulder again. 'Then someone else, the boss – anyone.'

'The Chief Inspector is out as well, but I'll get you his inspector. She picked up the phone and dialled Ali's extension. While she was waiting for an answer, she said, 'Can you give me your name?'

'It's Billy, Billy Emmott, and you can tell 'im I know who's done it and I want a new 'ouse and me name changed.'

chapter eleven

Ali and Warrender appeared to be sharing a joke as they waited for Handford outside his office. Whatever had amused them it was good to see them at ease with each other for once.

'Is it private or can anyone join in?' he asked as he unlocked the door.

'We've found Billy,' Ali said as they followed him in. 'At least, he found us. He came into the station about an hour ago.'

Handford pulled off his coat, hung it up and then looked at his watch. Thirty minutes before he was due to see Noble. 'Why?'

Ali grinned. 'He wants a new house and his name changed.'

'Of course he does.' Handford smiled and sat down, indicating that the two men should do the same. 'Why would he want that?'

Warrender made himself comfortable, one ankle balancing on his knee, and crossed his arms. 'He reckons Gott killed his elderly aunt,' he said.

'His elderly aunt?' Warrender nodded and grinned widely but didn't reply. In all the time Handford had known him, he'd had a penchant for spinning out information, a need to leave the best until last. Normally his boss would go along with him, knowing the information would be good; today he was not in the mood for the constable's amateur dramatics. He turned to Ali. 'Tell me,' he said with a sigh.

'According to Billy Emmott, Annie Laycock was his aunt.'

Handford's eyes widened. Surely, if she was related to him,

he should have been found earlier. He was about to make comment when Ali cut in.

'We didn't know of him because she wasn't a biological relation, but a neighbour who looked after him when his mother left him to his own devices, which was most of the time, apparently; in fact, Annie just about brought him up. He went on a lot about how he had learned of her death from the newspaper, said Blakely should have told him and about Gott being out as well. Now he's convinced Gott killed her as a warning to him because he grassed him up and equally convinced he will be next. I've got to say, guv, he's quite cut up about it, although to be honest I'm not sure whether he's more afraid than grief-stricken. Either way, he's positive he's the next on Gott's list.'

'He obviously doesn't know Tom's dead?'

'No, we didn't mention it and he asked specifically for Tom when he arrived at the station. The woman on the desk was very diplomatic and told him he'd retired so he asked to see Clarke instead.'

Handford wasn't sure that was what he wanted to hear. It suggested that whatever Blakely had given or promised or persuaded Emmott to say, Clarke was at best a witness to it, at worst part of it. He ran a hand through his hair. As if he hadn't enough problems of his own. He would have felt better about it had it not been Andy on the receiving end, but at least he knew what the man was feeling. Pretty much what he was feeling. Surreptitiously, he checked his watch again and wondered for a split second if he could end the discussion now and suggest they resumed first thing in the morning, using the fact that he had to be somewhere else as an excuse. At this rate he was likely to be late for his interview with Noble, and while he knew the officer would understand that Handford was busy and that five thirty didn't necessarily mean five thirty, he would prefer to be on time. He saw Ali observing him as he pulled his shirt cuff back over the watch, saw the frown that formed vertical creases down his forehead as it always did when he was puzzled, and decided against it. He'd worked with Ali for a good few years and reckoned the inspector probably knew him better than most. At some time he would be certain to ask what was wrong and Handford wasn't at all sure what he would or could tell him.

For the moment he avoided Ali's concern. 'OK, let's assume Emmott is right,' he said, 'what's his story?'

Ali referred to his notes. 'He says he saw Gott throwing a box into a skip the day after the burglary and when the picture of Mr Widdop's injuries was in the paper and he read about what had been stolen, he passed the information on to Blakely. Not that his reasons were totally altruistic; he wasn't a bone fide informant so no money was exchanged, just a promise that Blakely would drop the charges against him for stealing lead from church roofs with a group of other lads. Blakely agreed he would if his information was good and when the box was found to contain both the war medals and Gott's thumb print Emmott's name never came up.'

'And the charges against Emmott were dropped?'

'Yes, lack of evidence.'

'But the other lads were charged?'

'Got six months each,' Warrender said.

If it wasn't for the fact that Blakely was dead, that Gott had used his own arrest as his reason for revenge and Andy Clarke would be made the scapegoat, Handford would have suggested they forget it. So an officer had made a deal with a petty criminal to catch the bigger fish – they'd all done it at some point in their career. It was a pity Blakely had picked Gott as his *bête noir*.

He leaned back in the chair. 'Do you believe Emmott?'

'I don't know,' Ali said. 'But I have to say it sounds plausible and he definitely wasn't charged over the theft of the lead. In itself it doesn't mean Blakely set up Gott or that he was corrupt, but it does say he might have been acting on information that should have been passed on to the defence and wasn't.'

Which meant if Gott went to appeal over his sentence – and he probably would because there would be some lawyer out there with pound signs before his eyes – his conviction could be quashed on the grounds that it was unsound and he could be in line for compensation. 'Are you sure nothing came out at the trial to suggest Blakely had used an informant?' Handford asked.

'Yes, positive.'

'So how did Gott know Emmott had informed on him?'

'He reckons Blakely reneged on his promise,' Warrender said. 'Although I doubt it; I think it's much more likely Emmott boasted about what he'd done and Gott found out. He's not the brightest.'

Handford shifted his position and avoided the temptation to glance at his watch again. 'What worries me about this in relation to our cases,' he said, 'is that if what Emmott alleges is true, Annie Laycock may not have been a random target. Whether he meant to kill her or not, she may well have been chosen deliberately. If that's the case, it looks as though it was a calculated act on Gott's part to leave his DNA all over the place. He wanted Emmott to know he has paid him back for informing on him – and let's face it, it's worked. I doubt it worries Gott that he may end up back in prison – he's spent so much time there, he'll be pretty much institutionalised by now. All he'll care about is that he's succeeded in what he came out to do. Annie Laycock, Billy Emmott, Tom Blakely – if it is all down to him you have to admit he's made a meal of taking his revenge.'

He paused. 'Did she have money?'

'According to Emmott she was loaded. Kept it in a box in her bedroom.'

'And we didn't find it?'

'No, I think we can assume Gott has it.' Ali said.

'There's something else, boss.' Handford knew by the excitement in his voice, this was Warrender's best until last. He let a smile cross his face as the detective paused for maximum effect. 'When I drove Emmott back to his place, he was telling me how Mrs Laycock was a lonely old lady. If it hadn't been for him and Bronwyn Price, he said, she'd hardly ever have spoken to anyone.'

The best until last had maximum effect. Ali and Handford stared at each other and then in chorus said, 'Bronwyn Price?'

Ali added, 'You never told me.'

Warrender threw him a glance laced with contempt. 'Well, I'm telling you now, Ali.' Warrender shifted his position to face Handford, his back to the inspector. 'Until she disappeared Bronwyn Price spent a lot of time with Mrs Laycock: did her shopping, sat with her, even introduced her to her new boyfriend. In fact, that was why she thought she didn't come any more, because she was busy with the boyfriend.'

'Does Billy know who he is?' Handford asked. If he did, this could be the first real lead they had in the investigation into Bronwyn's murder.

'No, except that he's a foreigner, Mark or something that sounds like Mark.'

'Not Tom Blakely?'

'No, it's definitely not Tom Blakely. I'm already checking it out, boss. I'll go through Mrs Laycock's personal things – birthday cards, Christmas cards, things like that. You never know, she may have received one from Bronwyn and boyfriend. The chances are if he isn't an illegal he'll crop up somewhere and I'll find him.'

'Good.'

Warrender sat up straight and leaned towards Handford. 'I don't know about you, boss, but I can't help feeling that everywhere we look there are links between the victims – Blakely and Gott; Emmott, Gott and Mrs Laycock; Mrs Laycock and Bronwyn Price and even Blakely and Bronwyn. It's weird, guv, don't you think, really weird.'

Warrender was right; it was weird. There were too many links for there not to be some connection, yet the only one with any substance was that between Emmott, Mrs Laycock and Gott. It was doubtful Bronwyn Price and Tom Blakely were having an affair, unless she had told him it was over when the new boyfriend came along and that had angered him. It was a known fact that Tom always ended the affairs. Even so, to kill her because she took the initiative seemed a bit excessive. And even if he had, it would be impossible to prove, since both parties were dead. Mentally he crossed out that possibility and turned his attention to Bronwyn's relationship with Annie Laycock.

Emmott had said Bronwyn told his aunt everything. Had she told her something that had led not only to her death but to that of the old lady? Given the length of time between the two murders, Handford doubted that as well. What was more possible was that the burglary at Dart Insurance Company was linked to Tom. His was the only office to be touched and Handford didn't buy Graham Dart's suggestion that the thieves had been disturbed and therefore hadn't time to go through the rest of the building. He had checked whether there had been any other such break-ins, but nothing had been reported. Then on a whim, he typed Graham Dart's name into the computer. He wasn't sure why, except he wondered why Dart had given him the impression of a man, if not exactly in torment, certainly one who was suffering. In all honesty, he hadn't expected the computer to give him an answer, but it appeared that although Dart's outward mask was that of a man settled in marriage with a wife, three children and four grandchildren, he also seemed to have a penchant for rather young boys, so much so that he frequented the local gay club and over a year ago had been picked up by the police with a thirteen-year-old rent boy. Since he hadn't got round to having sex, he had been let off with a warning, but it was enough for a man with a reputation to keep up both in business and at the golf club. There had been nothing since, and Handford tucked away the information – it may mean something, but on the other hand nothing at all and have no bearing on the case. He lay back against his chair and rested his feet on the open bottom drawer of his desk. So many ideas and precious little to back them up. Up to now, they'd dwelt on the revenge theory, now they needed to think outside the box. Was the location of the bodies important? Was it possible that Bronwyn's death and that of Tom Blakely were linked somehow to the old coal mines? God only knew how, if they were.

As Handford made his way to Noble's office he wondered how long it would be before the press worked out a possible link. It wasn't rocket science – three bodies in as many days, two found in the same location, one that of a retired police officer. He'd give them two days, three at the most, before they were forwarding their own theories and it wouldn't matter how the police played it, 'keeping an open mind', 'no such link has come to light' or even 'we can't make comment at the moment', the journalists would put their own spin on it and the clever ones like Peter Redmayne would take it that step further. Handford knew Redmayne of old. Officially the crime correspondent of the local newspaper, but unofficially he was more than that; he was an investigative journalist who was good at ferreting out information the police were prevented from acquiring thanks to the shackles of the Police and Criminal Evidence Act, the Data Protection Act and even the Human Rights Act. Redmayne on the other hand would worry about none of those and would delve into backgrounds, probably find Blakely's predilection for other women, attempt to link at least him and Bronwyn and if past encounters were anything to go by, do a better job than the police. Not that he was against sharing his information with the police – he would, but only if he could have the exclusive. Perhaps Handford ought to bring him on side sooner rather than later – trade information – and place an embargo on what he knew until it was over and then give him free reign.

Noble was waiting for him. As always, his desk was littered with files, some of them, judging by their covers, from the archives. He'd never been the tidiest of officers, except where it mattered – in his head, where he was able to painstakingly compartmentalise. Handford was sure each victim, suspect and witness was carefully salted away in their own drawer in his memory. He would have his own soon, although whether it would be as a suspect or a witness he wasn't sure.

It had been a long day and the cold case investigator looked as tired as Handford felt. When he walked into his office, Noble stood up and said, 'We can do this in the pub if you like; I could kill for a drink.'

'I'd like to take you up on it, Brian,' Handford said. 'But given what I have to say, I don't think the pub would be an appropriate place.' Perhaps afterwards, although he doubted it.

Noble sat down and leaned back in his chair. 'Do I gather from that you've spoken to your brother and he hasn't seen sense?'

'Yes I have and no he hasn't. I spoke to him last night – well, spoke is hardly the word. We had a row, which ended in him walking out and me getting drunk. Anyway the result is that he won't give a sample of his DNA.'

Noble showed his anger. 'The stupid man. Did he give you a reason?'

'According to him he'd had sex with Josie earlier that evening and the chances are you'll find his DNA on her clothing.'

'Which means nothing unless we can link it with that of the other women.'

'On its own, no. But she was under age at the time and he's worried about his job if that gets out.'

'He'll be a lot more worried if I have to bring him in. Did you tell him that?'

'It didn't make any difference. As far as he is concerned you have my statement that he was with me at the time Josie alleged she was raped. That says he couldn't have done it.' Handford took a deep breath, 'Except ...'

'Why do I get the feeling I'm not going to like your "except"?' Noble said.

As he always did when he was embarrassed, Handford scrutinised his hands. He felt a bit like Warrender leaving the best until last – and he was sure this would be as good as anything Warrender could come up with. Finally, he looked up and said, 'I lied.'

Noble pushed himself forward and picked up a file. He leafed through the sheets of paper and pulled one out and skimmed through it. 'You mean this statement is a lie?'

Handford cleared his throat. 'Yes.'

'Which part of it precisely? Some of it or all of it?' Noble, if not exactly shouting, was raising his voice a few decibels.

'I said Douglas had been with us all evening. He hadn't; in fact, for quite some time I'd no idea where he was.'

'For God's sake, John, a girl had alleged rape, what were you thinking of?'

'I was seventeen; I wasn't thinking of anything. He was my brother and he asked for a favour. I gave it to him and anyway at the time, no one believed Josie Renshaw. Why should they?

She was the village whore; she loved sex and didn't care who with. Why would anyone need to rape her?'

'So why didn't you tell me this yesterday instead of compounding the lie.'

'I suppose because I assumed that when you had Douglas's DNA it would eliminate him and there would be no necessity to take it any further.'

Noble threw the statement down. 'And how many times have you heard that from people you've interviewed?' As he spoke he pushed himself out of his chair and stood up. 'You idiot,' he said in a falsely controlled voice. Then he walked towards Handford and leaned over him. 'I've a bloody good mind to take you to an interview room and turn on the recorders and then charge you with perverting the course of justice, except that it probably won't stick because legally you were a minor at the time.' He slowly regained his seat, his face red with the exertion, his top lip beaded with sweat.

Handford let out a long breath. He wasn't sure whether it was one of relief or disbelief, probably both. He wanted to apologise, but knew it would sound hollow, so instead he waited for Noble to speak again. When he did his voice was calmer, but his words measured.

'I want a retraction of your previous statement; you can do that in your own time, but now you tell me about your brother. Take me through exactly what he asked you to do, his relationship with Josie Renshaw and anything else you know about her and anyone else who might have been involved in the alleged rape.'

As he talked, Handford realised he had never discussed the events of that night. He'd pushed them deep down inside him and left them there to rot. Now the stench of what he was saying was making him sick. That night he'd accepted his brother's explanation of where he was simply because he was his brother. Douglas had vociferously and angrily denied the rape when he'd refused to attend the girl's funeral, and for the first time Handford acknowledged that he hadn't believed him. If he had he would have stood by him. Instead he had kept his distance and never mentioned it or him again until now.

He doubted many people in the station were aware he had a brother; possibly Clarke, but certainly not Ali. Soon everyone may well know.

By the time they had finished, Handford knew a drink was out of the question and as he ended the interview, Noble, his voice stripped of the earlier anger, said, 'I'll keep this as quiet as I can, although obviously I can't promise anything. I'll write up your new statement myself and you can sign it. In the meantime, I'll ring your brother and suggest he comes into the station voluntarily. But make no mistake, if he declines I will go to him and if he continues to refuse to give a sample of his DNA, then I'll arrest him on suspicion and take one.'

Handford nodded, not daring to think of the consequences to either of them if Douglas had to be brought into the station.

Noble hadn't finished. 'Please keep your distance from him tonight, John, and if he contacts you, tell him nothing, not even that you have spoken to me. I'll see you in the morning.' His final words and the telephone simultaneously and effectively ended the interview. He picked up the receiver, Handford replaced his chair at the side of the room and made to leave, but Noble waved him back. 'You're sure about that?' he asked into the phone. Then with a sigh, said, 'Thanks, I'll get back to you.'

For a few seconds Noble maintained an uncomfortable silence. Finally he said, 'We have the results from the DNA on Josie Renshaw's clothing. Unfortunately the sample had degraded somewhat but they got possible matches from it. We have six and obviously we'll need to check each of them out, but we do have the name of one person on our list who may well have had sex with her, but who up to now has denied any such relationship.'

Handford felt a prickle of fear. Why, he wasn't sure. Maybe it was Noble's expression or maybe his obvious embarrassment. 'Who?' he asked.

Noble gave him a long look that this time Handford couldn't read.

'You,' he said.

*

Christine Blakely was exhausted when she reached home; the visit to Marek Kowalski had taken more out of her than she realised and en route back she'd been to the supermarket, partly because there was little food in the house but mostly because she needed a plausible reason for going out. As she pulled into the drive, she saw Connie Burns sitting in her car. It hadn't occurred to Christine that if the liaison officer arrived back first she wouldn't be able to get in. Connie climbed out of her car and walked over to her. When she spoke, her tone showed her concern – or was it anger? 'Where on earth have you been? I was worried sick.'

Christine pulled the supermarket bags out of the boot. 'I had to do some shopping.'

'I could have done that for you.'

'I needed to get out, do something.' She handed one of the bags to the police officer. 'I wasn't supposed to ask permission, was I?'

'No, of course not, but it would be useful to know where you are in case Mr Handford needs to talk to you again.'

'Sorry. Next time I'll leave a note – and a key.' She placed the bags on the kitchen table and looked at Connie Burns. From her expression it was obvious she was not enough of the grieving widow for the officer, who was no doubt salting the information away for the next briefing. Christine pulled out one of the chairs and sat down. She attempted another apology and an explanation. 'I'm sorry, really I am, but by tomorrow the results of the DNA test will be known and ... well, I wanted to go out and do the shopping without people stopping me to offer their sympathy, or worse still to ignore me, which is what they'll do once they know.' Before the family liaison officer could comment, she pushed back the chair. 'I'm going for a rest before my sister arrives,' she said abruptly. 'Perhaps you could put the groceries away for me.'

In the bedroom she took the framed photograph of her husband from the dressing table and held it to her. She wanted to see him for one last time and while they couldn't actively prevent her, she knew they would counsel against it. 'Remember him as you knew him, not as he is now.' Even John Handford had prevaricated when she had asked him on the day they came to tell her he'd been found; had there been any reason not to see Tom he would have taken her himself once his body was at the mortuary. Didn't they realise that she wanted – needed – to talk to him but not through a closed coffin at his funeral? She didn't care how he looked now; it couldn't be worse than anything her imagination had manufactured.

Exhausted, she closed her eyes, unwilling at first to fall asleep, but she must have done for she was awoken by the door bell. She heard the television as Connie opened the lounge door, then a few seconds later her sister's voice. Christine pulled herself off the bed and sat at the dressing table. She looked at herself in the mirror, failing to connect with the woman she saw there. The face staring back at her belonged to someone else, a face that was gaunt and grey, the eyes sunken and empty. Tom had left her before, but never like this; before he had always come back. Now she couldn't imagine life without him.

Ian Gott had spent most of his days in prison imagining life without Tom Blakely. It was one of the few things that had kept him going. Now he was near to his goal, he had never felt better. Killing a man didn't bother him; killing Tom Blakely and Clarke would be a pleasure. With the old lady's money he'd bought himself as much as he needed – clothes from various charity shops and toiletries and cans from the supermarket. He'd also picked up a cheap suitcase from the market so that when he asked for a room, he looked like a traveller. He'd booked himself into a small but comfortable B&B, paying the lady cash. Once settled, he went out, bought a local paper and nipped into McDonald's for a burger and chips. While he was eating his Big Mac, he leafed through the pages. The front page was taken up with a picture of a young woman who'd been missing for eight weeks and whose body had been found the previous day. He smiled to himself. It had taken them eight weeks to find a body that, according to the journalist, had not even been buried. If that was the kind of Mickey Mouse police force they had in this area, he'd nothing to worry about. By the time they found Blakely and Clarke, he'd be long gone.

He finished his meal and wiped his mouth with his sleeve. The young lad who was tidying up the tables said goodnight to him. He smiled, not at the politeness, but because he had every intention of having a good night. For the first time in almost seven years he had his own key; he could come and go as he pleased. He would spend part of the evening enjoying the luxury of drinking beer and watching television in the peace of his room and then later in finding himself a woman – any would do, providing she was willing and able. He'd even pay if he had to. At least she wouldn't mind if he was a bit rough. He had a lot of catching up to do in that department.

Tomorrow he would make a start on phase two of his project. He smiled again, but this time not to himself. Project. He liked the sound of that. It gave authority and legitimacy to why he was here. Yes, project was a good word.

chapter twelve

Handford was astounded. 'That's ridiculous,' he said. 'It can't match mine, not partially, not any way.'

Noble remained unruffled. 'It's what the results show.'

'But I hardly knew her and I certainly didn't have sex with her, consensual or otherwise.'

'The results don't agree, John; they say you might have.'

'Then the results are wrong.' Handford slumped into the chair he had replaced against the wall, panic firmly establishing itself. He tried again this time more calmly. 'It's impossible for mine to be on her clothing, Brian,' he said firmly. 'I haven't lied to you; I never once had sex with Josie Renshaw.'

'You've lied before.'

Handford took a deep breath. It was warm in the room, but it wasn't the heat that made him sweat or caused his hands to tremble; these were the basic ingredients of the guilt he had witnessed in others in his position – except that he wasn't guilty, just very nervous. 'I know and I wish I hadn't, but I was seventeen and I did it for my brother not for me.'

'Come on, John, it's not such a big step to cross over the line to cover your own back, as you well know.' Noble played a good devil's advocate.

'Except that I haven't taken that step.'

Handford's head was reeling. One naïve lie thirty years ago and he was in deep shit. He'd been on the wrong side of an interview before when he'd been accused of racism, but it was nothing like this, for six years ago his innocence had been more easily proven, today Noble had science on his side and it was difficult to argue with that. This wasn't over, not by a long way.

Noble stood up, walked to the door and opened it, signalling the end of the interview – for the time being. As Handford passed him, Noble said, 'If it's any consolation, John, I believe you. But if I'm to have any chance of questioning the current results Douglas has to cooperate. You're brothers and you will share the same maternal mitochondrial DNA; it could be that his will also show a partial match. But until we have a sample, we won't know.'

Handford drove home on automatic pilot. Had anyone asked, he couldn't have described the route he took or whether he'd been over the speed limit and been caught on camera. The way things were going it would be just his luck to have hit the only one that was working. His instinct told him to talk to Douglas yet again, pointing out the problems he was causing by refusing his DNA, and more than once he grabbed at his mobile to ring him, but then replaced it because his instinct also told him that the way he felt about his brother he would probably have landed him a left hook rather than entered into a rational discussion. And if the truth be known, deep down he knew it wouldn't do any good; Douglas had been adamant last night and he couldn't see that changing; and anyway he'd been told by Noble to keep his distance. Noble wanted the element of surprise when he contacted Douglas, and Handford understood that; he would have wanted the same himself.

As usual, his mother had their meal almost ready, and the house was filled with the aroma of one of her curries. He had to hand it to her, when it came to cooking she had a wealth of knowledge and expertise which could only be described as cosmopolitan. The girls too were pleased to see him; he hadn't been home so early for a while. Even though he knew they understood his job was not nine to five he often felt guilty that he didn't try harder, particularly now with Gill away. They missed their mother as much as he did and as much as they loved her, and as hard as she tried, their grandmother was two generations away from them and didn't always approve of their lifestyle.

As soon as he had taken off his coat, he hugged them and apologised for being so grouchy the previous evening. They ate, talked and then he suggested they went to the bowling alley and had a contest between youth and age. Youth won, but at least it gave him the opportunity to release some of his anger on the skittles and he had more fun than he'd had in ages. It also helped to push his own problems to the back of his mind. But once they were home and the girls had gone up, his mother brought them flooding back.

His father had been asked to go to the local police station to give a sample of his DNA which would be passed on to the Wetherby Forensic lab for processing. It seemed the whole Handford family were to be involved. Inwardly, Handford cursed Noble for not mentioning it, although common sense told him there was no reason why he should have done. They were targeting all the men who had lived in the village, whatever their age or profession. A headmaster was just as capable of having sex with a young girl as anyone else. Thankfully, his mother didn't see it as a problem. She accepted that whoever raped Josie Renshaw, if she was raped – and she wasn't at all convinced of that – could well have lived in the village but not been at the hall. Never for one moment did it cross her mind that her family would be involved, as far as she was concerned DNA from them was for elimination purposes only. Handford kept his silence about Douglas, his fleeting relationship with Josie and his refusal to give a sample of his DNA, nor did he mention that unless he cooperated, he could well be taken into the station the next day for questioning. He also kept quiet about his own lie all those years ago. For the moment it was better she didn't know.

The next morning, sitting in his office, however, he wasn't so sure. If everything came crashing down around them, she would have to cope with the whole mess at once, not least that one of her sons had been involved with Josie Renshaw and – heaven forbid – could not only have been the one to rape her, but could also be accused of three more rapes. He was furious with his brother for putting them through this and furious with himself for being so stupid in the first place.

For a while, he remained motionless at his desk, a poly-styrene container of coffee in his hand, and stared at the wall opposite, seeing not the map or the noticeboard, but the images of yesterday's interview being played out. They were as clear as though someone had painted them and he half expected the tag of the graffiti artist in one corner. He would like to have blamed Noble for the way he had been treated, but he couldn't; had he been on that side of the desk as investigating officer, he would have been as cynical as his colleague. How could you make someone believe you when you'd already admitted to a lie? Compounding one lie with another wasn't unusual in a suspect, and that, Handford knew, was exactly what he was, in spite of the fact that Noble seemed to believe him. Sadly that wasn't enough; to give him a fighting chance his brother had to cooperate. But even with Douglas's DNA they would need a lot more than two partial matches to charge either of them with thirty-year-old rapes, unless of course Noble had more than he was making public. And that was possible, for to bring Douglas in for questioning was one thing, but Noble had said he would arrest him on suspicion and to do that he'd have to be pretty sure of his ground. If he was sure, Handford couldn't begin to count the cost to his family, particularly his parents. When he'd spoken to Gill after his trip to the pub, he'd been flippant about the headlines in the newspaper. Now, suddenly, they seemed ominously close.

He shifted in his chair, took a sip of the coffee and grimaced. Neither the drink nor his thoughts were palatable, but what was worse was the feeling of impotence; there was nothing he could do. Except ... except perhaps make a visit to Josie's parents. Maybe Josie had told them or at least given them some clue as to who it was had raped her. Talk in the village had been that she didn't know; he had jumped her from behind, she'd said. No one had believed her. After all, Josie had a reputation, a reputation of which her parents were ashamed. But what if Josie had told her parents who it was and they were too afraid – too ashamed even – to say because the idea that Mr X would ever do that to anyone was preposterous or because they'd been warned off going to the police. The village hadn't been without its thugs. Noble had told him to keep his distance from Douglas and that he would do, but he'd said nothing about the Renshaws. Tomorrow was Saturday; he would afford an hour or two in the afternoon to visit them.

The decision made, he glanced at the clock. A quarter to eight. Douglas, Josie Renshaw and his own problems would have to wait. He had three murder investigations to supervise and his in-tray was overflowing with statements and interim reports from the pathologist. There was also a note from Paynter telling him that uniform had been told to look out for Blakely's car and that he had organised more bodies to help Clarke check through the papers in Tom Blakely's office at Dart Insurance and to interview the employees. Paynter had also set up a meeting with DS Russell to find out more about the break-in at the insurance company. Handford smiled to himself; he would love to be a fly on the wall at that meeting.

For the next hour he read and made notes ready for the briefing, then listed the two teams to go with Clarke into Dart Insurance as well as one to trawl through Annie Laycock's things to see if there was a photograph of or a greetings card signed by Bronwyn and her boyfriend, or indeed anything that might give them some idea as to who the mystery boyfriend was. Finally, he rang Connie Burns to let her know he was sending a couple of officers to remove Tom's computer and any papers that were associated with his work.

He was about to ring off when the liaison officer said, 'It might be nothing, sir, but yesterday after you'd gone Mrs Blakely went out. She was away for some time. As I said, it might be nothing, but I thought you ought to know.'

Handford frowned. There was no real reason why Christine shouldn't leave the house, but he had to admit it was unusual behaviour in a wife who'd just been questioned about her husband's murder. Normally they found that exhausting and wanted to do nothing but rest or talk. 'Did she say where she'd been?'

'The supermarket, she said. She came back with some groceries, so she'd certainly stopped off there. I told her I would have done it for her but she said she didn't want to be alone in the house and since there was hardly any food, it was better to get it done before Tom's name was in the papers. She didn't want people stopping her to offer their sympathy.'

Again, a reasonable explanation, but Handford couldn't help feeling Christine Blakely was good at reasonable explanations. 'Do you know what time she left?'

'One of the neighbours had seen her getting into her car shortly after twelve. She'd called out to her to ask if everything was all right, but got no reply. There was a lot of activity at the house yesterday and the neighbour was worried there was a problem and wanted to know if she could help. I got the impression she wasn't aware Tom was missing, let alone dead. It was after two when Christine came back. She only had three bags with her, sir, so it couldn't have taken her two hours to do the shopping, even if she'd stopped off for a coffee or something to eat. I'm probably fussing about nothing, but it seemed odd. In my experience, victims who've just been told a close relative has been murdered and then been questioned for an hour or more can't bear to go out at all, let alone go shopping.'

He had to agree, but for the moment didn't want to make too much of it. 'Don't worry about it, Connie; it's probably no more than her coping in her own way. Just let her know someone will be over to collect the things.'

Thoughtfully, he replaced the receiver. It wasn't like Connie Burns to be uneasy. She was an accomplished FLO and had seen and dealt with most fluctuations of behaviour from a complete lack of interest, through deep grief to suicide attempts, so if something concerned her, it was worth following up. Two hours or more was a long time for a supermarket run, which meant Christine must have been elsewhere; but where he couldn't begin to imagine. As he'd said, it could be no more than a woman dealing with the death of her husband in her own way and for the moment he would do no more than pigeonhole it. If there was anything it would crop up eventually and either end speculation or become another piece in Tom Blakely's jigsaw.

David Younger kept Detective Inspector Ali and Detective Constable Warrender waiting as they stood on the doorstep in the driving rain. It was coming from the east and from the colour of the sky and the heavy clouds it appeared there would be no let-up. Through the patterned panel in the door, the two men could see him on the telephone and whatever the exchange was about he was gesticulating wildly, obviously angry and not about to stop to let in two police officers until he had made his point.

Ali pulled up his collar and stood while Warrender rapped again and shouted 'Police' through the letter box. Younger looked up, spoke into the phone then banged down the receiver. He grabbed at the handle and as the door jerked open the stink of body odour and alcohol wafted in their direction. Dark stubble covered the lower half of his face, his clothes were creased, as though he'd slept in them, and from the look of the bloodshot eyes and pallid complexion he'd been drinking for some time.

Ali introduced himself and Warrender as they flashed their warrant cards, though they might as well have been Sainsbury's loyalty cards for all the attention Younger gave them. Instead he said, 'Where's the other policeman? The one who's hardly been away from the house and now is nowhere to be seen?'

Ali brushed the rain from his hair, showering drops over Younger. 'Detective Chief Inspector Handford? He's busy with another investigation. He's asked me to—'

'Presumably that's the investigation on the body found with Bronwyn's?' Younger interrupted. 'Ex-policeman, wasn't he?'

When Ali made no reply, Younger sneered, 'Isn't that just typical? A dead copper warrants a chief inspector but when it comes to a girl you're supposed to have been seeking for the past eight weeks he doesn't want to know. Instead, he sends an inspector and,' he looked derisorily at Warrender, 'a constable.'

Ali was too wet and too cold to argue with him. He stepped forward so that he was half in and half out of the hall. 'Mr Younger,' he said purposefully, 'I have no intention of conducting an interview on the doorstep in the pouring rain. Either we ask our questions here, inside, or we ask them at the station, but I'm sure you'll find your own home more hospitable than an interview room.'

Turning abruptly, Younger walked in front of the two men, leaving Warrender to close the outer door behind them. The room they entered suggested the station might have been the better of the two options: for far from hospitable, it was a confusion of newspapers, cans and dirty plates and smelled of stale cigarettes and beer. It told the story of the trauma that had dogged the Youngers' lives for two months and from which they might never recover. But beneath the surface was a chronicle of happier times, for it was well furnished and had, back then, been well cared for. There was a profusion of potted plants, in need of water, an expensive plasma television and a plush leather three-piece suite, both too big for the size of room and both covered with a film of dust.

Ali glanced round; there was no sign of Mrs Younger. 'Where's your wife, Mr Younger?'

'She's gone to stay with a friend.'

'When?'

'Yesterday, if it matters.'

It did matter, but the explanation was probably better coming from her. 'We will need to talk to her; do you have her friend's address?'

Younger picked up a book from the sideboard. 'It's in there under Pauline Driver.'

Warrender flicked through the pages and wrote down the information, then handed it back.

As he took it David Younger turned to face Ali. 'Is this going to take long?'

'I don't know; it depends on how quickly and how fully you answer our questions and whether we're satisfied with the answers. Why?'

'Because I need to get to the office. I've spent too much time away as it is thanks to Bronwyn and your Chief Inspector and houses don't sell themselves.'

The two officers glanced at each other. 'You're going in to work even though you've just learned your daughter has been murdered?' Warrender said in mock surprise.

Younger glared at him. 'Bronwyn wasn't my daughter, Constable; she was my stepdaughter, and she hated me and I didn't like her, so I'm not shedding any tears. Add to that the fact that my wife doesn't need me and my office does, what else would you suggest I do? I'm only here at all because I was told the police would have to talk to me. So if you don't mind, I'd like to get on with it and get you out of my face.' He spat out the final word as he leaned towards the inspector.

'Then we'd better do just that, Mr Younger,' Ali said and without being invited to do so he shrugged out of his coat, handed it to Warrender and made himself comfortable in one of the chairs. Warrender raised his eyebrows to Ali in an unspoken question. The inspector understood and nodded.

'I'll put this in the kitchen to dry out,' Warrender said, 'and make us all a coffee while I'm there.'

'Not for me.' And to illustrate his point still further, Younger picked up an open can of beer and swallowed the last dregs, crushed it and threw it on to the already overflowing wicker basket. Then he took another from the cupboard in the sideboard and pulled at the ring. It fizzed as the white foam escaped and he put it to his lips and took a long drink.

Ali watched him while he played out the charade. If it was the man's intention to appear unconcerned, it wasn't working for the tell-tale signs of anxiety were there, the aggression, his reluctance to make or retain full eye contact and the difficulty he had keeping his hands still, so that as he drank the beer spilled and ran down his chin and on to his shirt. Ali was adamant. 'DC Warrender will make coffee for all of us,' he said. 'You've had enough of that for one morning.' He nodded at Warrender who slung the wet coat over his shoulder and left the room.

When Younger finally sat down, Ali said, 'Was it your decision your wife should stay with a friend or hers?'

'Not that it's anything to do with you, but it was hers.'

'Did she give a reason?'

'She gave a reason all right; in fact, she gave a dozen reasons, none of them worth anything.'

'Like what?'

'Like I don't care about her; like I don't care that Bronwyn's dead; like I'm no help to anyone. Take your pick,' Younger said bitterly. He let his fingers trace the rim of the can and then, as though admitting his concerns for the first time, said, 'I'm not sure what she expects from me and she won't tell me. All she's done since we were told they'd found Bronwyn is sit in that chair and cry. She won't eat, she won't talk; she just sits there staring at a photograph of Bronwyn. What good does that do anybody? It wasn't as if we didn't expect it.' He gave Ali a jaded look, then took another drink and wiped his mouth with the back of his hand. 'The truth is it's nothing to do with me not caring or being any help to her, it's because she blames me, that's why she's gone.'

'Blames you for what, Mr Younger?' Ali asked.

'Bronwyn. Anything and everything to do with Bronwyn. She's forgotten that she was the one who told her to get out in the first place.' Younger was restless. He pulled himself from the chair and walked away from Ali. 'She forgets what that girl's done and what she's said since we met.' He stood at the window, staring into the garden. Ali joined him. There were still signs of the digging carried out by the scenes-of-crime officers. Eventually, once permission had been granted by those who held the purse strings, the police would send someone to restore it, but for the moment it was a muddy bog.

When Younger turned back, his expression had softened. 'I suppose Lynne's got to find someone to point the finger at and I'm the nearest. She'll be back when she's had time.' For a long moment he remained motionless, his thoughts elsewhere, until suddenly his face reverted to one of loathing. 'You know what, that bloody daughter of hers has finally got what she wanted.'

'And what's that?'

'She's finally broken us up. By getting herself murdered she's finally destroyed our marriage.' Unable to contain his hatred towards his stepdaughter, he flung the can across the room, causing Ali to duck. It crashed against the wall, beer spilling out to run down the patterned paper and pool on the carpet. 'The bloody, bloody woman,' he yelled, his face flushed with drink and anger.

Ali brushed the drops of beer from his jacket and his hair. 'You've got quite a temper there, Mr Younger,' he said quietly.

Ali's calmness annoyed Younger and he made no attempt to pick up the can or to wipe away the liquid, which was rapidly discolouring everything it touched. Instead he faced the inspector, jabbing at him with his finger. 'You'd have a bloody temper if you'd had to put up with what I've had to put up with.'

Unsure how far the man's temper would stretch, Ali continued, 'Did you ever lose your temper with Bronwyn?'

Suddenly Younger became cautious. He knew where this was going and when he spoke his voice was hesitant. 'Sometimes.'

'When?'

'When she treated me like something she'd brought in on her shoe.'

'Did she do that often?'

'Often enough.'

'Often enough to make you angry?'

'Yes, often enough to make me angry.'

'Did you kill Bronwyn when you were angry, Mr Younger?'

Younger was no fool and it was a question he had probably anticipated. When he answered, his bitterness was muted and his words measured. 'No,' he said. 'I didn't kill her at all, not in anger, not in cold blood.'

'But you did dislike her? Would it be reasonable even to say you hated her?' Ali persisted.

Younger took a deep breath and met the inspector's gaze. There was a touch of venom in his eyes, but whether it was directed at the police or at his stepdaughter, it was difficult to determine.

'I've never made a secret of what I felt about her. Bronwyn was a bitch. She'd had all the attention until I came along and when Lynne and I got together she did everything she could to break us up. She spent most of her time trying to blacken my name.'

'In what way?'

'Anything from me running a dodgy business to me having affairs. She complained I drank too much and that I left Lynne alone most of the time. She said I wasted our money so that her mother was worse off than when she was single. In fact, I was everything her father wasn't.' He gave a rasping laugh.

'Well, she was right there. He was the biggest wastrel you could ever wish to meet. Why did she think Lynne left him? Left him long before I came on the scene, I might add. And as for having affairs, Bronwyn could beat me on that any day. She made a speciality out of one-night stands; she even had one with a copper once.'

'A one-night stand?'

'They'd had a break-in at the travel agent's and he'd come to investigate. The next thing I heard she was sleeping with him. I soon put a stop to that, I can tell you.'

'Why?'

Younger sighed, as if the implication shouldn't need explanation. 'She told lies about me, man; think what she could say to a copper. She wouldn't walk in to the police station in broad daylight and make the allegations, but in bed with him would be a different matter. She could have been saying anything. I own an estate agency; all that would be necessary would be to suggest I ran a dodgy business and I've have you lot all over me.'

'How did you put a stop to it?'

'I told his bosses. I don't know what happened to him, but he didn't see Bronwyn again. She wasn't pleased, I can tell you; said I wasn't content in ruining her mother's life, I was trying to ruin hers as well.' By this time Younger was breathing heavily and he sat down and rested his elbows on his knees and cradled his head in his hands. Finally he looked up, countering Ali's level gaze. 'Whatever she said, and whatever I might think of her daughter, I love my wife, I always have and I wouldn't hurt her by killing Bronwyn. I didn't even complain when they saw each other from time to time, even though I knew she would be poisoning her against me.' Then he sat back, as though the speech had answered all the questions the detectives needed to ask.

Not so; Younger couldn't make accusations against a dead girl and expect them to lay dormant. Ali said, 'The affair you say Bronwyn had with a police officer, when was it?'

'I don't know, six, seven years ago.'

'Do you know who the officer was?' He would like to have

asked straight out if it was Tom Blakely, but didn't want to put ideas into the man's head.

There was a moment's hesitation before Younger answered. 'No except that he was a detective. Bronwyn never did things by halves.'

Ali wasn't sure he believed him, but left it for the moment. 'Can you give us names of the other men with whom she had affairs?' Ali asked. 'It's possible one of them might know who this officer was.'

'Not all of them. She went out with Peter Bolton for a long time, until he dumped her. She said she dumped him, but he told me she was two-timing him.'

'When did their relationship end?'

'A year ago, more; I'm not sure exactly. I only know what Bolton told me. I said he ought to be grateful. Let some other poor sod have her.'

'Did he say who the other man was?'

'Not really, except that like many of her men he was a lot older. Bolton couldn't understand why she would bother. I think she was looking for a father figure.'

'Were any of them foreigners?'

'As far as I know there was only the one and he was the latest.'

'But generally the others were older than her?'

'From what I've been told.'

'It occurs to me, Mr Younger, that for someone who was not interested in his stepdaughter, you seem to know a lot about her.'

'People tell me things, and she spent a lot of time with Annie, as did my wife, so things got back.'

'Annie?'

'Annie Laycock.' He looked at Ali with contempt. 'Do old ladies who've been murdered mean so little to you that you forget who they are?'

Ali could barely control his anger. 'No, Mr Younger, they don't. I was simply confirming whom you were talking about.' Then, unable to contain himself, he said, 'I saw what the killer did to Mrs Laycock. If you think I could forget that, you are very much mistaken.' He wanted to add, 'and I saw Bronwyn's body and I'm not likely to forget that either', but was saved from what would surely have been a grave mistake by Warrender returning with the coffee.

To give him the opportunity to calm down, Ali moved the pile of papers from the coffee table onto the floor and the constable set down the tray. He passed a mug to Younger who placed it next to him, and one to Ali. Before he sat down, he whispered in Ali's ear. Ali nodded and Warrender seated himself in the chair opposite Bronwyn's stepfather.

Nervously, Younger watched him. 'Don't you know it's rude to whisper?' he growled.

Warrender took a sip of his coffee and after a moment's thought said, 'I do know it's rude to whisper, but I'm a police officer and it goes with the territory when I have something to say I don't want anyone else to hear.' He leaned forward conspiratorially. 'Really you ought to feel sorry for me, Mr Younger; the inspector wears some of the most disgusting after-shave I have ever had to get near to.' Then as though it was all part of the same conversation he said, 'Tell me about Help International.'

For a moment Younger seemed unnerved, but he continued to hold the constable's gaze. Finally he growled, 'Never heard of them.'

'I think you have; you were on the phone to them while we were waiting for you to answer the door.'

'What makes you think that?'

'One four seven one; it's a great system.'

Younger flushed. 'You have no right—'

'This is a murder inquiry, Mr Younger, I have every right. Now, tell me about Help International.'

'It was one of those junk calls.'

'And that's why the conversation was so heated.'

'Yes. They're a bloody nuisance.'

'Yes, you're right, they are.' He took a drink. 'Bronwyn's body was found at the entrance to one of the old mines. Was she in the habit of going up there?'

The suddenness in the direction of Warrender's question

added to Younger's nervousness. First he scratched at his palms, then crossed his legs and tried to look unconcerned, but the familiar signs of unease were surfacing again. 'How the hell should I know? Perhaps she was interested in dead miners as well as live men. I don't know.' He stood up and went to the sideboard to take another can.

Warrender stopped him. 'You've had enough, Mr Younger,' he said.

Younger turned. 'You don't tell me when I've had enough.'

Warrender smiled at him. 'Perhaps not, but if you pick up that can, the inspector and I will take you down to the station, throw you in a cell to sober up and then begin our questions again, and if we do that I promise you you'll not be selling houses today.'

Angrily, Younger sat back down.

'Does the old mine mean anything at all to you?' Warrender persisted.

'No.'

'Have you ever been up there?'

'No.'

'Have you read about it in the newspaper?'

'No.'

'But you know about the dead miners? You mentioned them just now.'

'I probably heard about them on the television. Does it matter? I didn't kill Bronwyn and I didn't put her body up there – any more than I buried it in the garden.'

Ali watched as Younger's level of anxiety climbed sharply. He had deflected questions about Help International and now he didn't want to discuss the old mine. Ali wondered why. Perhaps there was some link between them, something Younger didn't want them to know. It was obvious he knew something about one or both of them; but where did Bronwyn fit in? At the moment they weren't asking the right questions and until they did, they wouldn't get any further. He stretched out to place his mug on the table, pulled himself from his chair and walked to the window to give him a moment to think. It was raining more heavily now and the clouds had turned to a deep blue-black. A streak of lightning flashed across the sky, followed almost immediately by an ear-splitting crash of thunder directly overhead. As a second exploded above them, David Younger pushed himself from his chair and went to the sideboard where he grabbed another can.

Ali placed his hand on his arm. 'No, Mr Younger, no more beer.'

'If I want a beer I shall have one.' His hands were trembling and as he saw Ali looking at them, he said, his voice tight, 'I need a drink. I hate this weather, always have. My friend was killed by lightning when we were little. I was there; I saw it.' He reached out to the cupboard.

Ali's hand remained where it was, restraining him. 'Have you ever met or do you know of Tom Blakely, the man whose body was found up at the mine?'

The thunder crashed again and Younger tried to pull his arm away, but Ali's grip was firm. This wasn't fair and he knew it, but it was the only way. 'No, not until you've answered my question. Have you ever met or do you know of Tom Blakely?'

Warrender pulled a photograph from the folder on the table and moved towards the two men. He handed it to Ali who took it with his other hand.

'I'm asking you again, Mr Younger,' he said firmly, 'do you know of or have you ever met Tom Blakely?' He pushed the picture in front of David Younger. 'This man,' he said.

At first he thought Younger wasn't about to answer him, but the lightning was streaking across the sky and the thunder rumbling overhead and he was desperate for a beer. 'All right, I knew him.'

Ali gripped him harder. 'How?'

Deflated, Younger said, 'We had a burglary at the estate agency about four months ago. They took our computers, although God only knows why; they weren't exactly up-to-date. I put in a claim and Blakely was the investigator. He suggested I had managed the break-in myself and was making a false claim. We have a new-for-old policy and he decided it was my means of replacing my computers.'

'And was it, David?' His voice was softer and the use of the man's first name had its effect.

Younger sighed. 'No. It was a legitimate claim. I wouldn't care because I wasn't the only business the toe-rags had done over that night and the police caught them within days. Even so, Blakely kept going. I thought the insurance company wasn't going to pay out at first.'

'But now they have.'

'Yes, but thanks to Tom Blakely go-slow and Bronwyn's disappearance, it's all I can do to keep the business going. I've nothing to thank either of them for.'

And every reason to kill them. The storm was passing and the sky beginning to lighten. Ali released him. 'Let's sit down, Mr Younger.'

The man nodded and moved away from the sideboard to sink into his chair. He was drunk and exhausted.

When they were seated, Ali said, 'But they did pay out?'

'Eventually, when Blakely couldn't find any evidence against me. He didn't care that he almost bankrupted me, but I suppose I ought to be grateful he didn't fabricate facts just to get his own back.'

Ali frowned. 'What do you mean, David, to get his own back?'

Younger lifted his head. 'It's what Blakely was doing. He was the officer Bronwyn had slept with and against whom I made the complaint.'

Christine Blakely spread the local paper out on her bed. Staring up at her was a photograph of Tom. It had always been her favourite: a slight smile and the knowing look he often had in his eyes. Wearily, she stood up and walked to the dressing table where she opened a drawer. From it she took a flat curved box in blue velvet. She opened it and picked out a necklace in blue and white stones. She didn't think they were precious; Tom couldn't have afforded that, but they were a present. She'd only worn them once before he'd disappeared; now she knew she would never wear them again. The pain would be too much to bear.

She glanced once more at his picture in the paper. For the first time in more than ten days it was real. Tom was dead and he wasn't coming back and now everyone knew it: his relatives, his friends, the people in the street and the women with whom he'd had affairs – particularly the women with whom he had affairs. She hoped for his sake they were as distraught at his death as she was – but she doubted it.

Marek Kowalski sat in the day room, his eyes also firmly fixed on the newspaper. The body found with Bronwyn's was Tom Blakely – the man he had tried so hard to talk to. His wife had said he was away, but she hadn't said he was missing. Had he been dead then? Had Leon Jackson or Martin Neville killed him? Had they killed Bronwyn? Both knew about them and their scam; now there was no one to stop them – except him, and he couldn't; he daren't, just as he daren't tell Mrs Blakely what he knew. Each breath he took caught like a knife on his broken ribs and the pain he was feeling was a warning; next time they would kill him. It was a nightmare. He'd cried out in his nightmares when he'd been a child and his mother had come and stroked his hair and caressed them away. Now there was no mother to cry out to; he had never felt so lonely. His longing for Poland had never been more acute. There was nothing he could do; Leon had insisted he would pick him up from the hospital when he was discharged and Mrs Blakely had said she would tell the police. There was no way out of this, unless ... Would he dare? The man in the next bed had discharged himself. The doctor and the nurses had made a fuss, but they couldn't stop him, just made him sign a paper. He would do that, go back to his flat, pick up his passport and return to Poland. If he did it today he would be back in his homeland before anyone at Help International knew he had gone.

Ian Gott was in what had become his favourite restaurant since he had skipped prison. The Big Mac, the pack of fries and the beaker of tea in front of him were untouched as he glared at the newspaper. He fumed at the injustice of what he was reading. Tom Blakely was dead. Not that that concerned him; the man deserved everything he got. What infuriated him was that someone had got there before him and if he ever met the man who had done this, he wouldn't shake his hand, he would knock the living daylights out of him. Tom Blakely had been his and he'd been robbed of the one act that would have made his stay in prison worthwhile. The other customers looked round as he banged his fist on the table. He glared at them, but realised he shouldn't have done that; he shouldn't draw attention to himself. He had to stay free and couldn't risk being recognised; there was still one more on his list: Detective Constable Andrew Clarke.

chapter thirteen

Khalid Ali bumped into Handford in the car park.

'How did it go?' Handford asked.

Ali shook his head. 'Not brilliantly. Younger was drunk, his wife has moved out to stay with a friend and he was eager to get to work. He was having a heated phone call with someone at a charity called Help International when we arrived and insisted it was a cold call, but the conversation was too long and he was too angry for it to be that, so I've sent Warrender to their offices to see what he can find out. Otherwise he ranted a lot, mainly about Bronwyn and what she had done to their lives. According to him she had several affairs, including one with Tom Blakely.'

Handford's brow furrowed. 'I asked him about boyfriends when Bronwyn first went missing, but there was no mention of Blakely. I wonder why?'

'Probably because it happened six or seven years ago when he was in the CID and he didn't think it was relevant.' Ali described what Younger had told him about the insurance claim. 'According to him, Blakely's go-slow almost killed his business.'

The frown on Handford's forehead deepened. 'I'm sorry, but I don't buy this. If Tom was suspicious, he had to have a reason. There has to be more too it; I would say Mr Younger isn't telling us everything.'

'I agree, which is why I've told him to come into the station tomorrow, sober and with his solicitor. I'll have another go then.'

Handford climbed into his car and let his window down. 'I'll leave it with you then and when I've interviewed Blakely's brother and his solicitor, I'll talk to Christine again, make sure she really had no idea about Tom's liaison with Bronwyn. In the meantime, ask Clarke if he got the same impression of Bronwyn from the staff at the travel agency and see if anyone remembers the break-in and the police officer who investigated. Check it out in the archives as well and with Tom Blakely's boss; oh, and a press conference has been called for four o'clock. I'd like you there.'

Ali pulled a face. 'Do I have to be? I hate the things.'

Handford smiled and climbed into his car. 'It's all part of the learning curve, Khalid. I'll see you there.'

As his boss drove away, Ali made his way into the station. It may have been the light in the car park, but it seemed to him that Handford looked tired, ill even. He'd almost asked yesterday if something was troubling him but had decided against it. Handford didn't always take kindly to people prying and now wouldn't be a good time, what with three difficult cases to oversee and the possibility of a miscarriage of justice on his mind.

Predictably the reception area was seething with people waiting to be seen and not for the first time, he found himself surprised that it was just as busy as it had been before they moved further out of the centre and its location wasn't so convenient. Easing his way through the crowd, he ignored the shouts of 'get to the back of the queue' and the comments regarding his ethnic origin, and leaned towards one of the civilian workers. 'Anything for me?' he asked.

'No, Inspector, but there's a letter for DC Clarke.' She turned to one of the pigeon holes and pulled out a brown envelope. 'Would you mind taking it up?' Inwardly blessing her for referring to him by his rank, Ali smiled, took it from her and pushed his way to the lift, the comments silenced.

Peace reigned in the third-floor incident room, which apart from Clarke, who was in deep conversation on the phone, was devoid of personnel. The detective ended the call and pondered for a moment as he brushed the receiver against his cheek.

Finally he replaced it on the rest and began to make notes on the pad next to him.

'Problem?' Ali asked.

Clarke leaned back in his chair. 'I don't know whether it's my brain getting old, whether Tom Blakely was hiding something and I can't find it or whether he was doing no more than hanging on to information until he had the big picture,' he mused. 'I can't make sense of anything: where he was going, what he was doing or who he met before he was killed. The only thing I can be sure of is that he was investigating a group organising a scam into staged car accidents and that they are based somewhere in Keighley and big names are involved.'

'But he hasn't given any indication as to who they are and who the big names are?'

'No, at least not to people I've talked to or in the few reports I've seen. I've had a word with the Fraud Squad, but he hasn't been in touch with them either and so far they know nothing of any such insurance fraud. The trouble is since the break-in at Dart Insurance, his hard drive has gone and we don't know what's missing from his filing cabinet, if anything. I'm hoping I might find more on his home computer.'

'What about his lifestyle? Any women involved? The senior partner at Dart Insurance suggested there could be.'

'No idea. If there were he didn't talk about them.'

'Even so, it might be worth checking on his past liaisons in case we have a husband who wanted his revenge. According to Younger, he had a fling with Bronwyn Price, but it's a good few years ago. He also alleged she was fond of sleeping around, particularly with older men. It might be worth looking them up as well – someone must know who they are.'

Clarke scribbled down the information. 'If they do, it won't be any of her work colleagues. Not one person at the travel agency suggested she was anything but the quiet, unthreatening girl-next-door. But then they also said she kept herself to herself; didn't let much out, so perhaps her life's waters were murkier than her colleagues thought.'

'Possibly, but you need to keep in mind that she wasn't Younger's favourite person so he could have been exaggerating.

I doubt he would murder her because she was having affairs, although ... ' He explained about the insurance claim. 'He blames Bronwyn as well as Blakely for the attempt at sabotaging the application; apparently it harmed his business financially, so there's no doubt he has a motive to kill both of them, but I can't help feeling there's something more to all this, something we're missing.'

'The staged car accidents?'

'Possibly, although I wouldn't like to hazard a guess as to how he's involved.' Ali scratched his head. 'He's coming into the station tomorrow morning with his solicitor; sit in if you like and let's see if we can get to the bottom of it.'

'Thanks, I will.'

Ali nodded and was about to move into his office when he remembered the letter. He handed him the envelope. Brown, A5, nothing to suggest who it was from, just the name of the recipient printed across the centre. Clarke scrutinised it, front and back. Why did people do that? Ali wondered. Why did they check out the envelope first, why not just open it? As he reached his desk the telephone rang. He picked up the receiver and listened, a smile lighting his face. 'Thanks,' he said, 'I owe you one.' It was exactly the news he had been hoping for: the thumb print on the box of medals was Gott's. It was looking less and less likely that Gott had been set up. He shrugged out of his coat and hung it up and was about to call Clarke when the man himself tapped on his door. 'Can I have a word?'

Before Ali could answer, he held out a plastic folder in which he had placed the envelope he had received and another in which were its contents. 'I think you should see this,' he said.

Ali took it from him. The report on Tom Blakely's death and his picture had been torn from the newspaper and with it was a note on which was scrawled, *One down, one to go.*

He stared at Clarke. 'Gott?'

'I think so, don't you? He's telling us he killed Tom and he's giving me fair warning that I'm next. Perhaps John was right and seven years has given him a lot of thinking time.'

Ali picked up the telephone and punched in the reception number. 'This is Inspector Ali. You gave me an envelope for

DC Clarke a few minutes ago. Do you know who brought it in?' He listened for a moment then replaced the receiver. 'It was a young lad. He didn't give his name, just said it was for you, that it was urgent and to make sure you got it.' It was warm in the station, too warm, and Ali was beginning to sweat. He took off his jacket and hung it round his chair. 'Don't let's get ahead of ourselves; it may not be from Gott. Let's get it to forensics and see what that tells us.'

'And in the meantime?'

'In the meantime we check the CCTV footage from outside the station and in reception, step up our efforts to find Gott and you need to be extra vigilant. Does he know where you live?'

'I don't think so, although if he's determined enough he could probably find out.' Clarke pulled up a chair. 'Do you think he did kill Tom?'

'I think he wants us to think he did, just like he wants us to know he's in the area. I also think he's not going to show himself any more than he has to. If he did kill Annie Laycock, and there's no reason to suppose it was anyone else since his DNA is all over her house, then he must have some money, so it's unlikely he's sleeping rough. It's also unlikely he's in a hostel where he might come across someone who may know him, which means he's going to keep his head down, probably in a B&B somewhere, probably way out of the city.'

Clarke shook his head. 'I doubt he's that far away. I know Gott; he's not the brightest, but he's cunning enough to stay close by.'

'Not out in one of the villages?'

'I wouldn't think so.' Clarke shifted in his chair. 'Think about it, Khalid. Where do you hide a letter you don't want someone to find? Among other letters; it's the last place they'll probably look. So where does someone like Gott hide? In a B&B where people come and go, probably stay a few days at the most and then move on. In that way he's seen and forgotten.'

Ali seemed unsure.

Clarke pursued it. 'That's why we don't know how many young women Fred West murdered – because he chose them from a moving population where even under normal circumstances they were not in one place long enough to become known.'

'So what are you saying?'

'I'm saying that if finding him will be like looking for the proverbial needle, then let him find me. Flood the media with his picture; warn the public to be vigilant, pander to his nature by telling them he's dangerous and not to be approached, but to contact the police if they see him. Let me be the face on the television, the voice on the radio; give out my name and my number. That way either we'll pick him up or he'll come to me.'

Ali studied Clarke. He was buoyed up, excited. For a man nearing retirement he certainly had guts. Balding, silver haired and on the wrong side of fifty, he had joined the service later than most, but had persuaded the bosses to let him complete his thirty years. That was coming up on the rails – too fast to let a toe-rag like Gott prevent him from enjoying it. And while he agreed with Clarke's suggestion, he couldn't see John or Chief Superintendent Paynter going along with him putting himself so firmly in the spotlight. They'd have to find another way.

As Chris Warrender walked into the offices of Help International, Martin Neville and Leon Jackson were leaning on the curved reception desk reading the local paper. Had it been the sports page they were looking at the detective could have understood the hint of a smile on their lips. As it was they were scrutinising the front page. Nothing much to smile about there.

Neville looked up. 'Can I help you?' His voice was smooth and welcoming and Warrender wondered how long that would last once he knew why the detective was here. Warrender glanced at their name badges and then showed them his warrant card. 'Bad job that,' he said, pointing to the picture of Tom Blakely.

'Yes. Yes, it is.'

'Did you know him?'

'No.'

'He worked for Dart Insurance and I notice you have their public liability certificate on your wall.'

'We never met him; we dealt with someone else.' Outwardly Neville didn't appear unsettled by Warrender or his questions, but there was flicker of something in his eyes – no more than a flicker, but it was enough to peck at the edges of the detective's interest. Neville changed the subject: 'I don't imagine you're here for advice, Detective Constable. Unless of course you're investigating Mr Blakely's death, in which case I'm not sure how we can be of help.' He smiled, the kind of smile that he might use if he was about to stab a person in the back, Warrender thought. He'd had a teacher like that at school, a woman who would give him a sweet smile followed by a clip round the ear. He'd never forgiven her.

Warrender reciprocated. 'No, Mr Neville, neither, but I have come for information. I'm investigating the death of Bronwyn Price. Have you heard of her?'

Neville hesitated for several seconds. Whether it was because he was trying to bring the name to mind or whether he knew of, but would prefer not to be linked with, her it was difficult to tell. Perhaps he'd been one of the many lovers Younger had talked about. Now there was a thought, but not one to put to Neville here – perhaps later at the station, because he was sure there would be a later.

'Is she the girl who went missing?'

Went missing. Warrender hated that phrase; it sounded as though she'd gone off and then got herself killed on purpose. 'Yes. Her body was found a couple of days ago.'

Finally Neville glanced round at Leon Jackson. 'We don't know her, do we?' Jackson shook his head. Obviously, the strong silent type.

'Might she have been a friend of one of your clients?'

Again Neville appeared to be attempting to bring her to mind. 'It's possible I suppose, but I don't think so,' he said slowly. 'It's difficult when the name has been in the papers to know whether you're remembering that or the fact that at some point you have come across her. But no,' he added emphatically, 'I can't bring her to mind at all.'

Warrender turned to Leon Jackson. 'What about you?'

The smirk that seemed glued to Jackson's lips now curled

into a smile that could only be described as feral. When he spoke his voice was guttural, laced with a hint of menace. 'No, she hasn't been in here and if she had we couldn't tell you. Confidential, you see.'

Warrender groaned inwardly; he'd be quoting the Data Protection Act before long. As he watched Jackson resume his position in his lair behind the desk he wondered why a man as smooth as Martin Neville chose someone like him as his partner in a charity designed to help people. He made a note to check them both out later.

'I wondered, you see, because we understand she had a foreign boyfriend. If she had, it's possible you might know of him and I accept it's a long shot, but if he needed your help she might have come with him, particularly if he had a problem with English.'

'Do you have a name for this boyfriend?'

'Possibly Mark or a foreign version of that. Do you have anyone of that name or similar on your books?'

'No, no one.' The answer was quick, almost too quick and Warrender felt the beginnings of a game. Well, if that was what they wanted, he was prepared to join in. He turned to Leon Jackson. 'You have records of all your clients?'

'Yes, on the computer, but I've told you, you can't see them.'

Neville took over. 'You must understand that while some of our clients are foreign, many are single mothers or pensioners who need help with debts or benefit claims. Some of them, particularly the pensioners, are ashamed they can't manage and have to ask for money from the government – even though they're entitled to it. We promise them complete confidentiality.'

Warrender leaned over the desk. 'And this is a murder investigation, Mr Neville. A young girl has been brutally killed and I need to know the identity of her boyfriend, if only to eliminate him from our inquiries. Now either you can show me your records or I'll get a warrant.'

'Then that's what you'll have to do, Detective.'

Warrender sighed. At this stage of the investigation a

magistrate would throw out any application for a warrant, and to trawl through National Insurance numbers and council tax lists, always assuming he was registered, would take for ever. By which time they'd have either destroyed or deleted their information. The question was why should they feel the need to deny any knowledge of him and particularly of Bronwyn? After all, they knew her stepfather.

He stood back and kept his expression as neutral as his voice. 'You see, my problem, gentlemen, is that I don't believe you. You can't tell me you haven't a single Mark or foreign equivalent on your books. Now what I suggest is that you close up and we go into your office where we'll try to get to the bottom of this.'

Neville and Jackson looked at each other and when it seemed as though they were about to reject that as well, Warrender said, 'Of course, I could arrest you for refusing to cooperate in a murder inquiry.' That wouldn't stand up either, not yet, but what was a little white lie in the scheme of things? Nothing, providing they weren't well versed in criminal law.

They weren't and Jackson lifted the flap to let Warrender through while Neville locked the door and turned round the OPEN notice to CLOSED.

Unlike the reception area, the office, though quite large, was haphazardly furnished with two second-hand easy chairs and two plastic garden seats, one against a desk that had seen better days and the other at a table on which stood an elderly computer and printer. Packs of leaflets and A4 computer paper were stacked on shelves and in one corner was a battered filing cabinet, which Warrender decided would be easily broken into. He took one of the more comfortable seats and Leon Jackson leaned against the cabinet, still smirking. He wondered if they kept information of their clients in there as well and this was his way of refusing the detective entry. Warrender controlled the urge to kick his legs from under him and tear open the drawers. Instead he stared at him until Jackson looked away.

'You do understand why we can't let you see our records, don't you?' Neville said, sitting next to the desk.

'I understand perfectly, but you must understand why it's important for me that you do. A list of names is all I need at the moment. If this boyfriend is on it, we can locate him, question him and eliminate him from our inquiries. I'm not interested in anyone else.'

They sat in silence for a few minutes. Warrender reclined in the chair, the calf of one leg resting on the thigh of the other. He turned his head as he scanned the office. 'This seems a useful charity to be involved with – I assume you are a charity?'

They were on safer ground now. 'Yes, we get a grant each year from the council if we're lucky, but the rest of the money we have to raise ourselves.'

'It would be a pity then if you had to close down because of a criminal record. Refusing to cooperate with the police might not seem much, but it *will* give you a record and I can't see the council looking favourably on a grant then, can you? After all, if you can commit one crime, they will ask themselves, how many more are you committing? Smoke and fire and all that.'

Neville sat forward and challenged Warrender. 'I think you'll find that the law is on our side here. Data Protection Act and all that.'

The man was clever and for the moment it was worth allowing him to believe he had the upper hand. Warrender stood up and walked to the door. He looked into the reception area, picked one of the foreign language leaflets off the desk and returned to his chair. 'Do you speak these languages yourselves?'

'No, but we can call on translators if we need to.'

'How many people work here?'

'Just the two of us; we can't afford to take on staff – so we use volunteers.'

'And do you have many?'

'A couple, plus the translators, of course.'

'How often do they work?'

'As I said, we call on the latter when we need them but as far as the volunteers are concerned, it's up to them. They decide on their own days and hours to fit in with their lives.'

'Today?'

'No. We've been here on our own today.'

The answer gave Warrender permission to go for the jugular. 'You say you don't know Bronwyn Price.'

'How many times? We've said no.' Jackson was edgy.

'But you know her stepfather?'

'I don't think so.' Neville gave him that stab-in-the-back smile again.

Warrender parried it. 'David Younger?' His eyed flitted between the two. Neville remained cool, his face as blank as a tailor's dummy, while Leon Jackson's expression contorted between dislike of the policeman in front of him and panic at the name he'd just heard. If Neville hadn't been in the room Warrender was sure the man would have jumped him.

'Mr Neville, do you know David Younger?'

'I've already told you that I don't.'

'So who was he speaking to on the telephone this morning? One four seven one said it was somebody from this office and you said yourself there were no volunteers here so it had to one of you two.' He let them digest that, then linked his hands behind his head and leaned back in the chair. 'I've got to say, he seemed very angry with you. What on earth had you done to get him into that state? Killed his stepdaughter?'

He knew he was walking a thin tightrope and for a moment he thought Leon Jackson was about to sever it until Neville put a restraining hand on his partner's shoulder. 'You need to watch him,' Warrender said casually. 'He's got quite a temper and it's not a good idea to assault a police officer. Now I ask you again, do you know David Younger?'

Neville took a deep breath. 'He's an estate agent; sometimes he rents out a flat to a client in need. There's nothing illegal in that, but we keep his input confidential.'

The Data Protection Act again. My God, they were milking that one this morning. 'And?'

'One of the tenants was in arrears with his rent and it appears he's done a runner. Mr Younger was very angry.'

'Now that is interesting, Mr Neville, because David Younger gave us a completely different story. I have to admit, it wasn't quite as original as yours; he told us it was a junk call. Now, gentlemen, let's get down to business and stop farting about, shall we? I'd like you to tell me what you know about Bronwyn Price and her foreign boyfriend, your movements eight weeks ago and, just for good measure, your movements ten days ago. For instance, have you been up to the old mine workings lately?'

The answer was predictable. Neville spoke for the two of them. 'If you intend to question us as though we're suspects, then I insist on having our solicitor present. He's James Amery. Perhaps you know him.'

Warrender knew him all right, but not in the way Neville's overconfident pronouncement was meant to imply. James Amery was Tom Blakely's solicitor.

John Handford was about to open the door to Patrick Blakely's shop when his mobile rang. 'Handford.'

'It's me, boss, Warrender. I've just come from Help International, they're—'

'Yes, Inspector Ali told me. What have you got?'

'Three things, none of them much in isolation, but they could add up to something. They're insured with Dart Insurance, although they insist they've never met Tom Blakely. Second, they also said they didn't know David Younger until I reminded them they'd been on the phone to him this morning.'

Handford chuckled. 'And how did they get out of that one?'

'The usual: their dealings with him are confidential, but finally they agreed he sometimes lets out flats to their clients and that was what their call had been about.'

'That's possible, he is an estate agent.'

'Entirely possible, except that Younger told us it had been a telephone sales call. Whatever his reason, he obviously didn't want us to know he was associated with them, and they didn't want me to be aware of their association with him. One or both of them is lying, boss, and my feelings tell me it's both.'

'And the third thing?'

'They use the same solicitor as Tom Blakely.'

*

Marek knew something was wrong as soon as he opened the door to his flat. It smelled of more than the staleness expected in a room whose windows hadn't been opened for a couple of days or of the rancid fat from a plate and frying pan dropped in the sink before he left for the cinema. He wanted to believe that the odour from disinfectant and illness in the hospital was still clinging to his clothes, but he knew that wasn't it. There was a sharpness to this which invaded his nostrils, a sharpness familiar to him. It was Leon Jackson's aftershave. Since he had seen the TV advert suggesting it added to the macho man's sexual appeal, Jackson had worn nothing else. Its odour dominated the office at Help International just as it did here.

Marek leaned against the door as it clicked shut. Then he turned and locked it, sliding the chain across before he shuffled painfully into the kitchen. Nausea threatened to take over and he picked a glass from the draining board, filled it with water and gulped it down. His emotions lurched between fear and incomprehension. Why would Leon Jackson come into his flat? What could Marek possibly have that he would want? Or had he done it just to let Marek know he could? That he was the one in control? As if assaulting and hospitalising him wasn't enough. Never had he felt so frightened and so alone, for whatever Jackson's reason it was not in Marek's best interest. Quite the opposite. He had to get away – away from the flat, away from the town, away from the country. Until then he wouldn't be safe. He didn't care how much it cost; he would travel to London tonight and from there to Poland. He had money, dirty money Bronwyn had called it, but it didn't matter any more because Bronwyn was dead, Tom Blakely was dead and the dirty money was his way out.

Exhausted, he stumbled into the bedroom where he lay on the bed for a moment to regain his strength. He stared at the ceiling, wondering if the owners of Help International knew he was out of hospital. It hadn't been easy to persuade the doctor to let him discharge himself. 'I would be much happier if you stayed a couple more days; that was a nasty beating you sustained,' he had said. Eventually, when Marek promised he would ring his GP should it be necessary and lied that his neighbour would pop in from time to time to check on him, the doctor had given in. Even more difficult had been persuading the nurse not to contact Jackson to drive him home. It was the middle of the day, he said, and Leon – the name stuck in his throat – would be busy. He would prefer not to bother him and would take a taxi instead.

The journey had been bad; he had felt every bump, every twist, every turn. Travelling back to Poland would be even more of a nightmare, but he couldn't wait until he was better, not now that Jackson had been in his flat. Once they were aware he was out of hospital, they would come looking for him and another beating would be the least of his problems. Jackson had already insinuated he would kill him if he caused any more trouble – and he would enjoy doing it. Martin Neville would stay out of it, he wouldn't soil his hands, yet he was probably the more dangerous of the two. As Marek saw it, either he had to keep his head down and continue to work for them, saying nothing to anyone – not that there was anyone to talk to now Tom Blakely was dead – or he had to return home to Poland. There didn't seem to be much of a choice.

Cautiously he pulled himself into a standing position and struggled from the bedroom to the bathroom, from the sitting room to the kitchen. Everything was the same as he had left it. He pulled open cupboards and drawers and as far as he could see nothing had been disturbed; nothing was missing. Even his money was safe. He'd never dared put it in a bank because he'd been frightened they would want to know how he had got it. So why? Why had Leon Jackson come to his flat; how had he got in and what had he hoped to find? One thing he was sure of, if the man had been here once he could come again. Marek had to go now.

Back in the bedroom, he glanced at himself in the mirror. He was deathly pale and gave a good impression of a destitute. The clothes he was standing in were those he had been wearing when Jackson had attacked him. The trousers were torn and the coat streaked with the mud from the alleyway. He would attract less attention if he changed, but there was no time; he would have to do it later. The pain dragged at his arms and across his chest as he pulled his bag from the top of the wardrobe and began to stuff in what he could. He would take as little as possible, just what he needed for the journey, and buy the rest in London or in Poland when he arrived home. He wasn't sure where to hide the money; the customs people would be bound to search his bag, but he couldn't leave it. In the end he wrapped it in a towel and secreted it at the bottom of the bag. The chances were they wouldn't bother to unravel it. Finally, he picked up the photograph of Bronwyn from the dressing table and placed it on top. He couldn't leave her behind; indeed, he hated the though of leaving at all.

When he'd arrived in England at first, everything had been strange, but it had been good and when he had met Bronwyn it had been even better. Before he'd begun to work at the stables he'd used to wander the town, watching as people rushed about their everyday lives, as they sat in cafés in the shopping centre and drank in pubs. Later, he'd cared for the horses and enjoyed the company of the young riders, kept an eye on them out on the hills, walked round the ring holding the lead rein as the little ones learned the rudiments, and waved them goodbye at the end of their lessons. They'd been happy and they'd made him happy. But his happiness had evaporated when he'd taken Neville and Jackson up on their offer. It had been wrong – right from the start it had been wrong, but fool that he was he'd never envisaged how much worse it would become. At no time had he ever considered babies and toddlers would be involved. The image of the mother and her children in the car he had forced to slam into him would remain with him for ever. Each time he closed his eyes he saw the terrified face of the young woman and heard the screams of the children. He had done that to them; he could have killed them and everyone would have agreed it was her fault because she'd been driving too close. If only he could believe that. He slumped onto the bed and put his head in his hands. It hadn't been her fault; it had been his, his and Martin Neville's and Leon Jackson's and everyone else involved in the insurance scam. He had their names, but their identities would have to stay with him, he couldn't divulge their names to anyone, not now that Tom Blakely was dead and not if he was to avoid the same fate.

The first knock on the door was determined and insistent. His heart beating wildly, Marek jerked his head in its direction.

It came again, louder this time.

'Kowalski, I know you're in there.' The voice was guttural and unmistakably that of Leon Jackson. 'Open the door,' he shouted.

Globules of sweat began to form on Marek's forehead, his stomach lurched. For a moment he thought he was going to be sick. 'I'm in bed – resting. I don't want to see anyone. Tomorrow perhaps.'

'Kowalski, open the bloody door or I'll break it down.' The door shuddered as the man outside kicked it.

Marek pulled himself from the bed. 'Please. Please leave me alone.'

'Are you going to open this fucking door?'

Frantically Marek pushed the half-filled bag under the sheets and dragged a dressing gown over his outdoor clothes. 'Just a minute.'

He took his time, but inevitably he had to do as Jackson demanded. He turned the key in the lock and opened the door as far as the chain would allow.

'And now the chain.'

Marek released it and Jackson pushed the door open. He flicked at the dressing gown. 'Often go to bed in your clothes?' he said.

Marek made no reply; there was nothing he could say.

Jackson grabbed him and Marek held in the scream as the pain seared across his ribs. 'You discharged yourself from hospital,' he sneered, his eyes cold. 'Not a good move in your condition.'

Marek wanted to step back, preserve his own private space, but Jackson held on tightly.

'I didn't want to bother you.' His voice was no more than a whisper.

'Or you didn't want me to know you were leaving.' Abruptly Jackson released him. He pushed past Marek and strode into the bedroom to return seconds later with the bag. 'Going somewhere?' he asked. 'Poland, perhaps?' He turned it upside down and shook it until the contents scattered on to the floor. The towel holding the money unravelled and the notes spilled out. Jackson took a step towards Marek and seized his cheeks between his thumb and forefinger, squeezing hard. 'And to think I left you the money; you don't deserve it, you little shit.'

Then suddenly he began to laugh, a deep belly laugh that ended in a spasm of coughing, pitching spittle into Marek's face. 'Keep your money, Kowalski, I have something of far more use to me.' He put his hand in the inside pocket of his jacket and pulled out a small book which he waved in the air. 'You won't get very far without your passport, you little runt.' He pushed Marek away, then bent down and began to scoop up the money. 'On second thoughts, I'll keep it until you know who you're working for.'

'Why you do this, Leon?' Marek shouted. 'Why you hurt me like this?' Unsure where he got the strength, he kicked out at Jackson's legs, but the man flicked him away as though he were a fly teasing a horse.

'Please, Leon, let me go home. I don't want to do it any more. It's bad. I won't say anything to anyone. I'll just go.'

Jackson smiled. 'I don't think so, Kowalski. In fact, now you're fit enough to be out of hospital you're fit enough to go back to work. I'll let you know when the next job is.' He stood back and let his eyes wander over Marek. 'You know those injuries of yours are better than all right. Just think what we can screw out of the insurance company for those. And they're absolutely legit.'

chapter fourteen

Sport and Leisure Hire, the latest of the three shops owned by Patrick Blakely and his late father, was situated on the main street leading to the railway station in Leeds. It was sited in a tall stone building constructed, according to the date above the door, in 1863 and stretched almost the length of the block – the end shop being a mini-market, useful, Handford decided, when the staff ran out of milk. Each of the three large windows was decorated with the theme of a different sport: rock climbing, canoeing and skiing. Handford surveyed them. Whoever was responsible was an artist. He'd not seen better in the large stores in London.

Although he had always been based in a city, Handford was not a city man at heart; it was too claustrophobic, the more so today because he had to park his car in a multi-storey in the central shopping area and make his way through the crowds of office workers who were taking their lunch-breaks and pensioners who, judging from the rolls of patterned paper jutting from their bags, appeared to be going about their early Christmas shopping. What was it? Five or six weeks to go? Handford had put in for leave this year so that he could spend it with Gill and the girls and unless anything serious cropped up, he would no doubt get it. Paynter had come as near to a promise as it was possible in this job.

The bell tinkled as he walked into the shop. There were no customers and the man behind the counter was unmistakably Patrick. It was almost uncanny – he could have been looking at Tom, except that as he drew near he could see his face and

hands were marked with the black slivers of coal that had penetrated the skin to leave their own trade mark. He looked up as
Handford entered, his expression registering that he knew the
man was a police officer.

'I don't talk to policemen and if you've come to talk about
my brother, I'll tell you now he's of no interest to me.' Patrick
Blakely returned to the order form he was working on.

This was no more than Handford expected, but if Blakely
thought he would simply walk away he was sadly mistaken. He
looked round. The shop floor was large, with plenty of space
to set up the leisure and camping equipment, as well as rails
for the outdoor clothing and even in winter the impression was
that the business was doing well. The miners' strike and the
closure of their pit had done Blakely senior and son quite a
service, although he doubted Patrick believed that, and if he did
he would never have admitted it. Either way, Handford could
see why he didn't want to share the business with his brother.

'You still here?'

'Yes, I'm still here and I will stay here until you talk to me,
Mr Blakely.' It was a pity there were no customers; he could
have used their presence to force him to take him somewhere
more private; as it was, the open shop would have to do. He
leaned over the desk. 'Your brother has been murdered; you
hated him for being on what you consider the other side during
the strike and you hated him for inheriting half of this business
– a business I can see is doing well. Now add those together
and I think you'll agree you're in the frame for his death.'

Patrick opened his mouth to respond, but Handford gave
him no opportunity. 'Even when she told you he was missing,
you continued to harass his wife. I could arrest you right now
for that alone. And if you think I won't do it as well as call a
police car and have you taken out of the shop in handcuffs then
you are very much mistaken.'

The bell above the door of the shop tinkled again as a woman
with two young children walked in. Handford nodded towards
them. 'In front of those youngsters if you like,' he whispered.
'Now get your assistant to serve them and we'll find somewhere
more private to talk.'

'Janet's on her break,' Patrick Blakely said sullenly.

'Then get her off her break.' Handford pulled out his mobile phone and began to thumb in a number.

'All right, all right.' Blakely walked to a door behind the desk and called out, 'Can you come up here, Janet?'

Handford closed his mobile.

Janet ran up the stairs, dressed in a jogging suit and with a lithe figure that belied her age and grey hair and a leathery neck that didn't. She was probably somewhere in her fifties, and as she smiled at Handford, he wished he was in as good shape and determined for the umpteenth time to do something about it before Gill got home. Blakely nodded in the direction of the customer, 'Can you serve Mrs Peterson, Janet? I'll be upstairs if we get busy.'

Handford followed him up the steps at the back of the shop, through a large stockroom and into a small office. Unlike the shop, which was organised with almost military precision, this room was a mess, with papers scattered over every available surface as though they had been left where they dropped. Some envelopes were unopened – today's post? Yesterday's? An untidy desk, his teacher had always told him, suggested an untidy mind – or was it a worried mind in Blakely's case?

Patrick Blakely banged the door shut and before Handford could say anything he said, 'This business is mine; I'm entitled to it.'

'Not according to your father's will.'

'Bugger my father's will.' Patrick sat down behind the desk, leaving Handford standing. Like all the others who tried it, Blakely thought it granted him an air of authority. But it was a ploy Handford was used to and when eventually Blakely indicated that he should take the chair opposite, he didn't take him up on it immediately; instead he said nothing but folded his arms, leaned against the wall and stared at him. He had learned early on in his career to keep his eyes quite still while they worked on the other's psyche. It was disconcerting; forced them to wonder what was going through the detective's mind. What was he thinking? How much did he know?

It worked. Apprehension began to take the place of bravado

and Patrick snapped, 'Well get on with it then; I haven't all day.'

Now Handford sat down.

'You haven't visited your sister-in-law since Tom died,' he said.

'Why should I?'

'Because her husband has been murdered and she may need your support. Because, like it or not, you're family.'

Patrick snorted. 'Family. Tom was never part of our family.' He prodded his chest with the tips of his fingers. '*I* was family; *I* was the one who went down the pit; *I* was the one who helped to support my parents; *I* was the one who built up this business. What did Tom do? He went to a posh grammar school in a posh uniform, then to university and when we thought he just might give something back, he turned on us and joined you lot.'

There was no doubt Patrick was jealous of his brother. Would he have liked to wear the posh uniform and go to the posh school and then on to university? Would he have liked a life different from one underground in the pits? He was certainly capable of more, the successful business proved that. But did he convert that jealousy into action, perhaps when his father willed his part of the business to Tom? The final straw.

If he had then it had not dissipated his jealousy or his anger, for now, at this moment, he was taking it out on Handford – the policeman; the effigy that he could pierce with barbed needles. 'And not content with that,' he went on, 'he stood against us when Thatcher wanted to close our pits. He was as close as I am to you, pushing and shoving us. Have you ever been hit with a truncheon held by your own brother?'

That needle pierced and unannounced, a torrent of emotions overtook Handford. Physically, Douglas might not be wielding a stick, but the blow he was about to land would do as much harm psychologically. He wondered if Noble had had to pick him up, or whether his brother had seen sense and taken himself to the station. If he hadn't Handford couldn't begin to imagine what he would return to at work or the row that would ensue when he broke the news to his mother. If Patrick only knew it, he and the police officer he hated were not that far apart.

But he didn't know it and took Handford's silence on face value. 'No, I don't imagine you have. Well, that brother who turned against his own family and came at us with sticks now has my share of the business.'

Handford had had enough. 'He has nothing, Mr Blakely,' he said quietly. 'He's dead,' and before Patrick could argue it, he added, 'You might not have got it back completely, but you're pretty damn close.' He leaned back in his chair and prepared to change the subject. 'Tell me about your father,' he said.

'Why?'

'Because I need to know why he took his share of the business from you and left it to Tom instead. When did he die?'

'A couple of months ago, although he'd been dying in his own lung fluid for a long time. That's what being a miner does to you. The death certificate said pneumoconiosis; black lung disease is what we called it. It's not pretty, whatever name you give it.'

Handford nodded, but remained silent. Patrick was prepared to talk, and he was prepared to listen.

'He used to get out in the fresh air as much as he could. He would do gardening for his friends, particularly those who had been disabled in pit accidents. He got paid for it; miners are proud people; they didn't want anything for nothing. He liked gardening; when we decided to set up in business it was a toss-up between a garden centre and the hire business.'

'And what made you decide on this?'

'We knew what the people round us wanted. They wanted to get away; have a holiday they could afford and if they could hire a tent then they could have a cheap one. It made sense.'

Handford watched the man as he talked. Memories of his father had mellowed him. It was a pity the detective would have to break the spell. 'Your father left his half of the business to Tom. Did you consider contesting the will?'

The spell was indeed broken. 'No I didn't. My father had black lung not dementia.'

'Did you ask him why?'

'I didn't bloody know, did I? Not until the will was read. But I'm fairly sure Tom did. Didn't bat an eyelid at the reading; didn't look surprised, nothing. He knew all right. If he'd had a decent bone in his body, he'd have refused it and handed it back to me. But he's one of you lot, decent doesn't come into it.'

Handford had lost him and he knew it. 'You have knives in the shop?'

'Why?'

'Tom suffered several stab wounds as well as blows to the head.'

Patrick smiled. 'So whoever did it meant it, wanted him dead?'

Handford nodded.

'Well, it wasn't me. I would've given him a fair fight, not like the one you lot gave us. I would've let him see my face and my eyes; you hid behind your shields.'

He wasn't going to let it go; it was too deeply entrenched. The miners' strike had broken families, turned father against son, brother against brother, and forgiveness was in short supply, even now. Handford knew that, but he was also getting tired of it. 'That was over twenty years ago, Mr Blakely. I wasn't there, so I don't know whether the fight was fair or not. What I do know is that Tom and all the others were doing their job; some hated it, some enjoyed it – that's life and I am not prepared to waste any more time on discussing it. Now, Tom's body was found two days ago; we think he'd been dead about ten days. So I need you to tell me where you were between Tuesday the seventh and Friday the tenth.'

Patrick's lips curled. 'I can tell you exactly. Tuesday I was where I always am on Tuesday: at the wholesaler's and then onto the shops to stock up. On Wednesday I went to a camping exhibition at the NEC in Birmingham and came back on Friday evening. Ask anyone. I'll give you names and telephone numbers if you like so that you can check. Now if that's all ...?'

Handford pushed back his chair and stood up. 'For the moment. If you let me have the names and numbers of the people who can verify your alibi, I'll be on my way.'

Patrick wrote out the list and handed it to him.

As he reached the top of the steps, Handford turned. 'Just one more question, Mr Blakely. Tom was trying to persuade the council to provide a memorial stone for the miners who died all those years ago. Did he talk to you about it?'

'He mentioned it.'

'So, have you ever been up to the site?'

'Once.'

'When?'

'When I followed him up there after the will was read. I wanted to talk to him about the business. It was rightfully mine, and I hoped he would do the decent thing and give it back to me.'

'But he didn't.'

'No, of course he didn't. He must have expected me to turn up because he had his solicitor with him and his latest bit on the side. They were laughing and joking when I got there.'

That belied Christine's belief that Tom had given up women. 'Do you know who the woman was?'

'Not then, no, but I know her now. She's that girl whose body was found near his: Bronwyn Price.'

Brian Noble arrived at the office of the Director of Social Services at roughly the same time as John Handford arrived at Patrick Blakely's shop. He left some ten minutes later. The secretary watched as the police officer held Douglas Handford's arm and directed him down the stairs and into a waiting car, then she ran into the assistant director's office to relate what had happened and ask him exactly what was going on. The assistant director had no idea and said he hoped there wasn't a problem at home; he would try to find out. According to the secretary, it looked like Douglas had been arrested. Policemen held you by the arm if they were arresting you. Not that she could think of anything he could have done. She'd worked for him ever since he came and she considered him the nicest person she had ever met, although she had to admit he'd been in a dark mood for days now, snapping at her for the slightest thing. She had thought it was maybe a family problem; everyone had them, even social workers. But now she knew better. He was in trouble with the police and she wanted to know why. There was no way she was waiting for the assistant director to find out – he probably wouldn't tell her if he did. She'd do her own digging. You didn't do the job she did for as long as she had without knowing the right people, and she knew the right people – both in the police service and in the press. This was, as far as she was concerned, the most exciting thing that had happened for a long time and although confidentiality was the watchword at her level of seniority, she wasn't about to let it worry her. She closed the door, picked up the phone and dialled an outside number.

'Oh, hello, yes,' she said in a whisper. 'Newsroom please.'

By now the rain had stopped and a watery sun was beginning to penetrate the clouds, pummelling at them as it forced its way through to shine onto the wet road, so that the tarmac threw rays of light onto the car's windscreen. From Patrick Blakely's shop, Handford drove back into town for his appointment with James Amery, solicitor, it seemed, to half the district. He hadn't met him before, so obviously he had little to do with criminal defence work. It turned out he dealt with everything but criminal, including house purchases, wills, insurance claims and most things civil. It was obviously lucrative, for his clothes were expensive and the rest of him well-groomed. He was not unlike Graham Dart, except that he was at least twenty years younger. He was also willing to talk, although there was little he could tell Handford that he didn't already know. The will was watertight and Tom's father had been of sound mind when he made it – indeed, he was of sound mind right up to his death, as far as Amery could make out. Tom's death, as Ali had suggested, would make little difference to the will, except to slow it down. It would be necessary to make sure that Tom's brother wasn't guilty of the murder, of course, but even if he was, providing his wife and the children had no hand in the killing, Patrick's half of the business would remain his and his father's half would pass from Tom to Christina Blakely or even to Patrick's son, Greg.

'In all honesty, Chief Inspector, I can't see any reason why

Patrick should kill his brother.' He leaned back in his chair and steepled his fingers. 'Did you meet the children at all?'

'No, I didn't.'

'Well, I can tell you if Patrick had any thought that he would be able to persuade Greg to give up his part of the business, he would be very much mistaken. As soon as he's completed his A-levels, Greg wants in to it. He's got the same kind of business brain as his father and he's full of ideas. To be honest, it wouldn't have surprised me if Tom hadn't passed his half on to Greg once he reached eighteen. He did mention it to me once and asked how he could go about it.'

'Was Patrick aware of this?'

'It's possible. They met up at the old mine, you know. I'd gone with Tom to discuss the memorial stone and Patrick arrived. It was just after the reading of the will and he was furious. They had quite an argument and I did hear mention of Greg's name. I thought Patrick was going to hit him at that point. You can't blame him really; he had worked hard to build up the shops and he can be forgiven for feeling aggrieved at his father, but passing his half of the business on to Tom was Amos's way of forgiving him for joining the police. You know he fought the miners during the strike?'

Handford smiled. 'Yes, he told me, many times. Do you think Patrick killed his brother?'

'Oh, Chief Inspector, I wouldn't know. There was certainly no love lost between them, but if he killed him to get the business back he was fighting a losing battle. I don't think Patrick is as bad as people think he is. As far as he was concerned Tom was given everything: grammar school education, university – all the things he would have liked. But he lacked the one thing that Tom didn't and that was an academic brain. Patrick failed his eleven-plus examination, so everything Tom had was out of reach. Yet if you think about it Patrick has done as well as Tom, if not better and in a much shorter time, but the chip is still there and I suspect it always will be.'

'I understand you also act for Help International?'

Amery's lips tightened. 'My, you have been busy. Have you been checking up on me?'

'No, sir, of course not. David Younger, Bronwyn Price's stepfather, was on the phone to them yesterday when my officers arrived to talk to him. Apparently the discussion they were having was quite heated.' Amery's expression remained impassive. He was giving nothing away. 'When we questioned them they said they didn't know him until we pointed out the telephone call and then they agreed that he rented out flats to them occasionally. After that they refused to answer any more questions without you there. Yet this is a murder inquiry and you don't do criminal work; it just seemed odd, that's all.'

Amery shifted in his chair and suddenly Handford felt uneasy. He had come here expecting no more than information on the will and Tom's relationship with his father and now he felt an undercurrent of evasion, if not lies. 'I don't think there's anything sinister in that,' Amery said. 'I act for them and some of their clients; they probably assumed I would do the same thing in a criminal capacity. Although you surely can't believe they had anything to do with Bronwyn Price's death? I doubt they even knew her.'

'But you did, sir?'

Amery shifted again. 'No, I don't think so.'

'According to Patrick Blakely she was up at the old mine workings with you and Tom.'

Amery made no reply, but scrutinised his well-manicured fingers.

'Look, Mr Amery, I'm trying to find out who killed Tom and Bronwyn. I don't know whether I'm looking for one killer or two. What I do know is that Tom's wife insists there were no women in his life, yet here we have the woman whose body was found in the same location as his. He spent time up there and now, although you won't admit it, so did Bronwyn. I understand from Christine Blakely that you were friends as well as solicitor and client, so help me out here, was Tom having an affair with Bronwyn Price?'

The press conference was a zoo. They sniffed a serial killer, although they couldn't be sure. They wanted to know why the police hadn't yet caught whoever it was preying on people in the

Riddlesden area, an area they pointed out that was almost crime free until a few days ago. Detective Chief Superintendent Paynter said they were following a series of useful leads. The press asked what those leads were; Detective Chief Superintendent Paynter said he wasn't at liberty to say and everyone knew that meant they really didn't have a clue. They all asked their questions at once until it was impossible to hear any of them, let alone answer them. Handford saw one or two journalists from the nationals, but so far the majority hadn't got hold of the story or didn't think it was worth travelling north for. Once more of them saw it as a front-page feature, with the odd article inside, the problem would be preventing them from starting up their own investigation, questioning people like David Younger and, heaven forbid, his wife. Connie Burns would keep them away from Christine Blakely, which was as well, since Handford had several more questions to put to her. She'd said her husband was not having an affair with anyone, but had she known about Bronwyn Price? She insisted not when he had questioned her and said that she'd only heard of her from the media. But Tom had known her, had had a fling with her some years before. James Amery had laughed at Handford's question, but again there was that undercurrent of anxiety, which could have been no more than wanting to protect a friend and even maybe his wife, or it could have meant something else. That he knew Bronwyn had told Tom she wanted no more to do with him or that she had caught him out two-timing her, that he had killed her, leaving her body in a place he knew well but where it would be difficult to find.

What the police did give the press, however, was a picture of Ian Gott and the information that they wanted to talk to him about Annie Laycock's murder. DCS Paynter had agreed with Clarke and was prepared to let him flush the man out. They explained how he had walked out of open prison when he had been moved there as part of the government initiative to free up cell space in the overcrowded prisons. The press loved this. The chances were that by tomorrow the local papers at least would have Gott on their front pages. The journalists ran out of the station, their mobiles glued to their ears.

Only Peter Redmayne remained. He advanced on Handford who sighed and continued to walk away. He needed to get back to his office to ring Brian Noble, find out what had happened with Douglas. But it wasn't necessary; Redmayne answered the question with one of his own.

'Can you tell me, John, why your brother has been brought into the station?'

Ali looked surprised; Paynter puzzled. Handford swung round, his mind whirling. He didn't know whether to shake him or to walk away. How on earth did the man know? Douglas wouldn't have said anything. Was it Noble or someone on his team? And what *did* he know? He was about to demand where he'd got the information when Douglas appeared on the stairs.

Redmayne marched towards him. 'Have you been arrested, Mr Handford? Did your brother know? Was he the one who arrested you? Can you tell me what this is about?' The questions were fired as though from a gun.

Handford rushed the journalist, pushing him to one side and pulled Douglas by his coat, dragging him out through the door, away from the reception area and the ogling eyes.

But Douglas was having none of it. Beside himself with rage, he turned on his brother. 'You bastard,' he yelled, no longer the quiet director of social services, but an animal caught in a trap. 'You told the police; you told the press.'

Handford pulled at his arm. 'You're wrong; I've said nothing. Come on, upstairs, up to my office.'

Douglas wrenched himself away. 'I'm going nowhere with you. Call yourself a brother? I tell you, John, if I go down you're coming with me – all the way.' He rammed open the door and ran back out of the station. Handford made to follow, but Paynter's voice brought him to a halt as it thundered through reception. 'My office now, Chief Inspector.'

Redmayne smiled; he had his story.

chapter fifteen

'What the hell was all that about?'

Handford rubbed his hands over his face as though he could wipe away all that had happened. 'He's my brother,' he said.

'I know he's your brother, John. He's the Director of Social Services. I didn't ask who he was; I asked what that fracas out there was about.'

Handford was shaking. If it had to come out at all, this wasn't the way he'd wanted it to happen. 'Can I sit down?' he said.

Paynter pointed to the chair by the desk and walked over to the filing cabinet. He opened the bottom drawer and pulled out a bottle of whisky. 'Want one?' he said.

Handford nodded his thanks. If ever he needed a drink it was now.

The superintendent poured out two generous measures and handed him one. 'Will he be all right?'

Handford took a sip. The drink was warm and burned his throat. 'I hope so, but I honestly don't know.' For the first time in a long time, he realised he cared and it hurt. He'd spent too many years thinking he hated Douglas, when in fact he didn't. It was what he'd done he hated, not who he was. It was illogical, he knew, but he couldn't help feeling that he bore some of the responsibility for what was happening now. Somewhere, deep in his subconscious, was the knowledge that Josie's suicide was as much his fault as it was his brother's. If he hadn't given him that alibi, Josie may well still be alive.

Paynter picked up the phone. 'I'll get uniform to keep an eye out for him.'

Handford made to protest.

'Don't worry. I'll be discreet – for now.' He issued instructions to the duty inspector and replaced the receiver. 'You should have told me what was going on, John.'

'I know.'

'You do realise it'll be all round the station tomorrow – probably in the press as well?'

Handford shook his head. 'Not from Peter Redmayne, at least not yet. He's no hack; he won't do anything until he's sure of his facts.'

'In that case you'd better tell me so that I'm sure of the facts. Everything mind,' he warned. He sat down in his chair, leaned back, glass in hand and closed his eyes as though he was about to be told a bedtime story.

If only.

So Handford related the events of that night, of Josie Renshaw, her alleged rape, her suicide and the DNA found on her clothing, which was a partial match with his own. Paynter listened without interruption. When Handford had finished, his boss opened his eyes, sat up straight, put down his glass and said, 'Poor girl.'

'Yes.'

He looked towards Handford. His face, rather than flushed with anger, was couched in sympathy. 'Don't blame yourself, John. You were seventeen. Your brother asked a favour; you gave it to him.'

'But I shouldn't have. I didn't even think about it. In fact, it wasn't until he refused to come to the funeral, even though the whole village had turned out, that I asked myself why he would need an alibi. When he didn't give me a satisfactory explanation I should have said something.'

'And what would you have said? My brother doesn't want to come to a funeral. I repeat: stop blaming yourself. Right now Douglas is a very worried man. He knows that in his position, working with children – even though I'm willing to bet he doesn't set eyes on a child from one day's end to the other – he'll be pilloried for having sex with an under-age girl. That's what it's like nowadays; it matters little that it was all those years ago, that he was young himself, and that she was – what's the current terminology? – up for it? But it's not your problem, it's his; you're not his keeper; not now. It was his choice not to give his DNA, not yours, so he's got to sort this out himself.'

'And if there's more to it?'

'Then there's more to it and we'll deal with it.' Handford was grateful for the 'we'.

'Go home; talk to your mother; it will be better coming from you now than from someone else later.'

Handford stood up and placed his glass on the desk, the whisky almost untouched. 'Thank you, sir,' he said, 'but I have a briefing.'

'Then take it and then go home. Sort this out, John, and sort it quickly. I don't want it hanging over you and the team any longer than it has to.'

As he walked away from Paynter's office towards the incident room he couldn't help wondering how Russell would have reacted. Probably have given him a bollocking, which would have stretched back to a seventeen-year-old lying for his brother, and then suspended him for bringing the service into disrepute by putting himself squarely in the same frame. Paynter's method might be fairer, but he had still come away feeling humiliated. Being so forgiving had probably made him feel worse. At least with Russell, he could have banged the door and stormed off. Now all he could do was let the words 'Damn Douglas' spin round in his head.

He groaned inwardly as he met Ali on the stairs, his expression filled with concern.

'Are you all right, John?'

The smile was weak. 'Yes thanks.'

'I didn't realise you had a brother. Why didn't you tell me?'

Handford couldn't explain, not at the moment and not to a man whose culture demanded that family loyalty was paramount. 'We don't see much of each other,' was all he said.

They walked on in an awkward silence, which Ali was the first to break it. 'I don't want to pry ...' he said hesitantly.

'Then don't, Khalid.' The words were spoken a little too roughly.

'No. But if you want to talk, you know where I am.'

Handford sighed heavily and closed his eyes momentarily. Much as he liked him, Ali was the last person he wanted to confide in. 'Thanks, but just leave it, please,' then brusquely, 'I'll see you in the incident room in ten minutes.'

For what seemed hours after Leon Jackson had left, Marek Kowalski lay on his bed, trembling. Never had he felt so ill or so afraid. It had been a mistake to leave the hospital, but it was one he couldn't undo. Now, instead of being safe, he was vulnerable. Leon could return any time, could send him out on a job and use the injuries he had inflicted to his advantage. Shackled, without passport or money, he had no choice but to do the bidding of Help International, knowing that one day it could go wrong and innocent people would die – people like Bronwyn and Tom Blakely.

He slipped in and out of sleep, none of it dreamless, all of it violent, so that each time he woke up he was drenched in his own sweat. Later, although he wasn't sure of the time except that it was dark outside the window, he was conscious of someone knocking on the door, quietly at first, then more urgently. His heart missed several beats before it resumed its rhythm to pulsate through his body so that the pain was almost unbearable. It had to be Leon Jackson back to scare him even more. Perhaps it would be better, saner, to offer no resistance, let the man do his worst and end this nightmare.

So deep was he in his own fear, it was a few moments before he realised that the knocking had been replaced by voices. Not Leon Jackson's, but lighter and softer – women's. He couldn't make out what they were saying, but he was fairly sure one of them was Winnie's.

The knocking came again, this time accompanied by a voice. 'Marek, are you there? It's Winnie. I know you're in there. If you don't open this door I'll have to assume you're unconscious or something and get the police.'

The last word alone was enough of an incentive and he struggled from the bed and into the hall, shouting, 'I'm coming.' He turned the lock and then slipped the chain.

Exuding the aroma of the stables, Winnie stood in front of him, a shopping bag in one hand and a bunch of flowers in the other. When she saw Marek her expression registered horror but not her words. She lifted the basket and said, 'Groceries. The flowers are from the horses – I don't do flowers.'

He forced a smile as he felt the tears gathering. Instinctively she placed what she was carrying on the floor and stepped towards him to wrap her arms round him. The strength of the embrace caught the edge of his pain, but it was its warmth that was too much to bear and without warning he crumpled onto her shoulder, the tears flowing. For a few moments, they remained immobile, him clinging to her, her shushing him and stroking his hair as though he were a child. When he was calmer she held him at arm's length, her blue eyes scrutinising his as though she was delving deep into his soul.

'This was no ordinary mugging, was it, Marek?'

He shook his head, but couldn't bring himself to look at her.

She bent forward to make contact with him. 'Tell me.'

He moved his eyes away. 'I can't,' he whispered.

'Why?' She placed a finger under his chin and lifted it. 'Because whoever did it will do it again if you do?'

It was scarcely a nod, but it gave her the answer. 'Are you in some trouble, Marek?'

Again he nodded, not daring to speak in case he told her everything.

'Big trouble?'

'Yes.'

She took him by the arm, guided him to the kitchen and pulled out a chair. 'Sit there,' she said. 'I'm going to make a drink and then you're going to tell me exactly what you're mixed up in. And make no mistake, Marek, I'm not leaving here until you do.'

Handford wasn't at all certain he believed his own words when he'd said the newspapers wouldn't print until they were sure of their facts. As far as he knew, Peter Redmayne was the only journalist there, but the incident was something of a blur and he couldn't be sure of that. The truth was, if there were others in the background or if they had somehow got hold of the story they'd probably write it anyway with enough fact to make sure they kept on the right side of libellous. He'd been in this job long enough to know that some of the more unscrupulous journalist never let the truth get in the way of a good story. And a senior police officer and the director of social services brawling in public was a good story.

The babble of voices as he neared the incident room could be heard in the corridor, but as he stepped over the threshold there was no doubt that the scene being well ground in the gossip mill was not that of a triple murder. When the talking stopped the silence beat in his ears. What did they call it? White noise? As far as he was concerned it was brighter than white, it was brilliant white. He let his eyes wander the room. Officers either appeared uncomfortable or surveyed him with open curiosity. Even Warrender shifted in his seat. Most of them, he suspected, felt like Paynter that such a public display from a senior officer did none of them any good. And in all conscience he had to agree with them. He wondered for a split second whether he should apologise to them, but rejected the idea. Instead he said, 'Annie Laycock's murder, how far on are we?'

Ali broke the tension. 'We have a match with Ian Gott's DNA and fingerprints. He's made no attempt to disguise the fact that he was there. They're everywhere, even in the bedroom and on the door of the wardrobe in which she kept her money. According to Billy Emmott she had quite a lot of savings – at least two thousand pounds, he thought – and we couldn't find any of it.'

'Could Emmott have taken it? He's not beyond a bit of thieving,' a DC at the back of the room asked.

'He could have, but I think it's unlikely. He was fond of the old lady and from what we've been told he would have been more likely to bring gifts than steal from her. He has his own code of morality, which includes not taking from your own. She might not have been blood related, but she still came into that category. And anyway, there were no fresh prints from Emmott in the house and lots from Gott. Forensically we know he was there; what we don't know is whether he killed her or whether it was down to someone else, though it's quite a coincidence if it is.'

'Is that all we have on Gott, his fingerprints and DNA?' Not much for three days' work.

'No, the press conference has brought in a few sightings. The best are from a stall-holder in the market who sold a suitcase and two charity shop volunteers who sold clothes to a man resembling Gott. In each case he pulled out a wad of notes to make payment. They're coming in to the station sometime tomorrow to make statements.'

Handford turned to Clarke. 'Anything yet on his where-abouts, Andy?'

'No, guv, not yet, although he'll probably take his time. As I said before, he likes playing games. He will surface though – one way or another.'

Handford gave his friend a long look and wondered how nervous he was of *one way or another*. When the proposal had been put forward, he had been against it. Gott had killed once, probably twice. What was to stop him from killing again? If he was more of a threat than they envisaged, he didn't relish the idea of having to inform Clarke's wife that they had done nothing to dissuade her husband from acting as a target. Silently, he prayed that they caught up with the man before they were forced into dealing with *the other way*. He shook the thought from his mind. 'Let's turn to Tom Blakely. Did Gott kill him as well? He was stabbed and we know a knife was used on Annie Laycock.'

'But to frighten not to stab,' Warrender said. 'The pathologist said cuts were probably made by a knife being waved around.'

'But it does mean he was carrying one.' Handford turned to the board on which were pinned the photographs of the three victims. Radiating from that of Tom Blakely were three arrows, each pointing to the identity of possible suspects: Gott, Patrick Blakely and the nameless group organising staged car accidents. Handford pointed to the latter. 'Do we have any idea who they are?'

'Not yet,' Clarke said. 'I'm trawling through the information on his PC, but there's such a lot of it and so far I haven't come across any names. There is some mention of immigrants and asylum-seekers being involved, but he doesn't explain how or in what way.'

Warrender, who was slumped in his seat, suddenly pulled himself straight. 'Help International,' he said. 'I'll bet my pension they're involved somehow. When I went to ask about Bronwyn's immigrant boyfriend, they were cagey, lobbed the Data Protection Act at me. So for whatever reason they didn't want me to find him or talk to him. And the only reason I can come up with is that they had something else to hide.'

Handford was unconvinced; they were a charity, they wouldn't want anyone trawling their data base, not even the police. That said, Warrender was too experienced a detective to assume a connection to a person or persons without direct evidence but this time he'd done so. It was time to give him free rein, see what he came up with. 'So what do you suggest?'

'Nothing drastic, boss, we take over where Mr Blakely left off. We investigate the staged car accidents to see if there's a link with his death and if that link leads straight to Neville and Jackson. Maybe he was getting too close to them and they decided to do something about it. There's a lot of money at stake in a scam like this.'

Handford agreed. 'It's worth a look; work on it with Clarke. In the meantime, I want a couple of you to check out Patrick Blakely's alibi for between the seventh and the tenth. He says he was at the wholesaler's on the seventh and then went on to the shops with the stock. On the eighth to the tenth he was at a camping exhibition at the NEC in Birmingham. I have the name of the hotel where he stayed and a list of names of those he was with or whom he met. Check how long he was at the wholesaler's on the seventh, what time he arrived at the various shops – did he have time to go up to the mine? Similarly, with the NEC. Account for every second he says he was there and every person he met or talked to. Take nothing on face value.'

The men nodded.

Handford moved position and pointed to the photograph of Bronwyn. 'Suspects? Her stepfather, David Younger; her former boyfriend, Peter Bolton, and the latest boyfriend we know little about and whose name we're not sure of, but who is older than her and is possibly foreign. Not a lot to go on, I have to say. Was she having an affair with Tom Blakely at the time of her death? Patrick thinks she was. James Amery was with Blakely and Bronwyn at the old mine when he went up there to challenge him about the will, but he was not prepared to acknowledge that the two were having an affair. We know she had a fling with him some years ago when he was investigating a burglary at the travel agency at which she worked and we know her stepfather put a stop to it by making an official complaint to the Chief Superintendent.' He turned to Ali. 'Any news on that?'

'Yes, there was a break-in at the travel agency, Blakely was the investigating officer and it was common knowledge that she was seeing him. Younger did make the complaint and Mr Blakely was reprimanded.'

'Younger also maintains that Mr Blakely slowed down an insurance claim of his as revenge for the complaint. I don't know how true that was. Have you found anything to substantiate it?'

Clarke shook his head. 'Not so far. If it was a straightforward job, then it wouldn't be important enough for Tom to want to hide on his own computer.'

'And the hard disc was stolen from the insurance offices, so unless there's something among the papers, it will be difficult to verify,' Handford mused. He turned to a couple of the detectives. 'Go back to Dart Insurance after the weekend and see if they've come across anything yet. Talk to those working closely with him, see if they have any idea whether he was being deliberately tardy.'

Warrender stood up and crossed over to the picture of Bronwyn's stepfather. He stared at it for a moment then said, 'If, as Younger claims, he almost went bankrupt because the insurance claim was delayed, then perhaps he's involved in whatever scam Neville and Jackson are involved in? He certainly knows them and he's not too keen that we know he knows them. And neither are they keen that we know either.

He might have killed Bronwyn, although I doubt it; he might even have killed Tom Blakely, although I doubt that too. He pretends to be a big man, but most of that is bluff and I don't think he'd have the guts to do the deed himself. But that's not to say he doesn't know, or at least suspect, who killed one or both of them. He says the delay in Dart Insurance paying out his claim nearly bankrupted him. I'd be surprised at that. Even if he had to replace all his computers, most firms would let him have new ones without waiting for the claim to be settled, unless of course he owes money. He certainly spends a lot of money; he has expensive tastes, or his wife has. His furniture didn't come from IKEA, nor did his television or his two cars, both are top of the range. I think we ought to take a look at his bank balances – private and business. Perhaps when he comes into the station tomorrow that's the direction we should go – hit him where it hurts.'

Winnie had hit Marek Kowalski where it hurt.

'So,' she said when they settled down with a cup of tea, 'are you going to tell me what trouble you're in that forced someone to put you in this state?'

He was still beyond speech, able only to shake his head.

'Is it drugs?' When there was no answer she said, 'Prostitutes?'

Nothing.

'Do you owe money?'

He could hear the frustration in her voice and shook his head. 'Please, Winnie, don't ask. I can't tell you.'

That wasn't good enough for her. 'Are you involved in something illegal?'

Ambushed by the memory of the children and their mother, Marek lifted his head and for the first time since her arrival made eye contact. 'They won't let me stop. I don't want to do it, but they won't let me go. They've taken my passport and my money so that I can't go anywhere.'

'Who has?'

His voice cracked as though he was starting to break into little pieces inside, pieces that could never be glued together again and look the same. 'One day they will kill someone and they will say it's that someone's fault, but I will know it's mine.'

'Marek, I have no idea what you are talking about. Who will kill someone?'

Marek was beside himself. 'I told Bronwyn who and she's dead. I tried to tell Mr Blakely who and he's dead. I tell you and you die.' Part of him wanted to be left alone so that he could keep his secret, as awful as it was.

But Winnie wasn't going to leave him alone. 'If you know who killed Bronwyn and Mr Blakely, you have to tell the police. I don't care what you're mixed up in. In fact, if you think I'm going to let you keep that kind of information to yourself, then you're sadly mistaken. I saw Mrs Blakely when her husband was missing; she came up to the stables looking for you. From what I gather when she told you her husband wasn't at the house you ran away. She was worried sick about him; she had no idea where he was; she would have liked to have known why you had gone to find him. But no, you weren't prepared to tell her, just as you're not prepared to tell me now. How do you think she feels now that he's dead – and not just dead, but murdered? How do you think she would feel if she knew that you could have helped her then, that you could tell her now who killed him and you won't because you're scared?' Angrily, she pushed back her chair and grabbed the mugs. 'I'll tell you something else, Marek. The pain you're feeling now will go away, your bruises will fade; hers will not.'

Marek stayed silent, the nerves of his stomach coiling and recoiling until he could stand it no more. He pushed himself up from the table and rushed into the bathroom where he retched. There was nothing on his stomach except the tea he had just drunk and each time he heaved pain shuddered through his body. Eventually he straightened up and regarded himself in the mirror. A man, white faced and covered in cuts and bruises, stared back at him. The skin round his right eye was deep purple and still swollen and a line of black stitches curled across his cheek. He sluiced himself with cold water then pulled the towel from the rail and buried his face in it. What had become of the son who had come to England for a better life? Of the immigrant who had met and loved Bronwyn? How had he turned into a person neither his family nor his lover wanted or envisaged? He replaced the towel and returned to the kitchen.

'I will tell you,' he said.

Winnie placed a glass of water on the table. 'Drink this,' she said and sat down and waited.

It was beginning that was hard, but once he had started, said the first words, he couldn't stop. He told her how he had met Bronwyn and how he wanted to buy her presents but couldn't afford to on his wages, and how later he had accepted Martin Neville and Leon Jackson's proposals so that he could give her what he thought she deserved. He told her about the staged car accidents and his part in them and how he knew that it was wrong and how ashamed he was. Then he told her about how Bronwyn had left him when he had told her where his money was coming from and how he had learned that Tom Blakely was investigating the accidents for the insurance company. 'I tried to tell him, but I couldn't find him. I looked him up in the telephone book; there was only one Blakely listed there and I waited outside his house but he never came. Then his wife said he was away. I don't know how, but Leon Jackson found out that I had been to Mr Blakely's house and he hit me and kicked me and said the next time he would kill me. I came home from hospital early so that I could go back to Poland, but he had been here and stolen my passport. Then he came again and took my money as well.' Finally he told her the names of those involved.

As he talked he sobbed, sometimes hanging his head, sometimes resting it on the table so that he couldn't see Winnie's eyes and read the disgust in them.

When he finished the silence lay cold in the room. Eventually Winnie spoke, but this time her voice had lost its hard edge. 'What are you going to do?'

He knew what the right answer was, what she was expecting him to say, but he couldn't.

She understood. 'I'll come with you to the police,' she said.

Exhausted, he nodded. There was no fight left in him.

'Tomorrow?' It was a question not a statement. It could have been an order, but the tone of her voice said she was aware it was his decision.

'Yes,' he whispered. 'Tomorrow.'

She stood up. 'I have to go,' she said. 'The horses will need bedding down.'

He raised his head. 'Please don't leave me. I can't stay here on my own.'

She smiled at him. 'I had no intention of leaving you,' she said. 'Get dressed and pack a few things. You can stay in the flat above the stables. It smells a bit of the horses, but at least you'll be safe.'

chapter sixteen

The wind that had started out as no more than a breeze earlier in the day had now developed into something more excitable and was driving the heavy rain on to the car as Handford took the journey home. The spray from the vehicles in front blotted out his view as the wipers rasped across the windscreen and in the glare of the street lamps, patterns of light shifted and danced as they splayed across the road and over the car, coating it in intervals of orange as he passed beneath them.

The tension in the muscles of his neck was beginning to form into a headache and he took one hand off the steering wheel to massage it in the hope of some relief. It was a vain hope. Nothing, neither massage nor analgesics, would alleviate the uncertainty of what he had to tell his mother, of how he was going to do it and, worse, of how she would take it. How did you tell a mother that her son had been arrested on suspicion of rape? How do you tell two daughters that their father had probably, although unwittingly, aided and abetted in suppressing information that might have led to a conviction and a young girl's peace of mind? He had given this kind of news to strangers and broken their lives in the process, but that was part of his job and although he didn't find it easy he could walk away. Not this time; this time it was *his* family, *his* mother and *his* daughters.

As always, the aroma of the evening meal played with his senses as he walked into the house. He had already spoiled one meal for them this week so he had made the decision to leave the bad news until after they had eaten. Nicola and Clare talked excitedly about some event that had happened or was about to happen in school – he wasn't sure which. His mother made suitable noises; he played with his food. As they were clearing away, his mother said, 'What's wrong, John? Is it the case you're working on? You can't tell me the details, I understand that, but if there's anything I can do to help.'

He wanted her to stop talking for one minute, to let him think, to say that it wasn't anything to do with the case; it was personal to him and her and the girls and it could destroy them. Trembling, he placed his arm round her shoulder and said, 'Leave those and come into the lounge, Mum, I have something to tell you.'

She looked up at him, her eyes fearful. 'Is it about the girls? I wondered why you insisted they get on with their homework when they have the whole weekend in front of them.'

He manoeuvred her into the room and waited until she sat down. 'No, it's not about the girls. It's about Douglas,' he said as he took the chair opposite.

'Douglas? I don't understand; is he ill?'

If ever he'd wanted to be called back into work it was now, but the telephone was mute. 'No, Mum, he's not ill.' And for the second time that day he explained as carefully as he could exactly what had happened.

He wasn't sure what reaction to expect from his mother. First she said, 'I don't believe you. Douglas is no rapist; even if he did have sex with that trollop, which I don't believe, she would have led him on,' and then, 'How could you let Douglas down like that?'

Exasperated, he said, 'He has been arrested on suspicion of rape. They don't do that without some evidence. He refused to give his DNA because he'd had sex with her; he told me that himself.'

'And you told them.'

'Yes.'

'But you gave him an alibi.'

'It was a lie, Mother, a lie Douglas asked me to tell. Now why would he do that unless he had something to hide?'

He'd had this argument with himself so many times since

Brain Noble had talked to him on Tuesday. Was it only four days ago? It seemed like months. Then he was missing Gill and his main concern at work was the whereabouts of Bronwyn Price's body. Now his brother was in the frame for rape, he was branded a liar and God only knew what his mother was thinking. He watched her as she held back the tears. She was – had always been – such a dignified woman, but a woman who cocooned herself in her family, understood their failings but would always, *always*, stand by them. Why else would she give up her friends and social life to look after him and the girls for so long? But by the very nature of his work, Handford was firmly connected to reality, no matter how painful, and he had to look at the picture as it was, not as he would like it to be. To her he was a Judas; to him he had done what any honest police officer would do – and that wouldn't change.

He attempted to limit the damage. 'It may come to nothing; they haven't kept him overnight and they haven't charged him with anything yet. And if the results on the other girls' clothing point to someone else then proving he raped her would be impossible and they'll probably forget about the under-age sex with Josie. After all, he was young and she was consenting.'

'And you, John, what will happen to you?'

'I don't know. Nothing probably, perhaps a reprimand for keeping quiet about the lie when I was first interviewed.'

'Will Douglas lose his job?'

'A lot will depend on the outcome, I suppose. If it comes out that he has been arrested, then yes, I suppose he could.'

'What do you mean "come out"?'

'In the press.'

'Is there any reason why it should?'

She was persistent, he'd give her that. But then she always had been. Being a full-time mother, didn't mean she was stupid; in fact, she had always been astute, too astute sometimes, for she was the best person he knew for catching them out in any wrongdoings when they were boys. They hadn't been able to get much past her and now he wasn't even going to try.

'Every reason, I'm afraid.' On a scale of one to ten, this conversation was nearing the top. In fact, it was proving far harder than facing Paynter. 'The press were there,' he said. 'At least one of them was – and he saw the whole scene between me and Douglas. He asked Douglas if he'd been arrested. The man was only guessing, but instead of keeping quiet, Douglas shouted out that I'd told the police and the press and that if he was going down, he would take me with him. I tried to stop him,' he added lamely.

'So you brawled in a police station, in front of everyone, including some journalists?'

He stood up and poured them both a drink: him a whisky, her a brandy. 'Yes.'

'And all you will get is a reprimand?'

'Probably.' She obviously thought he deserved more. But then she'd often complained about lenient sentences handed out to criminals.

He handed her the glass. As she took it she gave him the look she had used when he was a boy. 'Tell me truthfully, John, do you think Douglas raped Josie or the other three girls?'

For the first time, he lost his nerve. 'No, Mum,' he lied, 'I don't.'

Ian Gott lay back on his pillow and gazed at the television news with a mixture of interest and anger. It was obvious they'd taken his note seriously, otherwise why this? Well good, at least he'd got them on the run if not exactly frightened, but they'd have to try a lot harder than that old copper inviting the public to contact the police if they saw him. It was a game to them – hunt the criminal. But what really angered him was that they hadn't mentioned Tom Blakely – not a peep. They'd showed a picture of the old biddy who'd tried to stop him having her money. Why her? She'd been no more than a means to an end, a casualty of war because that was what it was between him and them. Collateral damage, they called it. He sniffed. A good phrase that; it ran off the tongue with ease and precision and described what her death was – unintended. Not that he lost any sleep over it; she only had herself to blame; if she'd handed over her money he would have left her alone. They were so fucking possessive, these wrinklies. Like the old man and his medals. What did he need with a box of old medals? It wasn't as if they'd been worth anything.

He scrutinised Andy Clarke's image. He was older than he remembered, his hair whiter, but then it was seven years since he'd last seen him. Seven years for it to go white; he'd seen men younger than him turn white overnight in prison. That's what people like Blakely and Clarke did to them. The detective's name and telephone number rolled across the bottom of the picture. He didn't need the name, but he wrote down the number on the back of his hand; it might be useful to lure him out when he was ready.

The camera zoomed in to a picture of him the detective was holding up. It was an old one, taken when he first went inside, and it wasn't flattering, but it was a close enough resemblance for him to be recognised. So that was how they meant to flush him out? He'd have to bloody move now, just when he'd got settled. His landlady was out at the moment, he'd seen her go, but all this would probably be repeated on the late-night news or in tomorrow's papers, front page probably, and sooner or later she would see it. He needed to leave before she realised and got in touch with the police. He didn't want them picking him up before he got to Clarke. He might have missed Blakely, but he was damn sure he was having his side-kick. He hadn't intended to stay here much longer anyway; it wouldn't do to get too settled. The problem was he hadn't had time to plan where to go next. It couldn't just be anywhere. He didn't fancy sleeping rough again, particularly in this weather. It was teeming down outside and the wind was getting up. Even the far side of the lake, warm and hidden as it was, was not to his liking and he'd got used to a bed and a McDonald's every day. He'd have to try further out, perhaps somewhere busier – a pub, maybe, where they took in overnighters. There it would be too noisy and too crowded for them to notice him.

He pulled his suitcase off the top of the wardrobe and packed his clothes into it, locked it and placed it by the side of the bed. Then he hunched himself into his coat and carefully and quietly slipped out of the B&B. He remembered he'd seen a pub in the town about ten miles away. It was noisy, lots of people standing outside smoking, and according to the poster in the window they took in lodgers. There was even a supermarket with a café across the road and a McDonald's ten minutes' walk away. As he'd come in on the bus he'd noticed an estate of warden-assisted houses, useful if he ran out of money, and he'd also found out where the prossies worked. It must have been fate that he'd caught that bus. He'd suss it out properly tonight; see if they had any rooms and move in tomorrow. He smiled as he waited in the shelter; he would make the most of tonight, some beer, some sex and a few laughs because tomorrow things would become serious. Tomorrow he would teach the police what was really meant by games.

Douglas Handford had driven miles without realising where he was or what he was doing. He'd rushed out of the police station and taken a taxi back to his office, hoping no one was there – at least no one who mattered; he couldn't bear any more questions. Those the detective had asked him were bad enough – they had brought back too many memories. But those flung at him by the journalist were the ones that frightened him. They were the ones that could bring him down.

When he arrived back at the Social Services headquarters, his car was still standing forlornly in his reserved space. The building was lit up, but except for the cleaners it was deserted. He had no idea what he was going to do, but whatever it was he needed things from his desk, things he kept away from Mary and now things he needed to keep away from the police. They hadn't said they were going to search his house or his office, but it was probably only a matter of time.

He took the steps up to the second floor two at a time. There was a light on. He pushed open the door.

'Hello, Mr Handford,' the cleaner said. 'I thought you'd gone. Do you want me to come back and finish off later?'

He forced a smile. 'If you don't mind, Mrs Bennett. I've got one or two things to do. I won't be long.'

She picked up her cleaning box and dragged the vacuum through the door. 'You know your trouble; you work too hard,' she said as she left. 'You ought to get home early, particularly on a Friday.'

She disappeared from his view. Swiftly he closed the door and pulled open the drawer of his filing cabinet from which he pulled a rectangular red box and some files. He pushed loose papers into his briefcase and locked it. Then, looking round, he walked out and into the car park.

He wasn't going home; in fact, the last place he wanted to be at the moment was home. He loved his wife and children very much, but he needed to sort out his head and decide what he was going to do and he couldn't do that with Mary chattering on and the kids fighting over the television controls. So he threw the box, the files and his briefcase into the back of the car, climbed in the front and drove.

It was nine o'clock when he reached the north shore in Scarborough. He loved the sea, always had. He loved the serene, glassy quality when the ripples lapped the beach, quiet and at peace. Conversely, he marvelled at its strength and beauty during a storm. Tonight it was rough and as the waves hit the wall they sprayed over onto the pavement. He drove down the hill and onto the road that leads from north to south. As he reached the headland, he stopped the car and watched. In its most ferocious moments the sea buffeted the vehicle, attempting to drag it back into its waters. If only he could capture some of its strength. He'd had it when he was younger, but not now – now he was tired, too tired to fight.

As he surveyed the scene, the headlights of a car came towards him. It stopped and a man got out. Huddled in his coat, the police officer knocked on the window and motioned that he should wind it down. Douglas froze; surely they couldn't have come after him so soon. They couldn't have, they knew nothing yet, not even the results of his DNA swab. But the choice was minimal and he did as he was asked.

The policeman leaned in, water dripping from the peak of his cap. 'Bad weather is forecast for tonight, sir,' he said, 'gale-force winds and high tides. We're closing this part of the promenade to traffic. It'll be dangerous here and you don't want to be pulled out to sea. So if you wouldn't mind moving your car.'

Douglas murmured his assent, closed the window then switched on the engine. Turning the car, he drove back the way he had come.

On his way in he had spied a pub a few miles out of town. He pulled into the car park. In spite of everything he was hungry and they might still be serving. They were and he ordered a plate of sandwiches and a lager. It was winter and it wasn't too busy even though it was Friday night, and he chose a table in the corner. A fire was burning in the grate of the ornate fireplace, a pile of logs at one side of it and a scuttle of coal at the other. It was comforting, more comforting than anything he had encountered today or probably would ever again. He wondered what John had told their mother, whether indeed he had told her anything. He probably had, given that their brawl in the police station had been witnessed by at least one journalist. He was ashamed of that; he rarely lost control. He hadn't since Josie Renshaw. At the time, he hadn't thought of it as rape. But that was what it was. He had never done it before and he hadn't done it since. Test all they liked, they wouldn't find his DNA on the undergarments of any of the other victims. But once was enough, even if it couldn't be proven. He'd gone to the church the next day – the church from which she'd thrown herself – tried to ask forgiveness, but hadn't known what words to use, so he'd come away and lived with it ever since. The funeral had been held in the same church – that was why he hadn't gone. But he couldn't explain, particularly to John. Saintly John, whose only sin was to lie for him.

A woman in a flowered apron came over to the table with his sandwiches and his drink. He smiled his thanks. 'Do you have rooms?' he asked as she was about to walk away.

'Yes, we have a couple. We don't usually open them up in winter, no real call for them, but it's a lousy night, so I don't mind making an exception. Forty pounds with breakfast be all right?'

He nodded, took out his wallet and gave her two twenty-pound notes.

'Just for one night, would it be?' He thought she sounded

hopeful that he might stay longer. It must be hard up here in winter.

'Yes, just for one night, maybe two.'

That would be enough for him to reject or accept the decision he had made on his way here. He owed it to his wife and his children to do the right thing.

On Saturday morning John Handford left home late. He wanted to make sure his mother and daughters were coping with the news. His mother assured him they were and said that she had decided to take the girls shopping. 'A bit of retail therapy will do them the world of good,' she said. 'Then I might go and see Douglas.'

Handford frowned. 'With the girls?' He wasn't sure he wanted that.

'That's up to them, John, don't you think? It's not as though they're children any more.'

So he'd set off, but not to work. He wanted to see if he could talk with Josie Renshaw's parents. He wasn't sure why. At first it had been because he wanted more information, now it was because he wanted to apologise, to salve his own conscience and that of Douglas if he couldn't do it himself. But first he wanted to see the grave. It was ironic, but thirty years on he found it easily, perhaps he'd never forgotten. The rain of last night had settled into a fine drizzle and the grass round it was slippery and he had to hold on to the other headstones to get close. He stood for a moment looking at the simple inscription, which told nothing of her life and even less about her death. Was that all that was left of her – thirteen words? Her final resting place was neglected, as though no one wanted to know her, but someone did, for someone had left flowers, still wrapped in their paper.

'Hello again.'

The voice behind him startled him. He turned.

'Oh, I'm sorry. I thought you were the man who came a few days ago. You're very similar from the back.' He pulled off his glove and held out his hand. 'I'm the vicar, by the way.'

Handford accepted his greeting. 'You say a man came a few days ago,' he said. 'Can you describe him?'

'He was very much like you, same build, same features. You could be twins. They always say everyone has a double, don't they?'

'Yes, they do,' Handford said thoughtfully. It had to have been Douglas; it couldn't have been anyone else.

The vicar had the policeman's eye, perhaps they too had to develop it to search out the sinners. Quizzically he scrutinised Handford. 'He said he used to know Josie. Did you know her?'

'I used to. Actually I'd like to meet up with her parents if that's possible, pay my respects. Do they still live in the village?'

The vicar hesitated. 'Well they do, at least Mrs Renshaw does. I'm afraid her husband died on Thursday. Found dead in bed apparently.' Before Handford could say anything, the vicar went on. 'Actually, I feel a bit guilty about that. I asked the man who was here earlier in the week to go and see them. He didn't seem too keen, but he might have done. We'd talked about the state of the grave and I secretly hoped he would persuade them to do something about it.' He let out a deep sigh. 'Ah well, we all do things we'd rather we hadn't done, don't we? The human psyche is very frail.' He turned to go. 'The funeral's on Monday if you're thinking of coming, ten o'clock.'

The clergyman was on the path when Handford caught up with him. He handed him his card. 'If the man who was here returns could you let me know? On my mobile preferably.'

The vicar read the words. 'A police officer? I hope the man in question is not in any trouble. He didn't seem the type to be of interest to the police – although I suppose you can never tell. '

Handford tried to smile reassuringly. 'No, nothing like that, sir; it's just that it would be good to meet up, since he must have known Josie, perhaps we knew each other.'

The vicar looked again at the card in his hand and then raised his eyes. 'You know, Chief Inspector, Josie died some thirty years ago. I gather from what I've been told that there was a good turn-out for her funeral. Since then her grave has become neglected and very few people have visited her until this week.

I appreciate you can't tell me, but I can't help wondering why now.'

For a moment they maintained eye contact, which for once Handford was the first to break. The vicar said, 'I'm sorry, I have to go, I have a wedding at eleven o'clock, though why anyone wants to get married in November beats me; it's hopeless for photographs, but probably easier to get a venue.' He turned and set off towards the church, then he waved Handford's card in the air. 'I'll let you know if your brother turns up.'

Handford smiled to himself; the man had searched out the sinners after all.

David Younger arrived at Central Police together with his solicitor, James Amery, at precisely ten o'clock. As requested, he was sober, not only in body, but also in his dress. Wearing a dark suit, striped shirt and plain tie, Younger was the epitome of an upstanding member of the public. 'Everything that will persuade a judge not to send him down for life,' Clarke whispered to Ali when he saw him. Although not quite everything. His slightly bulbous eyes were ringed with red and together with the heavy drinking of the past few days, the lack of the sleep and the worry, he was not as together as he wanted to appear.

A constable escorted them to the interview room where Ali introduced himself to James Amery. 'I didn't realize you were involved in criminal work sir,' he said.

'I'm not usually but Mr Younger is a friend as well as a client and I agreed to help. It is a problem?'

Ali shook his head.

'More to the point as far as I'm concerned,' Amery said, 'is why you felt it necessary to bring us in on a Saturday morning, Inspector?'

'This is a murder inquiry, we have to make the best use of the time – even it means working at the weekend.'

'And you think interviewing my client, who is, after all, a victim, in that he is the dead girl's stepfather, is the best use of your time?'

'You wouldn't be here if I didn't.'

Amery let out a well-rehearsed sigh. 'In that case, let's get on with it and then we can all go home.'

Clarke said, 'Can I get anyone a coffee?'

Irritated, Amery snapped, 'No, I'd prefer we got on.'

Unfazed, Clarke sat down. 'Just let me know if you change your mind.' He unwrapped the cassettes and placed them in the recorder and then proceeded to ask everyone to identify themselves. Finally he cautioned Younger, reminding him he was not under arrest and could leave at any time.

'Tell me about your business, Mr Younger,' Ali said when the preliminaries were out of the way. 'You're an estate agent, I believe.'

Younger ran a twitching hand over his shaved head. 'You know I am.'

'Is it doing well?'

Amery intervened. 'You don't have to answer that question, Mr Younger.'

Younger shrugged. 'I can't complain,' he said.

Ali looked through the interview transcript in front of him. 'But you did complain when you thought Mr Blakely was shuffling his feet over your insurance claim.'

'He was. It was legitimate. He did it to get back at me because I'd made a complaint to his bosses when he was having an affair with Bronwyn. His job was to investigate their burglary not screw one of the employees.'

Ali let it go; he didn't want to get embroiled in Younger's bitterness. 'When we questioned you at your house you said, and I quote, "thanks to Tom Blakely's go-slow and Bronwyn's disappearance, it's all I can do to keep the business going", and later, "he [meaning Blakely] didn't care that he almost bankrupted me". That was roughly four months ago. Are you telling me that now your business is doing well? Because it seems to me that it hasn't taken you long to recoup your losses, particularly as you also blamed Bronwyn's disappearance for keeping you away from the premises. You can't have spent too much time there during that period.'

Younger gave Ali a long look filled with resentment 'I have good staff.'

224

'You must have.'

Ali closed the file, an indication that Clarke should take over.

The detective constable steepled his fingers for a moment and then asked, 'What is your relationship with Help International?'

Younger sat back, crossed his legs and tried to look unconcerned. But to the trained eye, his face was more taut than usual, his lips tighter and the muscles twitching beneath his skin. 'Not that again. I don't have a relationship with Help International. I told you that was a junk call.'

'Yes, you did. Unfortunately, Martin Neville, one of the leaders of the charity, told us differently.'

Younger and Amery looked at each other and the solicitor whispered something in his client's ear who in his turn nodded.

'I think this is time for us to leave, David,' Amery said, placing the top on his pen and his writing pad in his briefcase. 'Mr Younger does not wish to answer any questions about Help International, Inspector, so I think there is no reason to keep him here.' He stood up.

Ali pushed back his chair. 'I can't stop you, but I must advise against him going. Help International is fast becoming a major part of our inquiry. It will be easier on everyone if he answers our questions.'

Slowly, Amery regained his seat. 'You think Martin and Leon are in some way involved in the death of Bronwyn Price?' There was a high level of incredulity in the solicitor's voice, although to Ali it seemed overdone, more like play acting than the real thing. 'That is ridiculous.'

'I didn't say they were involved, I don't know if they were involved, but somewhere there is a link between them, Mr Younger and his stepdaughter and I simply want to find out what it is. It's no more than one line of inquiry.'

Amery held on to his next question for a moment and when he spoke he articulated each word as though he were in court. 'Can you tell us how Help International has entered into your inquiry into the death of Mr Younger's stepdaughter?'

'No, sir, you know I can't.'

'In that case, can you tell us what their reaction was when you questioned them about my client here?'

'I think so. They said he rented out flats occasionally to a customer in need. It appeared that one of them had left without paying his rent. Apparently, and quite understandably, Mr Younger was very angry. What I can't understand, though, is why your client chose to lie about it – unless, of course, Martin Neville was lying, in which case I have to ask myself why they both chose to do so.'

Younger glanced at his solicitor who shrugged, as if to pass the decision to answer over to him. He sat forward, his arms resting on the table and gave himself a moment to formulate a reply – or was it to formulate a lie? – then he shifted in his chair, licked his lips and swallowed hard, no doubt hoping his reply was better than admitting he was part of whatever Martin and Jackson were involved in. 'All right, I'll tell you. I didn't want you to know that renting out the flats to Help International is a side line.' When neither of the detectives spoke, he said impatiently, 'It has tax implications.'

'You mean the money they pay you goes into a box under your bed and not through the business?'

Younger held Ali's gaze, his own full of hostility. 'Something like that.'

'How much have you earned from them?'

'Not much. They only come to me when they're desperate.' He let out a deep breath. 'It paid for the television and the music centre and once we used it to go on holiday to Florida.'

'But not for the rather expensive kitchen you have in your house?'

'No.'

'I'm sorry, Mr Younger,' Ali said, 'I'm not satisfied with your response. I have to tell you we have applied to a magistrate for a warrant to open up your bank accounts and credit card transactions. Business and personal. That warrant came through this morning.'

The colour drained from Younger's face. His solicitor was

226

apoplectic with anger. 'On what grounds, may I ask? And why wasn't I told?'

'I'm telling you now, Mr Amery,' Ali said quietly.

'Then I demand time with my client.'

'Of course.' Ali turned to Clarke and smiled. 'Perhaps now would be a good time for that coffee, Constable.'

chapter seventeen

Marek Kowalski had passed a good night. The flat above the stables while small was comfortable, with the addition of the familiar smell of the horses. He hadn't realised how much he had missed them. When they had arrived, he had gone to the stables and been greeted like an old friend. Winnie had insisted on bringing his breakfast up to him, although she said when he was better he could do his own chores.

'You can stay here as long as you want,' she offered. 'Give up your flat in town if you like, live here permanently and in return keep the place secure, be my security guard if you like. It will be good to have someone on the premises.'

He wished he could say yes immediately, but he wasn't sure what the meeting with the police would bring. Would he go to prison? What could he expect from Martin Neville and Leon Jackson when they found out what he had done? They had made it clear what would happen to him if he tried to contact anyone again. Now it was not the insurance investigator, it was the police – a much more frightening prospect. He hadn't had anything to do with the police since he'd been in England and those he'd seen on the streets had seemed nice enough, but he'd heard from some of the men in the pub that the English coppers treated you badly – beat you up to get information out of you. He wasn't sure how true it was, because they were laughing when they were talking about it, but he hadn't wanted to risk it. Now he was doing just that. He'd asked Winnie to stay with him and she'd said she would if they let her. He wasn't sure what that meant, perhaps if they wanted to beat him up they would send her away? He'd almost said he'd changed his mind, but Winnie was adamant that he had to go to them. 'If you don't,' she said, 'I will. I promise you that whatever they decide to do with you, it will look much better in court if they can say you cooperated.'

Like it or not, she'd bundled him in the four-by-four and driven him to the police station. Leon Jackson's car was parked outside his empty flat as they drove past. By now he would be aware that Marek had gone and if he'd talked to the neighbour, he might know where. After all it was the woman next door Winnie had been talking to the previous night. She wouldn't have been able to stop herself from telling Jackson Winnie had been at his flat and since Help International had found him the job at the stables, Jackson would know exactly where they had gone. That would put Winnie in danger as well as him and that wasn't fair. He had no choice but to tell the police everything.

For a while he sat nervously on the blue plastic seats in the reception area. Winnie told the woman on the desk that they knew something about the deaths of Bronwyn Price and Tom Blakely and needed to talk to someone and then they'd waited, Winnie sometimes clasping his hand to give him physical support. Finally, a detective who introduced himself as Chris Warrender came down to meet them. He was a pleasant-looking man with cropped ginger hair and freckles. He shook hands with them and led them through a door and into a small room.

'Let's go in here,' Warrender said. 'We'll be more comfortable.'

It was not what Marek had expected. In fact, he wasn't sure what he'd expected. Something more austere perhaps. Something like the interview rooms portrayed on television. But in this one the walls were a light shade of yellow and in the centre was a low table on which stood a vase of flowers. The chairs were blue and comfortable. To one side was a small kitchen and Warrender asked them if they would like a cup of tea. They said yes and while they were waiting he asked Marek if he needed an interpreter. Marek declined; he understood and could speak English quite well, he said, and if he was stuck then Winnie was here to help him. There didn't seem to be any reason why she shouldn't stay or at least she wasn't told to go. Warrender explained that he would record everything that was said, so that there could be no mistakes later on then he asked Marek how he had come by his injuries. It took a while, but with encouragement from Winnie he told the whole story. Anything the detective didn't understand or wanted clarification on he asked a question, but otherwise he remained quiet until Marek finished.

'Now, let me get this clear,' he said. 'You are saying that Martin Neville and Leon Jackson organise the staged car accidents, that some of the immigrants on their books help out as phantom witnesses or phantom passengers.'

'Yes.'

'And those people are either short of money or illegal?'

'Yes.'

'And which one were you?'

'I am legal, from Poland. I have permission.'

'So you needed money?'

'For presents for my girlfriend.'

'Bronwyn?'

'Yes, but she found out where the money had come from.'

'What did she do then?'

'She left me and then she died.'

Warrender leaned towards him. 'Do you know if she told any one what you were doing?'

'I think her father.'

'Mr Younger?'

'Yes.'

'And what did he do?'

'I think he told Mr Neville and Mr Jackson.'

'What makes you think that?'

'Because she went and then she was dead.'

'And you think Mr Neville and/or Mr Jackson killed her.'

By now the tears were flowing freely. Warrender put his hand on Marek's shoulder. 'Would you like a break?'

Marek nodded and laid his head on the back of the chair, his eyes closed. He was very pale and Warrender wished he didn't have to go on, but this was probably the break the investigating teams were looking for.

Once he was more composed, Warrender said, 'You're doing really well, Marek, but there are other questions I need to ask. How much money were you paid to drive these cars?'

'Five hundred pounds each time.'

'It's a lot of money.'

'Yes.'

'And where did the cars you drove come from?'

'I think Mr Neville went to the auctions or bought them out of the paper or over the internet. They never cost a lot of money.'

'Now, you told me that you pull in front of the victim's car, brake and then it hits you from behind. Were you never injured?'

'Sometimes, but not badly. The driver who is coming off the roundabout is not going too fast and Leon taught me to relax so that I am not shaken too much.'

'What happens to the car you are driving? The damage can't be too severe.'

'Most times the driver in the car behind does not want the police to come so they give their insurance details and we give ours. Then I take the car somewhere and crash it again to make the damage worse in case the other insurance company want to look at it. Then I take it to our garage.'

Warrender was fairly sure he knew the answer, but he asked anyway. 'Which insurance company do you name as yours?'

'It is Dart Insurance. I give them the name of Mr Graham Dart.'

This was getting better and better. With difficulty, Warrender suppressed a smile. It was always good when the cracks became enormous crevices. 'You say there are people who help with the insurance claims, the medical reports and the repairs to the vehicles?'

'Yes.'

'Do you know who these people are?'

Marek nodded.

'I've asked him that, but he's too frightened to say,' Winnie interjected. 'He believes that Bronwyn was killed because he told her, and Mr Blakely because he tried to tell him.'

'What do you mean, tried to tell him?'

'He went looking for him at his house. He met his wife and she said he was away. Then after Mr Blakely's body had been found, although Marek didn't know at the time it was his, she visited him in hospital to ask why he wanted to speak to her husband.'

Warrender turned to Marek. 'When exactly was this?'

He thought for a moment, all the days had slipped into one and he had difficulty separating them. 'Thursday, I think, in the afternoon.'

'You're sure that was the day? Think carefully, it might be important.'

Marek screwed up his eyes as though that helped him to consider his reply more clearly. His head was aching badly now and all he wanted was to go home to bed, but he had to answer this question; it was important. He had come out of hospital yesterday, the day after he had read in the paper of Mr Blakely's death, and had thought that his wife must have known he was dead when she was talking to him. 'Thursday afternoon; yes, I'm sure.'

The answer seemed to excite the detective, but Marek didn't know why.

Warrender's brow furrowed. 'I don't understand how she found you. It doesn't sound as though she knew who you were.'

'That was my fault,' Winnie said. 'She had no idea who he was, but she said she smelled horses on him. That's the trouble with working in a stable all day: you tend to take the scent home with you. Anyway, she had visited at least one other centre before she came to us. When she described him, I said it sounded like Marek and she saw his photograph on the wall. We keep them up there for the children, so that they know who works for us and who doesn't. You can't be too careful nowadays. It was his day off and she said she'd come back the next day, but by then he was in hospital.'

'You told her that?'

'Yes, I didn't want her trailing all the way up to Moor Top when it wasn't necessary. Perhaps I shouldn't have done.'

Warrender placated her. 'No, you did the right thing.' He turned to Marek. 'Can you tell me the last staged accident you were involved in?'

Again he thought hard. 'That was Tuesday. It was a silver Ford Mondeo.' This was too much. He didn't want these memories. He could feel the tears run down his cheeks again and drip onto his hand. 'There was a woman and three children in the car. They were so frightened, screaming and crying and the woman was shouting that there were no brake lights on my car. And I had to show her that there were.' He was becoming hysterical by now, but still the policeman listened. 'I could have killed them; it would have been my fault and not hers. I tried to get out of it but Leon wouldn't let me. He beat me up and told me he would kill me if I told anyone else. He came to the hospital and showed me a picture of Bronwyn in the paper. He said he hadn't killed her, but he must have done because he told me not to contact the police. Then he went to my flat and took my passport and my money so that I couldn't go back to Poland. He said he would let me know when the next job was and that I wouldn't even have to pretend to be hurt this time.'

Warrender leaned over to him. 'You've done really well, Marek. Now I want you to give me the name of one of the men helping Mr Neville and Mr Jackson. You can tell me the rest when you feel ready. But one name would really help.' He passed him a sheet of paper. 'Write it down if you'd rather.'

Marek took the paper from him. He wasn't sure how to spell it, but it was close enough. He handed it back to the detective who pulled himself from the chair and said, 'I'm going to take this to my boss. I want you to stay here while I do that because I'm sure he will want to ask you some questions. In the meantime, I will ask our doctor to take a look at you and make you more comfortable. And if he says you are not well enough to answer any more questions, we'll leave them until later.'

When Handford returned from the churchyard his in-tray was full and if it wasn't to swamp him, he needed to make some inroads into it. He settled down to the paperwork. That was one of the drawbacks of his rank – the paperwork, a lot of it form-filling and governmental or local authority surveys, which seemed to them were more central to the job than the job itself. He pushed those to one side. They could wait.

The most important of the others was an interim report from Ali on the complaint made by Ian Gott. Handford was impressed. Ali had been thorough, more thorough than the original investigation, but he had come up with the same answer. Gott was guilty and nothing had been found to suggest the man had been set up. Handford closed the folder, as far as he was concerned Clarke was in the clear, although he doubted he was in Gott's mind. The man had to be found.

So far there had been no more useful sightings. Those that had come in were from a couple who had seen him in McDonald's and from the usual cranks who had seen him anywhere and everywhere. A detective had been sent to check out the McDonald's angle, but the information was not good. He had been reading a paper and had suddenly banged his fist on the table, which was why the couple noticed him. According to one of the managers, he'd been in once or twice over the past few days, but the problem was the employees didn't work regular shifts and no one could be sure exactly when or if they had seen him.

There was also a note saying Tom's car had been found in the playground of one of the schools closed during reorganisation. It had been torched and the assumption was that joyriders had stolen it, driven it and then destroyed it to wipe out any forensic evidence. Handford wasn't too sure. That was too neat an explanation. He rang the duty inspector to ask for it to be brought in for examination. 'I doubt you'll find anything, sir.'

He was not in the mood for argument. 'Just do it,' he growled.

The detectives given the task of checking out Patrick Blakely's alibi had drawn a blank so far. He had been where he said he was on the Tuesday and the timings suggested he couldn't have killed his brother and taken his body up to the mine. Nor would he have had time to meet him up there and kill him in situ. They were still checking with the organisers of the camping exhibition and with the names they had on the list. It was made more complicated by not having a time of death, but contrary to popular opinion he knew how difficult that was to determine. What was the pathologist's comment on this the first time he had asked for time of death? Find out when the victim was last seen and when he was found dead and the time of death is somewhere in between. Not very helpful, but all they had to go on. They knew the latter and Clarke was working on the former. He had no doubt they would get there.

There was also little on the staged car accident angle. He had spoken to the DCI in the fraud squad who knew from Clarke that it was occurring, but so far had no information on who was involved. Handford said he didn't want to muscle in on his investigation, but it seemed possible it was linked with theirs and would he mind if they either took it over or ran parallel. 'Be my guest,' the DCI said. 'Just let me know what you come up with.'

Handford sat back in his chair and stretched. Four days in and they had a lot of information, most of it not verifiable and none of it as yet leading anywhere. But that was police work. Carry on digging until something broke, and sooner or later, fingers crossed, it would. They had three murders, all linked somehow, all they needed was the right bit of information on one and it could well break the rest. He wondered how Ali and Clarke were getting on with David Younger and James Amery. Was it coincidence that he was the solicitor to just about everyone in these investigations, even though he didn't do criminal work? Handford didn't believe in coincidence and he made a note to check Amery out. He'd never come across him before, but someone must have.

He was about to start again when Warrender burst in.

'Don't you ever knock, Warrender?' he said angrily.

'Sorry, guv, but you really are going to want to know about this.'

'Now that you've had time to discuss your situation with your solicitor I need to ask you some more questions, Mr Younger,'

Ali said when they were settled. 'However, if you decide to leave, I will arrest you on suspicion of tax evasion and when you have been processed, I will continue my questioning. I'm sure you would prefer to cooperate now rather than sit here for twenty-four hours or longer. Cells are very boring and not very comfortable.'

Younger glanced at his solicitor who agreed they were prepared to continue.

'In that case, let's start with your business. You said that when Mr Blakely slowed down your claim, it almost bankrupted you. Does that mean you had little money in reserve?'

'Yes.'

'Why? Estate agents haven't done too badly over the past few years, surely you made reasonable profits.'

Younger made no reply.

'Then tell me how you organised the money that went into the business. What about tax, VAT, council tax, that sort of thing?'

'I have separate accounts, one into which the money from the clients is put and from there moneys needed for leasing the shop, paying the staff and myself plus everything else you have mentioned are transferred into another one and the rest into the business account. Everything has always been paid, ask my accountant.'

'So what is left is profit?'

'Yes.'

'And where does that go?'

'At the end of every financial year some of it stays in the business account as a safeguard ...'

'A safeguard against what?'

'The market going down. Property is volatile; it's the indicator as to how the economy is doing. I tell you, when it slides it does so with incredible speed, just as it looks set to do now. Take my word for it, by July next year property will be stagnant, nothing will be moving. Any estate agent worth his salt would make sure his business is safeguarded.'

'And the rest?'

'The rest is put into a high-interest savings account.'

'In the name of the business or in your name?'

'Mine.'

'Now, bearing in mind that very soon we will get all your statements from your bank and we will have our experts go through them with a fine tooth comb and will therefore be able to judge just how well the business is doing and how much money you have, can you tell me why you thought you were likely to go bankrupt and why you found it necessary to salt away the money for renting out flats to clients of Help International?'

Younger pondered for several moments. 'My wife had nothing when I met her. She was trying to bring up Bronwyn on three lousily paid jobs. She wanted a nice house with nice things and I gave them to her. Eventually she wanted more than I could afford. It was my fault, I should have told her but I didn't and she assumed I had more than I actually had. It can disappear as quickly as it's made, you know. When Help International asked me to rent out flats to some of their clients, I agreed.'

'Where do you keep the money from the flats?'

'More or less where I told you, except it's not under the bed. It's in a safe in the loft.' Pressure was beginning to take its toll and Ali was not sure Younger was telling the truth. It was all so slick.

'And how do they pay you, presumably not by cheque?'

'No cash. They get the rent from the clients and they pay me.'

'That means the clients are not on benefit, otherwise their rent would be paid direct to you from the council.'

Younger became flustered. 'I suppose so.'

Ali sat back and looked at Clarke who shook his head. Then Ali stood up and walked behind Younger's chair. It was time to become the invisible interrogator, to wrong foot Younger so that he didn't know whether to remain where he was or turn round. There was nothing more off-putting than having a question directed to your back. You cannot see the eyes of the interviewer so it's like he was wearing dark glasses. 'I'm sorry, Mr Younger,' Ali said, 'I don't believe you. Either you are running a scam or Help International is and you are benefiting from it.'

Younger remained where he was and Ali couldn't see his expression, but Clarke could. 'You appear worried, Mr Younger,' he said. 'Perhaps you would like to tell me why. Perhaps the inspector is too close to the truth.'

Younger opened and closed his mouth like a fish gasping for breath. There was nothing he could say. He sat hunched over the table, his gaze directed onto its surface. Nor was there anything he could do to relieve the agony; cigarettes were banned and he had drunk his coffee. He picked up the polystyrene mug and began to shred it. Then he looked up but as it appeared he was about to speak, there came a knock on the door.

'What?' Ali called, furious at being interrupted.

Handford's head appeared around the door. 'I need a word,' he said. 'I have a name you might be interested in.'

Christine Blakely felt as though she was in a goldfish bowl. The press had swarmed round the house once Tom's name had been released and as much as the police tried to move them on, there was little they could do when they weren't actually on her property. 'Give her some privacy', 'leave her alone to grieve' seemed alien concepts to some of them. Tom had been a police officer; his body had been found near to that of a woman who had been missing for several weeks and that was all they were interested in. They surmised and assumed and the headlines read, MURDERED EX-COP IN LOVE TRIANGLE? The question mark put it just on the side of the law because they weren't actually saying he was. But people wouldn't read it as that. People would believe he had killed Bronwyn because she had ended it; people believed what they wanted to believe, the more salacious the story the better.

Connie Burns had tried to talk to her about it, but Christine hadn't been a police officer's wife for thirty years not to know what the job of the family liaison officer was. It was to keep her in touch with the investigation and to get as much out of her as possible – mainly the latter. Every now and again Connie's mobile would ring and she would go out of the room, to come back and ask yet another question. They seemed to be particularly interested in her movements during the time Tom must have been killed. What more could she tell them? Her diary said it all. Apparently Patrick's alibi was so far proving accurate and why wouldn't it? She hated Patrick, hated what he had put them through, but she knew he wasn't Tom's killer. Why would he be? As far as Patrick was concerned he was to have complete managerial control, so why would he put that in jeopardy by killing him when it would pass to her and he would lose it?

Now it appeared they had found Tom's car, burned out in some school playground. Had he gone to work in it the morning he disappeared? 'Yes,' she had said. 'What else would he use?'

The inquest was to be held on Monday, but she knew it would be opened and closed and if she was lucky the coroner would give his permission for his burial. He had wanted to be cremated, to burn in hell, he used to say, rather than eaten by maggots. He'd always had a fear of maggots. Well, for once he'd have to overcome his fear. He was a murder victim; his body had to be available when it came to trial in case the defence wanted another post mortem. She couldn't understand why they should. What more could they want to know? He'd been stabbed eight times and then hit with something like a golf club. They didn't need any more than that. Poor Tom, even his final resting place had been blocked by the law. She wondered whether Bronwyn Price's had been.

She pulled herself off the settee and turned on the television. There was nothing on she wanted to watch, but her sister had gone out and Connie was in the kitchen making yet another pot of tea. She was drowning in the stuff. She didn't think she'd ever drink another drop once this was over. And that mobile, that bloody mobile, with a tune she knew but couldn't name. It had rung earlier. John Handford – except Connie referred to him by his rank. He was coming over again; he had some questions to ask her. She knew what they were and she didn't want to answer them. She didn't want to answer questions ever again. He needed answers. She needed answers. The answers to why: why did he have to leave her like that? Why had he done it again and why had he lied to her? But most of all, why did he want that woman more than he wanted his wife? She didn't blame her; the sin was his; it had always been.

It was ten minutes later when Connie Burns heard the front door close and the car engine start up. She had no idea where Christine Blakely was going, but the DCI would be furious if she lost her yet again. Grabbing her coat and her car keys, she rushed outside to see the car disappear onto the main road and speed away to the roundabout. If Christine got beyond the roundabout Connie would lose her. It was damp and her car didn't like sitting outside; it preferred a warm dry garage, so that when she turned the key all she got was a rasping sound. Angrily she banged on the steering wheel. The bloody woman. She knew she was grief-stricken, but that didn't mean she'd to keep running away. With a deep sigh, she climbed out of the car and let herself back in the house. Thumbing in the DCI's number, she waited for his answer. All she got was his voice mail and she left a message.

Detective Inspector Ali returned to the interview room accompanied by Detective Chief Inspector Handford.

'I hope you don't mind, but I need to ask you some questions, Mr Younger.'

Amery stepped in: 'Is this really necessary, Chief Inspector? Mr Younger and I came here in good faith and all you have done is question him about his finances. What can they possibly have to do with the death of his stepdaughter – or Mr Blakely, for that matter?'

'Quite a lot, I think you'll find, sir.' Handford sat down and nodded to Clarke to turn on the recorder again, but this time he asked for the video recorder as well. When they were ready Clarke went through the preliminaries, this time adding Handford's name to the list, and reminded Younger that he was still under caution.

'Staged car accidents, Mr Younger, what do you know about them?' Handford asked.

Younger floundered. 'Nothing,' he said. 'I've never heard of them.'

'Oh, I think you're mistaken there, Mr Younger. We have a witness who has told us you are very much involved, as are Martin Neville and Leon Jackson – the men you say you get money from for renting out your flats to some of their clients. Now I don't believe that any more than Inspector Ali does, so I would like you to tell us the truth. What exactly is your part in it?'

He turned to Amery, his eyes pleading.

'I am advising my client to say nothing,' the solicitor said.

'I'll bet you are,' Handford said.

'I object to your manner, Chief Inspector,' Amery announced, looking up at the camera. 'When you have released Mr Younger, as you will have to, I shall make an official complaint against you.'

Handford let the comment pass; he'd heard it too many times. Ask a question or make a statement someone doesn't like and the first thing they think of is making a complaint. 'As you wish, but in the meantime I ask your client once again what his part in the staged car accident fraud is?'

Pressure was beginning to take its toll and Younger's voice had risen a few decibels. 'I don't have a part in it,' Younger screamed at him. 'I don't know what you're talking about.'

'Right, so let's come at it from another angle. Do you know Marek Kowalski?'

'Never heard of him.'

'In that case, let me refresh your memory. He was your step-daughter's boyfriend for quite a long time.'

'I haven't seen my stepdaughter since she left home. How would I know who her boyfriends were?'

Ali interrupted. 'You knew about some of them. When we came to your home and asked about the affairs she had had, of which you said there had been many, you told us about a Peter Bolton with whom she split. You actually spoke with him. You also knew she had been going out with a foreigner – Marek Kowalski.'

'Now according to our witness, she split up with Kowalski because he was involved in the staged car accidents,' Handford said.

'Then question him and leave me alone. I've told you I know nothing about staged car accidents.'

'Except, of course, after he had told her she was furious with him, let him know in no uncertain terms that what he was doing was immoral and illegal and that the presents he had bought her had been bought with dirty money. They fought and during the fight he told her that you, Mr Younger, were also involved and it was her mother's fault because she demanded more than you could afford. Your savings were diminishing, you were dipping into the business finances and you needed money. Not money from renting out the occasional flat, but real money. What did you do, Mr Younger? Drive the car that caused the accident? No, that, among others, was Marek Kowalski's job. Perhaps you were a phantom witness or passenger? Unlikely, people who do that are ten a penny. Now you're not a doctor or a solicitor or a garage mechanic, you're an estate agent, so why would they need you? It seems to me that the only thing you could offer them were addresses – addresses to where the correspondence could be sent regarding the fraudulent claims.'

James Amery banged on the table. 'I'm sorry, Mr Handford, but I must insist that this stops now. This is nothing short of harassment. Mr Younger has said more than once that he is not mixed up in any deception involving car accidents and you have no right to continue this line of questioning. Apart from anything else, it has nothing to do with Bronwyn's death.'

'It has everything to do with Bronwyn's death, Mr Amery. After she had thrown Kowalski out of her flat, she went straight to Mr Younger. We know that from our door-to-door inquiries when she went missing. We also know that she was very angry, both when she arrived and when she left. We don't know what she said to you, but we do know what she told Annie Laycock, because the old lady told your wife. Half an hour ago I sent DC Warrender round to ask Lynne about it. Apparently she thought Annie had been killed because you had sent someone to warn her off and it had got out of hand.'

Younger shook his head vigorously. 'No. No, I'm not having that. I wouldn't have hurt a hair on Annie Laycock's head. She was lovely lady.'

Handford would like to have let him sweat for longer, but that would have wasted time. 'You've no need to worry, Mr Younger, Annie's murder was a burglary gone wrong, that much we do know. We have put your wife's mind at rest on that, told her you weren't involved. As for Bronwyn's murder, well that's another story.'

Younger pushed himself from his chair; if he could have landed a blow on Handford he would have done. Ali and Clarke made a move to stop him and Amery grabbed his arm. 'I know you're angry, David, but I advise you sit down and say nothing,' he said quietly.

'But I didn't kill Bronwyn; you know I didn't.'

'So answer no more questions. Now, Chief Inspector, Mr Younger is still not under arrest, so unless there's something else, I intend for us to leave here.'

'Yes, there is one more thing.' He nodded to Ali who stood up, placed a hand on David Younger's shoulder. 'David Younger, I am arresting you on suspicion of fraud. You do not have to say anything. But it may harm your defence if you do not mention when questioned something which you later rely on in court. Anything you do say may be given in evidence. And now, Mr Younger, I think we'll search your house and your business premises. After which we'll release you while we check out the details and make further inquiries.'

Amery stood up and put his pad in his briefcase. 'I want it noting that this is preposterous, Chief Inspector. You are arresting him on the flimsiest of evidence from a man who obviously has a grudge to bear because Mr Younger's stepdaughter refused to see him again. In the meantime, David, unless you want me with you while they carry out the search, there's nothing much I can do. Let me know when you're released and I will come over and we can talk.'

Clarke took the tapes out of the cassette player and began to write on the cover. He passed one to Handford who passed it over to the solicitor. 'Actually, Mr Amery, I would like you to stay for a moment,' he said. 'I have one or two questions to put to you.'

'There are no questions you could ask that I would be prepared to answer.' He walked towards the door.

'In that case, sir, I shall be obliged to arrest you too. You see, when Mr Kowalski came into the station this morning, he was very loathe to give us any names of the "experts", shall we say, who are also involved in the fraud. We didn't push him but finally he agreed to write down just one for us. It was your name, Mr Amery. So, yes, I do think you have some questions to answer.'

chapter eighteen

At last the case was coming together. Handford told DCS Paynter at his midday meeting.

'You've done a good job, John; don't let this business with your brother ruin it,' the chief superintendent said.

They were sitting away from the desk on the chairs reserved for visitors. The briefings Paynter held were less formal than those of DCI Russell, when it was the senior officer at one side of the desk and the junior at the other. It might have led to a more efficient meeting, but not always to a particularly comfortable one.

'I went to the graveyard this morning to see Josie's grave,' Handford said. 'There were some flowers there. From what the vicar told me it must have been Douglas who left them. Why would he have done that if he hadn't raped her?'

Paynter's expression was neutral. 'I realise it looks bad,' he said evenly, 'but I'm telling you what you would tell relatives: don't get involved. Leave it to Brian Noble. He knows what he's doing.'

'I know, sir, but—'

'John, that wasn't a suggestion, it was an order.'

Handford didn't like it, but he knew Paynter was right and raised his hands in submission.

'If it makes you feel any better, I've had a word with DCI Noble and he has promised to keep you informed through me. It's the best I can do.'

'Thank you, sir, I'm grateful.'

'Well, let's leave it at that.' The superintendent turned his

245

thoughts to the case. 'I assume you're bringing Martin Neville and Leon Jackson in.'

'Yes, I've sent a team out to find them. Jackson was last seen outside Kowalski's flat – at least, his car was. I'm concerned he will go up to the stables, so I sent a car with Winnie and Marek and told them to check the whole area.'

'Have you spoken with Graham Dart yet?'

'Not yet, no.'

'Then when you do so, question him about his sexuality. Let him know we know. Find out who else knows about his special interests and who might use it against him. It seems to me we have a tight little team here – everyone seems to be linked with everyone else – and those we know about joined Neville and Jackson either because they needed the money or maybe because they had something to hide, like a secret life. That burglary was convenient to say the least, probably set up by the two at Help International and they could only have done it with Dart's help. He's mixed up in it and most likely with a leading role. '

Handford nodded his agreement; he had been thinking on the same lines himself.

Paynter moved on. 'What about Younger and James Amery?'

'I had to let Amery go. I don't have enough on him yet to arrest him, let alone charge him, but I've told him to keep himself available. I'll put some surveillance on him, but I don't have the money to do that for too long.' It irked that money was always the bottom line, particularly as Amery's name was the only one Marek had been prepared to give them, but surveillance was a budgetary nightmare and he didn't want finances adding to those already stacking up. 'Younger's still with us. We're searching his home and his business premises, but unless he gives us something more, I'll have to release him pending further inquiries.'

'Do you think he killed Bronwyn?'

'I think he's mixed up in it, but I doubt he actually did the deed, although I think he knows who did. According to Warrender, after Marek left Bronwyn, she went to see Younger and challenged him, said she knew exactly what he was doing. I suspect he told Neville or Jackson or both and they decided to get rid of her.'

'But why leave her body at the mine? It seems an odd place.'

'To implicate Tom Blakely. Blakely was on their backs, probably getting close, so why not solve two problems at once? They would know about the memorial and if they didn't Younger probably would, and Amery definitely did. Tom had been having an affair with Bronwyn, which Amery also knew about, so it would look as though she'd finished it and in a fit of temper he killed her. I don't think for a minute that's what happened, to him women were like buses, when one passed by, another one came along soon. But they wouldn't necessarily know that. Tom was a charismatic man and he knew it. Women fell in love with him by the dozen and he used them until he got tired of them when he dropped them often without telling them. He didn't care who he hurt and he must have hurt a good few in his time.'

'Including his wife?'

'Certainly, including his wife. In fact … ' A thought struck him, a thought he would rather not have had, but some aspects of Christine Blakely's alibi and her cool efficiency had been niggling at him for a day or two. He'd put them to the back of his mind, thinking that it was because she'd lived with a police officer for so long that she'd picked up some of his characteristics – he knew Gill had. But now …

'In fact what?'

'I'm not sure. It's just that there are a few discrepancies between her actual movements and what her diary tells us.'

'Such as?'

'Such as on the day Tom disappeared, she wasn't where it says she was. She should have been at the charity shop in the morning and she arrived late, a couple of hours late, in fact. The volunteer working there says she remembers it clearly because she had a dental appointment and didn't want to have to cancel it or close the shop. Tuesday's a busy day, apparently. Christine said there'd been a crisis at home, something to do with Patrick. That's possible – she's been having real problems with him – except it was the day he was at the warehouse and driving round to his other shops with stock. If he didn't have time to kill Tom, then he certainly didn't have time to visit her. As much as anything else, it would have been well out of his way. According to Patrick he saw him with Bronwyn when he went up to the mine after the will was read. Amery was there as well, although he insists there was nothing going on between them. That's not what Patrick thinks, and that's not what he told Christine, yet when I asked her if she knew of Bronwyn, she said she hadn't heard of her except through the media.

'My other misgiving is that Kowalski had gone to Tom's house to tell him what he knew about the staged car accidents. When Christine asked him what he wanted, he ran off. So she trawled the equestrian centres until she found him. Apparently she could smell the horses on him and assumed he worked either at some stables or on a farm. What's more worrying is that she visited him in hospital the day we told her we had found Tom's body, yet she never mentioned that to us, she said she'd been shopping.'

'You think she killed Tom?' Paynter asked.

'I hope not, but I think it's possible. She wouldn't be the first wife to rid herself of an erring husband in a fit of rage. Bronwyn might have been the last straw.'

Paynter raised his eyebrows interrogatively. 'A fit of rage? Surely you don't think that?'

'No I don't and that's my problem. The pathologist said he died where he was found, so whoever killed him went up there with a knife intending to do just that. And let's face it, stabbing is a woman's crime.'

'Not necessarily; it could have been kids or teenagers, knives are a status symbol to them. He could have disturbed them.'

'Possibly, but we've had no report of teenage gangs in the area and I doubt many young people go up to the mines. To be honest, I would have expected more damage to the body from kids – kicking that kind of thing.'

'What about the blow to the head?'

'One, possibly two, but not several kicks. The pathologist

believes it may have come from something like a golf club, he suggested a nine iron.'

Paynter smiled. 'Always the joker that man.' Then more seriously: 'Does Christine play golf?'

'I don't know, but Tom did. In fact, he always carried a set in the boot of his car, even when he was in the police. We've found his car, burned out, but I'll bet they're still there.'

Paynter's expression showed concern. 'You do realise, don't you, John, that if it is her and she went up there with a knife in her pocket then she intended to kill him. That would make this murder and not manslaughter.'

'Yes, I do and I wish I didn't.' He scrutinised his hands for a moment. 'Look, sir, can we keep this between the two of us, at least until we know more?'

'I think we'd better. I also think it would be sensible for you not to go to see her alone.' He walked over to his desk and picked up a few files only to let them drop. 'I swear this paperwork breeds.'

Handford stood up. 'I'll leave you to it. Connie Burns will be at the house; she can sit in with me.'

'I'm not sure that's a good idea, experienced though she is. No, I feel like getting my hands dirty and this will keep. I'll come with you to question Christine Blakely.'

Winnie and Marek arrived back at the stables with a police escort. There was no sign of Jackson's car, so if he had been there, he'd gone. The officers scoured the buildings and the fields until they were satisfied he wasn't hiding somewhere and then left.

Marek was exhausted. It was partly the result of the beating, but Winnie knew that going to the police had taken a lot out of him as well so she'd shipped him off to bed. She'd been quite proud of him; it hadn't been easy for him, but he'd told them everything, and thank God they hadn't arrested him for his part in the staged accidents. But that didn't mean they wouldn't. DC Warrender had been honest with them. He'd said he would do all he could to keep him out of court, but in the end it was up to his boss and the CPS.

The staff at the stables had struggled on until lunch-time without her and she'd told them to take a break until the first lesson at two o'clock. She would prepare the horses herself. She hadn't told them where she'd been or why, nor had she explained the presence of the police. Perhaps she would one day, but not yet. The last thing she wanted was any of them gossiping about Marek. For the moment they thought he'd been mugged and that was how she preferred it to stay.

The air inside the stables was heavy with the familiar smell of the hay and horse dung and as she went in the horses pricked up their ears and put their heads out of the stalls. Mister whinnied. He was a big horse, sixteen hands, but as placid as they come. He looked at her with those big brown eyes and she knew she'd do what he wanted and take him out for a canter in the field before she prepared the others. She let herself into the stall, pushing him to one side as she did so. When she swung the saddle over him he shifted and pranced and she slapped at his rump and pulled lovingly at his ears then fastened the girth and put on the bridle. Finally she led him into the yard and stood looking round for a moment before she mounted him.

His hooves clattered on the concrete as they rode on. As they neared the gate, Leon Jackson stood in her way, a smirk on his face. He must have given the police the slip earlier or he'd only just arrived, though she couldn't see his car. Her heart missed a few beats and she swallowed hard, but whatever was in his mind he couldn't do much to her while she was on Mister.

The horse must have sensed there was something wrong, for he reared up, whinnying as he did so, and it took all her strength to stay on his back. 'You idiot,' she yelled at Jackson. 'What the hell do you think you're doing frightening the horse like that?'

Towering above him she had him at a distinct disadvantage for he had to look up at her. 'Marek Kowalski, where is he?'

She held on tightly to the reins. 'None of your business.'

'I think you'll find that it is.'

'And I think you'll find that it isn't.' Mister snorted and attempted to wheel away. Winnie turned him, stroking his neck to soothe him, but he was not to be appeased. He lifted his hooves and pawed the ground.

Jackson took a step backwards. 'Just tell Marek to get out here.'

'You want to hold the horse while I do?'

'I'm warning you.' Jackson threatened, making no attempt to come closer.

But the threat didn't seem that frightening when he couldn't take his eyes of the horse. She tapped at Mister with her heels urging him on. Jackson backed off even further. As they neared the gate, she lifted her whip in case he made an attempt to pull her off. If he did, she wasn't sure she could control the horse and hit out at him and if she was unseated, Mister would run off into the fields and she would lose the advantage, not to mention break a leg or dislocate a shoulder. In the end she needn't have worried. The horse was just too big for Jackson and he was plainly scared of it.

'Get that bloody horse away from me,' he yelled, backing away still further.

She continued forward at a slow pace. As they reached the gate Jackson leaped for safety then turned and ran, slipping and sliding on the rough path. Seemingly from nowhere, the two policemen appeared. 'Mr Jackson?' she heard one of them say. The wind blew away most of the words but she was sure she caught 'arrest' and 'caution'.

She leaned over and slapped Mister on his neck. 'Walk on,' she said.

The message from Gott to Clarke came through at a quarter to two. According to the officer who took the call it was from a Mr Michael who'd been walking his dog and had seen Gott near the lake in the National Trust grounds of East Riddlesden Hall. Clarke wasn't sure how that was possible, given that the Hall was closed for the winter, but he unhooked his jacket from the back of his chair and grabbed the first detective he saw. 'You're with me,' he said. On his way out, he popped his head round Ali's door. 'Gott's been in touch,' he said.

'Personally?'

'He called himself Mr Michael. Out walking his dog, apparently.'

'So how do you know it was Gott?'

'Mr Michael – Michael was his father's name. He died while Gott was in prison, cancer I think, so I imagine he hasn't forgiven me for that either. This is his way of letting me know where he is or sending me on a wild goose chase. I told you he was good at playing games.'

'I'm sorry, Andy, but I'm not happy about this. He could be hidden anywhere in those grounds. If he jumps you, you'll not stand a chance.'

'He won't jump me. That will defeat his object, which is to make me suffer, particularly if he missed the chance to kill Tom. He wants to enjoy this and I'm going to make sure he doesn't.'

'Then take back-up.'

'Of course, I'll need a car to bring him back in. I'm not putting him in mine.' He gave Ali a huge grin. 'Don't worry, guv, I'm not stupid. I want to enjoy my retirement when it comes.'

Christine Blakely wasn't at home when they arrived at the house and Connie Burns had no idea where she'd gone except in the direction of the roundabout. 'She rushed off shortly after I'd told her you were coming to ask her more questions. It seemed to upset her. I'm sorry, sir, but she was in her car and at the bottom of the road before I could catch her up.'

'That means she could have gone in any direction,' Handford said.

'Yes, up to the Dales if she wanted.' Paynter was plainly angry. 'She's done this before, Burns; you should have kept a better eye on her.'

That wasn't fair; Christine wasn't a prisoner and Connie was FLO not a warder; her job was to be there but not keep Christine in her sight every minute of every day. She might be a possible suspect, all family members are in a murder inquiry, but she was also the wife of a murdered man and they hadn't to forget that. 'Did she say anything or give any indication of where she might have gone?' Handford asked.

She shook her head in mute apology. 'Not really, sir. She's ad a bad day today. I mean you've only got to see the head-nes to know how she's feeling. She's been harassed by the ress, particularly the nationals since they've decided it's a good tory, but because they weren't on her property, there's little I an do except ask them to respect her privacy. Not that they've iken any notice. I've tried to talk to her, but at the moment he seems to treat me as the enemy. And I suppose she's right ecause we didn't believe her when she said he was missing nd we didn't believe her when she said he wasn't with another /oman. She talks a lot about wanting to sit with him. When I xplained why it wouldn't be a good idea, she said something bout us not being able to stop her sitting with his spirit. I'm ot sure what she meant by that.'

'I think I do,' Handford said, 'and I think I know where she night have gone.'

Trust Ian Gott to expect me to drive out to Riddlesden on Saturday afternoon,' Clarke grumbled to Lawrenson, the etective he had grabbed hold of on his way out of the inci-ent room. The roads were a nightmare at this time of day, vith traffic bumper to bumper most of the way, even on the elief road. What should have been a half-hour journey took lmost an hour and if Gott was there at all, Clarke was sure he vouldn't have waited.

The large wrought-iron gates were closed and Clarke was bliged to park the car on the roadside, the police vehicle draw-ng up behind him. As far as he could see, the grounds were leserted. He rang the bell and waited. No one came.

Gott came out of the gloom on the other side of the lake. You'll have to climb over,' he yelled. 'That's if you can, old nan,' and he laughed.

'Try the wall in the next-door garden,' Lawrenson suggested. You should be able to manage that.'

Clarke glared at him, but it was a reasonable suggestion. The vall was lower and manageable. 'You wait here; I'll call if I eed you, but if it seems I'm not going to then come in.'

The young detective made to argue, but Clarke said, 'I want

him talking and he's not going to if you're there.' He pulle
himself up the wall and swung his legs over, allowing himsel
to drop to the other side. The ground there was soggy and a
he landed water rose above his shoes.

'Not bad, old man.' Gott had moved and the sound cam
from the side of him. So he was playing that game – attemptin
to confuse and unnerve.

Clarke sidestepped through the reeds and round the bank o
the lake. The scene was surreal: the seventeenth-century hous
the lake, the swans and the ducks and a man waiting to ki
him. A heron suddenly rose up flapping its wings and flew to
nest high in the bare branches of one of the trees. He'd neve
realised they were so big and so beautiful. If he hadn't been i
such an extreme situation he would have stopped to watch i
As it was, the beating of its wings matched the beating of hi
heart and he waited for it to slow down before he said, 'I expec
you're seven years older as well. It was seven years, wasn't it?

'You know bloody well it was.' The voice was behind hir
now, louder and more menacing than he remembered. Clark
hadn't heard him move, so prison hadn't affected his craftines
in fact it had probably improved it. 'My father died while I wa
in that prison,' Gott said. 'I couldn't even go to his funera
Cancer he had, ate away at his insides.'

'I'm sorry for your father, but you can hardly blame me fo
that.'

'I can blame you for me not being at his funeral.'

'It was you who broke into Mr Widdop's house, you wh
stole his possession, you who beat him up.'

'It was you what got me sent down.' The voice was neare
now.

'It was the jury who found you guilty, the judge who sen
tenced you. I only did the spade work.'

'It was you who framed me.'

'I didn't frame you; neither did Tom Blakely, and you kno
it.'

Without warning, Gott grabbed Clarke round the neck, hi
face so close he could feel his breath. The stink of bad teet
and beer made him want to retch. Gott was strong, he'd giv

im that; he'd obviously worked-out while he was in prison. Clarke tried to pull away but the grip was relentless. Inside he was a mass of quivering coils, a mixture of fear and adrenalin; his mind told him he could get out of this; his body told him otherwise. He was as Gott had said an old man and no match for him. Better not to struggle, better to persuade Gott to think he'd surrendered.

'Giving in, are you, old man? I'd rather you didn't. Tom lakely didn't. He struggled and ran and struggled and ran.'

Early though it was, the day was turning into evening and the sun that had attempted to penetrate the clouds had yielded to the inevitable. The first few drops of rain were falling, big, heavy. Soon they would have a downpour.

'You didn't kill Tom Blakely. You're too much of a coward; you prefer to kill defenceless old ladies.'

Gott pulled tighter on Clarke's neck. 'There was nothing defenceless about that old crone. She fought like an alley cat.'

'But she still died; you still killed her. You're going down for that if nothing else.' He lifted his hands to clutch at the sleeve of Gott's coat, to try to release the tension, but it was hopeless.

'I'm going down for nothing.'

'Well not for Tom Blakely's murder, that's for sure,' Clarke gasped.

'He deserved it.' Gott was faltering. 'Same as you will.' It was then that Clarke felt the knife against his neck. Perhaps he was wrong about who killed Tom.

'Using the same method, are you?'

'Straight through the jugular – just what I did to Blakely.'

Clarke breathed a sigh of relief to be followed immediately by the feeling he was about to be sick. Gott hadn't killed Tom; he didn't know how it had been done. Not that that mattered to Gott. If nothing else he was arrogant and currently had the advantage. He lived by no code whatsoever, except perhaps 'look after number one'. Not that he'd done too well with that in the past. But at this moment he wanted blood, literally in Clarke's case, and he was going to get it. Where the hell was Lawrenson? Was he actually going to wait for Clarke to call or was he going to use some common sense?

The rain was coming down in torrents now and Gott pulled them both under the trees. If he made it all the way, Lawrenson would take an age to find them. A long low branch sliced against Clarke's cheek and bounced back, catching him on the thigh. If he could grab it he could use it to pull on and in that way he might stand a chance of turning this round. Releasing the hand clinging to Gott's sleeve, he felt behind him. As he made contact, he pulled and slipped, taking Gott with him. Arms flailing, the two men slithered over the grass and into the lake. The ducks and the swans retreated, flapping their wings and complaining loudly, incensed at being disturbed.

The bottom of the lake was thick silt, the water shallow and very cold. Clarke coughed and spluttered as he backstroked himself into a standing position. Gott seemed to be swimming in the surface as he plunged his hands downwards. 'Lost something, Gott?'

Clarke bent over, his arms waving gorilla-like in front of him and as he struggled towards his enemy, his feet dragged as though he was wading through treacle in the sediment and the sludge. 'It's gone, Gott,' he gasped.

Gott flung water at him in attempt to discourage him. It was cold and it was filthy, but not enough of a deterrent. As he continued to battle forward, Clarke yelled for Lawrenson. Where was the man? Having a smoke in the police car no doubt. Gott became more frantic, hitting at the water.

'I wouldn't bother, Gott, you're only burying it deeper.'

'Fuck you, Clarke.'

By now Clarke was close, close enough to jump him. He sprang as though he was attached by glue, his body not quite reaching, but he landed near enough to grab him with his hands. 'Not such an old man now, am I?'

Gott struggled and splashed. 'You bastard,' he spat.

'At last you've got it, you piece of excrement.' Without turning his head he yelled, 'Lawrenson!'

'I'm here behind you, try to keep hold of him.'

The younger detective pulled off his shoes.

'For God's sake, man, I'm trying to hang on to this bastard and you're going for a paddle.'

'Sorry, Andy, but they're new. If I ruin them my wife will kill me.'

'And if you take your socks off and roll up your trousers, *I'll* kill you.'

Gott struggled and flailed as he attempted to turn over and to scrabble out of the lake, but Clarke held on tight. 'Lawrenson!'

Gingerly, the detective stepped into the water and snatched at Gott's thrashing arms, finally getting purchase, then pulled him out of the water as though he were a baby. Two uniformed officers grabbed him and hauled him through the reeds.

'Wait,' Andy Clarke shouted as he followed them. 'Before you throw him over that wall I want to arrest him for the murder of Annie Laycock.' He turned to Gott and between coughs and wheezes he said, 'Ian Gott, I'm arresting you for the murder of Annie Laycock. You do not have to say anything. But it may harm your defence if you do not mention when questioned something which you later rely on in court. Anything you do say may be given in evidence.' Then he seized the lapels of his coat. 'But not,' he said, 'for the murder of Tom Blakely. I don't know who killed him but I do know it wasn't you because you haven't got the balls.'

chapter nineteen

John Handford found Christine Blakely exactly where he expected to – up at the crime scene. Not that it appeared ever to have been a crime scene. Except for a small piece of police tape attached to a stake and flapping in the wind, no one would ever have known one body, let alone two, had been lying there.

The village too was deserted. No children playing out or huddled in groups chatting. Parents making sure they collected them from school, from the bus stop and from their music, dancing or swimming lessons and once home refused to let them out to play anywhere but the garden. The fields and the hillsides were out of bounds as were late-night clubs and parties. That's what murder did to a community. No one trusted anyone. They held meetings to which the senior detectives were invited. They asked questions. What were the police doing? Why had no one been arrested yet? Even why had they let this happen, as though they could keep an eye on everyone twenty-four hours a day, seven days a week. And eventually, as the meeting wore on and tempers became frayed, the questions and the comments became more aggressive. Why couldn't they get off their fat arses and do something?

The press picked up on the anger and blamed the police for non-activity. The fact that all leave had been cancelled and overtime stepped up, that the detectives involved would not see their own families for days if not weeks meant nothing to them. The police were fair game.

As he and Paynter looked at Christine, Handford wondered who she was blaming. Them or someone else? She was crouched more or less where Tom had been lying – almost on top, as if she knew the spot exactly. She was not making a sound, neither crying nor moaning, just sitting playing with the grass he had been lying on and staring into space. Could she have killed him or could they be so wrong? She seemed to have shrunk; grief did that to people, but so did acute anxiety, shame and fear. Which one was she feeling? Perhaps all of them.

Handford approached her. 'Come on, Christine, let's get you home. It's beginning to rain. I'll drive you and Mr Paynter will take your car.' She made no attempt to argue but allowed him to lead her away from the scene and down the hill. She didn't look back.

It was a short drive back and once there Handford suggested she go to bed. She refused – she didn't want to go to bed. Connie had said he wanted to ask her some questions and she wanted to get them over with. They went into the lounge where the fire had been switched on and the curtains drawn. It was welcoming and homely, not at all the kind of room in which to ask the questions he had to ask.

'Christine,' he said, 'we have found ...'

She sat straight-backed, her fingers pulling at the flock on the chair, the only sign that she was anxious. 'What you really want to know is whether I killed my husband or not.' Her voice was small and tight, as though it was hiding in its own dark corner, but the look she gave him was jaded.

Handford threw a glance a Paynter. 'Did you?'

She nodded.

'Do you want to tell us why?'

She walked over to the curtains and opened them. The rain had stopped and it was dark but not so dark that it obliterated the sky, which was clear blue and cloudless. Against it, the bare branches of the tree were set in silhouette. 'We often used to look out of this window when the sun went down,' she said. 'I think it was one of our favourite views. Somehow it seemed to protect Tom from the wickedness he saw each day.' She closed the curtains again, shutting out the picture and the memories. 'Now it's just another tree and another sky.'

When she was seated, Handford knelt in front of her.

259

'Christine, if you are admitting to killing Tom then I'm sorry I will have to caution you, otherwise everything you say will be inadmissible. Are you sure about this?'

She nodded. 'I know the law as well as you do. And before you ask, I don't want a solicitor, at least not yet. Who would I use? James Amery was Tom's solicitor for a while but he only changed to him when he thought the man was up to no good. When I have a solicitor I want one I can trust. So for the moment, recite your caution.'

Handford hated what he was about to do. He began the caution once, stopped, cleared his throat and started again. This suddenly seemed too close to home. Sometime soon Noble or one of his team would reel off those same words to Douglas.

Paynter, sensing his discomfort, interjected: 'I'll do this, Chief Inspector.'

Gratefully Handford stood up and moved away, his feelings ambiguous, relieved and at the same time sad. Relieved that it would soon be all over but sad it had to end like this.

The superintendent delivered the caution and then said, 'Do you want to tell us what happened?'

She thought for a moment. 'Bronwyn Price happened and with her I lost everything: my dignity, my hopes and my marriage. You were right, all of you, he *was* screwing a woman, although in one way I was also right when I said he wasn't, because by then she was missing. I'd never seen him so lost. It must have been the first time he'd really loved one of the women he had affairs with. Before that it had been more to do with what was in his trousers, rather than what was in his heart. It took me a long time to realise what was happening – I was aware there was someone but not that it was serious.'

'How did you find out?'

She smiled a sad smile that reached her eyes. 'I don't know what Tom was like at work, but he was not very tidy at home. He put things down and could never seem to find them. The week before he heard about Ian Gott, he left his mobile phone at home. It wasn't the first time and we had an arrangement that if I found it I would keep hold of it until he rang me on it. That day it rang but it wasn't him, it was a woman. She asked for him, didn't seem to mind that she was talking to his wife. I knew immediately that something was different. Except to those close to him he never gave out his mobile number, only ever his work number. In that way if he didn't want to talk to someone he could pretend he was busy or driving or that someone was in the room. It was a ploy and it worked.'

'What did you do?'

'I asked if I could help or pass on a message. She said, "Just tell him Bronwyn called."'

Handford lowered his eyes. David Younger had said his stepdaughter was a bitch. Perhaps he wasn't that far wrong after all. 'Did you challenge Tom with it?'

'No, I'd had enough of challenges. I waited until he rang me and told him he'd had a call from Bronwyn. He was quiet for a moment and said she was someone who was helping him with an investigation he was on. She may well have been, but I knew by his voice that that was only half the story. He was screwing her as well. Then when Patrick told me he'd seen Tom up at the mine with her and how they were acting like young lovers, I was sure. I knew Patrick was only being nasty, trying to get his own back on his brother, but he said I ought to have had enough of the humiliation and do something about him and he was right. I thought about it, decided divorce was too slow and too acrimonious and anyway he might well have begged my forgiveness again and persuaded me to change my mind. Husbands who betray their wives through sex are no different from those who beat their wives. They're found out, promise they won't do it again and plead for forgiveness – until the next time when the whole cycle starts over again. Anyway, I don't know what happened to me, whether it was a mental aberration or what, but for the first time ever I wanted him dead. I tried so hard to quell the feeling but when he was told Ian Gott had escaped it seemed the perfect opportunity to rid myself of him and lay the blame at someone else's door.'

'So what did you do?'

'He'd said he was going up to the mine. He seemed to have an affinity with those dead miners, probably mining was in his genes. The idea of a memorial might also have salved his conscience for fighting against his father and his brother during the strike – for in spite of what Patrick thought and said, he did feel the most awful guilt. For some perverted reason the old mine seemed the obvious place for him to die, among the remains of those he loved the most, so I took one of the kitchen knives – they say women kill with knives, don't they? – and I followed him up there. His car was there, close to the entrance. When he saw me he looked surprised and pleased at the same time and made to put his arm round me. It was only a little thing, but it hurt so much. He'd been up here with her, probably made love to her on the very spot, and he tried to put his arm round *me*. Perhaps if he hadn't done that I would have changed my mind, but we hadn't made love since she came on the scene – a peck on the cheek morning and evening and that was all. I was so angry with him and before I could stop myself I pulled the knife out of my pocket and stabbed him five or six times then once in the back as he fell.'

'And then?'

'He wasn't dead; he tried to crawl away from me so I looked for something to hit him with. There was nothing I could see until I remembered his golf clubs. I opened the boot of his car and pulled one of them out of the bag, went back and hit him with it.' She pointed to her right temple. 'There.'

'Did you see Bronwyn's body?'

'No.'

'Go on.'

'I think I panicked. I wiped the blood and my fingerprints off the club and threw it in the boot and drove away. I wasn't sure what to do with the car it until I saw the boarded-up school so I took it into the playground and left it there. I didn't burn it, I just left it. No one noticed or if they did, they made no attempt to stop me or to report it. I caught a bus, picked up my own car and went into the charity shop. I told Janet that I was sorry I was so late but there'd been a crisis at home. The next I heard was from the police that Tom's car had been found burned out where I had left it. I assume joyriders or children had destroyed it. Either way, they'd done me a favour because they'd destroyed any evidence of me in the process.'

'After you'd killed him you went through the process of reporting him missing?' Paynter said.

'Yes, I know in the cold light of day it might seem heartless but I needed to make it appear I was worried. It would have looked odd had I not reported him missing and anyway I wanted him found. It might not seem like it but I loved my husband, Mr Paynter; I couldn't bear the thought of him lying up there, his body slowly decomposing or being eaten by foxes and crawling with maggots; he had a real fear of maggots, you know. It never occurred to me that the police wouldn't take me seriously.'

'And Marek Kowalski?'

'He had come to find Tom and I didn't know why. Everything that happened had to have an explanation so that I could stick to my story or change it if necessary. I wanted Ian Gott to be prime suspect. Marek Kowalski could have altered that.'

Handford wasn't sure what they had here, a crime of passion or a cold-blooded murder – probably a bit of both. Tom Blakely had had so many affairs, had hurt his wife beyond measure, until finally he had broken her. His colleagues laughed at him, some of them probably secretly envied him. So perhaps they were all a little bit to blame for the outcome.

'What now?' she asked.

Handford was sure she knew. 'I'll send the file to the CPS for a decision, but I imagine they will decide to charge you with Tom's murder.'

'And until then?'

'You can stay here with Connie.'

'You're not frightened I'll try to take my own life?'

'Will you?'

'No. It's the inquest on Monday and the coroner will probably release his body. I'll need to organise his funeral. I owe him that at least.'

Handford doubted she owed him anything, but he understood. 'If you'll excuse me, I'll put Connie in the picture.' As he walked out of the room and down the hall he thanked God that he had never, and promised he never would, put Gill through what Tom Blakely had put his wife through. And at this moment he knew he wanted nothing more than her home safe and sound and in his arms.

The interviews with Martin Neville and Leon Jackson were not going well. When asked if they wanted a solicitor, both had asked for James Amery. He was the last person Handford wanted to represent them. If he was part of the staged car accident fraud it would be unethical, not to mention stupid, to allow him near these two men and he asked for authorisation to refuse their request. In the event it wasn't needed, for when the custody officer had rung Amery when they had first asked for him, he was told by the secretary that he wasn't in his office and she didn't know when he would be back. 'Confidentially,' she'd said, 'he came back after representing Mr Younger, said he was taking a holiday and to transfer his files to the other solicitors in the practice.'

'Did he say where he was going?'

'No, but he said if his wife rang, I was to say he'd been called away and would ring her as soon as he could. So wherever he is he isn't with his wife.'

Handford told Warrender to put out an all-points bulletin on Amery, sea, airports and Eurostar. Apart from that there was little he could do. The man had given them the slip and Neville and Jackson would have to make do with a duty solicitor.

The two men were interviewed simultaneously and while Jackson refused to answer any questions, Martin Neville insisted he knew nothing about staged car accidents, fraud or even Marek Kowalski. If they ever got him to court, presumably that would be his defence. It was up to the police to prove his guilt, not to him to prove his innocence. When the details of Marek Kowalski's statement were given to him, he showed a flicker of anxiety but no more than that. The solicitor finally said that if the police had evidence of fraud then they should charge him, if not they should let him go. Handford said he was going nowhere except back to his cell; the twenty-four hours were not yet up.

Handford was about to go back to his office when the custody sergeant told him there was a call for him. Graham Dart was in the station. He called Ali out of the interview with Jackson.

'Graham Dart's here. I want you to interview him. If Marek Kowalski is to be believed he is mixed up in the fraud somehow; I want you to find out how. In the meantime, I'll give Jackson a change of face and join Warrender.'

When Handford walked in to interview room two, Leon Jackson was leaning back in his chair, arrogance written all over him. 'Sit up properly, Mr Jackson. You are in serious trouble here and it's about time you realised it.'

'What's he been saying?'

'Who?'

'Neville.'

'It doesn't matter what Mr Neville has been saying. I'm interested in what you have to say, which I gather isn't very much.'

Jackson smirked.

'You had a lot to say when you beat up Marek Kowalski, though, didn't you?'

'No comment.' Handford always thought the phrase 'no comment' was as damning to the person being questioned as a lie.

'Are you telling me you didn't beat him up and put him in hospital?'

'No comment.'

'Well, Mr Jackson, that's not what he says.'

'Then he's a liar.'

At last words that meant something. There was always a question that thugs like Leon Jackson had to answer.

'His injuries say he isn't.'

'He was mugged.'

'Yes, by you.'

'That's what he says?'

'Yes. And he's prepared to go to court and say it again. And sadly you won't have Mr Amery to defend you. He's gone, you know; you have been told I suppose. Do you know why he's gone?'

Jackson's tongue flicked over his lips. 'Nothing to do with me if he wants to go away.'

'The trouble is, Leon, I think it is. Because he's as mixed up as you are in the staged car accident scam – what do you call it, slamming?'

'Don't know what you're talking about.'

'Well, let me give you an example. A silver Ford Mondeo registration BN06HOR leaves the day nursery with a mother and three children in it, one a very young baby. You follow them. The baby is hungry, screaming for food, and the mother is desperate to get him home. It's raining but not too much, but there are stretches of water from the earlier downpour lying on the road. She reaches the roundabout on the relief road. A Mercedes driven by Marek Kowalski approaches and he puts his hand out of the window to straighten his wing mirror – a clear signal to let you know his brake lights are disabled and he is ready. Seeing the roundabout is clear, the mother pulls out; Marek cuts her up then slams on his breaks. Since there are no lights she isn't aware of what he has done and crashes into him. The children are screaming, she is upset and Marek enables the lights so that when she shouts at him that he has no brake lights he is able to show her she is wrong. Are you with me so far?'

The tension in the air had thickened and Jackson was sweating.

'A group of people who had been talking at the side of the road run over, while a grey Fiat Punto pulls to a halt, the driver gets out, ostensibly to help, and almost unseen the passengers in his car transfer to the Mercedes. Kowalski gets five hundred pounds, the witnesses blame the driver of the Mondeo, the passengers claim for whiplash and other injuries, which have been verified by a doctor working for you, Mr Amery does all legal work, David Younger gives addresses of vacant properties to which the various insurance companies can send their cheques, a garage reports that the Mercedes is a write-off or they repair it and inflate their bill and the final claim runs in to tens of thousands. Forgive me, but I'm not absolutely sure what Graham Dart's part is in this, but Inspector Ali is currently questioning him and will no doubt find out.'

'Quite a fairy story, Chief Inspector,' Matthew Cavendish, the duty solicitor said. 'Do you have one iota of proof of this?'

'Oh yes. I have Marek Kowalski's statement to which he is prepared to swear in court.'

'Not him; he's part of it; he'll go down with the rest of us.'

It was a few moments before Leon Jackson realised what he had said. He looked over at his solicitor who shook his head.

'I expect you'd like a few words with your client,' Handford said. He nodded to Warrender to turn off the recording machine and walked out of the room.

'You're good at that, boss,' Warrender said when he caught up with him. 'Ever thought of taking it up professionally?'

Handford laughed. 'Do you want to tell Neville's solicitor the good news or shall I?' he said.

By next day both Neville and Jackson had admitted their part in the scam and Handford had sent the team out to collect and verify evidence. Jackson became garrulous and talked about how Bronwyn Price had 'stuck her nose in', as he put it, but didn't go as far as to admit that he had killed her.

Graham Dart, on the other hand, had confessed his part in the scam. He acted for the driver of the rogue cars. None of his staff were aware of what he was doing and none were brought into it, not even his secretary. He was fairly sure Tom Blakely was getting close, which was why he had arranged for Neville and Jackson to break in to the offices, steal the computer and mess the place up a bit. He was horrified when Blakely's body was found and was quite convinced that Neville or Jackson or both had killed him.

'Did you put him straight?' Handford asked.

'I thought it only fair. I didn't tell him who had, but I did say it wasn't the two from Help International.'

'Did he tell you how he had become mixed up with them?'

'It's an old story,' Ali said. 'While he is married, he also visits gay clubs, has sex with men and sometimes uses rent boys. Neville blackmailed him. Help us and we'll say nothing. Then when Mrs Dart was diagnosed with Alzheimer's and eventually became too ill for him to look after, he had to let her go into a nursing home. The cost was bleeding him dry and the only way he could cope financially was to carry on working for Neville and Jackson. They're nasty pieces of work, the more so because they operate behind a façade of helping people. I'd like to see them sent down, but I'm not sure we have enough evidence to charge them.'

'The CPS lawyers think we're almost there and since they're on police bail for the next few weeks it will give us time to find the rest. We'll do it, Khalid, if we have to rip the whole of their lives apart.'

Ali was silent for a moment then he said, 'What about Bronwyn Price, did they kill her?'

'I'm sure of it, although that will be a lot harder to prove. Except for a few fibres found on her body which, according to the lab, have come from a carpet that was probably used to wrap her in to transport up to the mine, there's not that much forensic evidence. It'll be a slog, but when we know exactly which kind of carpet they have come from, and find it, we'll be halfway there.'

'Presumably she was taken to the mine to implicate Tom Blakely?'

'I would think so. Poor Tom was getting just that bit too close to them and to be honest his conscience did the rest. Christine believed he was pushing for a memorial to alleviate his guilt at being on the police lines in the 1984 strike. James Amery used it.'

There was still a lot of work to do and Ali had left Handford's office when the telephone rang. He picked up the receiver. It was Brian Noble. 'Just to let you know the DNA from the three girls who were raped does not match that from Josie Renshaw.'

Handford closed his eyes and let out a long sigh of relief. 'So what now?'

'Nothing – at least nothing as far as you and your brother are concerned. We'll be dropping Josie's rape allegation because it will be impossible to prove. Douglas has admitted having sex with her but insists it was consensual. She's dead, we've no witnesses. We'd never prove it one way or the other. So you're both off the hook, although I'm not sure either of you deserves to be.'

Handford accepted the reprimand without argument. After a moment he asked, 'Has Douglas been informed?'

'No, not yet. I've tried to get hold of him but his wife says he's not there and hasn't been home since we brought him in to the station on Friday. I assume by your question you didn't know?'

'No.'

'Christ John, don't you talk to each other in your family?'

Handford maintained his silence; there wasn't a rational explanation he could give Noble that wouldn't sound like a lame excuse. Perhaps one day, but not now.

'She's in quite a state, actually.' Noble continued. 'She obviously knows nothing of what's been going on. Forget your differences, John, and go and see her. She could do with some support.'

Handford put down the receiver. Again for the second time in twenty-four hours, conflicting emotions were swirling round his head.

He tapped in Ali's number. 'Khalid, I have to go out. Look after everything, will you?'

'Are you all right, John? You sound worried.'

'I'm fine. I'll tell you about it when I get back.' And this time he would. Ali deserved an explanation.

He was about to switch to voice mail when the phone rang again. He was in two minds whether to pick it up, but it was difficult to ignore.

'Detective Chief Inspector Handford?'

He thought he recognised the voice, but wasn't sure. 'Yes.'

'This is Edward Harris, vicar of St Andrews. We met yesterday. Look, I'm sorry to bother you but we seem to have a bit of a situation here.'

Handford's stomach curled. 'A situation?'

'Yes. Your brother – he is your brother, isn't he?' Without waiting for a reply, the Reverend Harris went on: 'I'm afraid he's on top of the church tower threatening to jump.'

Handford ran up the steps leading to the church and looked up at the tower. He could see Douglas standing where Josie

Renshaw must have stood. It was dry, but there was quite a stiff breeze and Douglas's hair was blowing round his face. According to the uniformed officer who'd been called, he'd been there for some time. 'That's a good sign, isn't it, sir? It means he's not sure he wants to kill himself. We're trying to get a negotiator to talk him down, but it's Sunday and they're not readily available. They'll get one to us as soon as they can, they said.'

'And in the meantime we wait and hope, I suppose,' Handford responded angrily.

The fire brigade had arrived and the fire fighters were standing around, not quite sure what they could do. An ambulance had come right into the churchyard, the crew unsure as to whether they would be needed, but obliged to stay anyway. They were talking and laughing. Jumpers were not high on their agenda. Members of the congregation had been moved behind the police cordon, but were not ready to go home yet. What did they think he would look like as he fell to the ground? What did they think the sound would be as he hit the concrete path? Why couldn't they give him some dignity?

He turned angrily to the uniformed constable. 'Get rid of those people,' he spat.

The officer walked away, his arms outstretched as he tried to herd them back to their homes.

The vicar walked to stand next to Handford. 'What's this about, Chief Inspector? Is it something to do with Josie Renshaw? Your brother comes to her grave and leaves her flowers, you come as well and now your brother stands on the same spot on the tower from where she threw herself to her death. It's over thirty years since she died, why this sudden interest in her?'

Handford ignored the question. 'Can I get up there?'

'Well yes, I'll show you, but are you sure?'

'Just show me.'

It was higher than Handford had expected. He'd never been good with heights and he took a deep breath as he came out of the door at the top. 'Douglas, it's John.'

Douglas remained as he was, not moving, not turning. 'Go away, John. This is my problem, my decision.'

'What, to kill yourself? I can't let you do that, particularly when there's no reason for you to do it. I've heard from Brian Noble. The DNA on the clothes of the three girls who were raped doesn't match that on Josie's garments. He knows they weren't raped by you – or me, if it comes to that. They're closing the case on Josie Renshaw.'

'It will never be closed for me. I'm finished.'

'No you're not. Now after your arrest they've got your DNA like the rest of us in the village, they'll see that it's not a match.'

'Except with that on Josie.'

'A partial match, Douglas. There are at least six others whose it could be.'

'But only one who raped her.'

Handford pulled himself closer. 'Are you saying you did rape her?'

Douglas laughed. 'You sound just like a policeman, do you know that?'

'Are you saying you did rape her?' Handford articulated the words carefully and slowly, trying to keep the accusation out of his voice, but a hint of it remained.

'You know I did. But it was Josie Renshaw; if she said no she meant yes.'

'It was a long time ago; things were different then.'

'But it doesn't make it right.'

'No it doesn't.' Handford inched forward. 'Do you want to tell me what happened?'

Douglas sat down and Handford could almost hear the collective sigh of relief from those watching below.

'Had you had sex with her earlier or was it just the once?'

'Just the once, except she'd said "no".'

'And you forced her?'

'Yes, I forced her. No one said no to Douglas Handford, particularly not a tart like Josie Renshaw. After all, she was always up for it and I'd just come from university with my degree. Who was she to tell me no?' His voice was edged with bitterness and lined with shame.

'It was a long time ago, the seventies when love was free.'

'Not always. Sometimes it was expensive. Sometimes it took away a life.' He stood up. 'Rape is rape, whenever it was done. And Josie paid the price.' He turned to Handford and held on to him. Then he said, 'Tell Mary and the children that I'm sorry,' and before Handford could stop him he had run to the edge of the tower and let himself fall just as Josie Renshaw had done all those years ago.

chapter twenty

It was Christmas Day, five weeks exactly since Douglas Hand-ford had jumped from the church tower. The press had written in detail about why the Director of Social Services and the brother of Detective Chief Inspector John Handford of the Homicide and Major Enquiry Team should want to commit suicide. Many reasons were put forward, none of them anything to do with Josie Renshaw or an ongoing investigation into the rape of three young girls over thirty years ago. Mostly they blamed pressure of work and, depending on the colour of the newspaper, the government for heaping that pressure on those who worked with the public. Peter Redmayne alone picked up on the fact that Josie Renshaw had also killed herself by jump-ing off the tower some thirty years ago following an allegation of rape she had made. He didn't make judgements or suggest either that she had made it up or that she hadn't but com-mented instead that the police hadn't bothered to investigate it in any depth.

He wrote that the case of the rape of the three girls had been re-opened and DNA samples had been taken from all the men in the surrounding villages. So far no perpetrator had been found, but DCI Brian Noble had said it was still early days. Asked if there was any DNA on Josie Renshaw's undergarments Noble answered that yes there was but it did not match with that found on the other victims. Redmayne made no mention of the fight between Douglas and John in the police station. Perhaps he was leaving that until later.

John Handford sat by his brother's bed in the side ward of

the general hospital. Douglas had been in a coma since he was brought in. First he had been put on a life support machine, but when it was turned off he was able to breath unaided. He had many injuries, the head injuries were the most worrying, his pelvis broken as well as both legs and one arm. The internal damage was less severe, although the surgeons had to remove his spleen. No one had been sure whether he would survive, but survive he had, although it could not be known whether there would be any permanent brain damage until he woke up. What his psychological or emotional state would be was anybody's guess. Whatever the result he would need a lot of care.

Handford looked up as Gill and the girls tiptoed into the room. He smiled at her; it was so good to have her home. She had loved America and although she would return to Cliffe Top Comprehensive at the beginning of term, she wasn't sure that was where she wanted to be.

'How is he?' she said.

'About the same. No sign of him coming round. I keep talking to him and reading to him and I've played the CDs you girls gave me, although to be honest I'm not sure the music is quite to his taste.'

'What does he like then, brass band music?' Nicola said and Clare laughed.

Handford was a devotee of brass bands. He had played in one for a long time until he went into CID when he could never guarantee getting to rehearsals let alone concerts. Now he satisfied his love of them with CDs in the car and at home when the girls would let him. Usually when he played his music it was met with groans. When they played theirs they were met with 'Turn that down', something he had always said he would never say to his children – but when he had become a parent to two teenagers he had changed his mind.

'No, I think he is into light classical.' Handford realised he didn't really know and he wondered if he would ever be able to find out. He could ask Mary, of course, but she still blamed him for not stopping his brother from leaving and from jumping. She'd asked him why so many times and so far he hadn't told her, at least not the true version. Gill said he ought to, if

274

it was her she'd want to know. But he wondered if she really would and whether their relationship would ever be the same again. Pressure of work was a more palatable lie. It would be up to Douglas to tell Mary, not him. It had to be his choice.

'I'm going to take the girls home,' Gill said. 'There's a lot to do if we are to be ready for everyone arriving for dinner at seven.'

He stood up and kissed her. 'I won't be long, I promise,' he said. 'Mary's coming with Mother at three so I'll just stay another half-hour.'

When they had gone, he stretched his legs round the small room. It had been decked out with a few Christmas decorations and people had sent cards and presents. Handford wondered whether Douglas would ever see them or open them. *Happy Christmas, Get well soon* – all meaningless in this situation. There was one from his parents. He read it. It was one of those blank ones so that you could write your own greetings. It said, *We love you, Douglas, and we want you back with us.*

Handford picked a few of them up and sat down next to the bed. He took hold of Douglas's hand and grasped it. His mother had never quite forgiven her second son for not continuing the lie he had told confirming the alibi. He found that difficult to understand, since she had always been such an honest woman. He'd spoken to his father about it. 'He's her first born John, you've got to understand that,' he had said. 'She wants him safe. And there's no way she'll ever believe he raped anyone, let alone Josie Renshaw.' Handford was not sure whether his father agreed.

He opened up some of the cards and read out the greetings. The doctors and nurses had said to talk to Douglas and to read to him, to bring music for him to listen to, because although he was in a coma he may well be able to hear. It is one sense that often remains. The trouble was he was running out of things to say. He could hardly tell him about the case. Christmas greetings seemed the next best thing.

He was reading the last one when he felt it. Slight pressure on his hand. He looked down. His was clasped over the palm of Douglas's hand, which was warm but limp. Nothing. No movement. Had he imagined it? Probably. He was about to let go so that he could put the cards back on the shelves and the window-sill before he left when he felt it again, that slight pressure. Then he saw it, an almost minuscule movement of the thumb. Was it a muscular spasm or was Douglas beginning to come round? He wasn't sure. He pulled away from the bed and rang the bell. A nurse appeared a few moments later.

'I think he moved, nurse. I can't be sure, but he seemed to squeeze my hand.'

The nurse lifted the lid of one of Douglas's eyes and flashed a light over it and then over the other. 'I think you may be right,' she said. 'He's not quite with us yet, but it's a start. I think you're going to have your brother back, Mr Handford.'